Right
Where
We Left Us

ALSO BY JEN DEVON

Bend Toward the Sun

Right Where We Left Us

A Novel

JEN DEVON

ST. MARTIN'S GRIFFIN
NEW YORK

First published in the United States by St. Martin's Griffin, an imprint of St. Martin's Publishing Group

RIGHT WHERE WE LEFT US. Copyright © 2024 by Jen Devon. All rights reserved. Printed in the United States of America. For information, address St. Martin's Publishing Group, 120 Broadway, New York, NY 10271.

www.stmartins.com

Library of Congress Cataloging-in-Publication Data

Names: Devon, Jen, 1978– author.
Title: Right where we left us : a novel / Jen Devon.
Description: First edition. | New York : St. Martin's Griffin, 2024.
Identifiers: LCCN 2024003636 | ISBN 9781250822024 (trade paperback) | ISBN 9781250822031 (ebook)
Subjects: LCGFT: Romance fiction. | Novels.
Classification: LCC PS3604.E8873 R54 2024 | DDC 813/.6—dc23/eng/20240201
LC record available at https://lccn.loc.gov/2024003636

Our books may be purchased in bulk for promotional, educational, or business use. Please contact your local bookseller or the Macmillan Corporate and Premium Sales Department at 1-800-221-7945, extension 5442, or by email at MacmillanSpecialMarkets@macmillan.com.

First Edition: 2024

10 9 8 7 6 5 4 3 2 1

For Mom and Dad.
My favorite real-life second-chance romance.

Part One

CHAPTER ONE

Temperance

$\mathcal{D}$r. Temperance Madigan had slept for only four of the past twenty-eight hours, kept on her feet by stubborn resistance to the limits of human biology and a truly indecent amount of hospital break-room coffee. Even on a normal day, sleep was low on her list of priorities. But today wasn't a normal day. Today, she was an accomplice to a marriage proposal between two of the people she loved most in the world.

The Brady property was on one of the high points in Vesper Valley, up a gravel lane on a ridge barely wide enough for two cars in either direction. Through the patchwork of trees out her driver's-side window, the midday sun was a smoky gold shimmer on the lake nestled in the crook of the vale. At the top of the drive, a tall wrought-iron gate sat rusted permanently open, more of a trellis for morning glory and honeysuckle than a barrier to entry.

Passing from the shade of the tree-lined lane onto the main drive of the Brady land always felt a little like emerging into a new world. Temperance had to squint against the flood of sunlight. Under a May-blue sky, rolling lawns of soft grass and clover spread up and away, marked with mow lines as tidy as green corduroy.

The Brady home sat at the center, a medley of architectural styles that reflected its century of different inhabitants. It should have looked strange, with its brick to the west and the stone face to the east, its different-shaped windows and mismatched shingles on the roof of each wing. The composite of varied but equally interesting parts only added to its charm. Like the Brady family itself.

The place was usually alive with activity—a far-off hum of lawn equipment, music through open windows and screen doors. Rowan zipping around in her little utility vehicle or a tractor, and her vineyard crew buzzing like bees in and out of the trellised grapes. Now, it was preternaturally silent. Like the land itself had taken a big breath and held it. Waiting.

At Harry's request, Temperance drove the gravel access road along the eastern perimeter of the property to avoid being seen from the vineyards or the house. The bumpy road took her past the massive stone bank barn, around the pool and pool house that seemed to be a perpetual source of plumbing problems, and up to where the old Victorian greenhouse sat on the highest point of the land like the center jewel in a crown. Temperance pulled around to the grassy clearing behind the greenhouse and parked her car next to the only other vehicle there. A hulking black pickup with its windows all the way down. Aviator sunglasses hooked over the rearview mirror.

Duncan was here.

Temperance's belly gave a little thump.

A faded pink bandage was still stuck to a shallow dent on the rear bumper. Temperance had been there that day, when one of the Brady kids let their bike fall too close to the truck. Little Grey had attempted to "make it better" with one of his sister's Band-Aids.

For almost a month, Duncan Brady had unabashedly driven his big growly pickup all over the valley with Hello Kitty faces stuck to the bumper.

Again, something inside her felt noisy and hot. She ignored it and got out of her car.

Temperance started to sweat the moment she stepped out of the air-conditioned microclimate of her tidy little Corolla. Even though it was only four days into May, temperatures had already climbed into the high eighties. It had been a record wet spring as well, so the humidity was problematic. With the back of her hand, she swiped her damp jaw and nudged her glasses up. A bead of sweat raced down the center of her chest.

She should've worn a different bra.

The heavy greenhouse door was half-open. Its hinges groaned when she pushed through. "Harry?"

No answer.

Hesitantly, she said, "Duncan?"

Temperance knew Duncan wasn't inside the greenhouse even before she called out his name. After nearly twenty years, she was attuned to the man's presence the same way a songbird knew it was about to storm. He was neurochemically branded into her brain.

God, it was hot.

The blades of an exhaust fan on the far wall rotated too slowly to push any air. It sliced intermittent shadows through the citrusy sunlight that flooded through the glass walls. A dusty cassette-deck radio played an old Guns N' Roses ballad. Even with a wire coat hanger sticking out of the radio's top as a makeshift antenna, Linden's classic rock was the only station that played static-free that deep in the valley. An old refrigerator itself made its own music—an intermittent creak that sounded a lot like the rhythm of particularly athletic sex on a squeaky bedframe.

Temperance checked her phone. No updates from Harry.

Green transcended color here. It was an actual taste in the air. A mood. An entire *experience*. Rows of heavy tables stood three across and at least ten deep. Every horizontal surface was occupied by photosynthetic things: herbs, baby grapevines, vegetable seedlings, roses in brazen bloom. Dozens of other plants that Temperance didn't recognize. Some of the plants went vertical, wandering up the iron window frames to drape down from overhead beams.

Signs of Rowan were everywhere. Her old khaki hat hung on a nail near the door. Every other table seemed to have a notebook on it, the pages wrinkled by water stains. Three abandoned coffee mugs were visible just from where Temperance stood at the door—one of them filled to the top with potting soil. There were twice as many pairs of gardening gloves nestled between pots, on stools and benches, and hung from clothespins on a little line strung over a rust-stained sink.

It was organized chaos. This place was an ecosystem of its own, and what looked like utter disarray to Temperance was likely her best friend's intentional and thoughtful organizational system. It felt like she'd stepped directly into Rowan McKinnon's big, beautiful brain.

Temperance felt kind of shitty that she had to mess it all up.

There was a limit to how long anyone could plausibly keep Rowan away from her greenhouse, so a lot had to happen here in less than three hours for Harry to pull off his proposal later tonight. He wanted all the seedlings and haphazard flats of ornamental plants and herbs moved, replaced on the tables with potted native plants in full flower. Grapevines and greenery were to be woven throughout, accented with glass lanterns with candles inside.

Temperance lifted and lowered her arms like an awkward baby bird in an attempt to circulate air around her body. The waistband of her ancient Levi's cutoffs was already damp, and she'd barely been there five minutes. And yeah—she *definitely* should have worn a different bra.

In a complete failure to consider the heat, she'd worn the same kind of underthings she wore every day—approximately three hundred dollars' worth of high-end lingerie. She'd always favored a minimalist wardrobe with sleek lines and solid colors, but she'd been instantly hooked on the frothy lace and sumptuous fabrics of the sample pieces Frankie had gifted her after she'd modeled for a lingerie designer. From then on, Italian and French intimates became the one indulgence she allowed herself whenever she had a bit of extra money—which had been rare on a medical resident's salary. It felt private and personal at a time when she gave a near-totality of herself in service to others.

Temperance was deep inside her head weighing the aesthetic virtues of fancy bras against their shortcomings in the management of underboob sweat when the door to the greenhouse banged open behind her. She whirled so fast her braid arced around and smacked her between the eyes.

"Oh my *god*, where did you come from?" she said.

An enormous cardboard box obscured the upper half of the person carrying it, but she didn't need to see a face to know who it was. Hands, big. Arms, bigger. Tattoos began at a crisp line at his wrist, each piece connected to the ones beside it to create a colorful, unrelieved mosaic that disappeared into the snug sleeves of his T-shirt. Button-fly jeans with two blown knees hugged thick thighs with the kind of sartorial precision that only came with years of regular wear.

That faded denim knew the body beneath it as well as she did.

Duncan Brady lowered the box with a breathy baritone grunt. "Well, it all started back when Will Brady met Gia Vega in Spain—"

"Where's Harry?" Temperance flung her braid back over her shoulder and shoved her glasses up her nose.

A lock of his hair arced down, glossy and black as a crow's eye. He pushed it off his forehead with a quick sweep of his thumb. "Harry is the only person on this planet who can distract Rowan from coming into this greenhouse. Do you want to talk about how he probably accomplishes that?"

Temperance's cheeks flushed. She lifted a huge bag of potting soil and popped her hip sideways to balance it there. "No."

Duncan's mouth twitched. "I didn't think so."

"Where's everyone else?"

The interconnectedness of the people they both loved meant forced proximity was a fact of life. But despite their attempts to exist in a sort of emotional demilitarized zone, they had more than a decade-long record of messy behavior whenever they found themselves alone together like this. Prolonged contact tended to result in verbal battles, hastily discarded clothing, or their tongues in each other's mouths.

Sometimes all three at the same time.

It was like she had one of those fill-in-the-blank safety compliance signs hung inside her brain. *It has been three hundred ninety-five days since we couldn't manage to keep our panties on while alone with Duncan Brady.*

Thirteen months was a new record for them, actually. At least the last few times she'd been smart enough to not let him kiss her. Her mouth seemed to have a direct line to her heart, and the aftermath of being kissed by Duncan Brady was way harder to get over than anything they did with the rest of their bodies. Vivian Ward in *Pretty Woman* had been onto something.

"I assume Harry's put them all to work, too, but I don't have everyone's social calendar. Colby Everett will be here in about an hour with all the flowers, though." He lifted the heavy bag of soil away from her with one hand, like it was a five-pound bag of sugar instead of the size of a kindergartner.

Temperance watched him walk to the back of the greenhouse. Even in that worn-out T-shirt and the old denim, Duncan Brady was the kind of gorgeous so audacious he was distracting to be around. When her best friends had met him, Rowan had said he was the hottest person she'd ever seen in real life. Frankie'd said he'd be a dream to photograph, with a face and frame suited for a spread in an edgy fashion editorial. It had been easy for Temperance to imagine—he'd smolder at the camera in some gritty, subversive location, like the parking lot of a run-down motel or a mechanic's graveyard for vintage cars. It would be nighttime in the shoot, but maybe he'd wear his vintage aviators anyway, looking sulky-hot and intimidating. But there'd be something about the way he carried himself that made you want to figure out the ways he was soft. Once the camera was off, he'd make half the crew laugh and the other half fall in love, because what really made Duncan Brady so damned compelling wasn't a corporeal thing like the angle of his jaw or a pair of cocoa bedroom eyes. It was in the way his expansive smiles felt like they were *for* you instead of at you, and how, when you had his attention, it felt like you were the sole object of his mind.

It was the same thing that made him so hard to stay away from, even though he'd repeatedly cracked her heart open like a pistachio.

He caught her looking at him. "You mad again, Madigan? You look like you could suck the yellow off a lemon."

She shook her head and met his eyes. "I'm good."

"You here to help, then? Or are you just going to scowl at me?"

"I don't scowl. This is just my face."

He breathed out a bland laugh that was the nonverbal equivalent of *"Bullshit, but okay."* Without hesitation, he picked up a terra-cotta pot full of rosemary that was as big as her torso. It had to weigh at least a hundred pounds.

"Surprised you're here today," he said.

"I've been here a lot lately."

"I noticed."

"Then why are you surprised?"

"You worked a twelve-hour shift at the hospital last night." Over by the sink, he set the massive pot down on the ground so gently it didn't make a sound. Then he picked up a tray of baby trees from an adjacent table. "And you were at the clinic most of the day before."

"How do you even know that?" Temperance grabbed a flat of basil seedlings and headed to the back of the greenhouse.

"Your sister is married to one of my brothers. One of your best friends is marrying another brother." There was a rueful slant to his smile as they passed each other. "You come up in conversation."

"Rowan hasn't said yes yet," she said to his back.

Duncan turned and cocked his head to the side. "Temperance. Come on. Harry wouldn't be proposing tonight if he wasn't already sure of her answer." Quieter, he said, "That's how this usually works."

That felt like a personal dig. *"I heard that,"* she wanted to say. She didn't.

They worked for half an hour, shuttling plants off the tables in silence, giving each other a wide berth. When they finished, Duncan left to get something else from his truck, and Temperance peeked inside the boxes he'd brought in earlier. They were both knee height and filled to the top with strand after strand of tiny fairy bulbs.

"Oh my god." She slumped back against a table. "We're so screwed."

Duncan came back into the greenhouse with a twelve-foot ladder. "Ah, ye of little faith."

"Me of reasonable expectations." She skirted sideways when he drifted toward her.

His eyes were on the ceiling. He palmed the back of his neck and rubbed. It made his biceps bunch and flex, and Temperance was absolutely positive he did it on purpose.

"I have a plan. We've got this." He wrapped his hands around the edge of a heavy table and dragged it toward him with a grunt and a quick jerk of his arms. "You trust me?"

"Hm. Situationally."

His shoulders shook in a quick laugh. "Good enough."

* * *

THEY worked together, stretching the strands of lights lengthwise on the empty tables to plan spacing and remove any tangles.

Through lowered lashes, Temperance watched his hands while they worked. The middle finger on his right hand was slightly crooked at the end. It'd healed wrong after it'd broken in a Brady game of Team Tag years ago. Today, two fingers were wrapped with adhesive bandages, and his knuckles were scraped. He was always hurting his hands.

The outer edge of his left hand was dark with a gray metallic sheen—something she hadn't seen on him in at least a decade. Duncan Brady was one of the tiny percentage of the human population who was naturally ambidextrous, but he'd always claimed he had more control when he sketched with his left hand. The consequence of that had always been a blur of graphite or charcoal on his skin where he moved it across the paper.

Temperance was intimately familiar with a few other things he preferred to do with his left.

When they were younger, those smudges were ever-present on his hands, well before he'd begun to decorate his skin with tattoos. That final summer they'd been together, his sketchbook went everywhere they did, tucked above the passenger's-side visor in his truck. A kit with pencils, a sharpener, and a soft eraser lived in the glove box.

Lightly, she said, "You sketching again?"

Something unreadable passed across his features, but it was gone before she had time to dissect it. He rubbed his hand on his jeans and said, simply, "Yeah."

This man was not known for frugality with words. A one-syllable, one-word response from him was a blatant dismissal.

"I'm just making polite conversation," she said.

"Is that what we do now?" A single eyebrow boosted high on his forehead. "Polite conversation?"

"Seems like a thing we've never tried." A jaw-stretching yawn snuck up on her as she untwisted her final strand of lights. She pressed her mouth into her shoulder and shook it off.

"Do you ever sleep?" Duncan watched her with a faint crease of concern between his eyes. "You look like an extra in a zombie movie. The one who tries to hide it from everyone else that they got bitten."

"Shut up."

He *tsk*'ed with his tongue and smirked. "That's not very polite conversation."

Lightly, she said, "Kiss my ass."

Another upward hook of that right eyebrow. "Not where I usually prefer to start, but okay."

Temperance rolled her eyes, but she had to pin her lips between her teeth to keep from smiling. That one was straight out of the Duncan Brady playbook. Funny, with shades of innuendo. And quick, too. It was like he kept those quippy little comebacks tucked under his tongue, waiting for the chance to deploy them.

In her back pocket, her phone suddenly blared with the dissonant staccato of the *Halloween* movie theme. She lowered a strand of lights and groaned.

"Mommy and daddy dearest?" Duncan said. He went to grab the ladder where he'd left it propped against the wall.

"How'd you guess?"

He made a vague sound in the back of his throat. "You gonna answer?"

"Nope."

The phone went silent. Five seconds later, it started again.

Duncan positioned the ladder under the beam at the front of the greenhouse. "You want *me* to answer?" he said over his shoulder.

That made her laugh. "Oh my god, can you imagine?"

"I have." He turned to face her, and he wasn't smiling. "Many times."

The phone stopped ringing, and for a moment, silence cushioned them against the weight of unsaid things.

Again, the phone rang. It almost felt like they knew she was alone with Duncan.

"Persistent," he said over the noise. "Is everything okay?"

"They want to collect on their investment." Temperance put the phone on silent mode—which she rarely did in case the hospital or clinic needed to reach her. "They need my help on a grant application."

Duncan shuffled a step closer. "You going to do it?"

"Maybe. It's—ah, a backup plan, I guess." Temperance blew flyaway strands of hair back from her face, then gestured to the ceiling to redirect them to the task at hand. "We should split up. You do the lower areas where you can reach, I'll use the ladder—"

"Absolutely not."

"It'll be faster—"

"No. These floorboards are crooked as a goat's hind legs. We'll do what we can with our feet on the ground, then I'll hold the ladder for you to reach the high spots."

She looked at him with narrowed eyes.

Duncan widened his stance and crossed his arms over his chest. "That's the way it's going to be, Teacup."

A swirl of something nameless stirred in her belly at the old nickname. "Fine."

The plan was to attach small magnetic hooks to the iron beams that extended from the center of the ceiling down to the side walls, then hang the lights from the hooks. Once they finished all the lower beams, Temperance packed all four pockets of her cutoffs with the hooks, so Duncan didn't need to keep handing them up to her. He fed her light strands while he kept a steadying hold on the ladder. They had a rhythm and routine down quickly.

The longer they were at it, though—the more her composure frayed at the edges.

Each time she came down the ladder, there were a few seconds on the lower rungs where his biceps bracketed her in. She'd lost count of the number of times her calves skimmed his forearms. She could even feel hot gusts of his breath on the backs of her thighs.

Another involuntary yawn overtook her when she came down, popping her jaw with the force of it. A sleepy tear tracked down her cheek, and her vision swam. For a moment, there were *two* Duncans.

Oh, boy.

"Seriously, when's the last time you slept more than a few hours?" he said.

"I'm fine." She flicked the tear away with the edge of her pinkie. "I haven't even started hallucinating yet."

"Christ, woman. That's not a flex."

For the past year, she'd been working per diem at the University Hospital where she'd done her residency instead of committing to a permanent position somewhere else. Most doctors she knew worked per diem so they could work fewer hours and maintain more control over their schedules while still earning close to—or even more than—a full-time salary.

Temperance leveraged that flexibility to work *more*.

She averaged five twenty-four-hour shifts most months, and

she'd often moonlight to pick up additional crossover shifts and call-offs. Her Wednesday evenings and Saturday mornings belonged to the student-run free clinic in Linden. The work she did there was what truly lit her up inside, and she'd built every other aspect of her professional life around it. If she could actually survive on the small stipend the university paid her as the clinic's medical director, she wouldn't hesitate to do it full-time.

It was time for them to shift the ladder, but Duncan wasn't moving.

He was a handful of inches over six feet tall, and even if she'd been wearing four-inch stilettos she'd top out at almost a foot shorter. The sharp aluminum edge of the step dug into the back of her thigh when she turned and braced her butt against the rung. At that height, she could look him straight in the eye.

"Not your problem," she said.

He held her eyes. "Maybe I want it to be."

With the back of her wrist, she wiped sweaty tendrils of hair off her forehead. She gave him a sardonic smile. "What, like, you want to be my *friend*?"

There was a subtle shift in his expression. A twitch in the tiny muscles around his eyes. The flicker of jaw muscles at his temple. And that damned beard—it framed his lips like they were an art piece. This man was built like a rugby forward, but his mouth was made for reciting poetry and kissing collarbones.

Quietly, he said, "I don't think that's what I'd call it, Temperance."

It had been years since she'd been this close to his face in daylight. The terrain of his body was charted in her memory with indelible ink, but the landscape of him had changed. Smile lines made tiny starbursts at the outer corners of his eyes, and his skin was a bit more snug over high cheekbones.

He ducked his chin and raised his eyes. "What?"

"I was just—ah—" Temperance stalled to think of a deflection. "Looking at your beard."

"What about my beard?"

"Just occurred to me I've never dated a guy with one."

"Do you want to *date* me, Teacup?" His attention was conspicuously fixed on her mouth.

She rolled her eyes. "Please."

"What's wrong with beards?"

"They're dirty."

He laughed. "That's a goddamned myth. They're no dirtier than the person under them." He paused for a second, then his tone dropped low. "I guess they can get *messy* sometimes—"

She knew exactly where his mind had gone, and hers eagerly followed right into a horny, high-fidelity flashback montage.

Duncan Brady had a memorably strong tongue.

"I don't like how they *feel*."

"If you've never been with someone with a beard, how do you know how they feel?"

"Inference, I guess." The man plucked her nerves like a mandolin. She pressed her knee forward into his chest. "Move."

He didn't. He nudged his chin toward her. "Touch it."

"What?"

"Touch my beard."

Temperance laughed and bumped her glasses up with a knuckle. "Absolutely not."

"I don't bite."

She gave him a long look. "Yes, you do."

When he still didn't move, she let out an exaggerated sigh and patted the dark hair along his jaw. She used only her fingertips, the way an elderly auntie would pacify a precocious child.

Oh.

Soft.

Temperance snapped her hand away and balled it into a fist.

The scent of him was baked into the weathered cotton of his T-shirt like a sensory transcript of his day. Smoky sawdust and clean, coppery sweat. A sweet hint of cloves. Something unidentifiable and a little volatile, like damp earth after rain. She wanted to press her face to the center of his chest and inhale.

He laughed, a single deep *ha*. "Weak. That was barely long enough to—"

She made an impatient sound and delved the fingers of both her hands into his beard. Curled, tugged. His cheeks gave a little beneath her knuckles. He rocked into her with a soft grunt. The tips of his ears were red, and his cheekbones were beginning to follow suit.

The ladder creaked where he gripped it, white-knuckled.

Her fingers loosened to splay gently around the bottom edges of his jaw. A muscle ticced there, and his breath was hot against her wrists.

"Temperance." Duncan's pupils dilated rapidly, conspicuous even within the deep brown of his irises.

Her muscles had turned to ribbons. "What?"

"Your glasses are fogging up," he whispered.

"They are not—"

"Am I getting you steamed, Teacup?" His smile was all mischief. She felt his low laugh deep in her belly. It set her temper to a simmer. She snatched her hands away and shoved him in the chest with her knee. "Go to hell, Duncan."

He took a few steps back, clutching both hands to his sternum where she'd pushed him. Still smiling that pain-in-the-ass smile. "Ow."

Outside, two gray pickup trucks with the Three Birds Winery logo on the sides pulled up and parked behind the greenhouse. Colby Everett and his brother Brennan hopped out and lowered the tailgates to reveal hundreds of potted flowers.

Temperance was so relieved by the interruption she felt light-headed. Duncan's smirk slipped away.

The look they shared in that moment was a familiar one. A look loaded with mutual want and mutual disappointment. Temperance was the first to avert her eyes.

Duncan Brady wasn't for her. He was made for folly and flirtation. Together they were binary stars built vivid and hot—unstable by nature and destined to catastrophically explode.

The biggest and brightest ones always did.

CHAPTER TWO

Duncan

After more than a decade of practice, Duncan Brady had it down to a science how long he could look at Temperance Madigan before anyone who noticed could call it staring.

In the flat stretch of lawn between the big sugar maples at Cloud Tide, everyone sat around a dying campfire, glancing intermittently at the greenhouse on the hill. It gleamed like an amber gemstone on the highest point of the property, lit from within by the thousands of fairy lights he and Temperance had hung earlier that day.

They'd made a damned good team.

The eerie songs of night creatures pulsed all around them, like the earth itself had a heartbeat. A particularly warm and wet spring meant fireflies in early May. They rose from the grass by the hundreds, lighting the dark spaces beyond the halo of firelight. Duncan couldn't remember seeing this many in the past ten years.

His family was uncharacteristically quiet; all of them chatting in hushed tones, pretending not to be fixated on the greenhouse. A few big candles burned on two outdoor tables pushed end to end, dimly illuminating what remained of the earlier picnic feast. His sister Arden pinched cake crumbs between her fingers and nibbled them like a nervous bird gathering seed. Temperance and Frankie Moreau had their heads together at the opposite end of the table, whispering to each other.

Temperance laughed quietly at something Frankie said. Night wind drew threads of her long hair across her face, and her cheeks bloomed pink around a subtle smile. She looked soft. A pale Mona Lisa in a Monet palette.

Up on the hill, the lights in the greenhouse turned off. Everyone gasped in unison. Breaths were held.

The lights flicked back on, then off again, then back on. Harry's signal.

Ma whooped. "She said yes!"

"Of course she did," Dad said. He used the heel of his palm to swipe moisture from the outer corner of his eye.

"All right, then," Duncan said. He stacked a few new logs on the fire. "Let's have a party."

* * *

THE Bradys never needed an excuse to have a bonfire, but that night, they had a reason to celebrate. Everyone sat around the fire, intermittently roasting marshmallows and affectionately roasting the newly engaged couple.

"You two thought you were so clever." Nate laughed.

"Oh, please." Maren nudged him in the arm. "You'd have never noticed if I hadn't told you."

Rowan's cheeks were crimson in the oversaturated light of the fire. "You knew?"

"Honey." Maren's smile was gentle. "Once you've felt it for yourself, it's pretty easy to recognize. I know what falling in love with a Brady boy looks like."

Duncan didn't miss the way Maren's eyes flicked over toward Temperance.

"I heard you two whispering at each other in the library the morning of Patrick's and my wedding last April," Mercy said to Rowan.

"And I saw you banging on the door of the carriage house last May, Rosie," said Patrick.

Mercy was the newest Brady as of her wedding to Patrick last spring. Patrick and Nathan were the oldest Brady brothers, identical twins who were becoming more difficult to tell apart now that Patrick had decided to grow a silver-flecked beard like Nate's.

"Jesus, I think the real thing we need to talk about tonight is what else Patrick and Mercy have seen—" Harry said.

"If we want to go there"—Patrick squinted one eye and pointed at Malcolm—"I've definitely got a few stories about that one—"

Mal cut him off. "No."

Malcolm was the next oldest after the twins—Duncan's tallest, grumpiest, and most antisocial brother. Until recently, at least. For the past six months he'd been driving down from New York to stay at the vineyard a few weekends a month with his daughter, Charlotte. Duncan had a feeling it had a lot to do with Frankie Moreau.

"I hate"—Temperance leapt to her feet with a screech of frustration, slapping at her legs—"mosquitoes!" She bent at the waist to swat the back of her calf, then pirouetted to try to reach her back, whipping her ponytail around her face.

Everyone watched her, wide-eyed.

"You look like one of those wacky-armed inflatables they put outside car dealerships," Frankie said.

Again, Temperance swiped at her legs. She almost elbowed Frankie in the face. "Oh my god, why aren't they going after any of you?"

"Me? I taste disgusting," said Frankie.

"I seriously doubt that," Mal muttered into his can of ginger ale.

"Listen," Duncan said. "If you want to hang with the fireflies, you have to brave a few mosquitoes."

Temperance glared.

"Nice." Harry chuckled. "Life lessons from Duncan Brady."

"Did you know fireflies find mates based on specific flashing patterns?" Rowan's cheeks bulged with a jumbo marshmallow. She swallowed and cut her eyes over to where the kids were preoccupied, dropping her voice to a stage whisper. "We're sitting in the middle of a big bug orgy right now."

"Thank you, David Attenborough," Frankie deadpanned.

Harry glanced at Duncan, then back to Rowan. "So, what you're saying is—that communication and good timing are essential when it comes to a successful romance?"

"Communication is everything." Rowan queued up a new

marshmallow on the end of her stick and held it in the fire. "In some species, the females mimic the signals of a different species, then when the male of that species comes swooping in to mate, they become dinner instead." She smacked her free hand on her thigh.

Temperance sat back down. "Well, that got dark real fast."

Harry laid a hand on Rowan's arm. "You're on fire, sweetheart."

"Fascinating, right?" Rowan said.

"Yes—but I mean, ah, the marshmallow," Harry said.

Rowan gasped and blew out the flaming end of her stick, then she crinkled her nose and gave Harry a messy kiss on the mouth.

To Duncan's left, Nate was rapid-firing questions at Arden. She was a few weeks away from the end of her senior year of college, and she planned to hike a portion of the Appalachian Trail later in the month. Nate had a morbid fascination with the lack of reliable toilet access.

"I gotta know, Arden," Nate said. "How will you poop?"

Arden blinked a few times. "The same way you do, Nathan." Her eyebrows twitched. "With my butt."

Everyone laughed.

"How's work, Doc?" Duncan said to Harry.

"So many babies born last month. What the hell happened last August to make everyone so horny?"

"Neat how my patients come in a nine-month lag behind yours." Temperance smiled.

"I don't get it," Nate said.

"Pediatrician joke," Harry clarified.

Across the fire, Duncan's eight-year-old nephew, Grey, piped up, "What's *horny* mean?"

Ma shot a withering look at Harry. Nate barked a laugh and stuffed a piece of flatbread as big as his hand into his mouth. Maren elbowed him in the side.

His niece, eleven-year-old Alice—"call me Ace"—held her marshmallow over the fire at a distance optimized for browning instead of burning. Without taking her eyes off the end of her stick, she wisely said, "It's when you can't wait to have breakfast with someone."

All the adults were silent for a beat. A few nodded their heads. Dad covered his face with his hands.

"Well, then." Harry raised his plastic cup. "To having breakfast!"

Everyone laughed and raised their drinks.

"Speaking of babies . . ." Mercy's eyes glittered as she laid an affectionate hand on Patrick's thigh. "A new Brady will be arriving early next year."

Patrick pulled her closer and kissed her forehead. "Mercy's pregnant."

Murmurs of happiness and congratulations went up around the circle. Ma rushed to Mercy, arms wide for a hug.

Duncan thumped Patrick on the back and laughed. "Better you than me, big brother."

Patrick chuckled. "Ah, come on, bud—there have to be at least a few little Duncans running around out there in the valley, don't you think?"

Nate groaned, and Harry launched a marshmallow that hit Patrick in the face.

Duncan pasted on a tight smile and muttered a lukewarm "Yeah, yeah," but his insides felt hollow and hot. When he caught Temperance's eye across the fire, the hurt in her expression hit him like a brick in the mouth. The heat of the fire made the air shimmer between them, and he had to look away.

When she'd left for college all those years ago, she'd stayed out of the valley for most of that entire first year, and the distance had given him a wildly overestimated sense of closure. He'd tried to reinforce it with an impressive—or embarrassing, depending on who you asked—number of hookups that only left him feeling emptier afterward. But there was no such thing as closure when it came to Temperance Madigan. Every time he thought he'd fully buried his feelings, they came heaving to the surface with just a glimpse of her face in a crowded room. Sometimes, all it took was overhearing someone say her name.

You couldn't starve away a hunger.

Duncan chanced another glance at Temperance. She was still looking right at him. Close enough to touch. Completely out of reach.

"I thought you were quitting that thing, Malcolm?" Patrick slashed his hand through a cloud of sweetly fragrant smoke from Mal's pipe.

"One vice at a time," Mal said. The mellow bass of his voice seemed at odds with his angular frame.

"He still has writer's block," Duncan said.

"The hell does that have to do with the pipe?" said Nate.

"He's channeling Sherlock Holmes," Duncan said, as if it were the most obvious thing in the world.

"Holmes wasn't a writer," Arden said. "He's a fictional detective."

"But he solved mysteries." Duncan tapped a finger to his temple. "Mal *writes* mysteries."

Nate whistled softly. "Sometimes I worry your train of thought left the conductor at the station, bud."

"Fuck off." Duncan laughed.

"Language," Ma said as she set three unlabeled bottles of wine on the picnic table.

"Crime fiction," Mal said. "I write crime fiction."

Duncan shrugged. "Same thing."

"It's not." Mal lowered his head and pinched the bridge of his nose.

Patrick flicked an aluminum beer bottle cap at Mal. "I wonder what all your broody edgelord fans would think if they knew you were actually soft as baby shit."

Mal gusted a plume of smoke from his nostrils and looked bored.

"He's definitely more Jessica Fletcher than Jessica Jones." Arden patted Mal on the knee.

At the table, Rowan and Ma put out fresh plastic cups for everyone to try the first grape-to-glass Brady wine—a Chambourcin from last October's harvest. Excitement was high, expectations were low. The vineyards were still in their relative infancy after Rowan had restored them from wild ruin over the past two years.

Once everyone had a cup—though Mercy and the kids got plain grape juice, and Mal declined in favor of his ginger ale—Dad stood for a toast.

"When we bought this place two years ago, we had no idea what we'd gotten ourselves into. Everything we've done here has been more difficult, more expensive, and more messy than we'd ever imagined it could be." He paused for a moment to stare into the fire with a reflective half smile on his face. He held his red Solo cup to his chest like it was fine crystal. "I've gotta tell you, though—I've had the time of my life. This place has brought our family together in a way we never could have anticipated, and you know what? Turns out, it's a hell of a lot of fun to do hard things when you're doing them side by side with the people you love."

Everyone raised their cups in agreement.

When they tried to drink, Dad held up a hand. "Wait, wait—not yet. I have a few more things to say."

Patrick and Nate groaned. "Shocker," Arden muttered.

Dad turned to Duncan, pointing to him with the same hand that held the cup. "You, Duncan Callum. I can't imagine anything we've accomplished here in the last two years happening without you. You've become the backbone of Brady Brothers. Watching the way you've handled the family business while also helping to bring this land back to life has been a privilege and a joy." Dad paused to swipe a tear away for the second time that evening. "Hell, maybe we should rename it to Brady and Son."

Around the fire, everyone smiled at him with pride and affection—even Temperance, though she looked away as soon as his eyes met hers.

Duncan gave Dad a stiff smile. It should have felt good. But it felt like utter shit.

Of the six Brady kids, Duncan was the one Ma and Dad relied on the most. While all his siblings had gone off and gotten their advanced degrees, he was the one who'd stayed. How the hell would he explain to them—barely two years after he'd agreed to take over management of the family business—that he didn't actually want to manage the family business?

Will Brady had barely been in his twenties when he and his older brother Iain founded Brady Brothers Contracting from the dirt up. It eventually became a design-build firm that employed both architects and contractors. Duncan had been sixteen when Uncle Iain died, and more than once throughout that first year, he'd overheard Dad working through his grief with Ma. *"It's not Brady Brothers without my brother."*

Duncan started working for Brady Brothers after school, mostly helping with surveying and job site cleanup. By the time he was seventeen, he'd taught himself 2D and 3D design in two different computer-aided design programs. By eighteen, he was generating leads for jobs, and shadowing the senior project managers and design teams. Dreaming of a future as an architect.

By nineteen, he'd given up.

Again, everyone raised their cups to drink, and again, they were interrupted. This time, it was Ma.

She looked to where Temperance and Frankie sat together, smiling at them both. "They all know this"—she gestured to everyone else—"but my mother is Galician, and my father was Spanish. So, when I was growing up, we always did toasts and celebrations in both languages." Ma walked around the fire to stand by Dad. "Que el amor nos encuentre siempre dispuestos," she said in Spanish, raising her cup.

Across the fire, Harry leaned to whisper into Rowan's ear. His face was half-hidden by her billowy red curls, but by the way his mouth moved, Duncan could tell he was translating the words for her. Cheeks flushed, eyes dreamy, her fingers curled in her lap as she stared into the flames. To their left, Maren leaned into Nate with her head notched against his shoulder. He tipped his face sideways to drop a slow kiss on her windblown hair.

May love always find us ready, Ma had said.

Duncan felt something begin to unravel in him. Slowly at first, then faster, as the weight of it grew heavier and heavier. It was a hell of a lot easier to pretend that he didn't burn for that kind of visible, visceral love when it wasn't staring him in the face. He'd had it once, with Temperance. But it had been hidden. They'd never been able to share it, display it publicly.

Moving only his eyes, Duncan looked to where she sat.

She was looking right at him. The jolt it gave his nervous system felt like she'd physically pushed him. Eye contact with Temperance Madigan redefined the phrase. Connecting with those electric blues felt like a tangible, knock-you-backward collision.

Again, she looked away first.

"Para nós e para os nossos," Ma said, this time in Gallego.

For us and ours.

Temperance dampened her bottom lip with a quick dart of her tongue. With her free hand, she twisted the end of her braid around her fingers.

Dad put his arm around Ma and raised his cup. "Let's toast! To *when can we start,* instead of *how long will it take.* And to *what's next,* instead of *what if.*"

"To Cloud Tide," Ma said.

"To Cloud Tide," everyone echoed.

Cup high in the air, Nate shouted, "To the longest toast that has ever been toasted, Jesus Christ on a Jet Ski. Let's drink some wine."

Laughing, everyone tapped their cups against those of whoever they could reach. They smiled and murmured *cheers,* and *how exciting,* and *can't wait.*

When they took their first sips, silence fell.

Someone cleared their throat.

"Oh my," Maren whispered.

Harry coughed and banged his chest with the side of his fist.

"Um, I don't—I don't think—" said Rowan.

Frankie discreetly lifted her cup back to her mouth and dribbled the wine back into it.

"Well, that's, ah—" Dad tipped his head thoughtfully to the side. "That's—it's—interesting—"

"Satan's mouthwash," Nate muttered.

Arden cackled out loud.

Duncan forced himself to swallow.

Everyone turned to watch Ma.

For a few agonizing moments, she looked down into her cup before slowly setting it on the table behind her. She removed her glasses and let them dangle on the crystal chain around her neck. Without a word, she walked away from the campfire and stood with her back to the group.

More silence. Everyone shared concerned glances when Ma bent at the waist and put her hands on her knees. Her shoulders began to silently shake.

Nobody moved.

From Ma, a thin, high-pitched sound.

"Oh, Gia—" Rowan began, softly. She started to get up, but Harry grabbed her hand.

Ma stood up straight and turned back toward everyone, helplessly waving her hands in front of her face. Tears squeezed from the corners of her eyes. Another weird wailing sound came from her, but she wasn't crying.

She was *laughing*.

One hand over her chest and one hand over her belly, Ma was laughing so hard she was wheezing.

Everyone lost it.

Dad dumped his wine onto the ground behind him. Rowan teased that he was going to kill the grass, and everyone laughed even harder.

"Maybe you and Ma should stay in Spain for more than ten days next month, Rosie." Duncan chuckled. "Aunt Renata is going to need time to pull off a miracle."

"If we served this to guests," Ma howled, "we'd have to pay *them* as an apology!"

CHAPTER THREE

Duncan

*I*t was near midnight.

After everyone had left the campfire to settle in for the night, Duncan went up to the equipment garage to change the front tire on the Gator so it would be ready for Rowan and the vineyard crew in the morning. On his way back down the hill, he noticed a narrow wisp of smoke coming from where they'd had the campfire. The land around him was still and silent. No wind in the trees, no faraway sounds of cars on the county roads.

Temperance was there, alone in the dark. She sat on the picnic table bench with her arms wrapped around her middle, staring glassy-eyed into the remains of the fire. The embers cast her in shifting garnet and ruby and gold.

Duncan parked the truck and hopped out. "Hey," he said. "What are you still doing up?"

"Can't sleep."

"This can't be healthy, Temperance."

"Don't doctor me, Duncan," she said. "You're still up, too."

Duncan didn't reply. He sat across from her at the fire and stared at the embers until his eyes began to water, hypnotized by the pulse of heat and color.

After a while, Temperance wavered where she sat. In a sleep-husky voice, she said, "Fire seeds."

He chuckled. "What?"

"Embers are like"—she rubbed her eyes—"little fire seeds."

Sometimes, she was so cute, it caused him physical pain. He used to get to see this fanciful, unfiltered side of her all the time.

He missed her. How cruel, to have to miss a person who sat right across from you.

Duncan cracked his knuckles and stood. "Can I put this out?"

She shook her head and shoulders like she was coming out of a fog. "Yeah. I'm going back to the house soon."

He poured the water from a nearby bucket on the fire. Some of the charred wood continued to glow red in places, even after he doused it.

"They want to be fire again. The embers." She pointed to the tiny rubies near the center of the circle. "They're stubborn."

Duncan set the bucket down. "Nah, they're hopeful."

"Stubborn, hopeful." Temperance stood and stretched her arms high. "Same thing."

The embers hissed and sent up tendrils of steam and smoke when he poured on more water. This time, the fire went dark.

"You need a ride to the house?" he asked.

She breathed a little laugh through her nose. "Duncan, the house is fifty yards away."

"Just trying to help."

"Don't treat me like I'm fragile." The whimsy was gone from her voice, but her eyes glinted in the darkness. Like she'd drawn down the moon and banked its glow there. "Good night, Duncan." Temperance didn't bother to put on her sandals. She wandered toward the house with them dangling from her hand.

"'Night," he said, quieter than she'd have been able to hear. He watched her until she disappeared around the front of the house.

Duncan stayed for a while. The land was dark except for the muted blue of the solar lights through the hedges around the pool to the east, and the greenhouse high on the hill. It was almost supernatural in its pale inner glow, always seeming to catch whatever light the moon offered.

The window to Temperance's room lit with a cozy apricot glow a few minutes after she went inside. Ma and Dad always put her in the Primrose room because it was the best room in the bed-and-breakfast wing—complete with a double-sided fireplace between the bathroom and bedroom.

A tiny tuft of steam rose from the doused fire. Near the outer edge of the pit, a single ember remained.

Duncan picked up a pencil that had rolled off the picnic table into the grass. On the summer solstice, Spaniards would sometimes write a name or a wish on a piece of paper, then burn it at midnight to make the wish come true. They'd bring old items of clothing to burn, or jump over the bonfires to encourage good luck. In coastal cities, many people would walk backward into the sea for a new beginning. Duncan and his siblings never got to burn clothes or jump over fires, but Ma liked to keep her Galician and Spanish roots alive in the little ways she could.

Leftover squares of paper were weighed down beneath the candle tins on the table. Duncan slid a piece free and laid the pencil beside it. For a while, he simply looked at it.

His phone buzzed in his pocket. It was a text in the family group chat, from Arden.

> WELCOME TO THE
> FAMILY, ROWAN!

Since everyone but Mal had moved back to the valley, the group chat wasn't as lively as it had been when Maren and Nate and the kids had still lived in Westfall, and Patrick and Mercy were still in Philly. Recently, the chat was mostly selfies of Arden and her pet tortoise, Otis, and a video montage of farting dogs shared by Nate. Since Rowan had been added in the fall, she shared photos of plants and bugs and birds from around the vineyards, often with a brief treatise on some weird aspect of their biology.

Ma replied to Arden's recent text with a flurry of botanical emojis, including an entire row of eggplants. The chat then shifted into an explanation of why she shouldn't ever do that again.

Temperance had been added to the family group chat years ago at Maren's request, since there were often details shared about the kids' birthday parties and school events. She only ever participated in the chat if she was addressed directly, though.

Duncan wondered what it felt like for her, seeing the text from Arden welcoming Rowan into the family. On a summer night like this one when they were eighteen, Temperance had told him how jealous she'd been that Maren got to take the Brady name when she'd married Nate. How much she'd wanted to be a Brady.

"I'll see what I can do," Duncan had said.

"Is that a proposal?" she'd teased. Her hair had been in two braided buns, and she'd been wearing an old Foo Fighters T-shirt that kept sliding off her shoulder. She'd had a sunburn there.

And then he'd said, *"When I ask you to marry me, Temperance— you'll know it."*

Duncan looked again at the blank paper.

Her.

Write it, damn it.

Phone still in his hand, he tapped in Temperance's name. A single message from last fall was the only thing there, in lonely black pixels:

Are you there?

He'd sent it back in September after he'd impulsively driven to the city to see her at almost eleven o'clock at night. It wasn't until he reached the Philadelphia city limits that he realized he had no idea what the hell her address was. So, he'd pulled over on a tree-lined residential street, cut the ignition, sent the text, and waited.

Shortly after one o'clock in the morning, a police officer had tapped on his window and encouraged him to "get to wherever he was going."

Temperance never replied.

Hell. What did "Are you there?" even mean, really? Of course she was there. She was always somewhere out there. Doing life in her big, important way. Entirely separate from him. There wasn't a day since he'd met her nearly two decades ago that he wasn't acutely aware of her, even when they went months without contact.

> Are you there?

Duncan stared at those unanswered words for so long, they felt burned into his retinas.

He put the phone down and picked up the pencil.

Her.

Things between them were never easy or effortless. Either they stalled out for years or barreled forth without caution for consequences. He'd spent the last fourteen years being so preoccupied with the thought of not having her that it never occurred to him to attempt it. Now that he had the means, the motivation, and the clarity to try, the timing could absolutely not be worse. His literal dream was under his literal nose, and he didn't have the time or the bandwidth necessary to launch the most ambitious and high-stakes project of his life.

Duncan let the pencil hover over the paper until his hand began to shake.

Her.

When he looked up at the house again, she'd turned the light off in her room. Now, the darkened panes of glass stared back at him like a dead eye.

For several weeks after that pointless late-night drive into Philly last fall, his thoughts had been consumed by Temperance Madigan. The things he'd done wrong. The unfairness of it all. The possibility that there could be a chance for them again. All his other responsibilities began to slip, distracted as he'd been. It was the only time in his life he'd missed a deadline for Dad—and it wasn't even that he'd missed just one.

He'd missed three.

Duncan didn't write anything on the paper. Instead, he crumpled it in his hand and tucked it into his jeans pocket.

Stubborn, hopeful. It didn't matter.

Duncan put out the last persistent little ember with the heel of his boot and headed back to his cabin in the dark.

CHAPTER FOUR

Duncan

TWO WEEKS LATER

Duncan's day began as it often did—sprinting away from a donkey determined to take a bite out of his ass.

It happened at least once a week. Ears laid back, nostrils flared, the donkey broke off from the little flock of sheep she watched over and came at him like she had a taste for his blood. That morning, she was nearly on his heels by the time he kicked into high gear, rushing southeast through the luminescent morning fog that gave the property its name. Cloud Tide.

Duncan was a big guy, built for strength and endurance rather than speed. Even on a good day he had a hard time keeping ahead of the damned animal's hooves. Today, though—he wore a pair of shiny oxford dress shoes instead of his usual work boots. He had to windmill his arms to keep from slipping on the dew-slick grass.

From behind, someone honked a tractor horn to taunt him as he ran—a perky, high-pitched *beep-beeeeep!*

His whole family thought the donkey thing was funny as hell.

Without looking, he aimed a middle finger in the direction of the horn and hauled ass south toward the bank barn. He was pretty sure the donkey's aim was to incite terror rather than actually trample him, and he also knew she wouldn't get too far from her flock before she gave up the chase.

The lawn dipped and flattened, and the big stone bank barn materialized in the mist. The donkey veered off with a disrespectful parting *hee-haw* and cantered back up the hill toward the vineyards. Duncan slowed to a jog and stacked his hands on his head to catch his breath.

Harry stood in the open frame of the barn where two ten-foot doors would eventually hang. He wore a grass-stained UCLA T-shirt and a pair of cargo shorts so old and weathered they might disintegrate directly off his ass if he sat down too fast. He looked as natural in those clothes as he did in a white coat with a stethoscope around his neck.

"Ah, Ducky," Harry said. He poured black coffee into the gravel from a mug that read HOT BEAN WATER in vintage script. "I'll never get tired of watching her chase you."

Still winded, Duncan shot a glance over his shoulder. "Who'd have thought a donkey named after a fucking vegetable would be malevolence incarnate?" He undid the cuffs of his button-down to roll the sleeves up to his elbows.

"Asparagus is a sweetheart. She's just doing her part to ensure your cardiovascular health."

Up the hill, the donkey twitched an ear and blithely began nibbling clover.

Duncan grunted. "Should have named her *Asshole*."

"Hmm. Little too on the nose, don't you think?"

"Well. I'm not exactly known for subtlety, am I?" Duncan said.

"Good point." Harry used the empty mug to gesture at Duncan's clothes. "What's with the business casual?"

"What, these old rags?" He smoothed a hand down the front of his pale peach button-down.

"The only times I've ever seen you in anything other than jeans and T-shirts have been weddings and funerals," Harry said.

"I've got a thing in Linden today." Duncan crossed his arms and immediately uncrossed them when the seams at his shoulders and biceps strained.

His brother's brows twitched in curiosity, but thankfully, he didn't press.

"Now what the hell is going on?" Duncan said. "When you text me before seven in the morning, I know it's not going to be good."

"Well, I was taking coffee to my future bride." Harry set the empty mug on a stack of lumber. "When I found her, she gave me a kiss, patted me on the ass, and told me to get the hell out of her vineyard if I wasn't going to prune, pick, or plant something."

Duncan laughed. Rowan McKinnon could be prickly about people lingering in her vines if they weren't putting in the sweat equity. She had a bad habit of abandoning coffee mugs half-full, perched on the flat-topped trellis posts. At least once a month, Harry made a trip to the thrift store in Linden to stock up on old mugs. The family had an ongoing bet about how many they'd find in the vineyard later in the fall when the vines lost their leaves.

"Anyway," Harry continued, "I had some time, so I came down here to see how things were looking. It's—ah, I think it's best for you to just see."

The barn was a monolithic two-story structure that seemed to have sprung directly from the earth itself. With foundational walls of gray Pennsylvania fieldstone, it seemed as indigenous to the land as the forest of hemlock and red cedar that bordered it from behind.

When Duncan was a kid, Ma and Dad had taken him and Harry and Arden on a day trip to the historic Fallingwater house—Frank Lloyd Wright's most famous architectural achievement. It was perched at the top of a waterfall, tucked into surrounding forest and stone as if it had erupted there fully formed. In effortless, impeccable harmony with nature. For nearly two hours they'd stayed, touring the grounds and the interior, and even though ten-year-old Duncan had never heard phrases like *spatial quality* or *biomimicry* or *organic architecture*, that day at Fallingwater, he'd experienced what those words *meant*.

It felt a lot like what he'd recognize later as falling in love.

Since that day, he couldn't look at a building without noticing the way it met the land beneath it.

The upper story of the bank barn was level with the ground in front of him, with the basement level nestled partway into the sloping embankment that flattened to empty pasture. His family's winery was half-finished in that basement level. Since it was tucked into the hillside, humidity and temperature would passively stay perfect for aging wine year-round.

Projecting off the front of the barn was a bay that would be the future tasting room for the winery. About as big as a two-car garage, the front face of it was two aluminum-and-glass doors that opened and closed on a sliding ceiling track. "Rustic-industrial chic," Ma called it. Duncan had paneled it with reclaimed wood stained a deep espresso brown that contrasted beautifully with the pale gray stone around it.

He followed Harry to where the tasting room opened into the main interior space of the barn. The sweet mustiness of old wood and sawdust mingled with the damp mineral odor of fresh concrete. From both gable ends, gauzy light poured in through floor-to-ceiling casement windows, the glass so new it still had the protective film stuck to it. Bolts of sunshine slashed through the open cupolas on the roof, intersecting with the exposed planks and trusses overhead. It felt like standing in the belly of an enormous upside-down boat.

Harry quickly held out his arm to stop Duncan from crossing the threshold into the tasting room. Then he pointed at the ground.

It took Duncan's brain several seconds to process what he saw.

Last night, he and his crew had left the freshly poured black concrete floor as smooth as a mirror. Now, the surface was imprinted with dozens—no, *hundreds*—of tiny animal footprints, and the concrete had long since begun to cure.

"Jesus Jennifer Coolidge Christ," Duncan muttered under his breath.

Harry tilted his head sideways like he was appraising a painting. "I think it's artistic."

"Fuh-huck—" Duncan bowed his head and pinched the bridge of his nose.

"Raccoon, you think? Possum?"

Duncan groaned at the ceiling. "I don't have time for this. What—*why*—"

Harry pointed to the wall behind the bar. "I think whatever it was wanted your pastrami."

Perched on a two-by-four stud in the open wall sat the remainder of his lunch from yesterday afternoon, a half-eaten hoagie from Hogger's deli. He'd put the damned thing there intending to come right back to it after a call with the electrical subcontractor he'd hired to bring the winery level up to code. Until that moment, Duncan hadn't remembered eating at all. It had been at least a year since he'd finished an entire lunch on a weekday.

He turned away, swiped a hand over his beard, and muttered to himself. "—trip hazard—barstools won't sit flush—impossible to keep clean—"

That concrete had a ten-day cure time before furniture and appliances could be put down, and he still needed to finish the ceiling and drywall before he brought anything else in. He had about two weeks until the sink and refrigeration units were due to arrive, and he couldn't seal the hardwoods on the main floor of the barn until he moved out all the tables and chairs and barstools from where they were being temporarily stored.

He paced, still talking more to himself than to Harry.

"—crew coming Monday to install the ceiling fans in the barn, and I've got some electrical to finish in the back kitchen. Still need to move the rest of my crap out of the loft so Dad and Nate can move the office—could probably delay that. And—ah—" Duncan cut off and swore under his breath.

Harry frowned. "And what?"

And the leaking roof and lead paint in the cabin.

And the ruts in the drive into the vineyard, before another storm dumped enough rain to turn it into a fucking Slip 'N Slide again. The dry-rotted gasket on that ancient refrigerator in the greenhouse. The old pool house's plumbing issues were a recurring nightmare, and the roof on the old gambrel barn in the east pasture had finally collapsed after a bad storm in April. A hundred other little things.

It felt like a giant, expensive puzzle spilled out onto an eleven-acre table, and he was the only person who knew where all the pieces went.

Harry and Rowan wanted to have their wedding reception here next month. Ma wanted a fully functional event space along with the completed winery by late September—but Duncan's personal timeline was tighter. If everything went according to plan, he had about two months to figure out how to tell them he'd need to scale his workload back by at least half. And more important—that he couldn't run Brady Brothers anymore.

Duncan felt time bear down like the barn itself was collapsing around him.

"There's no way around it." He blew out a frustrated breath. "We're going to have to hammer out the whole goddamned slab and start over. There's no *time*—"

"Duncan." Harry put himself between his brother and the doorway. "What have you been doing in Linden? I've been watching you age before my eyes over the last six months."

Duncan strode around him and out of the barn. "I've just got a lot of plates in the fire."

Harry followed close behind. "You mix idioms when you're stressed."

Duncan grunted and kept walking.

It wasn't the first time Harry'd tried to talk to him about Linden. Everyone else in the family was so accustomed to his perpetual hustle that they never remarked on how often he was gone, or how tired he looked. The hours he spent in Linden could be explained away as vineyard or Brady Brothers business—site visits, client meetings, trips to the hardware store. Networking with local artisans, farm equipment auctions. Without exaggerating, he could give any of a hundred different reasons for spending a few hours a day in Linden, and his family would buy it.

The truth would actually be less believable.

It had been almost two years now, and nobody knew he'd gone back to school at Linden Community College. Duncan meant to keep it that way. If nobody knew he'd gone back, nobody would have to know if he fucked up and failed out again.

After classes, he'd head back to the valley by midafternoon, balancing Brady Brothers tasks with projects around the vineyard and the last of the guest room renovations in the main house. In the evenings, his retrofit work at his cabin would begin. Radiant heat in the floors, double-paned windows, low-flow everything. A new slate roof would go on the first week of June, and next would be solar panels.

Duncan worked each day until the sun was gone, or until his fatigue made it hazardous to handle power tools or sharp things or electricity. Whichever came first. Some nights, when his hands were too sore to function, he'd take a break from the cabin reno, make a cup of shitty coffee, and get ahead on reading or school projects until he fell asleep at the table.

Handling all the things became a passive process for him. A simple matter of maintaining momentum, sticking to routine. But all that careful equilibrium didn't account for regular close proximity to his ultimate distraction.

Temperance skimmed the outer edge of the Chambourcin vineyard on her morning run, airy as a dandelion seed in her short, short white shorts and yellow sneakers. Without bothering to cover her mouth, she yawned as she ran, and Duncan could almost hear the sweet little *huh* sound she always made at the trailing end of it. The sway of her body turned her ponytail into a white-hot flickering flame.

Even from that distance, she made his bones ache.

He tightened a fist in the front of his hair until his eyes watered.

The high-pitched *beep-beeeep* of the Gator horn sounded again from the direction of the Chardonnay vineyard. Rowan sat behind the wheel in an old khaki hat over twin ginger braids. From the back of the little utility vehicle, a dune flag jutted nine feet into the air on a flexible pole, bouncing and whipping in the air as it went. Duncan had originally attached the flag to the Gator so he'd be able to find it when Rowan inevitably left it parked in one of the vineyards overnight, and someone had made a game out of anonymously changing it. Today's flag simply read I BRAKE FOR POSSUMS in block letters.

Rowan slowed the Gator to a crawl alongside Temperance as she ran. Sunshine lit her up like an ember, and the muscles in her thighs shuddered with every footfall.

Duncan's mouth went dry. His bones felt unhinged from their joints. He started back up the hill, and Harry followed.

Around dusk last night, he'd spotted her jogging northward toward the greenhouse as he finished up with his crew at the barn. And now here she was, barely eight hours later, running again. He'd always been impressed and a little intimidated by her discipline, but he also knew what simmered just beneath her cool exterior. Temperance Madigan was a shaken bottle of champagne with a loose cork. She ran because she *had* to.

"Duncan?" Harry said.

Hell. He felt like a juggler who'd swapped one of his rubber balls for a hand grenade.

"I think you need a day off," Harry said.

"I'm like Cinderella, man. I can't go to the ball unless I get all my chores done."

"Anything I can help with? I kind of miss the days of you bossing me around this place, making me do your bullshit grunt work."

"Ah, Doc." Duncan dug deep for levity. "I'm sure all the calluses on your pretty hands have been moisturized away by now."

"Fuck off." Harry laughed, smoothing a hand over his belly. "God, I was so ripped last summer. Pretty sure I have you to thank for Rowan finally falling for me."

Duncan laughed, too. "She didn't fall for your abs, Harry."

"Really, though—I'll be on baby watch for four different patients soon, but if you need a hand over the next week, let me know."

"Hell. We should go into business together. Call it 'Parts and Labor.'"

Close to the house now, Temperance laughed at something Rowan shouted to her from the Gator. They were too far away to hear, but Duncan knew that laugh like a favorite song. Intense but quiet, punctuated at the end with a husky little *hmm* in the back of her throat. Her eyes would sparkle long afterward, like the laughter had left behind some kind of joyful residue.

"I'd love to see you two spending more time together," Harry said.

Duncan pulled up so short the soles of his shoes skidded on the grass. "I'm sorry, what?"

"You and Temperance. There's always been static between you two. I think you should try to be friends."

Friends.

With Temperance Madigan.

Duncan set his teeth against the frayed cuticle of his thumbnail and ripped sideways. Blood welled hot against his bottom lip.

Harry had been high-minded and big-hearted ever since he was a kid. To him, it was a logical request. Temperance had, in all the ways that mattered, been a member of the Brady family since the first summer she spent with Maren and Nate when she was in high school. Maren and Nate's kids were her niece and nephews, just like they were Duncan's. Harry'd been one of her closest friends since they were teenagers, and now her best friend since college was going to marry Harry. Temperance Madigan was woven through the fabric of the Brady family from multiple directions, impossible to extricate without leaving a hole.

But there was more to it than Harry knew. Friendship hadn't ever been on the table for Duncan and Temperance. Back when they first met, she was barely fourteen and he'd been a few months from fifteen. They couldn't be friends because they'd had nothing in common.

At seventeen, friendship wasn't an option because they couldn't keep their hands off each other whenever they were alone together.

At eighteen, they couldn't be friends because they'd fallen into devastating, soul-walloping first love with each other.

Now, they couldn't be friends because they hated who they became when they were together.

What if they tried true platonic friendship now, and Temperance decided it suited *her* just fine, but *he* sank even deeper into his feelings? Hell. He'd been treading water for fourteen years. Infusing his lifelong craving for her with the warmth and intimacy of true friendship would pull him permanently, unconditionally under.

"Maybe just try?" Harry studied him with a thoughtful downward draw of his brows. "This weird vibe between you two can't go on forever. Listen. If not for me, then for Rowan. For peace, for the wedding."

Duncan had a giant soft spot for Rowan, and Harry knew it. He exhaled a quiet laugh. "You fucker."

Harry grinned. "I'll take that as a yes."

CHAPTER FIVE

Temperance

*F*rankie Moreau had been a constant in Temperance's life since they'd been freshman dorm roommates in college. Today, their friendship leveled up into an elite and unexpected new tier as Temperance lay belly-down on a bed while Frankie tweezed wood splinters out of her left butt cheek.

"Anyway," Frankie said as she bent over Temperance's ass, "at the rehearsal dinner last night, bride number one's dad got so trashed on caipirinhas, he fell and gave himself a black eye trying to get into his Lyft. Bride number two texted me this morning to ask how good I am with Photoshop, but bride number one apparently thinks it's hilarious and doesn't want me to edit it out at all. Authenticity, she says."

Frankie sat up for a second to stretch her back. She wore a celery-green bikini top and a pair of denim cutoffs so short the front pockets peeped out under the frayed hems. Temperance's own swimsuits were in storage boxes at her parents' place in Linden, so earlier that afternoon, she and Frankie and Rowan had driven to Nelson's on County Road 25. A combination bait shop, gas station, convenience store, and pizza place, it was where she and Duncan used to buy condoms and Hank's grape soda the summer they were eighteen. Their fountain-drink dispenser also had the soft pelleted ice she loved.

Nelson's had only two swimsuits left in their dubiously named "summer aisle," stuffed on a shelf next to sunscreen that was most certainly expired, a few pairs of goggles that looked suspiciously pre-owned, and an impressive assortment of fishing lures. One of the suits was a camouflage bikini a few sizes too big, leaving Temperance with a hideous gold lamé one-piece for the bargain price of six dollars and ninety-nine cents. The fabric smelled faintly of hot dogs and old cigarette smoke, and when she'd pulled it on, the elastic in the left shoulder strap surrendered to dry rot and refused to snap back into place. It kept sliding down her arm.

Rowan had nabbed a trucker hat with a cartoon cactus and the phrase DON'T BE A PRICK on the front, and Frankie bought a long-stemmed artificial flower that was actually a pair of cheap red panties creatively folded to look like a rose. When Temperance asked what she planned to do with it, Frankie had simply answered, "The heart wants what it wants, T.J."

Frankie pinched her with the tweezers.

"Ow!"

Frankie hissed through her teeth and squeaked, "Sorry."

Temperance laid her head sideways on the pillow. Outside the cabin's bedroom window, sunshine was the clear gold of honey fresh from the comb. Notes of an old Indigo Girls song drifted in through the window screen. The faint tones of wind chimes from the porch were bright and familiar, and more than a little nostalgic. They'd been restrung many times over the years, but they were the same ones that had hung on the Bradys' old porch in Westfall as long as she'd known them.

"Why do so many people get trashed at rehearsal dinners the night before weddings?" Frankie mused. "Did I ever tell you about the best man who claimed he had *bird flu* the day of the wedding, and everyone had to get tested afterward? Turns out, he was hungover from too much Wild Turkey. What an asshole."

Listening to Frankie chatter on sometimes felt like wobbling in and out of rush-hour traffic on the back of an old bicycle. Temperance closed her eyes for a moment and enjoyed the ride.

"Anyway, this weekend's couple has a swing routine planned for their first dance at the reception, and everyone thinks they're coming out to some tepid Ed Sheeran song. They're doing 'Erotic City' by Prince—can you even imagine?" Frankie sighed happily. "I'm pretty sure it's going to be the best night of my life, and I'm just the photographer."

Frankie pinched her again.

Temperance pushed up onto her elbows again and twisted to look over her shoulder. "Oh my *god*, Frances—"

"I am doing my best, okay?"

"Aim for the tiny slivers of wood—"

"Listen, your butt is so pale—"

"—and leave my poor skin—"

"—it's like trying to thread a needle while staring straight into the sun—"

"—alone."

There was motion in the half-open doorway to the bedroom. Bare feet on old hardwood scuffed to a halt.

It was Duncan.

"What in the *MTV Spring Break* is happening here?" he said.

Frankie jabbed the tweezers in his direction. "Your dock tried to take a bite out of her ass, that's what."

"My *what*—"

"Your *dock*," Frankie enunciated.

"Her ass?" said Duncan.

Temperance yanked a pillow over her exposed butt cheek. "Do *not* look at my ass."

"That's my *pillow*—"

"Absent thyself." Frankie made a dainty little *shoo* motion with her hand.

Duncan pointed. "—on your *ass*."

It was hardly the first time her ass had been in contact with one of Duncan Brady's bed pillows.

"Out," Frankie repeated.

"I need some privacy. I have to make a phone call," he said.

"Five minutes," said Frankie.

His voice rose. "This is my place."

Temperance pushed up on her elbows again. "What do you mean, it's your place?"

"Mine." The single syllable was more of a growl, drawn out in the middle and rumbly at the end.

Frankie stayed silent.

"I thought your parents bought it to extend the vineyard—"

"Mine." He bent low and pointed out the window. "Four acres, that way. Inclusive of this bedroom."

"Why?" Temperance said.

Duncan did a double take. "Because I wanted it." He said it like it was the most obvious thing in the world.

"But *why*?"

He was motionless for a moment, save a flicker of muscle at his temple. "I guess I'm not at a place in my life where I pass up a chance to get something I want if I have the means to get it."

Close your mouth, Temperance.

Her phone blasted her parents' ringtone from where it sat on the bedside table. It vibrated against the wood as it rang, turning slowly counterclockwise as if it were possessed.

All three of them eyed the phone until it stopped.

"You still avoiding their calls?" Duncan said.

"I'm not *avoiding*—"

"Yes, she's avoiding their calls," Frankie said.

Duncan looked from Temperance to Frankie and back to Temperance again. "I'll come back later." He did a tense about-face and disappeared down the short hallway.

The pillow *did* smell like Duncan. She'd sensed it when she'd first lain down, but she'd passed it off as some phantom memory. Now that she knew the place was his, she felt absolutely surrounded by him.

"Wow," Frankie said once he was gone.

"Don't say it."

Frankie leaned back in with the tweezers. "Say what?"

"You're going to ask me when I plan to tell Rowan."

Through the window, Temperance had a clear view of Lake Vesper and the big T-shaped wooden dock jutting out from the shore. It was the solid, sturdy kind, with posts sunk deep into the lake bed. Rowan was there, launching herself into the lake—wild-haired, long-limbed, and awkward as a newborn giraffe.

Temperance loved her. So much.

Frankie and Temperance knew nearly everything about each other, from the mundane (Frankie couldn't get to sleep unless she had socks on, mint toothpaste made Temperance gag) to the strangely specific (cold SpaghettiOs straight from the can was Frankie's regular PMS craving, Temperance used to bite her toenails as a kid). There were things that Frankie and Temperance knew about each other that Rowan didn't know about either of them. It wasn't an exclusivity thing, or that their friendship was stronger than what either of them had with Rowan. It was simply that they'd already dealt with everything the year before they'd met her.

By then, Temperance had packed Duncan Brady away into a feelings-proof box and sank it deep inside her with metaphorical cinder blocks attached.

But the thing about burying feelings in feelings-proof boxes was that covering them up didn't actually make them go away. They'd still be there if you peeked under the lid, and they'd just be older. Hungrier. And ready to make you pay for ignoring them for so long.

And now—record scratch—Rowan was a few weeks away from becoming a Brady herself. Another permanent thread that tied Temperance to the Brady family.

Out the window, she watched Duncan pace the length of the dock, occasionally nudging at the wood with his bare toes. In his hands was a roll of gray duct tape. Every few steps, he ripped off a piece of the tape and crouched to stick it down, presumably marking spots where the wood needed repairs.

Temperance had to swallow hard while she watched him. Afternoon sun traced him in coppery light. He was *big*, but not so ripped with muscle that he'd gone completely solid. Strong by necessity rather than vanity—with powerful arms and thick thighs from using his body hard, every day. It had been a long time since she'd lingered in the space between his arms, but she knew firsthand that there was just enough give over the broad muscles there that the cuddling experience was truly world-class.

"Well." Frankie sat up to stretch again. "Since you mentioned it—"

Temperance groaned into the pillow. "Listen, you've never told Rowan *your* secret."

"Mine doesn't have any present-day relevance. My secret isn't around all the time, staring us in the face like a Spanish-Irish god with big brown eyes and a panty-melting smile."

"My answer hasn't changed, Frances."

"T.J. Come on. If I notice it, others are, too."

"No. You only catch it because you know the full backstory. Duncan and I stay in our corners. Nobody else notices."

"You go ahead and keep telling yourself that." Frankie gave her a single tap on her butt and stood. "You're good. Splinter-free."

"Thank you." Temperance reached back to pull her swimsuit into place and rolled to a sitting position.

Out in the lake, the Bradys played a game of Chicken. Maren and Mercy were on their twin spouses' shoulders, and they seemed to be teaming up against Rowan and Harry. Rowan laughed so hard she didn't seem to be breathing anymore. Duncan was in the water now, too, with Bess Everett on his shoulders. The eldest Everett brother, Colby, had been a year behind Temperance at Linden High School, and he'd been one of her closest friends from marching band. A late bloomer, Colby's teenage claim to fame had been his ability to burp the ABCs in one breath. Now, he was enormous, legitimately gorgeous in a rugged man-bun-and-flannel sort of way, and truly one of the sweetest human beings Temperance had ever met. He was the winemaker at Three Birds, the vineyard and winery a few miles down the road from Cloud Tide. They'd shared a field crew for almost a year now, and the Brady and Everett families had begun to feel less like business partners and more like friends.

The Bradys drew people into their world like dandelions drew bees.

Yelping laughter echoed off the water as Duncan and Bess moved in to defend Rowan against Maren and Mercy's joint attack. Temperance had never known a group of adults who loved games as much as the Bradys did. They seemed to acknowledge that it was a fundamental aspect of human nature to simply want to *play*, and they refused to believe the urge disappeared at a certain age.

By any material or superficial standards, Temperance had had a good childhood. As soon as she was out of diapers, she did everything—adventure camps, science camps, museum camps, sports camps. She had a live-in nanny who was also a music instructor. She was in the after-school STEM club. In high school, she'd been a cheerleader *and* in the marching band. At halftime, she'd have to scurry off the field, pull her band uniform over her cheer outfit, march in the show, then rush back to the sidelines to cheer for the rest of the game.

But after only a few weeks with the Bradys that first summer she'd stayed with Maren and Nate, she'd realized the way she was being raised wasn't a generous and indulgent one. It was that her parents had efficiently outsourced her upbringing in a way that minimized them actually having to parent her.

Temperance had been fourteen that first summer with the Bradys. Her mother had needed to move quickly to fill a gap in executive leadership in the family's nonprofit foundation after her grandmother passed away. But Laine Talbot-Madigan didn't go anywhere without Corbin Madigan, Corbin Madigan didn't go anywhere without Laine Talbot-Madigan, and they refused to let Temperance tag along with them, having convinced themselves that Maren's exposure to the humanitarian-aid world at a young age had been the true reason she'd washed out of medical school.

So, Maren became useful to them again.

Maren had jumped at the chance for Temperance to stay with her and Nate that summer. Temperance had grudgingly agreed at first—not that she'd actually had a choice. Initially, the biggest draw was that Westfall, the little valley town where Maren and Nate lived, was just a few county roads over from Linden, so she'd be able to see her friends every day if she wanted.

By the second week of June, she was head over heels for the entire Brady family.

They hadn't been perfect. There were dust bunnies under the couch and piles of shoes left haphazardly by the front door. There was bickering and moodiness, and a family photo on canvas in the hallway that fell off the wall every time one of the brothers slammed their bedroom door after a petty argument. But the occasional hot temper actually endeared them to her even more than the absence of it would have. The way she'd grown up, nobody felt enough or cared enough to bother raising their voice.

The Bradys paid attention. If one of them was going to the library, they'd make sure to round up everyone else's overdue books. Whenever anyone drove someone else's car, they brought it back with a full tank of gas. Gia Brady saved the burnt corners of brownies for Duncan, and Will Brady saved the half-popped kernels of popcorn for Harry. Cream for coffee would often spoil in the refrigerator because everyone who usually used it would leave it for someone else once they felt the carton getting low.

For the next four years, Temperance lived her real life during those three summer months. The other nine were just spent waiting.

Temperance swung her legs over the side of the bed and glanced out the window screen. Laughter echoed around the basin.

Again, her eyes were drawn right to Duncan. In a crowd, he was the first person she looked for when she arrived, and the last person she put eyes on when she left.

"T.J.?"

"Hm?" Temperance turned to where Frankie leaned against the doorframe. "Sorry, what?"

"I said—are you ready to get back out there?"

Temperance pushed the strap of her swimsuit back up and fluffed the imprint of her face out of Duncan's pillow. "Let's do it."

CHAPTER SIX

Temperance

*F*rankie and Temperance sat at the end of the dock, swirling their feet in clear cool water the color of sweet tea.

The air was pollen-hazy and heady with the musky scent of lake mud and sweet white clover. A glass of lemonade streamed condensation down Frankie's wrist, and her cropped hair was pulled into a glossy black nub. Sweaty tendrils clung to her neck. Temperance applied SPF 50 to the tops of her thighs for the fourth time that afternoon, dashing the leftover bit across her forehead and nose. Still, she could feel her skin turning pink.

Out in the deeper part of the water, Maren launched a waterlogged football to a crowd of people who shoved, splashed, and dunked each other to get it. Duncan caught the ball one-handed and fell backward. He disappeared for a few seconds and shot to the surface in shallower water, dark and sleek as a seal. Water beaded on skin slick with sunscreen, making the tattoos on his arms look freshly painted on. A wide cuff of an Irish county tartan around one biceps, an elaborate honeysuckle vine around the other. Blackbirds in flight, a flourish of red poppies, a bearded man with a long, curving pipe. Columns of muscle alongside his spine bunched and flexed as he fired the ball back to the group, and the thin fabric of his trunks hugged the high curves of an ass that was exceptional in the literal sense of the word.

When Nate broadsided Harry to get the ball, Duncan tipped back his head and laughed.

She'd always loved the way he laughed. Full-throated, uninhibited, loud. Sometimes his nose crinkled and his eyes squeezed shut, and the dimple on his upper cheek would appear. Sometimes he laughed until he cried.

Duncan Brady knew how to do joy.

With both hands, he pushed his hair back, squeezing water down his neck. He turned to look right at her. His big smile faltered, downshifting into a look so loaded it made the little hairs on the back of her neck lift. The force of his gaze felt like a physical shove—a compression in her chest, a tilt in her belly.

He turned and swam away with powerful pulls of his arms through the water.

Duncan Brady knew how to do pain, too.

Frankie bent to scoop water onto her legs. "I saw that."

Temperance made a vague sound in her throat and tipped ice into her mouth from her Nelson's forty-ounce Whistle Wetter travel mug. It had a cartoon groundhog on the side, giving a smiling thumbs-up. The damned thing was bigger than her entire head, and she'd had to pay eighteen dollars for it. She'd initially grabbed a Styrofoam cup at the gas station's soda machine, but Rowan's look of disappointment had flayed her alive. So she'd grabbed the reusable one, feeling personally responsible for the planet's polystyrene problem.

"You two have been playing eye-tag all day," Frankie said.

Temperance set the mug down and leaned forward, rubbing her temples.

"He can't keep his eyes off you, but he's shockingly good at making it seem incidental. Seriously. He deserves an Academy Award." She dropped her voice low and dug a knuckle into the side of Temperance's thigh. "Oh. Here we go—watch."

Duncan retrieved the ball again, pivoting sideways in the water.

"In three, two, one—" Frankie whispered.

As if on cue, Duncan scanned the shore, starting a little north of the cabin. Eventually, his eyes landed on Temperance, lingering for a few beats longer than they did on anything—or anyone—else.

Her heart pulsed like sonar, firing an aching *ping* into the deepest places inside her.

"God." Frankie did a melodramatic full-body shudder. "The secondhand angst is giving me a contact buzz."

Out in the lake, Rowan swam their way.

"Behave," Temperance whispered.

"No promises."

Rowan boosted herself onto the dock, raining cool water down on Temperance's legs. "What did I miss?" she said, squeezing her thick ginger braid. "Who are we talking about?"

Temperance looked at Frankie with pleading eyes. Frankie sighed.

"That's really working for me." Glittering droplets of lake water fell from Frankie's toes when she pointed them in Mal's direction. "I actively dislike him, but I also want him to back me up against the nearest wall."

Rowan laughed. When Temperance and Frankie didn't, she blinked, lowered her voice, and leaned in. "Wait. Seriously? He's at least ten years older than you."

"I don't get it either, but their age difference is the least of the reasons why I'm confused," Temperance said.

"You two have no imagination," Frankie said. "Look at him."

Malcolm Brady managed to be dark and broody even while sun-saturated and lounging in a massive avocado floatie that said HAPPILY AVO AFTER along the side. A black hat sat over his face, but his forearms alone made a compelling case for Frankie's argument. They were roped with lean muscle and a few prominent veins ran elbow to wrist. Big hands. Long fingers.

Okay, fine. He was legitimately hot—in a sullen, whipcord kind of way.

Abruptly, he lifted his head and tipped the hat off his face with a thumb to stare right back at them. Heavy brows crowded together in a scowl, and a swoop of black hair fell forward into his eyes.

"Put your tongue away, Frances," Temperance muttered into her giant plastic mug.

Mal let the hat fall back in place.

Rowan aggressively chewed a thumbnail. "I'm marrying his brother in a few weeks."

"I know," said Frankie.

"And it's very likely Mal will be here when you come to visit me."

"Now that you mention it, he *has* been here a lot more lately, hasn't he?" Frankie pressed a fingertip to her plush bottom lip. "Golly, I wonder why."

"You're the only person in this world who can use the word *golly* unironically and get away with it." To Rowan, Temperance said, "Did you know she has a nickname for him?"

"Oh god," Rowan groaned.

"Malcolm Baddie."

Frankie shrugged a bare shoulder. "I think it's perfect."

"I think *Scowlcolm* is a missed opportunity," Temperance said.

Rowan leaned in again. "Listen to me, Frances. Have you ever hooked up with someone whose family you have to play it cool around? Polite conversation gets impossible after you've seen all the different versions of their adult son's o-face."

"Oh, really?" Frankie swiveled to face Temperance. "That sounds tough. I can't imagine. Can you *imagine*, T.J.?"

Temperance tipped a few pieces of ice into Frankie's lap. "*Oops—*"

Frankie screeched and laughed. Once again, Mal lifted the hat from his face, just enough that Temperance saw a raised eyebrow and glinting black eyes.

Frankie regained her composure fast and leaned back on her hands. The movement boosted her breasts forward, and a streak of sweat traced down the center of her belly. Mal's glower darkened, and he laid his hat over his lap instead of returning it to his head.

"Boner alert," Rowan said under her breath, and the three women snort-laughed like piglets.

Temperance almost felt bad for him.

"It seems to have worked out fine for you, Rosebud," Frankie said. "Just think, if you hadn't followed your heart and taken the chance—"

"It wasn't my heart calling the shots at first, Frank." Rowan lay back on a towel and covered her eyes with her forearm.

"Doesn't matter."

Rowan said, "I didn't *know* I was going to fall in love with Harry when we started sleeping together."

"I did." Frankie raised her hand. "Just for the record."

"We know," Temperance and Rowan said in unison.

"Smugness isn't cute on you," Temperance said.

"Everything's cute on me." Frankie adjusted the strap of her bikini top. "Malcolm Brady would be cute on me."

"Dear god," Rowan said. "I already have concomitant embarrassment—"

"Stop," Temperance said. "Did you just use the word *concomitant* in casual conversation?"

"There is nothing *casual* about this conversation," Rowan breathed.

"This sounds a lot like when T.J. told you not to hook up with Harry, and you did anyway," said Frankie.

"Listen." Temperance held up a finger and slurred around a mouthful of ice, "I didn't *tell* her not to—"

Well. She definitely *had*. She'd warned Rowan and Harry away from each other after she'd noticed their instantaneous chemistry the night they'd met, and back then, Temperance had told herself it was out of a desire to protect them both from inevitable heartache. "Opposites attract" was a thing that only ever worked in romance books and rom-coms, and two people didn't get more opposite than Harry Brady and Rowan McKinnon. But there'd been a shameful, self-serving side to it, too. Temperance hadn't wanted yet another invisible string permanently tying her to Duncan Brady.

"You *strongly recommended*," Frankie said.

Rowan sat up on her elbows. "That was different, anyway."

"How so?"

"Malcolm is a cyborg. He probably plugs in at night instead of sleeping. He's also ten years older than you. Harry is—" Rowan's voice went soft and melty. "Well, he's Harry."

Frankie laughed and patted her on the leg. "Oh, how quickly the president of the Marriage Repudiation Club has fallen."

"I'm good at romance now," Rowan said.

Temperance stopped mid-crunch on a mouthful of ice and gave her a long look.

Frankie grimaced. "Wow."

A flush blotched Rowan's neck and cheekbones. "What? I am, damn it."

Frankie snorted. "Says the woman who thought *Me Before You* was a porn flick."

"Says the woman who reminds everyone at Christmas that mistletoe is a poisonous parasite," Temperance added.

"Says the woman who insists *Pride and Prejudice and Zombies* is the best Austen adaptation," said Frankie.

Temperance sniffed. "Obviously not. The 2005 version. No contest."

Frankie exhaled a sound of outrage. "Colin Firth would like a word—"

Temperance raised her voice to talk over Frankie. "Matthew Macfadyen is the superior Darcy; I won't be taking questions at this time."

"T.J., I swear to *god* I will push you off this dock—" Frankie bent down and scooped a handful of water at Temperance's face.

"Okay, okay," Rowan cut in. "I get it. Hilarious. Obviously, I've changed." She looked dreamily into the lake, where Harry leapt to catch the football. He missed by a mile, sinking backward under the water with arms flailing.

"He's a good one." Temperance smiled.

Frankie made a happy sound of agreement. Then she said, "Did you know my phone autocorrects Colin Firth to Colin Girth?"

"I think that's beautiful," said Rowan.

Temperance laughed. "You're typing Colin Firth's name into your phone frequently enough that you've noticed?"

They all laughed. For a while, they sat quietly and looked out over the lake. Fuzzy cottonwood seeds floated over the water like summer snow.

After a while, Rowan asked, "You have a date for the wedding?"

"I asked Bodhi, but it's too close to the end of the term for him."

"Aww, Tastykake," Frankie said.

Bodhi Rao was a neurosurgery fellow at Stanford now, and she hadn't seen him in several years. During residency, they'd had a near-perfect friends-with-benefits arrangement—he was sexy and funny and generous in bed, and had zero expectations once they were off the mattress. They'd come to each other's rescue a few times over the years—her as his date to a few family weddings, him as her date to a handful of work functions. Years ago, after a glimpse of his torso in a shirtless selfie he'd sent, Rowan and Frankie had begun calling him "Tastykake." Because he was an absolute snack.

Temperance didn't have any other prospects. Her last date had been a few months ago, dinner at an overrated bistro in Philadelphia where one of the courses had been a truly gruesome thing called *culinary foam.* The guy was a software engineer named Tyler who looked exactly like you'd expect a guy named Tyler to look—and he was shockingly as much of a ten in person as he'd been in his profile photo. But he'd quoted Internet memes at least six times during their dinner conversation, and at the end of the meal he'd wrapped his napkin around his pointer finger, dipped it in his water glass, and used the wet cloth to wipe his mouth. Temperance had swung her eyes around the room to look for a hidden camera crew, convinced she was on a prank show.

The culinary foam had been a precise metaphor for how unsettling and unsatisfying the whole experience was.

"Speaking of the wedding," Rowan said. "How's it going with you and Duncan?"

Temperance almost aspirated the chunk of ice in her mouth. *"Hnngh?"*

"Harry told me you two decorated most of the greenhouse for his proposal. It just occurred to me that I never notice you two doing anything together. I'm just glad you're able to be friends."

Again, Frankie dug her knuckle into the side of Temperance's thigh.

"I wouldn't go *that* far." Temperance rammed her knee into Frankie's.

Out on the lake, Maren and Nate's kids swam at Duncan from both directions, and he rapid-fire lifted them and tossed them backward in the water, squealing and flailing. Long ago, she could have written this entire day as a scene in a screenplay. The gauzy golden air, sweet with clover and Coppertone and campfire. The laughter. The family.

Alice and Grey were living renderings of what her children with Duncan might have looked like. They had the dusky Brady complexion and dark wavy hair, but Grey's mouth and the shape of his eyebrows were distinctly Maren's, and Alice had her nose. Baby Leo sat on a quilt with Gia in the shade near the cabin. He had the glacial Madigan-blue eyes, just like Temperance's own.

She hadn't let her imagination carry her to that place in years, but in that moment, her mind took her there without consent or warning. It was an emotional riptide, and she didn't even have a chance to take a breath.

"For peace. For the wedding." Rowan dipped her head to meet Temperance's eyes. "It would mean a lot to Harry," she coaxed.

Checkmate.

Duncan Brady was the embodiment of full-throttle joy. She knew just how it felt to be on the receiving end of that big way he loved and laughed and cared. She knew what it felt like to lose it, too.

Friends.

Temperance squeezed Rowan's hand and met her eyes. "Okay, honey. I'll try."

CHAPTER SEVEN

Duncan

*D*uncan had owned the cabin for a few months, but it had only been habitable for the past few weeks. The porch was nearly as large as its interior, and it greeted him with percussive creaks underfoot whenever he climbed the steps.

The cabin sat at an angle facing west instead of head-on toward the water as lakefront properties usually did. Whoever designed it nearly eighty years ago had optimized it for sunset views over Lake Vesper, and the corridor of pines and sugar maples that loomed around it was obviously far older than the cabin itself. Every one of Duncan's instincts told him that the place had been built to collaborate with nature rather than defy it.

To the west, a few other lonely cabins dotted the shoreline. Most mornings when he sat out there with his mug of tea, he felt like the only soul for miles, save the occasional old-timer in a canoe and a few loudmouthed kingfishers in the cattails. Now, the place was alive with the sounds of music and his family's laughter and conversation.

A cheap cork dartboard hung from a rusty wreath hook to the right of the front door. Patrick's first throw went high, his dart sinking into the weathered wooden plaque that hung above the cabin door: DOG STAR COTTAGE it read in rustic block letters.

"Watch it, asshole." Duncan reached up and tugged the dart free.

Patrick waved a hand toward the sign. "What does that even mean, anyway?"

"I don't know. The place didn't come with an owner's manual."

Duncan wasn't sure of the origin of the cabin's name, but it was one of the things that had made him fall in love with it. There was a grove of flowering dogwoods around the back, at the edge of the forest of taller trees. The porch also faced toward Sirius, the night sky's brightest star. The Dog Star. Harry had a more whimsical idea—that the place was somehow the inspiration for Keanu Reeves's band's name, Dogstar.

A FOR SALE BY OWNER sign for the cabin had lingered for about a year at the top of the gravel access road it shared with his folks' property. Its four waterfront acres were in a flood plain, and the cabin itself was a structural disaster that no potential buyers wanted to contend with. Duncan had glanced at that damned sign every day for months as he drove to and from the vineyard and Linden, or Vesper Notch, or the dozens of other places in the valley that Brady Brothers Contracting took him. He had watched the letters fade from red to pink to gray, until it was just OWN that remained legible.

He'd told himself that if it hadn't sold by March, he'd buy it. To flip, maybe. Fix all the mess that was too daunting for the average person, then maybe sell it at a profit to some suburban executive who wanted to pretend he was Ralph Waldo Emerson on the weekends. Maybe turn it into a glamping rental for bougie Philadelphians, or make it a premium lodging option for vineyard tourists once his folks opened the bed-and-breakfast at the end of the year.

Then he saw it up close, and he fell in love the way he always did: fast, hard, and under the most inconvenient circumstances imaginable.

It had been the last day in February, late in the afternoon. He'd turned down the muddy access road on his way back from Linden instead of continuing up to the vineyard, and he'd felt an odd sort of inevitability as the cabin came into view. Like he'd committed to an arranged marriage and was about to see his bride for the first time. When he'd closed the door of his truck behind him, a flock of starlings erupted from their communal roost in the trees behind the cabin. Scared the hell out of him. He was convinced that the resulting rush of adrenaline had amplified everything he felt about the place in those first few moments of exploration.

It was the same way he'd felt the first time he'd seen the stone bank barn at his folks' place. His eyes had seen a crumbling foundation and decades of water damage. His mind had quickly cataloged the financial and labor investments. But his soul had said—*bring it.*

What was one more project on top of an already overflowing bucket? The ocean didn't mind when the sky added a little rain.

Nate had the darts now. His first throw bounced off and fell into one of the moving boxes full of Duncan's belongings below the dartboard. When Nate went to retrieve the dart, he made a low whistle and pulled out a condom box instead. He held it in the air like he'd discovered an anthropological artifact.

"Holy shit," Nate said. "This is the biggest box of rubbers I've ever seen."

Mal's forehead creased in a thoughtful frown. "Who the hell still says *rubbers?*"

"You get that thing at Costco, Ducky?" Patrick laughed.

"What's the message you're trying to convey with this?" Nate said. "I'm imagining one of your dates, coming in for a drink or a movie, seeing that giant box, and thinking, *Wow, this guy wants me to know he has a* lot *of sex—*"

Duncan tossed back two fingers of bourbon in one go, hissing through his teeth against the afterburn. "All three of you can go straight to hell."

"Actually." Nate looked thoughtful and shook the box. "Based on how full this feels, it's not getting much use."

"Open the box, chuckleheads," Duncan said.

Nate slid the worn cardboard lid loose and peeked inside. "Huh." He tilted the open end of the box toward the others.

"Huh," echoed Patrick in an identical voice.

There were adhesive bandages inside. Dozens of them, in varied shapes and sizes. Gauze pads. Medical tape. A mostly empty tube of arthritis ointment for his achy knuckles, and some antibacterial cream.

Mal leaned forward to look in the box, then sat back and folded his hands over his waist. "I don't think you're doing sex right, man."

"Wow, you guys are *hilarious*." Duncan snatched the box away, closed it, and tossed it back where it came from. "I use my hands for a living." He held up his right hand to show three knuckles wrapped in white medical tape. Then he curled down all but the middle finger.

"You know I'm a pharmacist, right?" Patrick said. "I can get you a real nice first-aid kit."

"That box does the job. I like to recycle."

Laughter erupted down by the lake, and all the brothers turned to look where the women sat on the edge of the dock. Temperance was there, between Maren and Frankie.

Despite being half a foot taller, Frankie bent sideways to rest her head on Temperance's shoulder. That's the way it was with Temperance. In a crowd, she wasn't usually the most outgoing, or the chattiest, or the quirkiest, but she always seemed to be the social nucleus that others naturally gathered around. Like people could sense that her energy was a safe one to tether to. The solid, tough one, even though her physical presence was small.

Hell. Matchsticks were tiny. Only took one of those to start a wildfire.

Duncan could hear the low tones of her voice, but he couldn't make out the words. Everyone else laughed again, and he had to suppress the urge to smile along with them. Nobody had ever made him laugh the way Temperance could. Her sense of humor was dialed right in on the same frequency as his.

Abandoned buildings weren't the only things Duncan Brady tended to lose his heart to. He'd been in love a bunch of times since he was old enough to recognize what the feeling was.

Every time, though—it was with her.

"What's going on with that?" Mal used his cane to point to the dock.

"Well." Duncan averted his eyes and schooled his expression into a neutral mask. "I need to sand and pressure-wash the wood before someone else gets splinters in their ass—"

Mal interrupted. "Try again."

Duncan turned away and raked his fingers through his hair. "I should probably reseal it with some kind of anti-slip coating before anyone falls—"

"You know what I'm asking."

"Carport needs shoring up, too." He nodded in the direction of the wooden beams supporting a weathered roof next to the cabin. "That thing's coming down if anyone walks by it and *farts* too loud—"

Mal sighed. "You're a clown, Ducky."

But Mal was a bloodhound for interpersonal drama, and now that Temperance was under his skin again, Duncan felt flayed wide open. It didn't take much to shred his patience.

"What?" He took the darts from Nate and hurled one at the board. It sank into one of the outer rings.

Nate and Patrick fell in beside Mal. Identical curiosity crested like high tide in the twins' faces.

"I have no idea what this is about." Patrick grinned and rubbed his hands together. "But I'm listening."

"You're not here often enough." Mal's eyes were still locked on Duncan's. "If you were, you'd know."

"Oh. Temperance?" Patrick sounded disappointed. "I've known about that for years."

"Hell." Duncan launched a dart at the board as hard as he could, then another. The final one wedged into the cabin's wooden paneling.

"Wait—you guys didn't know?" Patrick blinked. "I've known forever. Seven years ago. Harry's wedding to Nicola. I saw T.J. sneak out of Duncan's hotel room. I figured it was one of those, like—open-family-secret kind of things."

"That doesn't mean anything," Mal said. "Maybe she was getting something for someone for the wedding—"

Patrick tipped his chin down and raised his eyebrows. "Oh, she'd definitely gotten *something*—"

"Don't," Duncan warned. He made a fist and popped his knuckles.

"—it was six o'clock in the morning, fellas."

"I hate all three of you." Duncan collected his darts from the board and slapped them into Mal's outstretched hand.

That night was after the reception at Harry's wedding to his first wife. Temperance had shown up at Duncan's hotel room door, puffy-eyed and as broken as he'd ever seen her. He let her in—why the hell wouldn't he?—and she'd been the one to initiate it, kissing him with an eager, open mouth. The fingers of one hand had twisted in his hair, the other greedily plunging into the elastic of his boxers.

"*Don't talk,*" she'd whispered against his lips, a tiny hitch of desperation in her voice.

At first, Duncan had been overwhelmed with joy and love and lust—and that finally, *finally*, she'd come back to him. It wasn't until they were naked and tangled that he'd noticed how desolate she was. The salt of her tears had stung his face.

Hours later, she'd asked him to simply hold her, and she'd cried herself to sleep on his chest after refusing to tell him why she was so upset. Duncan's deepest insecurities took him to dark places. He'd imagined she was mourning Harry marrying someone else. Using his body to soothe her pain. "*Don't talk,*" chanted over and over in his head, and he'd convinced himself it was because she'd wanted to imagine herself with Harry.

Christ, he was an idiot.

It had been a special kind of hell, and the first of dozens over the years where she'd come to him. Every time he'd start to cool off, she'd come around and start kicking at the embers.

Down at the dock, more laughter. Maren whooped, Mercy clapped her hands, and Frankie's loud, musical laugh danced over the rest. Duncan needed a misdirection fast, and she'd just delivered it to him, wrapped up in an olive-green bikini string bow.

He turned his attention to Mal. "Speaking of being here more than usual lately . . ."

It took a second for the words to sink in, but when they did, Patrick glanced at Frankie, snapped his fingers, and pointed at Mal, wide-eyed. Nate's eyebrows shot skyward. "Holy shit, you're right."

With his pipe in one hand, Mal took a dart from Duncan and fired it at the board with a tight back-and-forth snap of his forearm. "I write better here."

"It's not even your turn, man." Patrick grabbed the dart from the cork and kept it.

Again in the distance was Frankie's lilting laugh.

Mal grumbled.

Dryly, Duncan said, "Must be the fresh country air."

Mal shot two more darts rapid-fire at the board. They sank effortlessly into the bull's-eye ring, each close enough to the other that the flights touched. "I'm trying to be here more for Charlotte's sake. So she can have a better relationship with her family."

"Of course," Nate said. "And it has *nothing* to do with Frankie Moreau."

"Not interested." Mal pretended to check his watch, but his wrist was bare.

"Patrick, check his pulse," Duncan said.

"I said, I'm not *interested*"—Mal took a bracing breath and lowered his voice—"in some Hallmark-y three-brides-for-three-brothers crap—"

Patrick looked offended. "The hell's wrong with Hallmark, man?"

"Temperance and I are never happening," Duncan said to Mal, "so if you want to try it with the sublime Miss Moreau—"

"Goddamn it." Mal glanced to where the kids played kickball with Dad in the stretch of grass near the path to the vineyard. "Don't say shit like this where Charlotte could hear you."

"Charlie's lonely, Mal."

"I'm aware. But there are worse things than loneliness." Mal took a long pull from his pipe, followed by a slow exhale of cherry-scented smoke. "Loneliness hurts, but it's less likely to do damage. I'm not risking her heart with someone who might do what her mother did."

* * *

PATRICK left to join Mercy in the lake, Mal disappeared to parts unknown to recharge his social battery, and Duncan went inside with Nate to prep dinner.

The little kitchen smelled like sliced cucumber and watermelon, and a tinge of woodsmoke and hot sugar from scorched marshmallows through the open screen. Out the window, late-afternoon sun glazed the water with a candy-bright patina. Temperance wasn't out at the dock anymore—he'd barely have to glance at a crowd to be able to tell she wasn't in it. He'd had a lot of practice. He wasn't ever not looking for her.

Nate stood beside him at the counter, chunking fresh pineapple for Dad's grilled chicken skewers. "I can't believe I didn't notice sooner."

Duncan was up to his elbows in bubbly dishwater. He tipped his head up and sighed. Cobwebs splayed over a water stain on the ceiling that looked like a staring eyeball. He needed to make sure that leak was managed—

"You know," Nate continued, "I used to think all the time about what Maren's life would have been like if I hadn't come along."

"Man, you two have a fantastic life."

"We do now. But it was rough at the beginning. I hated myself for what she had to endure from her parents because of me. But I was too much of a coward to risk losing her. So, I let her."

"Nobody *lets* the Madigan women do anything," Duncan said.

"Solid point," Nate said. "Listen. When Maren and I first started out, I had to balance protecting her with supporting her as she tried to let her parents back in. When she was pregnant with Alice, we knew when they'd be in Philly for that foundation fundraiser thing they do every year, so we invited them to dinner that weekend. Maren bought onesies that looked like scrubs, and she folded them in a rectangle to look like napkins to set next to the plates." Nate stopped chopping and hung his head for a moment.

"They didn't show. Few days later in the mail, we got a gift certificate to some high-end baby boutique in Philly. The reality was that they weren't going to change their minds about us, and by then, Maren realized that the thing that hurt her the most was thinking she could solve the Corbin and Laine problem if she just tried enough different things. So, she finally let it go. But I couldn't make that choice for her, and I couldn't ask her to choose, either, you know?" Out the window, Nate watched Harry bounce baby Leo on his hip while Maren played kickball with the older kids. "You can fight for someone, but you have to be sure they're ready to be fought for."

Duncan didn't respond. He rinsed suds off a pan in the sink, and the water pressure blipped in and out. Pipes thudded in the walls.

"You know—" Nate wasn't done. "I think it's bullshit, the notion that two people who worked when they were younger can't work as adults. Some people really do just . . . fit. They have to get out of their own way to come together long enough to figure it out, though."

"You're just bursting at the fucking seams with folksy wisdom, aren't you?" Duncan finally said.

Nate chuckled. "Maren would disagree."

Duncan rolled his shoulders and hesitated. You couldn't un-ring a bell once it was hit. Sheer curtains at the window above the sink lifted in a warm breeze. Two white flags.

Hell with it.

Finally, Duncan said, "I've got a bit of a Corbin and Laine problem of my own."

"Well, you don't fall in love with your brother's wife's little sister and expect smooth sailing, Ducky."

Duncan grunted.

"They offer you money to stay away?" Nate kept his expression neutral and didn't look up from the cutting board. When Duncan didn't respond, he added, "They offered me five grand."

"No shit?"

"No shit."

Duncan took a big breath. "Ten grand."

Nate laughed. "They must have been way more afraid of you."

"Eh," Duncan said. "Either that, or inflation."

Again, Nate laughed.

"You didn't take it, though, did you?" Duncan said. "You didn't take the money."

"Wait—" Nate lay down his knife and leaned away. "You *did*?"

Duncan kept his eyes on the sink.

"Ahh, I see now." Nate started chopping fruit again. "Thus, the Madigan problem."

"You're a better man than I am," said Duncan.

Add it to the list of ways he envied his older brothers. If he were more like Nate, he'd have told Corbin Madigan to fuck off into space. If he were Harry, he'd have never made the mistakes he'd made with Temperance in the first place—but if he had, he'd have worked things out with her thoughtfully and thoroughly, and they'd be celebrating a double-digit wedding anniversary with a brood of baby Bradys by now.

But he wasn't like them. He was an idiot.

"Hell. I was much older than you, Ducky. If I'd been eighteen and hotheaded and emotional—I'd have taken the fucking money, too. Ten grand is Monopoly dollars to the Madigans."

Duncan's low *huh* was humorless. "The money itself isn't really the problem."

"Then what—" Again, Nate froze. "Oh, shit. Temperance doesn't know."

"Nope."

"What'd you do with it?"

Duncan pulled the plug on the sink and dried his hands. "Did what investors call a buy-and-hold, even though I didn't realize what I was doing at the time. I found the first name in an alphabetical list that I recognized and put the whole ten grand in it. Then I just—left it. Never touched it until about six months ago."

Nate made a low whistle.

Duncan flipped the towel over his shoulder. "I've been trying to give the ten grand back to them since the fall, but they won't return my calls. I've even tried sending checks to their goddamned foundation, but they never clear—" He cut off when the cabin's screen door opened. The way it squealed sounded like Rowan's demon donkey. Quieter, he said, "I can't do anything about Temperance until I get square with her parents. But they're not letting me. It's like they *know*—"

"Where's my pineapple?" Dad shouted from the little living room. The creaky door banged closed.

"Hey." Duncan put a hand on Nate's arm. "Later—tell me more about that annual fundraiser."

CHAPTER EIGHT

Temperance

While dinner was made, Maren conscripted Temperance to help fill water balloons for the kids to play with. The cabin kitchen was tiny, with just enough room for two adults to work together at the sink and countertop, so they sat on the ground next to the corroded outdoor spigot along the side wall. Sawhorses and lumber sat stacked under tarps, and a tangle of flowering vines rambled up a sagging wooden lattice.

The tangy scent of Will Brady's famous pineapple-molasses barbecue chicken skewers and the nutty smell of roasting corn drifted from the front of the cabin. Will had been grilling that same summer meal for as long as Temperance could remember.

"You're going to relax over the next few days," Maren said. She was eleven years older, and in all the ways that mattered, she'd been more of a parent to Temperance than their mom and dad had ever been.

"Yes, ma'am."

"I mean it." Maren handed over a filled balloon for Temperance to tie off. "I don't even want to see you fold your own laundry."

Temperance laughed. "Am I allowed to feed myself?"

"No. Nate will make an extra plate for you when he feeds the kids. I hope you like nuggies."

"Love 'em."

Temperance had learned early in undergrad that she could thrive on four or five hours of sleep each night, with no detriment to her cognitive function or physical health. She'd had a neurobiology professor who liked to say that life was a marathon, not a sprint. For Temperance, it was a marathon she sprinted through. Everything in her life was something she was running toward or running from.

She kept her body busy every hour she was awake, filling gaps and lulls with long-distance runs and high-intensity activities that would reliably spike her dopamine and adrenaline. Nearly everything she did was a vehicle to propel her from now to next, and she'd spent the last eight years avoiding deceleration at all costs.

Next was safe.

But *now* had finally caught up with her. For the first time in her adult life, she was stuck in a holding pattern, and rather than making progress toward getting out of it, everything she tried seemed to slow her down more. It was the only reason why her sister had managed to convince her to come to the valley for the week and try something so out of character. She was going to do . . . nothing. For seven whole days.

"If Mom and Dad call this week, I think you should give yourself permission to not answer—"

"They've called multiple times a day, for days," Temperance said. "I can't avoid them much longer."

Maren let out a disappointed sigh. "You know I try to not get involved when it comes to them—"

"I know." Temperance laughed.

"But you seem to be impervious to everyone's bullshit but theirs. Just—give yourself some space before they sweep you up into the Corbin and Laine show."

Temperance's phone rang.

"Oh my god, you conjured them," she said.

Maren made a face. "Wait—wasn't their ringtone the *Jaws* theme?"

"Yes, but I needed something louder. More dread-inducing."

They both side-eyed the phone.

"Don't do it, T.J."

"They're just going to keep calling until I talk to them."

"And you can just keep ignoring it."

The ringtone stopped.

As Laine Talbot-Madigan and Corbin Madigan's eldest daughter, Maren's destiny in humanitarian healthcare had been all but written on her birth announcements. She was a satellite to their planet, her worth contingent upon remaining within the orbit they'd designated for her. So when Maren eventually dropped out of med school to marry Nate Brady and start a family, it divided the Madigan family into two opposing factions of a very small war. Maren was cut off financially and emotionally, and Temperance had been caught solidly in the middle of it.

Temperance had been only thirteen and knew very little about the emotional politics of falling in love. But it was unmistakable that Maren Rose Brady was an elevated version of Maren Rose Madigan. She was unburdened and sparkling in a way Temperance hadn't seen in years. For that, she was solidly Team Maren.

But.

Maren's absence created a space for Temperance in their parents' lives that hadn't been there before, and wouldn't have ever been, otherwise. Young Temperance quietly resolved to not let them down in the same way Maren did, even though at the time she'd had no idea what committing to a career in medicine actually meant.

The Madigan girls had been born into a family of women who'd lived and breathed medicine for five generations. Their great-great-grandmother Louisa Capewell had been one of the faculty physicians at the country's first medical college for women in the late 1800s, and her eldest daughter, Theodora, became a physician as well. Theo married into money when she wed August Talbot, the eldest son of a Philadelphia iron and steel family. Theo and August had shared the same philanthropic spirit, combining their talents and resources to establish the Capewell-Talbot Foundation. Today, the foundation provided funding to the Vesper Valley healthcare system and an endowment to the University Hospital where Temperance, her mother, Laine, and Laine's mother, Helen, had done their residencies. But Capewell-Talbot's signature initiative was Domestic Relief and Aid—also known as DORA.

Founded in the 1960s by Helen Capewell-Talbot—Temperance's grandmother—DORA began as a small, secular humanitarian aid organization during the counterculture movement providing medical aid at protests and marches, and advocating for healthcare reform. Helen had a bohemian heart, a brilliant mind, and a larger-than-life personality that gained her name recognition amongst activist groups and the medical community alike, and DORA's scope and influence grew along with Helen's own reputation in the following decades.

Most of what Temperance knew about her grandmother she'd learned from books. Helen's own memoir, *Hippie Humanitarian*, had even been optioned for a film in the 1990s, but it never got made due to fundamental differences in vision between Helen and the studio. *Between Heaven and Helen: A Lifetime of Radical Compassion* was the tantalizing and fan-worshippy biography written after her death, and teenage Temperance had read it cover to cover more times than she could count. Helen Capewell-Talbot had been an influencer before influencers existed, a minor celebrity in humanitarian healthcare, and a household name within activist circles around the country. Even now, Temperance knew of at least two attendings whose LinkedIn profile photos were from two decades ago at the annual Capewell-Talbot fundraising gala, posing with an ageless Dr. Helen Capewell-Talbot.

Temperance's mother, Laine, was born and raised in the unconventional DORA lifestyle, and road-schooled by DORA's tight-knit nomadic community of doctors, nurses, engineers, and social activists. Temperance's father came from old Philadelphia money—the youngest grandson of a real-estate tycoon. Corbin Madigan had been a hotshot emergency medicine doctor fresh out of residency when he joined DORA, and he and Laine were married within the year. Helen eventually took on more of a figurehead role in the organization by doing keynotes and fundraising appearances, while Corbin and Laine ushered DORA into a new era of expansion. In the name of keeping DORA as nimble as possible, they strategically built five small brick-and-mortar locations throughout the country after cross-referencing social vulnerability indices with decades of FEMA disaster data, and they used humanitarian response as a platform for preventative health measures like vaccines and family-planning resources.

Objectively speaking, her parents were good people. They made positive change in the world.

It didn't mean they weren't shitty parents, though. Being Corbin and Laine's daughter was like being the child of superheroes. Eternally second to their higher purpose.

When Temperance reread her grandmother's biography a few years ago—the first time she'd done so as an adult—she'd realized that shitty parenting might be as much a part of the Capewell-Talbot legacy as life-changing healthcare was. The only mention of Laine in either of the books about Helen Capewell-Talbot was in the context of what a brave and progressive thing it was for Helen to have shrugged off the social stigma of single motherhood, defying the patriarchy by refusing to name Laine's father.

It hadn't occurred to Temperance until then that her grandmother's larger-than-life personality and legendary status as an activist might've meant she made little time to actually be a good mother. That realization had come during a particularly probing session with her therapist, after which Temperance had ugly-cried in the front seat of her car, blowing her nose into the (admittedly large) stash of Taco Bell napkins she kept in the glove box.

The phone blared again. When Temperance reached for where it sat on a low stack of lumber, Maren tried to snatch it away.

Temperance was faster. "Just let me get it out of the way," she whispered. Then she smoothed her hand down over her hair, pasted on a smile, and held the phone in front of her face. "Hey."

"Temperance, hello." Laine Talbot-Madigan's voice echoed a bit. "It's Mom and Dad."

"I can literally see you right now, Mom."

Corbin Madigan and Laine Talbot-Madigan were dedicated first to each other, a very close second to the family foundation, and a distant third to their daughters. They were so intertwined they didn't even have separate personal phones, so whenever they made a video call, it was both of their heads crowded in the frame. They were in their seventies but had the decades-younger look of two people whose wealth and privilege translated to lifelong wellness. Laine's hair was ash blond and white, twisted into a long braid just like Temperance's was. The glow of the phone screen made her eerily pale green eyes seem almost silver. Corbin's dark-blond hair was trained into an obedient side part that Temperance had quite literally never seen move out of place. She got her icy blue eyes from him, but she hadn't been gifted with the same dark lashes he had. Her own were blond and even paler at the tips, requiring a generous swipe of mascara to summon them from the ghostly realm and into the corporeal one.

"Hi, Teej," Corbin said.

"Are you"—Laine squinted at the screen—"in the woods?"

Temperance pointed a finger over her shoulder. "It's—ah, a virtual background. New feature."

"I hear people, though," Laine said. "And birds."

"Part of the feature, Mom."

"You look tired." Laine leaned toward the screen. "Doesn't she look tired, Corbin?"

"Are you exercising enough, Teej?" said Corbin. Not, *Are you resting enough, Teej?*

"Her iron might be low," Laine mused. "Her vitamin D, maybe."

Corbin said, "When was your last CBC?"

"I'm sorry," Temperance said, "are we doing a differential or having a conversation?"

Laine's version of a smile didn't involve her mouth, only a slight squint of her eyes. "Doctor humor. That's cute."

"I have a CBC every six months, Dad. Same as always. All normal. Platelets above one-fifty. Same as last time."

"You look pale," Laine said.

"This is just my normal face, Mom."

There had been a time in her life that she'd have gladly parted with a limb to have her parents fussing over her health. Temperance recognized it for what it was now, though. They were keeping tabs on a valuable professional asset.

Since the Capewell-Talbot Foundation was founded more than a century ago, every generation of Temperance's family had a woman doctor who'd made an important contribution to it by the time they were forty. Now, Laine was positioning a program to address the unique needs of children in natural-disaster responses as Temperance's chance to do the same. A two-million-dollar innovation grant was on the line, and they wanted her to write the proposal for it.

Two million dollars.

If DORA was awarded the grant—which they would be, because Temperance was damned good at what she did—the program would need to be underway within six weeks of receiving the funds. An initial progress report would be due by week eight, and after that, every four months. It would mean more than a year of administrative and operational work. Lots of paperwork, meetings, and red tape—and very little practicing actual medicine.

Deep down, though, Temperance knew it wasn't really her that her parents wanted. It didn't matter that she had a master's of public health and an MD from an Ivy. For them, the most attractive thing on her résumé was that she was their daughter. They got to leverage her expertise and her energy, *and* they got to maintain influence in a way they wouldn't have with another doctor.

Perhaps most important of all, they could groom her as the eventual successor of Capewell-Talbot Foundation leadership.

In another move that was far ahead of her time, Helen and her original board had written the Capewell-Talbot bylaws to require the organization's chief executive officer, chief medical officer, and chief operating officer to all be physician executives rather than MBAs and suits. Laine had been happy to take over that role after Helen died, and throughout undergrad and her first year and a half of medical school, Temperance had always assumed she'd be ready for it someday, too.

At first, medicine hadn't been something she'd loved like so many of her student peers, but the coursework came naturally to her, and she'd managed to convince herself she'd be satisfied with being a doctor as much as any other profession. Then, halfway through her second year of med school, she'd volunteered at the university's student-run free clinic in Linden, and she fell in love.

As was often the case when unexpectedly falling in love, things got complicated.

Temperance quickly found that she *lived* for that steady build of trust with the littlest patients. That visible transformation on the parents' faces when they realized their child was in safe hands with her. Even now, Temperance had a few patients in their early twenties who she'd originally seen in the clinic as teenagers when she'd still been a med student.

An executive role in Capewell-Talbot meant she wouldn't do clinical work at all. Not only would she not have time for it—it would also be a conflict of interest from a business perspective. She would spend most of her days doing personnel management and re-port writing and strategic planning of how donor dollars translated to clinical outcomes.

It was important work, no doubt. It just wasn't for her.

But her parents had another lever that they hadn't hesitated to pull.

"We heard about the clinic," Laine said.

"Of course you did, Mom. You're on the board."

Corbin cut in. "Your mother isn't the only trustee on that board, Teej. And the funding vote wasn't even close."

"Closing that clinic will mean more patients enroll in Medicaid, and they can get into facilities that receive government reimburse-ment," said Laine. "It's stronger and more sustainable."

"How do you think people in communities like this find out about the care that they qualify for, Mom?" Temperance's voice rose. "A huge part of what we do there is connect people with social workers to get them into programs and more specialized care."

"It's no longer a good investment," Corbin said.

"You make everything about money—"

"Everything *is* about money, Temperance." Laine Talbot-

Madigan never raised her voice, but the pace of her words picked up speed when she was irritated. "Money increases influence, and influence increases impact. Ninety percent of the med students trained at that clinic over the years haven't stayed in the valley, or even in the suburbs. That talent goes elsewhere."

Temperance glared at the screen. "You do realize that clinics like mine serve a purpose beyond teaching, right? Actual human beings come to them for care. It's not just a simulation to train med students."

Her mother disregarded that, a technique she'd employed since Temperance was a child. Laine was so good at smoothly skipping over questions or contributions to a conversation that sometimes Temperance wondered if she'd even verbalized them at all. It was an insidious, invisible sort of gaslighting.

In the background on her parents' end of the line, a forklift beeped over the sounds of muffled voices and two-way radio conversations.

"You could make a difference in tens of thousands more lives with DORA," said Laine.

"Sorry, never heard of her." Temperance made eye contact with Maren over the top edge of the phone. Maren slapped a hand over her mouth to hold in a laugh.

Laine made a sound that was the auditory equivalent of an eye roll. "Aren't you the comedian today."

"You can tremendously increase your impact by coming to work with us," Corbin said. "It's a numbers game."

"I'm ending the call if you say *impact* again."

Corbin pressed on. "DORA is bigger than you, Teej."

"Maybe I want to be small?" she said.

Laine sniffed. "Nobody wants to be *small*, Temperance."

Temperance did want a small life, and she resented the way her parents made it seem like a desire to care for individual patients and form community relationships was somehow a waste of her effort and attention.

"We made sure you had the kind of privileges and resources you do so you could do more with your life. Not less," Corbin said.

Abruptly, Laine said, "Does this have anything to do with Duncan Brady?"

Temperance's belly dropped. She did a double take at the screen. "Why would you ask me that?"

At the edge of her vision, Maren tipped her head in curiosity.

"Where are you right now?" Corbin said.

"I'm in the valley. Taking a little break."

"A break." The way Laine said it, Temperance might have said she was taking a little crime spree.

"With Maren?" said Corbin.

"Yes."

Strained silence. "Is she well?" Laine eventually asked.

"You could call her sometime, Mom. Ask her yourself." *Ask about your son-in-law, too. Ask about your grandchildren, you ghouls.*

Maren grimaced and made a horizontal slashing motion in front of her neck. *No thank you, please*, she mouthed.

Her parents shared a look but didn't respond.

"Okay. Well. This was fun, but I have to go," Temperance said. "Send me the grant application materials, and I'll take a look."

"Wonderful. Expect an email from Seraphine sometime tomorrow—"

"No promises, Mom. I'm just going to look. I have to go now," Temperance said, and ended the call. She lobbed the phone into the grass beside her and groaned into her hands.

Maren reached out to squeeze her arm. "They're not bad people. They're just bad parents."

"It might be easier if they were bad," Temperance said. "I'd feel a lot better saying no to what they want me to do."

"Why even consider it, honey? They can find someone else to write their grant. You don't need their money. Get a business loan. Open your own clinic once the Linden clinic closes."

Maren's sunny, simple optimism was clear proof that she was more Brady than Madigan now. The Brady family identified the thing they loved, and they went for it. Together. It seemed so simple.

"It's a little more complicated than that, Mare." Temperance took off her glasses and rubbed her eyes.

She told Maren everything.

Sometimes, she wished she'd hated medicine. Or at least been ambivalent about it. Either way would have made her life a lot simpler. Because once she loved being a doctor, she became protective of it. It was hers in a way nothing in her life had ever been, and she would fight for it if necessary.

A fight was what it had come to, and her parents' weapon of choice was money.

After those first two months of volunteering at the clinic back in med school, Temperance told Laine and Corbin she planned to pursue pediatrics, and she wouldn't be joining them at the helm of Capewell-Talbot and DORA after residency. They'd threatened to cut her off the same way they'd done to Maren. Temperance hadn't had any weapons of her own to fight with, so she did the only thing she could.

She disarmed *them*.

She rejected the Capewell-Talbot money and used federal loans to pay for her final two years of medical school tuition. It had made her feel powerful for the first time in her life. But now, it was painfully obvious that she hadn't actually reclaimed any power at all. She'd simply transferred it away from her parents and into the hands of loan servicers.

She'd cut the proverbial apron strings and sliced off her own leg in the process.

Now, Temperance found herself in the paradoxical position of being a double trust fund baby with six figures of student-loan debt and virtually no assets of her own beyond a ten-year-old Corolla and a gratuitous collection of couture lingerie—half of it second-hand.

And *time*. Time was another currency she didn't have. It couldn't be generated or borrowed, either. You either had it, or you didn't.

The announcement of the clinic's closure gave her a little less than three months to figure out how to keep the lights on—and covered by insurance—while she figured out a more permanent solution. But thanks to her parents' close management of her finances through the first half of her twenties, followed by a frugal cash-only lifestyle during residency, Temperance had a mediocre credit score that would slip into "fair" territory under the weight of too many simultaneous hard inquiries from lenders. So she couldn't simply cast a wide net of loan applications and hope one of them caught an approval. Her first two attempts hadn't even made it past the pre-qualification step, since her per diem work history wasn't extensive or consistent enough to indicate income stability. There were grants available through health-care foundations, but they tended to avoid funding nonprofit start-ups, and many of those required an invitation to even *apply*, anyway. Those invitations weren't exactly pouring into her inbox, and even if she knew where to begin with those, she didn't have time.

The clinic's impending closure had given her parents a sharp, shiny hook baited with the only thing that could possibly get her to bite: a fresh start. She'd write the grant for the Capewell-Talbot board so they could groom her for executive leadership someday. In exchange, they'd establish funding to make sure underserved Vesper Valley families got the aid they needed.

Temperance left out the part about how Capewell-Talbot was her very necessary backup plan in case coexistence with Duncan proved impossible once Harry and Rowan were married. Maybe she'd be *eager* to get the hell out of there by then.

Maren was quiet for a long time after Temperance was done talking.

"So, yeah. I started med school for them." Temperance raised her chin. "I finished med school for me."

"Bold choice," Maren said after a thoughtful silence. "A little stupid, maybe—"

"Thanks, Mare. That's super helpful."

That earned her a classic Maren look that said, *I'm not finished yet.* "—and emblematic of your privilege, rejecting so much tuition money. But bold, for sure. And probably—" Maren sighed. "The right thing."

Temperance wasn't a big crier, but the grudging approval from her sister made her eyes well with hot tears.

"Look." Maren took her by the shoulders and gently touched their foreheads together. "You say you want a small life. But even small things take work to build. You might need to do this thing for Mom and Dad to get started, but you have more negotiating power than you realize. Sometimes you have to turn around and take a different path to go forward, honey. But it's okay. It's still movement."

Temperance swiped away tears before she slid her glasses back on. "I love you. Even though you're bossy."

"I'm not bossy." Maren sat back and smiled. She pulled a new balloon over the faucet and turned it on. "I eagerly share my wisdom—and I'm right a lot. There's a difference."

CHAPTER NINE

Temperance

Maren had to bail on the balloon-filling when baby Leo wanted to nurse, so Temperance took over solo. Her glasses kept sliding down the sweat on her nose. With one hand squeezing the lip of a new balloon over the spigot, and the other on the faucet handle to control the flow of water, she had no hands free to nudge them back in place. Impatiently, she tried to use her shoulder to push them up, but all that did was make them sit lopsided on her face.

Duncan came around the side of the cabin and stood next to her. For a moment, he blocked the sun.

"Whatever you're doing back here is messing with the water pressure inside of the cabin," he said.

The faucet squeaked as she turned it off. "Take that up with Maren. She wants balloons for the kids to play with." An orange balloon swelled in her palm as water swirled into it, tiny bubbles racing up the inside. It was hypnotic.

Duncan lowered his butt to the ground and hooked his arms over his knees. Temperance watched him through lowered lashes. Every bit of him was beautifully proportioned—even the dark hair on his legs was impeccably distributed, as if it had been arranged on his skin by an algorithm.

"Need a hand?" he said.

"Nah. Almost done." She glanced up and wiggled her nose to lift her glasses back into place.

Duncan leaned in. "I meant, *you* need another hand." He hesitated for a moment when she met his eyes, then he put the tips of his fingers on the points of her glasses to readjust them on the bridge of her nose. He scanned her face from her eyes to her lips, then back up.

"You going to tell me you're looking at my beard again?" he said. "Or are you going to admit you're looking at my mouth?"

She didn't take the bait. "So is your beard essentially your entire personality now or what?"

"I have a *reason* for this beard, you know."

Lightly, she said, "Cosplaying Aquaman on the weekends? Khal Drogo?"

"My beard is better than Momoa's. I'm also far more charming."

"I think you both mistake mischief for charm." She tied off the orange balloon and lifted the strap of her swimsuit back onto her shoulder. It slid back down as soon as she let it go.

"I have no idea what cosplaying is," Duncan said.

"Costume play."

"Is it a sex thing?"

"It's—ah, performance art," she said. "You create costumes and dress up like characters from pop culture—"

"Sounds like it *could* be a sex thing."

She sighed up at the sky. "Why do you do that? You always do that."

He tipped his head. "Do what?"

"Make a joke. Or make it about sex. There always has to be this—this friction between us—"

"Friction feels *good*, Temperance."

"Friction also makes fire. We could probably burn down the sun."

Some of his playful mask slipped. "That has a certain poetry to it, don't you think?"

"Sure, if you're into planet-ending catastrophes."

"Does feel kind of selfish of us, when you put it that way." He squinted out at the lake. "Do you really want to know? Why I do the jokey shit?"

"Yes."

He looked at her for a long time before he responded again. "I keep it shallow with you, because every time I go deep, you disappear on me." His brows drew tight.

Whatever she'd expected him to say—it hadn't been that. Truthfully, she'd expected another quip or innuendo. She swallowed past the sudden tightness in her throat.

Duncan's chuckle was a little dark. "You asked."

They were quiet for a while.

Tentatively, he brushed a fingertip over a quarter-shaped bruise on her bare shin.

Temperance glanced down. "That's nothing. I bumped it when I was moving stuff out of Frankie's and my apartment."

Duncan grazed his thumb over a dime-sized bruise on her forearm.

"Edge of a sink at the hospital."

He touched another—a long streak of pale purple on her upper thigh.

"Edge of a countertop at the clinic."

Duncan drew his hand back and looped his arms over his knees. "You need to be put into a bubble."

"I'm fine, and I will continue to be fine." She tied off a pink balloon and plopped it into the bucket on top of the others. Condensation made them glisten like gems.

"I'm sorry about earlier," he said, quietly. "I saw you and Frankie go into the cabin, and you were walking like you were in pain—"

"Your dock bit me in the butt, Duncan." She laughed.

Duncan cleared his throat and pointed to the bucket of bigger balloons she'd filled earlier with Maren. "That looks like a private stash of ammunition."

Thankful for the redirection, Temperance scooted sideways to block his view of the bigger bucket. The move gave her an instant wedgie. "I don't know what you're talking about."

He wasn't wrong, though. Maren had planned to make room in the cabin fridge to chill the bigger balloons for a surprise attack on Nate and his brothers later that afternoon.

Duncan gave her a comical side-eye. "You put something un-wholesome in those?"

"What, like hydrochloric acid?" She tossed another filled balloon into the bucket.

"I was thinking red food dye, but you go on being diabolical, Teacup."

"I considered glitter, but Rowan would give me shit about polluting the environment with microplastics."

He chuckled. "She's offered twenty bucks to the kid who brings her the most balloon pieces after the game is over."

"Ah, yes. An economics lesson and an ecology lesson all in one." Temperance rolled another balloon onto the end of the spigot, and it suddenly seemed very condom-adjacent. There was no way she could unsee it.

Duncan reached past her to lift one of the bigger balloons. He smelled like sun-warmed skin. "The way you overfilled these big ones, they'll hurt like a bastard when they hit." He bobbled the balloon in his hand, testing the heft of it.

Temperance pitched her voice high and sweet. "Will they?" They both watched the balloon on the tap swell into her palm. She kept her eyes down. "It's physics. An under-filled balloon might just bounce off the target. Wasted ammo."

Duncan's laugh was dark. "Only you would science a water-balloon fight."

"Science is surprisingly versatile in its applications."

"Your strategy is risky, though." He slowly traced the condensation on the surface of the balloon in his hand. Then he rubbed the wetness between his finger and thumb. "Fill them too full, and they could bust prematurely."

Temperance met his eyes. "Mm, that's something you know a lot about, isn't it?"

His attention tracked downward to her breasts for an instant. She'd have missed it if she hadn't been looking right at his face. He made a low noise in his throat. "That's always been your fault."

Jets of water suddenly shot out around the rim of the balloon, speckling Temperance's glasses, spraying Duncan in the chest. She sputtered and flailed with the overflowing latex while Duncan reached forward for the valve. He twisted it the wrong way. A blast of water shot the balloon off the end of the tap and ricocheted up from the ground to soak them both. Dirt instantly became mud. Temperance held out her hands and screeched; Duncan shouted in surprise, reaching again with both hands to twist the creaky damned thing off.

For a moment, they sat there in stunned silence.

Water dripped placidly from the tap, from the end of her nose, from the tips of his hair. Tiny droplets glistened in his beard. He used the back of his wrist to swipe them away.

Then they started to laugh, and the afternoon seemed to pause. In the huge pines, the birds hushed, and there was a lull in the crackly music from the cabin. Even the sounds of wet revelry from the lake quieted. Like the world had stopped to listen.

She was close enough to him to see the tiny chip in the outer edge of his front tooth. It was a casualty of their first kiss. They'd been seventeen. She'd leaned in, he'd leaned out, thinking she was messing with him. Teasing, like they'd always done. When he'd realized that she was earnest, he overcorrected with a bit too much enthusiasm and came in hot.

Temperance had swallowed that little fragment of his tooth that day. Sometimes she imagined that it had lodged permanently inside her, like a grain of sand in an oyster.

Breathless, she said, "You did that on purpose."

Duncan stood, blocking the sun again. "Ah, Temperance." With a quick jerk of his chin, he whipped damp hair off his forehead and looked down. "When I'm trying to get you wet . . . you'll know it."

It might have been the smirk before he turned around, or the fact that she sat in muddy grass in a gross gas-station swimsuit while he had the audacity to look so aggressively gorgeous and unruffled as he walked away. Maybe she was lashing out at being stuck between her parents and him. On one side, their inescapable expectations, and on the other, her own inescapable feelings for him.

Does this have anything to do with Duncan Brady?

She wanted to scream and laugh at the same time. It would *always* be about Duncan Brady.

Temperance shot to her feet and hurled one of the big balloons at him with as much force as she could muster. It connected between his shoulders with a soul-satisfying *smack*, splashing water up his neck and down his back.

"Now who's wet?" she taunted.

He froze. Without turning, he put his hands on his hips and looked up at the sky. Rolled his neck, rolled his shoulders.

She picked up four more balloons and cradled them against her chest. One was filled so full it burst in her hand when she wound up another throw. Water raced down her wrist, her inner arm, her armpit. She hissed a breath through her teeth at the cold and shook it off.

Duncan exploded into motion. He pivoted toward her, startlingly nimble for his size.

Temperance whirled away with a whooping scream. She broke for the grassy clearing where cars and trucks were haphazardly parked like toddler toys. A balloon exploded across the backs of her thighs as she ran. Behind her, Duncan's big, booming laugh. The sound of it raced straight up her spine.

Another balloon sailed past her head, splashing against the trunk of a tree.

Laughing and bubbling over with silly, uncomplicated joy, Temperance spun around to fling another balloon.

He'd picked up the whole bucket.

He slowed to a walk, and didn't bother to dodge what she threw. One of her balloons soaked his chest, and the other connected just above the waistband of his trunks. She ducked around the back of Duncan's truck.

A green balloon sailed over her head and exploded against the window of Maren and Nate's minivan.

Temperance popped up and held out a hand. "Wait, wait."

Duncan rounded the truck, bobbling a red balloon in his hand. He wore the kind of smile she hadn't seen on him in a long time.

Playful and unmistakably sensual, his top lip curled a little higher on one side. "Shouldn't start something you're unprepared to finish, Teacup."

She was down to one balloon. Breathing hard, she said, "White flag."

"Oh, really?" Sunbeams streaked through the leaves above them, dappling his face with shine and shadow. He crowded her backward until she was against the passenger's-side door of his truck. "We playing flags again?"

Temperance swallowed hard. "I don't know."

There was a subtle shift in his features. The tiny muscles around his eyes tightened, two faint creases appeared between his brows. A little exhale flared his nose, and his mouth worked silently, like he was trying on words before speaking them.

He let the bucket hit the ground, and a few balloons wobbled out and rolled away.

Duncan's chest rose and fell a little faster, and his features darkened. The red balloon exploded in his fist. The water was warm from the heat of his palm, soaking her thighs. "I can't figure out how to act around you."

Temperance shrank back against the truck. It was hot against her bare skin. "You don't have to *act* any way—"

"I don't know what the rules are anymore." His words were clipped.

"There aren't any rules."

"No?" His breath stirred the tiny hairs around her face. "I've been trying to get you to talk to me since September, Temperance."

"We're talking right now," she said.

"We're not actually *saying* anything."

"What are we supposed to say?"

His brows did a subtle pinch and lift. "I can think of a few things."

The tip of his tongue swept the inner edge of his lower lip. He'd always done that when he was getting ready to kiss her, and she knew the exact trajectory he'd take. How he'd drop in easy at first, and fit his bottom lip flush with hers. Then he'd press in hard to spread her mouth wide against his. He always liked to keep his eyes open for the first few moments, to watch her react when his tongue made its first slow, purposeful slide across hers.

Her heart beat wild and loose. They never forgot how to kiss each other, even when they went months without doing it. The give and take, the push and pull, the way he'd lift her with a single flex of his forearm under her ass—

"Can I fix this?" Duncan looped a finger under the swimsuit strap where it had fallen down her shoulder again.

"Not sure what you could do without a needle and thread—" When she tilted her head down to watch his hand, his knuckles brushed the underside of her jaw. She looked up and away, over his shoulder. "And, ah, some spare elastic—"

He used the very tips of his fingers, careful to minimize how much of her skin he touched. Water from the burst balloon trickled off his fingers and down her arm. In two quick movements, he looped the loose material of the strap over itself and secured it in a tidy knot that stuck up from her shoulder like a little antenna. It was simple and functional and perfect. Temperance was a little embarrassed she hadn't thought of it herself.

"Thank you."

Quietly, he said, "I fix things."

Temperance looked up. Duncan's eyes were soft and hazy. He was close enough that the front of his trunks brushed her bare legs.

She knew him. The boy beneath the beard and the tattoos and the angst. The man whose cracked edges matched hers because they'd been broken by the same thing.

They'd always been as different as two people could be, but in the way a lock contrasted to the shape of its key. They'd fit because of their differences, not in spite of them.

She knew he couldn't bring himself to eat Oreo cookies because it was the last treat they'd given his childhood dog the morning they had to say goodbye. She knew the sensual bass of his rumbly morning voice, and she knew how the curve of her calf fit *just so* in the notch at his hip when she hiked her leg over him in her sleep. She knew his skin smelled like home to her, more than anywhere she'd ever actually lived.

Temperance was honey in hot tea—every bit of her softened and flowed toward him. *This* was the Duncan she'd fallen in love with all those years ago. This quiet vulnerability and keen emotional intelligence that most people missed because they were too distracted by the impressive breadth of his shoulders or the sexy slung-sideways smile he threw on like a shield.

They both climbed inside the moment and wore it like armor, safe from who they were outside it.

"Someone will see us," she whispered.

Duncan braced his hands against the truck alongside her shoulders. "Maybe they should."

Maybe they should.

A red mini truck rambled loudly down the gravel access road. Temperance and Duncan both turned to look. The vehicle was absurdly cute and obviously old, with one of those flat-fronted faces and circular headlights that made it look like it was straight out of a Miyazaki film.

It belonged to Camilla Bristow from Westfall.

Duncan cleared his throat and took a step backward.

Gossip and county roads were like neurons connecting each little valley town. Everyone knew which community festivals to go to for the food, which to go to for the nineties cover bands, and which were best to avoid entirely unless you wanted to flirt with gastroenteritis and a good chance of getting pickpocketed. They knew that Zinnia MacQuoid in Fort Hill would be happy to foster that litter of kittens you found under the shed in your backyard. It was a fact that Mambo's Deli in Chapel Ford had the best cheesesteak outside of Philadelphia, but if you wanted a hard roll hoagie, you went to Hogger's in Linden and hoped they hadn't sold out for the day. You knew the current status of high school football rivalries and high school marching band rivalries, and you knew the latter was even more savage than the former.

It also meant knowing when—and with whom—the boy you loved moved on with astonishing speed after you ended.

Aside from recognizing her unmistakable little truck, Temperance knew three things about Camilla Bristow—that everyone called her Millie for short, that she was assertively, undeniably likable, and that Duncan had been hooking up with her on and off since the month after they fell apart more than a decade ago. She was fair-haired and blue-eyed like Temperance, but where Temperance's blond was silvery, Millie's was an intense sunset-through-bourbon, and her eyes were an animated ultramarine instead of Temperance's crystalline cool.

Millie parked the truck and got out, waving. Duncan hung his head for the briefest moment, then he looked up to pin Temperance with heavy-lidded black eyes. His voice was low. "We're not done yet."

Then he jogged away to meet Millie. She gave him a megawatt grin and hugged him around the neck, and they disappeared into the cabin.

Temperance slumped against the truck and looked down at the white balloon in her hand. Millie Bristow was charming and sweet and uncomplicated. Everything about her was big and bright in all the ways Temperance wasn't. She felt drab and withered, standing there alone in her hideous bargain-bin swimsuit.

All that melty heat in her blood winked out.

CHAPTER TEN

Duncan

That night, Mal stayed well after everyone else was gone. They sat side by side in the deep Adirondack chairs on the cabin porch. Moonlight was a spill of glossy white ink on the surface of the lake. The air was humid and heavy, resonant with the eerie vibrato of night creatures.

"You going to talk to me about Temperance, or do I need to make it weird with a bunch of questions first?" Mal said.

Duncan put his elbows on his thighs and leaned forward. Palms up, his hands were a blue-collar canvas of calluses, rough skin, and fingertips darkened with engine grease. It didn't seem to matter that he scrubbed them a dozen times a day.

He'd learned pretty young that he was good at two things without really needing to try: building things and being funny. Humor was an important social lubricant for him now—his tattoos and dark beard paired with his sheer size tended to be intimidating for folks who didn't know him, so a well-timed one-liner or a self-effacing quip went a long way toward putting people at ease. Since he was a kid, humor was also what set him apart in his family of big brains and big personalities. His siblings would get novels and science stuff for birthdays, while Duncan got whoopee cushions and books like *500 Knock-Knock Jokes for Kids*. Literal clown shit. He'd committed to the persona and built it all on his own, though, and nobody had ever intentionally made him feel small.

He did a fine enough job of that himself.

"Harry and Temperance—" Duncan began. He cut himself off with a frustrated sigh. Christ, he was an idiot.

"Harry and Temperance . . ." Mal prompted.

"Forget it."

"I won't be doing that," said Mal.

Duncan was born a builder. A fixer. Hell, sometimes he broke things just to figure out how to fix them or put them back together in a better way. The thing with Temperance was the one thing he'd never figured out how to fix.

"Look. Imagine you're one of six siblings, and everyone but you is so accomplished. Med school. Pharmacy school, MBA. Goddamned bestseller lists, Mal. Literary awards." Duncan's laugh was dark and a little desperate. "And you're the only blue-collar one in the bunch. You couldn't even make it through your first semester of community college. But nobody ever expected anything more of you because you're funny and uncomplicated, and why did it fucking matter anyway, because you were good at swinging sledgehammers and resurrecting old engines, and you were going to take over the family business someday. Imagine constantly thinking you're less than the people you love most in the world. And then the goddamned *guilt* on top of it, because you envy them for it."

Mal was quiet for a long time. Eventually, he said, "You're not uncomplicated."

"That's your takeaway." Duncan narrowed his eyes. "Out of everything I just said."

"You're also not *that* funny—"

"This is really helping, thanks."

"We didn't come from a limited supply of genetic resources, Ducky. Ma didn't allocate more brainpower and talent to us at the expense of giving it to you."

Mal picked up a copy of a book from the moving box. *Walden* by Henry David Thoreau.

Duncan had been eleven years old when Mal had gifted it to him at Christmas, along with a copy of *Nature* by Ralph Waldo Emerson. When he'd unwrapped the books, he'd assumed they were mislabeled. Meant for Dad, or Nate or Patrick—literally anyone in the family other than him. "*Just read them*," Mal had said, and Duncan tried—he really did—but the wordy prose had only reinforced his assumption that they hadn't actually been meant for him.

He picked *Walden* up a few years later, and he devoured it. *Nature* soon after. Both texts had introduced him to the nature-centric ideals of transcendentalism that had inspired Frank Lloyd Wright's own design philosophy, further fueling Duncan's own fascination with organic architecture.

Mal knew him. Truly *saw* him. Years before Duncan knew much about himself.

Still did.

Duncan flipped through one of the tattered drafting sketchbooks from the box Nate had pulled his makeshift first-aid kit from earlier that day. There were a few dozen, layered like a fossil record in bedrock. The oldest ones were jam-packed with his shitty juvenile attempts at mimicking Frank Lloyd Wright and Marion Mahony Griffin. Later—Peter Muller, Ken Yeang. Duncan's renderings of texture and light and three-dimensional perspective grew progressively more sophisticated in each sketchbook, as did his handling of proportion and scale. Eventually, he'd experimented with his own designs of new buildings in harmony with their surrounding ecology, and he'd reimagine existing structures using more sustainable materials. Retrofitting with green roofs and conceptualizing adaptive reuse options, like turning an abandoned shopping mall into an indoor farmers' market entirely powered by solar. Old barns became art galleries, old churches became libraries. During a few months of his senior year of high school, he'd filled an entire sketchbook with ideas of what it would look like to rebuild in the ruins of an apocalyptic event.

Admittedly, those were pretty fucking weird.

"I can't believe a person capable of the things you're capable of, a person who looks like you do, carries themselves like you do"—Mal used one of the sketchbooks to gesture from Duncan's head to his feet—"can feel like they're not enough."

Duncan gave him a sardonic sideways smile. "Are you saying I'm just too damned pretty to be sad?"

"Fuck off." Mal chuckled. "What I'm saying is—if someone like *you* is truly 'not enough,' what the hell hope is there for the rest of us?"

Duncan stared at the wood floor between his feet for a long time. He'd used planks reclaimed from the crumbling gambrel barn in his folks' northeast pasture to fix up the rotted places on the porch. The result was a mosaic of old and new that made him feel even more connected to the place.

His own.

"You think nobody notices how hard you drive yourself," Mal said. "How you stack a mountain of responsibilities and tasks and bullshit sky-high on your back so you can barely breathe. Why do you do it?"

Duncan rolled his shoulders. "I have a lot of people who count on me—"

"Why do you do it?" Mal repeated.

"If I don't do it, it's not going to get done."

"You want to know what I think?" said Mal.

"No."

Mal watched him in profile for a few long seconds, then he nodded and sat back, silent. He flipped through Duncan's dog-eared copy of *Silent Spring*.

"What?" Duncan sat forward. "You're really not going to tell me what you think?"

"You're smart, Ducky. You'll figure it out." Mal put the book aside.

Duncan grumbled and popped his knuckles.

"This thing with Temperance, though—you need to rip it open at the seams and figure out how to fix what's inside."

"My history with her isn't a broken plot you can workshop."

"I'm not talking about writing."

"Ah, okay. You're talking about the way you fixed your healthy and thriving relationship with Charlotte's mom, then."

Mal sat back and linked his fingers across his waist. "Sometimes, you break a thing open and find there's nothing actually there. That's equally useful information."

Hell with it.

From one of the smaller moving boxes in an empty chair, Duncan set aside old CDs and books, a grass-stained Westfall High football jersey. Another stack of softcover sketchbooks strapped together with an oversized rubber band. From the deepest, darkest corner, he pulled out the wooden cigar box he'd gotten from Dad when he was eighteen.

It felt like an excavation of a long-buried skeleton.

The first thing Duncan handed to Mal from inside the box was a raggedy photo booth strip with four faded images. The only pictures of him and Temperance that existed from the summer they'd been inseparable. The summer when years of pining and horny infatuation had burst into full-blown, devastating first love.

In the photos, Temperance had a sunburned nose and cheeks that had started to peel, her hair bleached so pale from the sun that it appeared almost white in the glare of the booth's flash. Even fourteen years later, Duncan could remember the taste of her strawberry lip balm, and how she'd looked that night in the passenger seat of his shitty rust-bucket pickup truck, belting out the lyrics to "Everlong," wondering aloud if anything could ever be that good again.

In the first square at the top of the strip, they both wore awkward expressions of confusion, their lips parted in mid-speech as they tried to figure out how to initiate the booth's camera. Their heads were thrown back in laughter in the second image, and the third showed him cradling her face in both hands as they kissed, looking wide-eyed at each other. In the final image, she'd wrapped both arms around his head and pressed his cheek against her chest.

Her head rested sideways on the top of his. They both wore serene, serious expressions. Eyes solemn, mouths soft, lips gently quirked up at the corners as if to say: *We are each other's. Don't you wish you had this, too?*

Four hours after the photos were taken, he'd rushed her to the Capewell-Talbot hospital in Linden with a nose that wouldn't stop bleeding and softball-sized bruises on her thighs that he'd been terrified he'd given her.

Mal handed the photo strip back to Duncan. "You've been pining for Temperance Madigan half your life because of a summer thing when you were eighteen?"

Duncan took a small velvet pouch out of the box. He split his fingernail picking apart the tightly knotted drawstring. It had been tied tight for fourteen years.

He tipped the contents into his hand. Two rings.

Duncan slipped one of them on, and it barely fit to the first knuckle of his pinkie. The finish was dulled to a grayish-brown, and in the center was a tiny turtle with a round blue plastic stone in the center. "I bought her this from the beach gift shop. She wore it the rest of the summer. Left a green mark on her finger, but she didn't care." He tucked the ring back into the bag.

The other ring was a little diamond with a sapphire halo, with smaller diamonds on the shoulders. Vintage. Art deco, according to the antiques shop owner. The center stone was petite, but in the low light of the porch lamps, it sparkled like it had been carved right off the edge of a star. It looked absurd against the backdrop of his callused palm, but the weight of it was profound. Like he'd taken his soul from his body and infused it into metal and stone.

Duncan didn't really believe in supernatural bullshit, but in that moment, he was convinced that this must be what it felt like to see a ghost.

He held it out to show Mal.

Mal looked slowly from the ring to Duncan's face. "I don't think that's my size."

Duncan snatched the ring back and gave him a sour look. "I thought I was supposed to be the funny one."

He rubbed his thumb against the old platinum. It was cool to the touch, and utterly meaningless unless it was on her finger. A prism without light was just cold, empty glass.

"And I thought I was the one who told fictional stories." Mal gave him a thin smile. "Seriously, I'm impressed with the narrative you've sold yourself here."

"Well, you know me. I'm nothing if not fucking entertaining, yeah?"

Duncan tucked the ring away in the velvet. The drawstrings were shredded from the messy way he'd opened it, and they wouldn't pull closed. Impatiently, he folded it over on itself and stuffed it back into the cigar box, then tucked the whole thing back into its bottom-corner hiding place. He stacked all his other nostalgic garbage on top again.

"What does this have to do with Harry and Temperance, anyway?" Mal said.

Duncan stood and gripped the porch railing until the wood creaked in his hands. "I thought she'd end up with him." Until he'd spilled his guts to Rowan last September, it was a thing he'd never told anyone else. After he'd uttered the words out loud to her that night, he'd been overcome with such a sensation of simultaneous shame and relief, he felt like he'd be sick.

Now, confessing it to Malcolm—he just felt like an asshole.

Mal was quiet for a while, and when he eventually spoke, the words came slowly. "You were at a point in a relationship with Temperance where you bought an engagement ring"—he paused—"and you thought she wanted to be with Harry."

"I didn't think that while we were together." Duncan hesitated. "Well. I *kind of* did, that first summer. It was the first year Harry didn't come home from college—"

Mal did a low whistle. "These are Olympics-level mental gymnastics."

"She lived with him the summer after we broke up. And then

at family gatherings those years after, she'd cling to him like a little orbiting moon—"

"Reasonable, if you two had a messy breakup. He was a safe space for her."

Duncan shoved his fingers through his hair. He realized how ridiculous he sounded, but he couldn't stop. "They had that—that—marriage pact thing, where they said they'd marry each other if they were single by the time they were thirty—"

"That's a classic romantic comedy trope," Mal said. "The characters always end up together."

"Yeah, no shit, Nora Ephron."

Mal blinked at him, expressionless. "I'm sorry—are you intentionally missing the point, or are you that clueless?"

Duncan didn't respond.

Mal sat forward with his elbows on his knees. He steepled his fingers together. "Those are movies. This is real life."

"Then Harry and Nicola split, and he came home—"

"And you thought he'd come for Temperance," Mal finished for him. He dropped his head into his hands and rubbed his temples. His voice was muffled. "This is the stupidest fucking thing I've ever heard."

Mal armored up with cynicism the same way Duncan did with humor, so he usually got a free pass. He never pushed back, always took Mal's misanthropic teasing at face value. But tonight, his patience was fractured.

He swung around and got loud. "Why do you even want to talk about this, Malcolm? For the fucking schadenfreude?"

Mal looked up slowly. His face darkened, and his brows crammed together on his forehead. A vein in his neck throbbed, and his jaw worked, like he was trying to chew down the words. The corners of his mouth twitched a millimeter upward.

Duncan jabbed a finger at his face. "You're dying to make a shitty quip about me knowing a word like *schadenfreude*. Admit it."

One of Mal's rare laughs came out on an explosion of breath. "Guilty."

Duncan wanted to cling to that fortifying anger, but he couldn't. He laughed, too, and the tension was broken.

When Mal spoke again, there was a quiet reprimand in his tone. "I think you've told yourself this story as an excuse to not have to try with her, and your stubbornness and insecurity have kept it alive with a self-sustaining circle jerk inside your head. But the truth is staring you in the face now, and you can't use it anymore as an excuse to not go after her."

God, he was tired. "You know how, in any relationship, there's one person who settled and one who reached?" Duncan said. "Everywhere we go, people would see that with Temperance and me. It's obvious."

"That's ridiculous. And reductive. And who *cares*?"

Duncan didn't have an answer for that.

Mal wasn't done yet. "You must have thought so little of her to have believed this bullshit for so long."

"I thought so little of *myself*."

"You ever consider therapy?" Mal said. "Seriously."

"You first." Duncan cracked his knuckles again.

"Way ahead of you, brother." Mal grunted. "Does she know?"

"About the Harry thing? God, no." Duncan sank his hand into his hair. "Well, hell—maybe? I spilled my guts to Rowan about it last September. Maybe she told her."

"Harry is Temperance's home base, man. Warmth isn't the same thing as fire."

"Fire's pointless without the warmth, though." Duncan lobbed a dart at the board. It hit sideways and fell to the deck. "*Love must be as much a light, as it is a flame.*"

"Ah, we've gotten to the quoting-Thoreau part of the evening," said Mal. "It's questionable whether that quote is actually his, you know. Some say he was an insufferable misanthropic bastard."

"I can see why you were such a fan."

Mal sat forward in his chair. "People can be multiple things at once, Ducky."

"Yeah, well. I guess I've been tilting at waterfalls."

"Windmills."

"What?"

"Tilting at *windmills*. You just mashed up *Don Quixote* with a TLC song."

"Ah. My bad."

Mal looked at him for a long time. With an analytical narrowing of his eyes, he finally sat back and said, "I'll be damned. You do it on purpose."

Duncan kept his expression neutral. "People can be multiple things at once, Malcolm."

"Touché."

They sat in silence for a long time after that, listening to the muddy song of bullfrogs and the lap of tiny waves in the cattails. Little brown moths danced around the glow of the porch lamp, charmed by the light in a way they couldn't understand or resist.

Duncan could relate.

"Don't say anything to anyone about this," he said after a while. "Okay?"

"What, the fact that you've been trolling us your whole life with your bullshit mixed idioms and malapropisms?"

Duncan breathed out a helpless laugh. "Harry and Temperance, asshole. And I don't even know what that last word means."

"That won't be a problem." Mal got to his feet with a faint grimace and a sigh. "I'm not exactly Harry's first choice for a heart-to-heart."

"You want me to drive you back up?"

"Nah. I need to walk." Mal made his way down the steps and headed toward the vineyard path that led back to Cloud Tide.

"Watch out for crawdad holes," Duncan said to Mal's back. "It's a minefield of 'em."

Mal stopped and turned around. "Duncan." In his dark clothes, he was almost invisible, if not for the glint of moonlight on his cane and the white of his teeth. "Look—don't use your past as an excuse to not have a future. The main difference between a mess and a masterpiece is time."

CHAPTER ELEVEN

Duncan

The black of the room was absolute.

Duncan passed his hand in front of his face. Nothing. The darkness was so deep it went beyond not seeing. It felt like maybe his body didn't exist anymore at all.

Somewhere, Temperance was crying.

A candle flickered to life, but Duncan couldn't smell a blown match. He moved toward the light, and the closer he came, the wider the radius of the candlelight grew.

Bodhi Rao was there in full physician's garb. Navy-blue scrubs, white lab coat, stethoscope around his neck, scrub cap on his head. He sat in the chair from Ma and Dad's living room at the old house in Westfall. Temperance was on his lap, weeping.

Naked.

Bodhi had a hand clasped against her hip, another around her shoulders. His skin melted into hers like wax, fusing them into a single organism. Duncan approached, unable to stop himself.

He wanted to throw up.

A thin finger of blood stretched toward him from beneath the chair. It rolled and ran like it was leaking downhill, even though the floor was flat. It glistened black in the dim light.

This is a dream.

When Duncan looked back up to Temperance, Bodhi was gone. Now, she sat on Harry's lap.

Harry, no.

She wasn't naked anymore. They wore identical clothing—all the way down to the bruise-blue color of surgical scrubs and the way stethoscopes draped over their collarbones. A bubble of blood hovered inside her nostril, and it burst with a tiny audible *pop* before it streaked down her lip, then her chin.

The name badge clipped to her shirt read DR. TEMPERANCE BRADY, and Duncan knew she'd taken the Brady name because she'd married Harry.

Not him.

She'd always wanted to be a Brady.

Now *Duncan* was naked, wearing only a tool belt and work boots. The belt was bolted into his hip bones, fused to his body the same way Bodhi Rao's fingers had flowed into Temperance's skin. When he tried to take another step closer, he was fixed in place. The boots were filthy, cemented to the ground with mud and grime caked all the way up to his knees. Layer after layer continued to solidify, climbing up his body like masonry.

This is a fucking dream.

Now he was in a hospital waiting room. It smelled like sunscreen. Coconut, bananas. Salt and cream, and the mineral scent of healthy human sweat and hot sun on cut grass. Temperance smelled like that, just behind her ear, and beneath the crook of her jawbone. She'd worn that sunscreen every day he'd known her, even in winter.

It was dismal there in the waiting room, though. Monochromatic and bleak. That summer scent piping down from the ceiling was a misdirection and a lie. This place had never known warmth.

Duncan was the only person there. Jammed into a corner, in a chair too short for him. If he bent forward, just a little, he could touch his forehead to his knees. It made him feel paradoxically small. It wasn't the chair's fault, though. The problem was that he was too big. Too rough around the edges. Too everything.

He blinked, and there were more people in the room. A sea of bodies, shoulder to shoulder. The man in front of him turned. Slow and stiff, like a ballerina figurine in a music box.

It was Corbin Madigan.

"You're the Brady boy," he said.

He didn't answer. Kept his eyes on the ground. Duncan didn't know why, but it was important for Corbin Madigan to not know who he was. He needed to be like glass.

There was a chair beside him now. A nice chair, not the cramped thing that was trying to feed Duncan his own knees. The man in the chair was Corbin Madigan, too, even though Corbin Madigan already stood in front of him.

"Temperance was asking for you," the second Corbin Madigan said, and that time, Duncan looked up. He couldn't help it. You couldn't *not* look at a person when an exact copy of them sat next to you.

Temperance was asking for you. The words were a test that Corbin Madigan knew Duncan would fail.

Hundreds of people stood in the waiting room now. Thousands. Different bodies, different clothes. It seemed like there shouldn't be enough space in a hospital waiting room for that many people, but it also seemed like there shouldn't be thousands of versions of the same person there, either. Every one of them had the face and voice of Corbin Madigan, and they all turned to him in unison. Then they parted at the center of the room, and he saw Temperance.

Two Temperances.

The first Temperance was in a wheelchair and had streaky tear tracks on her cheeks. The second Temperance stood behind her, wearing a white coat and a scrub cap the color of blood.

They spoke at the same time, in the same voice. Temperance's voice. "You said we were all flame, Duncan. Have some light."

Light flooded the space until it was a molten-hot whiteout. The light shrieked in Duncan's eye sockets and ears, noise he could taste and brightness he could hear.

All the Corbin Madigans laughed. They laughed and laughed and laughed.

* * *

DUNCAN screamed himself awake.

He lurched upright in bed, huffing breath through his nose like a Clydesdale.

Jesus Christ.

It had been a while since he'd had one like that. Years ago, he'd gone through a period of months where nearly every night was a midnight showing of the Duncan Brady Nightmare Fuckery Cinematic Universe, and Temperance Madigan had top billing.

She was haunting him again. Right when he'd finally started to believe he didn't need an exorcism.

Part Two

CHAPTER TWELVE

Duncan

The Honey Moon Festival in Vesper Notch was held annually in June, on the weekend closest to the full moon. It started decades ago as a small gathering of area garden clubs and beekeepers to exchange seeds and socialize to celebrate the start of wildflower season. Now, it had expanded out of little uptown Vesper Notch and into the ten-acre park on the southern end of town. The festival began with a Saturday-morning 5K to raise money for a local charity—this year, it was for the animal shelter in Shelby—and later, the park would be filled with carnival rides, live music, food trucks from around the valley, and a bazaar to give Vesper Valley artisans and businesses a chance to showcase their offerings.

The 5K route zigzagged through the festival grounds, and every year a crowd of supporters lined up along it to cheer for loved ones. They fully embraced the festival atmosphere by waving flags, sparkly streamers, and noisemakers. Many of the runners wore flowers in their hair or dressed in colorful yellow-and-black tutus and bee costumes.

Harry and Rowan were in the 5K, and it would be Rowan's first. Duncan had secretly made T-shirts with Rowan's smiling face screen-printed in the center, and ROWAN KEEP GOIN' printed underneath. Dad waved a small pennant flag printed with the same. Everyone pulled the shirts over their regular clothes and waited for the race to begin.

The Bradys set up in a spot between Bennett Goodwin's dairy

table and Florence Holley's small apiary tent. While they waited for the race to begin, Dad chatted with Goodwin, a plainspoken dairy farmer Duncan had met a few times at the Linden agriculture equipment auctions. He offered rustic paper-wrapped cheeses with different fruits and honey, and a stack of paperback books he'd self-published about biodynamic practices on his farm. Talking to Dad was the first time Duncan had ever seen Goodwin smile. Beekeeper Florence Holley sold honey and beeswax candles, and also gave out samples of her award-winning mead to anyone who wore the bright yellow wristband that designated them of age. She had an elaborate honeycomb tattoo that covered the dusky skin of her entire left forearm.

Duncan had a clear view of the Linden Free Clinic tent, where Temperance worked with a few other volunteers. She was stacking informational flyers in a wooden display case when a young couple approached to chat with her. She came around the front of the table and gave them her full attention, occasionally bending to smile and coo at the baby in their stroller. Her long braid swung toward the little one each time. When the baby managed to grab it, Temperance laughed and sank down to her knees in front of the stroller to pull it free from the little one's fingers.

In a cream lace tank top and a bohemian patchwork skirt that had begun to fray along the bottom hem, she was a flesh-and-blood true north, drawing his entire consciousness like a compass needle.

Once the 5K began, there was an initial surge of runners followed by a trickle of slower folks over the next half hour. Harry and Rowan eventually brought up the rear, just ahead of two men who jogged with three elementary-aged children. Rowan was red-faced and shuffling but hanging on. Harry hadn't even broken a sweat.

Ma clanged the miniature cowbell she'd had since Duncan had played high school football, and everyone waved and cheered as they passed. When Rowan saw the shirts, her shoulders shook with laughter and she pressed both hands to her chest, turning an even more alarming shade of crimson. Harry turned to jog backward in front of her, grinning and clapping.

At the clinic tent, Temperance watched, but it wasn't Rowan

and Harry who had her attention. Her eyes were right on him. She twisted the end of her braid in her fingers. Duncan raised a hand in a subtle wave, and instead of turning to pretend she hadn't seen, she waved back.

Well. That was something.

* * *

AFTER the race, the Bradys began to make their way through the huge mown field where tents and pergolas were set up for the artisan bazaar.

They stopped at the tent for the hobby farm owned and operated by an honest-to-god, unironically named farmer named Barnhill McDonald. He raised goats for artisan cheeses, while his husband, Owen Flynn, made bar soaps with their milk, infused with herbs, dried flowers, and swirls of natural dyes.

Arden gasped and jogged over to the table. "The Boonies! You guys are bringing back the Boonies?"

On the table was a round glass aquarium with a few coins and paper bills in the bottom. A little sign on a wooden dowel poked out, hand-lettered with BRING BACK THE BOONIES.

The Boonies had been the drive-in theater between Linden and Westfall, originally built in the early 1960s. Like most other drive-ins in the country, it fell victim to the double-punch of rising expenses and home movie rentals. Now, it was a forgotten relic on a low-traffic county road.

Owen lined up honey-lemon soaps shaped like miniature honeycombs in a tidy row. "Trying. The property backs up to our farm. We bought it this spring."

"Everyone in this damned valley is trying to bring something back from the brink," Nate said. He wore nine-month-old Leo in a backpack carrier, and he had to bounce continually in place or the baby would pull his hair with tiny fists. Nate also cradled a basket of deep-fried cheese curds against his chest.

Duncan watched Temperance approach. Quietly, he said, "Shame not to try, when it's worth it."

Temperance greeted Maren and Mercy, and Arden gave her a quick hug, too. At the table directly across from Duncan, she lifted a bar of rose-scented soap to her nose. Her long braid seemed to have more hair flying free from it than what was bound inside. When she looked up at him, there was genuine pleasure in her eyes. He gave her a nod in greeting, and she slid her gaze away.

Arden tucked a crisp ten-dollar bill into the jar. "I was in junior high when the county tried to revive it the first time around. I went to a double feature of the first two Mummy movies with six other kids in the back of Grace Pennypacker's mom's conversion van. Chad Yearwood tried to touch my boob midway through the Nefertiri fight scene."

Duncan scowled. "Chad *whom*?"

"I know you've done far more at the Boonies than a thwarted boob grab, Duncan." Mercy hip-checked him.

"Holster your outrage, Ducky. I told Grace's mom, and she made him sit outside the van on a lawn chair with her." Arden sighed wistfully. "That scene was my bisexual awakening."

"You and me both," Owen said.

To Temperance, Duncan said, "Got any fond memories from the Boonies, Teacup?"

She lifted a honeycomb-shaped soap to her nose and shot him a warning glare. "Oh, I don't really remember much happening there."

Duncan chuckled. *Like hell.*

Their last summer together, the Boonies had been their favorite spot. Even on the weekends, attendance had declined so dramatically they'd often be one of only a few dozen vehicles there. In a lot designed for hundreds of cars, it meant plenty of privacy. They'd taken full advantage of every minute of darkness with an air mattress and an old comforter in the bed of his truck.

"I never noticed your tattoo, T.J." Arden pointed to the barely visible ink on the inside of Temperance's ring finger. "What is it?"

Temperance returned the honeycomb soap to the table and rubbed her thumb over her finger. Sometimes, she wore a Band-Aid over it, or a wide sterling silver ring. "It's just a little bee."

"Does it have a meaning?" Arden said.

"Because she's sweet," said Duncan.

"Because I sting," Temperance said at the same time.

She narrowed her eyes at him.

Arden and Mercy exchanged a long look.

"I've always liked bees," Duncan said, lightly.

"Do you?" Temperance raised a blond brow. "Remember that summer at Bethany Beach, and you got stung on the lip?"

"Obviously I *don't* like bees in my soda cans."

"Your mom made you keep a smear of toothpaste on the sting for hours—" She reached up to drift a fingertip across his upper lip. "It was hilarious."

Duncan's smile dropped, and Temperance snatched her hand away. She put distance between them, suddenly interested in Owen Flynn's assortment of lip balms at the opposite end of the table. Maren and Nate both stopped their silliness to watch. Even Owen paused restocking a line of lavender soaps to stare.

"Anyway," Temperance said. "When you mess with a bee, you should expect to eventually get stung."

He followed her around the table. "Ah. So, you're saying I got what I deserved that day?"

"I'm just saying it's not fair to get upset with bees for doing"— Temperance made a vague gesture with her hands—"bee things."

"I'm sorry. Are you two," Arden began, "*flirting*?"

"No," they said in unison.

Nate said, around a mouthful of fried cheese curds, "We used to call that place the Boobies." He chuckled, then hissed in pain when Leo ruthlessly yanked his head sideways by a fistful of hair.

"Who is *we*?" Mercy said.

"Me and—*ow*—Patrick."

Mercy rolled her eyes. "That's what I was afraid of."

"Plus a few of our buddies," Nate said. "Ah—most of the guys in my high school graduating class, actually."

"Gross," Arden said.

"Charming," Maren said.

"Listen, sweetheart," Nate said to Maren. "If Owen and Barney get that place running again, I will take you there and give you the most thrilling tit grab you've ever had."

"Aw, and they say romance is dead," said Maren.

Nate held his basket of cheese curds aside to go after her for a greasy kiss, and Maren spun away, laughing. In the carrier, baby Leo squealed and battered his dad's head with tiny fists.

When Duncan looked back to where Temperance had stood, she was gone.

* * *

"DUNCAN Brady!" Millie Bristow leaned out the window of the barbecue food truck she ran with her two sisters. She wore a purple bandana over her hair, and her cheeks were a lively red from the heat inside the truck. "Hey, handsome. You got a minute?"

"Always." He met Millie around the back of the truck. It was dimmer there in the shadows, and the air was heavy with the syrupy tang of caramelizing barbecue sauce and the savory scent of potatoes frying in peanut oil.

Millie took her bandana off and swiped the sweat away from her cheeks. She pulled out her phone to take a photo with Duncan, angling it so she captured the festival in the background.

"How do we look?" Duncan leaned in to peek at the screen.

She tilted the phone up so he could see. "Adorable, as usual. Possibly the cutest fake couple that's ever existed." Millie added the photo to her Instagram account and tucked the phone away in her back pocket. She gave him an affectionate smile. "I'm sorry to take you away from your family."

Duncan chuckled. "Nah. I'm going to miss this."

"Only a few more weeks of it, then you're off the hook for good."

"Have you figured out our sad-but-mutually-decided-upon breakup?" Duncan asked.

"I'll probably just say we decided a long-distance relationship wasn't a good idea while I was away at school. That's believable, right?"

Duncan barked a laugh.

"What?" Millie said.

"That's the story of my life, Mill. I can't escape it—in real relationships *or* fake ones."

Millie stuck out her tongue.

"I'm just teasing," Duncan said.

"I know. Mama really loves you, but I think all that will matter to her is that I'm a safe distance from Gavin. You really are a saint for doing what you've done for me, Duncan Brady."

"Just a friend helping a friend," he said.

"Once I leave, you're going to make a move on Dr. Madigan, right?" She knuckled him in the center of his chest.

Duncan grunted. "See, when you call her 'Dr. Madigan,' it reinforces how far out of my league she is."

"Mm. Sounds like a *you* problem, sweetheart."

He cracked his knuckles. "I'm going to look like a real piece of work if I start publicly chasing Temperance right after our presumptive breakup."

Millie's eyes went soft. "I feel terrible that this could interfere—"

"Listen. Don't. When we started this, the odds of me going to the moon were better than me ever having a chance again with her."

"You told her the truth, right? About us?"

"Ah, shit, Millie. It's complicated."

"Why?"

"I haven't told anyone I went back to school." He rubbed the back of his neck.

"So?"

"They'll want to know how you and I reconnected. I'm shit at lying."

"Just tell them we matched on Tinder or something."

Duncan's laugh was dark. "Temperance already thinks I've spent the last ten years fucking everyone in a fifty-mile radius."

"Haven't you?" Millie arched a playful eyebrow.

"Ah. Well—ten miles, maybe," he joked.

"You're not, like, using me for emotional leverage with her, are you?"

He twisted a bit of his beard between his fingers and made a thoughtful face. "Considered it."

She punched him lightly in the arm. "Jerk."

"Ow. Come on, I have *nothing* else on her. She's so far out of my league, we're not even playing the same sport."

"Duncan, you don't need to have something *on* her. That's not how it works. And even if it was, you're a catch." She rubbed his arm in the same place she'd popped with her fist moments ago. "If you don't tell her the truth before I leave, I'm going to tell her."

He jammed his fists in the pockets of his jeans and looked down at the grass between his feet. "Truth has always been complicated between Temperance and me."

"No. Truth is truth. It's never complicated, because it is what it is, and nothing else."

"Getting deep over here, Mill," Duncan mumbled.

Millie grinned. "Good thing you're tall."

"Listen, no offense, but—"

"Stop." She held up a hand. "Anytime someone leads with *no offense*, something offensive is about to come out of their mouth. Every time."

"Not true."

"It has the same linguistic flavor as *gentle reminder* and *just wondering*."

"What flavor is that?"

"A shitty one."

They both laughed.

Around the front of the truck, one of Millie's sisters jangled the antique dinner bell that hung from the awning. They did it whenever anyone left a tip of ten dollars or more. Millie smiled and swiped the back of her hand over her forehead.

"How'd your truck manage to get a spot at the Honey Moon?" Duncan said.

"Birdie came up with a new honey-mead barbecue sauce." She

tied her bandana back over her bright hair. "We slap some hand-cut fries into a paper boat, top them with our pulled pork, cheese curds from Goodwin's, then drizzle it all with that sticky, boozy sauce. We call it 'Valley poutine'—"

Inside the truck, a metallic crash was followed by an impressive string of profanity.

"Ooookay. I need to get back in there before Midge breaks something." Millie gave him an affectionate side-hug squeeze. "Try to have some fun today. You work too hard."

CHAPTER THIRTEEN

Duncan

Duncan found everyone at Praise Cheeses, a novelty grilled cheese truck out of Philly. With unique offerings like melted Brie and honey, apples and Gouda, and goat cheese with bacon and dates, they were one of the most popular trucks at events around the valley. They even had a vegan option with cashew cheddar on sourdough with a fat slice of heirloom tomato.

Nate wiped tears from his eyes after his first bite of a thirty-dollar sandwich stuffed full of half a pound of lobster and Gruyère. The bread was grilled crisp in Old Bay–infused butter. "I've peaked." He rested his hands on his belly. "I'll never feel this way about anything ever again."

Maren laughed and threw a wadded-up napkin at his chest.

The kids finished their sandwiches well before the adults did. They were bored, clamoring to go to the Linden Free Clinic tent. It always had a face painter and baskets of freebies—fidgets, pencils, lip balms—but Aunt T.J. was as much a draw as all the goodies were.

Grey tugged on Duncan's forearm. The little boy angled his butt backward to put his full weight into it, but Duncan didn't budge. He made a fist and flexed upward, lifting a giggling Grey off the ground.

"Pleeeease, Uncle Duncan?" Alice said. Charlie stood beside Alice with her little hands clasped beneath her chin.

Nate and Maren gave him a nod and a shrug when he raised his brows their way.

"Fine, fine," he said, and the kids cheered. "Let's get Aunt T.J. a snack first, okay?"

Temperance was talking to another member of the clinic staff when they got there. The kids ran ahead to swarm her in a group hug. She had a stethoscope looped around her neck, along with a lanyard identification card.

Duncan held a little brown bag toward her as he approached. "Maren said you skipped breakfast."

Temperance squinted and said, "Hmm," but her belly betrayed her with an audible growl. She primly peeked into the bag, then popped her head up in delight. "You *didn't*." The edges of her teeth pinned her bottom lip, and her pupils widened like inkblots into a thin ring of blue.

While the kids lined up to pillage the freebies, Temperance sat in the grass with Duncan under a nearby tree. She crossed her legs and arranged her skirt around her, then unwrapped the sandwich with reverence. The thick slices of bread were an alarming shade of orangey red, crusted with crushed Flamin' Hot Cheetos and grilled to a buttery crisp.

"You're a horrible influence." She took a bite, stretching the melty cheddar. She used her tongue to loop it into her mouth.

The sound of pleasure she made drilled straight into Duncan's id. Her eyelids fluttered in bliss. "Thank you."

"Look in the bottom of the bag," he said.

She pulled out a small plastic baggie filled with dill pickle slices. "You remembered."

The wistful sweetness in her voice made his throat tighten. "You know I'm violating my personal code of food ethics to enable this behavior."

"Don't knock it until you try it." Temperance tucked a few pickles into the sandwich and took a bite.

"Pass." He snagged a pickle slice from the bag. "I'm a pickle purist."

Temperance swiped at him as he leaned away to pop it into

his mouth. "Watch it. You know what happens when you take my food."

"Cutlery shouldn't be weaponized, Teacup."

She shrugged. "I expected you to be faster."

"You stabbed me in the *hand* with a *fork*."

"You shouldn't put your fingers into unauthorized plate space," she mumbled around a full mouth.

"You drew *blood*."

"It was the last piece of your dad's leche frita. The stakes were very high."

"Sadist." He laughed.

"Thief," she fired back.

They both smiled and held each other's eyes for a tiny beat too long.

Temperance was the first to look away. She dabbed her lips with a paper napkin.

"I've never had Flamin' Hot Cheetos, you know," Duncan said.

"I feel sad for you and your unsophisticated palate."

"Listen, if you want to talk about unsophisticated, please remember how many twelve-inch hoagies I've seen you take down over the years."

They both laughed.

Between bites, Temperance told him about her day. Coppery sunshine glittered on her face through the lattice of leaves overhead, and warm wind animated that loose ribbon of hair around her lovely face like a punctuation mark.

The kids ran over, calling her name. They still had on their ROWAN KEEP GOIN' shirts.

Temperance said to Duncan, "I hope you saved me one of those shirts."

"Of course I did," he said.

Grey took her by the hand when she stood. "Come listen to our heart beeps."

Thank you, she mouthed over her shoulder. She let Grey lead her back to the tent.

Duncan gathered the empty bags and followed.

Each year, the Linden Free Clinic was a regular presence at area fundraisers, festivals, and school events, offering a range of wellness tests like glucose and blood pressure checks. Brennan Everett was there in his Linden Township Fire Station ball cap doing car seat safety talks, and Reese Culpepper offered free haircuts. There were informational brochures and postcards about everything from nutrition guides to vaccination facts to Lyme disease symptoms. There were even boxes where people could donate old pairs of eyeglasses and old cell phones.

Temperance washed up at a portable sink with a foot pump. Grey side-eyed the digital blood pressure monitor when she approached with it. "Does it hurt?" he said.

"It's a little squeezy," she said. "And you have to sit very still. Can you do that?"

Grey thoughtfully pushed out his bottom lip. "Do Uncle Duncan first."

Their eyes met over the little boy's head, and Temperance comically raised her eyebrows.

The pediatric cuff she held would barely fit around his wrist. Temperance swapped the cuff on the portable monitor for the largest adult size they had and strapped it around his biceps. When she bent toward him, her braid fell heavy over her shoulder, bringing with it the cool floral scent of her.

"My usual patients are much cuter than you," she said, loud enough only for him to hear.

Duncan cupped his hands over his knees. "They probably don't follow directions as well as I do, though."

"Mm. Debatable."

As she attached the cuff, her fingertips grazed the sensitive skin of his inner arm, and her knuckles brushed against his rib cage. He twitched and cleared his throat.

"Still ticklish?" she said.

"Never was. I just couldn't handle being touched by you back then."

"Liar." Temperance's eyes twinkled. "Put your arm across your belly and be still."

He did. "See? Good listener."

She held his gaze and pushed a button on the monitor. The cuff squeezed.

Ow, he mouthed.

She pressed her lips into a little pout and made a faux *tsk* of sympathy. Her eyes danced.

Moments like this reinforced how much he just—*liked* her.

"Try to breathe normally, Mr. Brady," she said, and damn it if she didn't intentionally brush her breasts against his arm when she reached for a drink of water from her tumbler.

He chuckled. "Trust me, I'm trying."

A familiar tightness gathered in his chest, and his throat constricted.

Ah, shit.

Hiccup.

Temperance leaned back to look him in the eye. "You still get hiccups when you're nervous?"

"No."

Hiccup.

When the cuff released its pressure, Temperance removed it from his arm.

"Blood pressure is a little high right now, Mr. Brady. Pulse is elevated, too." Her tone was serious, but her expression was playful. "Have you been feeling okay?"

"I guess—" Duncan rubbed his arm. "Ah—doctors make me nervous."

"How did it feel, Uncle Duncan?" Alice said.

He gave the kids a reassuring smile. "Like a nice hug."

Hiccup.

Grey pointed at the stethoscope around her neck. "Listen to his heart beeps now, Aunt T.J."

"Ah, yes." She tucked in the earpieces and laid the chest piece flat against Duncan's upper back, then held a finger to her lips with her free hand. "Lung sounds first."

Duncan squared his shoulders and sat up straighter as she bent toward him again. His heart kicked like a stalling engine. She had a clinical front-row seat to the way she affected his physiology.

He focused on a spot on the ground to count individual blades of grass.

When she moved to the front of his chest, he said, "Might not hear anything in there."

"Hm?" She hesitated.

"Been living without a heart since I was eighteen."

"Wow." Temperance pressed her lips between her teeth. "Red flag." She laughed.

Duncan grimaced. "I know. That was bad."

She sighed through her nose, but her eyes twinkled. "No more talking."

"Yes, ma'am."

Temperance finished the exam and reported to the kids with a formal tone. "Well, my friends. My diagnosis is that your uncle Duncan has a very big and very strong heart."

Duncan stood. He thumped his hand against his chest and gave the kids a stoic smile.

"Me next!" Grey climbed into the chair.

Temperance gave all three kids the same treatment she gave Duncan, verbally guiding them through everything she did. She spoke to them gently, with clarity and a touch of humor, and she tailored her language and movement to each child. With Grey, she pretended to listen to his brain with the stethoscope in the middle of his forehead. "This brain is full of fart jokes and random facts about—one moment, please. I'm picking up a different signal." She moved around to the side of his head. "Ah, yes—sea turtles, Roblox, and, oh, my goodness—your favorite auntie, Temperance. I love you, too, buddy." Then she let Ace listen to her heart through the stethoscope, and she had a few dry one-liners for Charlie. Temperance had always treated

Charlie with the same affection as Ace and Grey, even though she wasn't her niece by blood.

Duncan and Temperance stood in momentarily awkward silence after the kids scurried away to line up for face painting. The little ones had provided a buffer between them that made the playful flirtation easier. Now that they were alone, the air seemed charged.

"So what's going to happen now?" Duncan said.

Temperance tucked a lock of hair behind her ear. "With—?"

"The clinic."

"I don't know. It's complicated. Remember the grant I mentioned to you a few weeks ago? My parents offered to fund the clinic through Capewell-Talbot if I help them. I've been trying to get a loan to keep the lights on. My codirector has talked a bit about fundraising, but that would take months for us to even begin. We could probably try an appeal to the university trustees, but that would involve a lawyer, which means money, and there's no guarantee it would even work. It's just so much uncertainty."

"So you only try for something if you know you'll succeed?" Duncan said.

She looked unamused. "Not the time for teasing."

"I'm serious."

"Well, maybe, I guess? It's a good way to never be disappointed."

"You must not want it bad enough."

Temperance slipped her thumb and forefinger beneath her glasses and squeezed the bridge of her nose. "Don't tell me what I want."

"You could just try. Trust the process."

She laughed. "Duncan, *trust the process* is one of those skeevy corporate heuristics used to gaslight employees. It's right up there with *assume positive intent*."

Duncan made a face. "I think *assume they tried their best with the information and resources available to them at the time* is much better."

"Hmm. That one wouldn't look as nice as a tagline on a motivational poster, though." Her throat tensed, her mood darkened. She looked away. "This clinic is where I fell in love with medicine."

The effort it took to not reach out and touch her knotted the muscles in his shoulders and cramped his fingers. "Tell me," he said.

"My second year of med school, there was a little boy brought in by his parents. A toddler. Bruises all over his legs, his arms. Bloody nose." She glanced at him, then looked down to nudge her foot around in the grass. "Some of the social work students got involved, and the parents were beside themselves once the questions made it obvious they suspected abuse. I butted in, advocated for an immediate CBC. Thankfully, the attending who was there that night agreed with me."

"He had ITP, didn't he," Duncan said.

"He did. He was so tiny, Duncan." Temperance rubbed her nose and looked up at the tent top. "It helped me finally feel some peace about my own diagnosis. Some meaning. Like I was meant to be there that night. Recognize what I was seeing." She twisted her name badge around in her fingers. "His platelets were so low by then, just a sneeze or a cough could have caused a brain bleed. For weeks after, I thought about how—if they'd tried to separate him from his parents that night instead of listening to me, and he'd started crying hard, like toddlers do—" She shook her head and took a shuddery breath. "It was the first time I felt like being a doctor was more than just what my parents wanted. It felt like it could be mine. Important."

Duncan didn't realize he was staring until she glanced up at him. She shielded her eyes from the sun slanting in through the open front of the tent.

"What?" she said.

"Ah—I was just thinking about how I never got to know that version of you."

The tilt of her head was stubborn, but her eyes were gentle. "I've always been the same me, Duncan."

"I'm starting to realize that."

Softness on Temperance Madigan was a double-edged blade. Any hint she might still feel something real for him had the paradoxical effect of making him feel that much worse. Give him adversarial

Temperance any day, or frosty Temperance, or the Temperance who rolled her eyes at his stupid jokes and mixed idioms. He knew exactly where he stood with her. That Temperance made it easy for him to not have to try.

This one, though. This Temperance he wanted to bury himself in—physically, metaphorically, existentially. This Temperance was the opposite of a distraction. She was the force that grounded him, made him want to slow down.

Hell. They were all the same Temperance, and he'd never stopped being in love with her.

"Hey." Duncan knuckled his jaw. "Can we talk later? Somewhere else?"

Temperance began to answer, then looked past him. Her posture drew up straighter, like an invisible hand had tugged marionette strings above her head. Duncan turned. Two men approached.

"Hey, Temperance," said the shorter of the two. He had a leathery tan and curly nineties-sitcom-dad hair. A lanyard ID similar to Temperance's hung around his neck. In his badge photo, he looked to be at least ten years younger. He smiled and extended a hand toward Duncan.

He glanced at the spotless skin of the doctor's palm and instinctively wiped his own hand on his jeans. No matter how much he scrubbed, the evidence of his livelihood was as indelible as the ink tattooed into his forearms. But the doctor didn't match Duncan's hesitation. His shake was firm and congenial—a strong-fisted *pump-pump-pump*. "Ike Elias," he said.

"Hi there." He nodded. "Duncan Brady."

The other guy appeared to be barely older than Duncan. He was so smoothly bald that the midafternoon sunshine gilded the top of his dark brown head with gold. His lanyard also identified him as a doctor. "Coleman Bello." The man smiled and nodded toward Duncan's forearms. "Incredible ink. I'm just getting started myself." When they ended the handshake, he turned his wrist up to reveal a tattoo of a stylized rib cage in the shape of a heart.

"Nice." Duncan returned the smile. "Hell of a tender spot for your first, though."

Temperance smiled up at both men. She was unmistakably fond of them. "Ike was my favorite attending at the clinic when I was in med school. He volunteers for us sometimes. I've known Cole since high school. He went to Duke for residency, but for some reason he left that lovely North Carolina weather to come back here. Now he's my codirector."

Another man approached. Tall, built like a fitness model, wearing teal scrubs. He had a disproportionately small head with an airy tuft of blond hair, and a weak chin that no number of hours in the gym would improve for him.

"Afternoon, Doctors," Weak Chin said. He stood close to Temperance and towered over her in a way that made her have to tip her head back to look at him.

She stood her ground. "Erik."

"Dr. Erik Uttridge." The guy met Duncan's eyes, and, unlike the other two men, he wielded the *doctor* honorific like a weapon. He turned his head to Temperance and grinned like a mule eating briars. "You going to introduce us?"

When she hesitated, Duncan felt a potent slither of shame in his gut.

"This is"—she cleared her throat—"my friend Duncan Brady."

Friend. An invisible cloud padded the word from either end— *just* a friend, and *nothing* more.

Uttridge snapped his fingers and pointed at him. "Hey, I think I recognize you, man. Were you the one who fixed the scrub sink in the SICU last week?"

Duncan gave him a blank look and crossed his arms over his chest.

Temperance ignored the question. "Why are you wearing scrubs for a wellness event, Erik?"

"Oh, I'm not here to volunteer. I didn't even work today." Uttridge gestured to his chest. "Impresses the little barista at the coffee shop in Chapel Ford."

Bello's answering look was sour. "Wow, you're a dick."

"Indeed." Uttridge owned it with a quick nod. "Gentlemen. Declan." Another nod, then he moved on.

"It's *Duncan*," Temperance called as he walked away.

Ike Elias huffed a laugh and shook his head. "What an ass."

"Good meeting you, Duncan," Coleman Bello said. "Back to it."

Once they were alone again, Duncan said, "That guy sucks."

"I'm sorry he was shitty to you. He has a tiny, tiny mind. Some of the interns last year called him Buttridge."

"Buttridge, really? I assumed doctors were above that kind of thing."

She laughed. "Assholes are assholes, even if they're *Doctor* Asshole."

The kids came back. All of them sported cartoon art on their cheeks. A butterfly for Grey (with half a wing smeared because he'd tried to touch it before it was dry), a grinning alligator face for Alice, and a flower with petals the colors of the rainbow for Charlie. Temperance gasped in delight when they came back, as if they'd been painted in gold and diamond dust.

"I'll be here the rest of the afternoon," she said. "I'll find you all later, okay?"

* * *

IT was nearly dark, and Duncan was nearly drunk.

Enclosed firepits were lit at dusk. String bulbs and lanterns flickered on in the half-light. The huge gambrel barn near the front of the park had dusty concrete floors and booths along the inner walls, all serving standard festival fare. Weathered wrought-iron chandeliers hung from the high ceiling, a permanent fixture from the Renaissance festival held there for six weeks every fall.

A storm was inbound. Armchair meteorologists in the concessions barn used phrases like *jet stream* and *wind shear*, and something called a *derecho*. Others mumbled about crop damage, or the threat of Lake Vesper flooding. For Duncan, severe weather had a new weight to it now. Instead of sturdy homes in the suburbs, his family had fifteen acres of land with outbuildings in various states of disrepair and an actively growing vineyard to worry about. And his cabin was smack in the center of a massive flood plain.

Duncan's first cup of Florence Holley's mead was intended to wash the taste of Erik Uttridge's disrespect out of his mouth. It was so strong that the first couple of sips made his eyes water. He knew more people there than not, so he socialized for a while, slipping into the neighborly, smiling veneer that everyone had come to expect from him. Good-time guy Duncan Brady. Youngest son of the Westfall Bradys, and all-around helluva nice dude.

Before he was done with his third cup of mead, he lined up for a fourth. He was halfway through the line when two of his architecture classmates from Linden Community College entered the barn through a side door. Maren and Nate were there, too—about ten yards from where Duncan stood. His brain connected the dots like string on a conspiracy board, and his belly bottomed out. He imagined the five of them converging, and the awkward moment where he'd have to explain how he knew these two fresh-faced twenty-one-year-olds.

Hell.

He bailed from the mead line and slipped around the deserted far side of the barn, where a gravel path gave way to hiking trails into the forest. A bank of bloated purple clouds hovered above a horizon of sooty orange.

Out there, the noise of the crowd inside the barn was muffled, overtaken by the shrill calls of tree frogs and katydids. Three picnic tables were snugged in a dark nook between the back of the barn and a strip of woods, illuminated by a lonely string of old-fashioned multicolored Christmas bulbs. They hung like an afterthought between a hook on the side of the barn and the branches of a tree.

What—*who*—Duncan saw there almost made him choke on his mead.

Malcolm sat on top of one of the tables, feet on the bench seat, legs wide open. A woman stood between his knees, leaning into him with her hands clamped high on his thighs. The two were engaged in a hungry, devouring kiss—so consumed with each other they didn't even come up for air when a twig snapped under Duncan's foot.

The woman was Frankie.

Mal had two white-knuckled fists buried in her hair, kissing her like he was suffocating, and she was pure oxygen.

What the *fuck*?

Before they saw him, Duncan turned and hauled ass around the dark side of the barn.

He almost laughed. Malcolm—misanthropic, surly Malcolm— was face-deep in Frankie Moreau ten feet away, while Duncan had spent the past hour drinking mead out of paper cups in a dusty-ass barn to try to cope with his feelings for a woman who was no longer his because of his own shitty choices.

Don't use your past as an excuse to not have a future, Mal had said, a week ago.

When he and Temperance ended, it wasn't only her he'd lost. His dreams and aspirations had been so tangled up in a life with her, unraveling the two would have been like separating a wheel from its axle and wondering why the damned thing stopped turning. His entire future felt like it had been ripped away. He'd been utterly unprepared for the emotional dead zone left in its wake, incapable of powering through, or moving on, or any of the other bullshit platitudes he was supposed to swallow like a pill then spew out positivity in the next breath.

Mal had been absolutely right that night at the cabin a few weeks ago. It *had* been far easier to live inside the false narrative that Temperance was meant to be with Harry instead of facing the fact that he'd fucked up so magnificently losing her *and* the rest of his future at the same time.

And he'd hated himself for it.

But now, he was trying to fix it. Fix his future, anyway. The sheer scope of Cloud Tide's renovations had lit the fire under him to get back to school and do the thing he'd always wanted to do. And now he was literal weeks away from wrapping up a two-year investment of his time and energy—the first two years of a seven-year plan down. A plan to finally finish his architecture degree.

God, he was tired, though. Already maxed out in every possible way. But Temperance was *right there*, all the time. His soul itself felt fragile, as if one more tap in just the right place would fracture it clean in two. Even if he had the extra bandwidth to try to make it work with her, there was no *time*—

"You stack a mountain of responsibilities and tasks and bullshit sky-high on your back so you can barely breathe. Why do you do it?"

Duncan stopped cold. More of his conversation with Mal a week ago came at him like a kick in the gut.

"You're smart, Ducky. You'll figure it out."

He'd spent the last fourteen years piling on responsibilities and distractions, convincing himself the burden was nonnegotiable so there was no way he could logically give it up. What everyone else saw on the surface was a competent, dependable man who got shit done. Underneath, though—he'd kept himself in a constant maxed-out state as one big, multidimensional coping mechanism. Filling the void she'd left. And now that coping mechanism was the very thing making it near impossible for him to even consider trying to make Temperance Madigan his again.

Fucking hell.

He'd figured it out.

Duncan tossed back the last drink of his mead and headed for his truck.

CHAPTER FOURTEEN

Temperance

*T*he approaching storm made the whole world feel ominous.

The craft bazaar and food trucks wound down with the sun, and festivalgoers congregated around the fires in stone urns and beneath the lights webbed between the branches of trees. In the flat field beyond the concessions barn, an Irish tin whistle and string quartet played folk songs for a crowd of contra dancers. The scroll of bruise-blue clouds overhead gave the merry music an eerie overtone. Wind snapped pennants and awnings against their moorings, whipping skirts and hair high. It all felt deliciously wild and pagan and free.

Maren and Nate had taken the kids home about an hour ago, and the elder Bradys went home with Rowan and Harry. Temperance had arrived with Frankie, who had disappeared. Frankie often went missing at social gatherings like this. It was usually more surprising when she stayed put for very long. It wasn't that Frankie was inconsiderate or flaky, or that she went where the wind took her. Frankie *was* the wind.

Temperance hadn't seen Duncan since the sun went down.

She knew he was there, though. Like all those times she came back to the valley for a visit or a break from school, there was a low-key hum of tension in her belly that she could run into him anywhere, anytime. Being around him made her restless, and she was restless when he wasn't around, too. He unbalanced her, simply by existing.

The last she'd seen him was an hour or so ago, through the space between the Crabtree's Garden Center tent and the Vesper County fire safety trailer. He'd been at the Bristow sisters' barbecue truck for the third time that day, carrying two big bags of charcoal under one arm. Another was propped up on his opposite shoulder. Millie Bristow followed close behind with a bag of her own. A low-hanging red-and-yellow pennant garland knocked his ball cap off his head when he didn't duck low enough to clear it, and Millie picked it up after him. Laughing, she put it on her own head and followed him around the back of the food truck.

When Temperance finally spotted him again, he was with another one of the Bristow sisters. Midge, maybe. Or Birdie.

Why did they all have to have such cute names?

Duncan stood at the edge of the field of contra dancers, his head bent low in conversation with Midge-or-Birdie. As he talked, his attention remained on Millie while she danced, and Millie smiled her wide sunshine smile at him, waving as she moved between partners. Duncan returned the wave with a raised hand and a tender smile.

Temperance looked away.

That comfortable camaraderie between them stung far worse than anything else. Millie Bristow got to have a different Duncan than Temperance had ever had. A man with maturity and nuance, and without the burden of angst and unfinished business.

When Temperance looked back up again, Duncan was on the move. He headed toward the corridor of forest that separated the festival from the parking field. The glint of firelight caught on the keys in his hands.

He stumbled, once.

Had he been drinking?

Temperance sent Frankie a quick text to let her know she was going back to Cloud Tide, and to not wait for her. Then she took off after Duncan.

When she fell into step beside him, they walked in silence for a while, arms jostling against each other as they moved through the crowd. When they reached the forest, it felt cooler there, and quieter, cushioned underfoot and overhead by fragrant needles of pine and red cedar. Fireflies winked and sparked in the dark spaces between the trees. They pulsed like tiny searchlights all around them.

"I'm driving you home," Temperance finally said.

"Nobody drives my truck."

She crossed her arms. "Oh god, you're one of those guys?"

Duncan stopped walking. "What guys?"

"One of those millennial *Mad Max* assholes whose vehicle is some kind of—I don't know, weird proxy for their masculinity."

He ran his tongue over his teeth. "It's a big truck, Temperance."

"You're not driving like this."

His long sigh was punctuated by a frustrated grumble at the end. "Look. I wasn't going to drive. I'm not a fucking idiot. I was just going to sit there for a while."

This Duncan was a very different Duncan than the flirty guy with the hiccups earlier at the clinic tent. She gave him an analytical once-over and said, "What's wrong?"

"Nothing. I'm just tired."

Liar.

In one quick motion, she snatched his keys away. He reached for her, and she feinted away from the arc of his hand.

"Goddamn it."

"You're letting me drive you, or you can find another way home."

When she emerged into the open field from the cover of trees, a wall of warm wind sideswiped her. Her skirt billowed sideways. Clouds bulged overhead, heavy with rain.

"I had my last drink thirty minutes ago," Duncan said.

"Blood alcohol concentration peaks thirty to forty minutes after consumption of a single drink. Impairment while driving is still a concern at the two-hour mark if you've had three or more drinks—"

He fell in beside her. "My pants get tight when you use your doctor voice on me, you know." His tone was bland.

Something was definitely wrong. Even his jokey innuendo was a faded version of the real thing.

Lightning blinked in the sky, followed by a roll of thunder. Temperance hit the lock on the key fob to make the truck's headlights flash. "As soon as this storm opens up, everyone at this festival will try to leave. Then we're going to be stuck bumper-to-bumper in this lot. You want to get home? We need to leave *now*."

Two fireworks exploded overhead. Behind them, the festival crowd cheered, and thunder answered back in kind.

Duncan hooked her arm and pulled her to a stop.

Three young women approached. They stood in a tight shoulder-to-shoulder battle formation. The shorter one in the middle said to Temperance, "Are you okay?"

"I'm okay," Temperance said. "But thank you."

The taller woman with a pixie cut frowned at Duncan. "Aren't you dating Camilla Bristow?"

Boom, boom. More fireworks, more far-off cheers.

Duncan closed his eyes and let out a ragged sigh. He let her arm go. "It's complicated."

"We're good," Temperance assured them again.

All three women gave him a final side-eye before leaving. Temperance overheard one of them say, "That was Duncan Brady. She'll be much more than *good* tonight."

Again, Temperance hit the fob to make the truck lights flash. Duncan stayed on her heels as she hustled to it. When they reached the truck, he grabbed her again by the arm.

She looked down at where his hand gripped her. "Who is Millie to you now, Duncan?"

He stared her down, expressionless. Tension rolled off him, and he dropped her arm. "You know what? Never mind. I don't want to do this with you. There's no point. We'll hash some things out, shit will get too real, and you'll decide we're done. You've always got your shoes laced tight and ready to run."

She put her hands on her hips. "I'm wearing sandals."

"It's a fucking metaphor, Temperance."

She bent down to slip out of her Chacos. Looking him straight in the eye, she hurled them overhanded, and they landed in the bed of his truck with consecutive *thunk*s.

"Okay, now I'm not wearing any shoes," she said. "Try me."

"You're a pain in my entire ass."

"Tell me."

"She's a friend."

"She's on the wedding guest list as your date, Duncan."

"So?"

Boom. She felt that one in her teeth.

"You don't bring a friend as a date to a wedding."

"Is that right?" Duncan quirked a brow. "You were Harry's date at Patrick and Mercy's wedding last spring."

"That's different," she said.

Boom. More explosions in the sky, sent rapid-fire, one after the other to beat the rain. The shower of sparks sizzled and hissed, lighting Duncan's face in green and gold and red. "Exactly. Whose bed were you in that night, Temperance?"

Well. She fell right into that one.

Duncan planted his hands on his hips and tipped his head back. He closed his eyes. "I haven't been with anyone since April."

"That's not what I asked."

"It's not my story to tell." His tone fell flat. "But Millie and I aren't together. I swear it."

More fireworks burst above them. Five, ten at a time. Each detonation seemed to echo inside her chest. It was hard to tell them apart from the pound of her heart.

"You called me Teacup today. In front of everyone."

Temperance smelled the sweet earthiness of mead on his breath when he sighed through his nose. She *tasted* it.

Duncan rolled his shoulders. "It slipped."

"You want them to find out. About us."

"Everyone in my family has a nickname. There's no way they'd think it meant anything."

"But it does mean something. That's why you say it."

"It slips, damn it. It's always there." He paced for a moment and breathed up at the sky. The muscles at his temples pulsed when he faced her again. "You're still holding a big piece of me hostage inside you, and I don't know how to get it back."

"Did you go looking for it in other women's pants? I've heard about the size of that box of condoms at your place—"

He laughed and pressed the heels of his palms against his eyes. "Ask Mal sometime what's in that box."

Temperance held his gaze. "Weird. But okay?"

"Great." He gave her a tight smile. "Let me know what you find out."

"Tell me why you're in Linden every day."

Duncan looked at her for a long time, and Temperance felt the tension in his body like it was an electric charge. A few fat raindrops fell, landing loud against the parked cars. In minutes, the field would be flooded with people trying to get the hell out of there.

"That—I can't tell you."

Temperance watched his face for any sign of reluctance or dishonesty, or anything other than a stony mask. But he was locked down tight in a way she'd never seen before. "This moment," she said, her tone tight. "Remember it. It was an opportunity to avoid a misunderstanding, and you missed it."

The fireworks were a barrage now, impossible to tell apart from the lightning and thunder.

"Ah, Temperance. You're so used to being the smartest person in a room, but there's a lot you don't know shit about."

"Why do you always weaponize my intellect? You're just as smart as I am. I've always been so *pissed off* at you for never trying to have a future outside the valley—"

That hit a nerve. His upper lip twitched. "*You* were my future."

"No." She thrust a finger forward. "You don't get to pin that on me, and you especially don't get to stay mad at me about it for fourteen years."

The fireworks were a geyser of sound and light now, blowing up the sky.

"You're still chasing your parents' validation—"

Boom, boom.

"No. I made my own plans and went after my dreams—"

An explosive laugh. "So, you left the valley. Chased your dreams. Congratulations. But now you're too fucking scared to stop running long enough to actually start living them."

"You're the one who's still stuck here in the valley, doing the same crap you've done since you were eighteen. I grew up."

Duncan moved fully into her space, crowding her against the truck. He radiated heat like a dark star. "You want to know how grown up I am now, Temperance?"

The words made her lightheaded and heavy-limbed all at once. Another burst of lightning. Answering thunder rumbled so loud and long she felt it in her lungs. Her body was a blood-and-bone barometer. The storm's agonizingly slow approach felt almost sexual, an elemental edging. A familiar lick of adrenaline lit through her veins, prickling her skin with goosebumps and raising the roots of her hair.

"Go to hell, Duncan." She pushed past him to get to the driver's-side door of the truck.

"Already there, sweetheart." He caught her by the wrist. Again.

The gentle cuff of his fingers against her skin lit up nerve endings through her entire arm. It would have been easier if he'd grabbed her hard. Squeezed, pulled, claimed. This touch was a plea, not a demand, and it was far harder to resist.

"How about this." Frustration pumped out of him like steam from a kettle. "How about *you* tell *me* why this matters to you? Maybe you could give *me* something for once? Why do you care?"

Warm wind whipped her braid sideways across her throat and thrashed her skirt around her ankles. Night creatures sang shrill and frantic around them, like they were egging on the storm.

"Is it a woman?" she said.

Duncan dropped her wrist. "You are something else." He studied her for a moment, tipping his head sideways like a curious Labrador. "For the past fourteen years, you barely look at me when you come around, Temperance. I don't owe you anything."

Those words landed like a blow. "Do you have a child? Multiple children?"

Duncan froze. "Are you serious?"

"You use these secrets as leverage—"

He barked a short laugh and swiped a palm over his face.

Temperance crossed her arms over her chest. "Why is that funny?"

"Leverage. Millie used that same word."

"You talk about me—with Millie?"

Behind his lips, he ran his tongue over his teeth. Headlights began to come on in the field as people rushed to their cars.

"You want me to be jealous," Temperance said.

"I don't want you to be jealous." His composure slipped, and he got loud. "I want you to be *with me*."

The words landed with unimaginable weight, knocking the wind out of her so completely she felt dizzy. It was a targeted emotional shot across the bow. A little seed of hope cracked open inside her, but it hurt even worse than the absence of it did. Hope was a stubborn, hungry thing. It devoured caution and good sense, and the more you fed it, the bigger it grew. But big hope wasn't a promise of big possibility. It just meant bigger stakes.

Bigger disappointment.

All at once, the sky ruptured wide, unloading rain like a belly split by a blade.

CHAPTER FIFTEEN

Temperance

They made it out of the festival grounds without incident, but they'd barely been on the road more than five minutes when the rain made visibility plummet to near zero.

Temperance's brain went a little haywire, juiced on adrenaline and emotion. She felt kinship with the chaos of nature on the other side of thin glass and aluminum, and the raw power of the big truck beneath her made her feel reckless and invincible.

The steering wheel shuddered in her sweaty hands.

"Slow down," Duncan said.

The truck hit a dip in the road where rain had pooled, sending a sheet of water up over the hood and the windshield. The wipers were already at peak speed. Their frenzied back-and-forth matched the thundering pace of her heartbeat.

"Do you know how a combustion engine works?" Duncan snapped. "It needs *oxygen*. You hit another flood in the road like that, you'll replace the air with a bunch of fucking water."

Temperance could barely see the reflection of headlights shining off the double yellow line in the center of the road. Again, the wheel rocked in her hands.

"Pull over." He shouted over the sound of the rain. "*Now.*"

Her sense of caution overrode the toxic flood of adrenaline that lit through her bloodstream. She slowly braked and pulled over. The truck tilted side to side as it dropped into the steep shoulder. She hit the gas to bring them back parallel with the road, but there was only the futile, dinosaurian roar of the engine and the spin of tires in waterlogged mud.

She tried again.

"Stop." Duncan's voice was low, but the single clipped syllable had the piercing power of a bullet.

Temperance took a shuddery breath and put the truck in park. She lowered her hands to her lap.

Shit.

Their labored breathing seemed to echo unnaturally loudly between the close walls of the truck's cab.

Temperance took a surreptitious glance toward the passenger seat. Duncan was utterly motionless.

The storm outside had carved itself into an avatar of bone and flesh, and she was trapped with it inside this glass-and-metal cage. His pale gray T-shirt clung to muscle-topped shoulders and the broad convexities of his upper arms. His nipples jutted in sharp relief beneath the wet fabric. Goosebumps lifted the fine hairs over his tattoos.

A starved and primitive thing stirred inside her. Sweat trickled between her breasts. Slicked the small of her back. She knew this darker Duncan, but she hadn't seen him in a while. When he went quiet like this, it meant only one thing. He was moments away from completely losing his shit.

This Duncan was a spool of chaos, and she knew exactly where to yank to unravel him entirely.

Headlights from an oncoming car illuminated half his face, painting his cheeks in shadowy streaks from the rain on the glass. Like tears. The road was soon deserted again in either direction.

Finally, he moved. He took his phone from his back pocket, then tossed it up onto the dashboard with a sound of disgust. "No signal."

She checked her own phone—also no signal.

Duncan unlatched his seat belt and pinched the bridge of his nose. "What did you say, earlier? Two hours? After drinking?"

"Yes." She unlatched her own seat belt.

"Well, we've got one hour down. So, we're going to sit here for another." Every word was quiet and measured, but his big chest heaved under the wet shirt like a locomotive wheel. "Then I'm going to push us out of this mud. Then I'm driving us home. Do you understand?"

"Duncan—"

"Do you—" He paused to take a long breath in through his nose. "—understand?"

"Yes."

"Good."

Abruptly, he reached across her and hit the button that locked all the doors at once. Then he twisted the keys in the ignition and yanked them away to cut the power. Tiny console lights remained on standby power, but the headlights winked out. With the side of his fist, he hit the button on the dash to activate the truck's hazard lights.

"This is why nobody drives my truck," he growled. There was something else in his voice, too. A tremor under the rage. He was shaken, but he hid it well. He hunched forward with elbows on thighs, head in his hands.

For an eternity, they simply sat there as the rain squalled against the roof and windows. With the truck turned off, the windows quickly went opaque with condensation.

Duncan's voice was muffled when he spoke again. "Did you ever really want me, Temperance? Or was I just convenient?"

Wind rampaged against the truck, pressing in tendrils of chill.

Temperance's good judgment was irreparably fucked. Her most inviolable rule was busted clean through: don't be horny, emotional, and alone with Duncan Brady.

"All the time, I want you. It's constant." She barely recognized the sound of her own voice.

Duncan was *shaking*. His eyes were closed. She could barely make out his whispered string of filthy, frustrated words: "*—fucking killing me—did I do to deserve this—I'm in actual fucking hell—*"

Then he looked up.

Her self-control collapsed like a landslide. They both burst into motion at the same time, and everything happened in a few chaotic beats.

Her, half-standing, the back of her head hitting the cab's ceiling, knocking the rearview mirror askew with her elbow.

Him, yanking her into his lap by her forearm with one hand, tossing the fabric of her skirt high around her waist with the other.

Her, activating the turn signal with her ass, hitting the horn with her foot.

It was a frantic choreography of sexual desperation.

Her heart felt like it might beat free of her chest. Duncan's fingers dug into her waist to pull her down to his lap, crushing the aching knot of nerves between her legs against the bulging seam of his jeans. Her sweaty knees squeaked against the vinyl surface of the seat.

Her head fell back. She could come like this, and he wouldn't even need to move.

"Wait," she said.

Duncan froze.

"You've been drinking. Duncan, you can't consent—"

He dragged his thumb along her damp jaw. The friction of it made her mouth sag open. "I am excruciatingly aware of what is happening right now."

Duncan drew his bottom lip between his teeth to dampen it with his tongue. He cupped the back of her neck, his jaw angled in a way that would guide them right into a kiss.

Temperance leaned away and pushed her fingers against his mouth. Outside, wind whipped the rain into a slash through the air. It battered the doors, and the truck swayed with each powerful gust.

"No. No kissing," she said. "That's not what this is."

Duncan groaned so loud she felt the vibration of it in her pelvis. His lips were drawn tight across his teeth, and his eyes were so black they reflected all the tiny pinpoints from the dashboard standby lights.

This man stripped her down to her most base sensation-seeking self—and that was only half of it. What frightened her more were the feelings his kiss would churn to the surface—and how much she'd inevitably want *more*. Kissing Duncan Brady was more than sensation. It was an intimate emotional exchange, and she was already dangerously close to giving all of herself away again.

Hot breath washed down the skin of her inner forearm. Goosebumps rose in its wake. Duncan set his teeth against the pad of her middle finger and tugged it into his mouth. He sucked the sensitive tip with a rhythmic pulse of his tongue. It amplified the throb at the opposite end of her anatomy.

Temperance pulled her finger free and scored her short nails through his beard.

"You're killing me," he said.

She pressed her palm to the center of his chest. His heart banged hard beneath it. "Still beating."

"*Temperance.*"

She tore her tank top over her head and threw it aside. She had no idea where it landed.

His big hands came up around her ribs, thumbs skimming the small lower curves of her breasts.

"You walked around—all day—wearing *this* under your clothes?" The bra was a creamy La Perla confection, expensive as hell and far fancier than the day deserved. Duncan closed his hand around where the shoulder strap met the upper edge of the cup, and one of his fingers burst through the lace. "Goddamn it—I'm sorry—"

"Stop talking, Duncan." She shrugged out of the straps and let the cups fall away from her breasts. The band stayed hooked around her ribs.

He buried his face in the tender concavity beneath her jaw, gasping and greedy. The feel of his beard against her skin disoriented her—it felt like someone *not* Duncan, even though her body and mind knew the scent and feel of him as intimately as she knew her own.

Her heart knew him, too.

Outside, a truck roared past, firing a surge of rainwater and road debris against the driver's-side window.

His teeth closed around her collarbone. "Tell me to stop."

"Do you want to stop?"

"God, no. Green flag." A moan rolled into his words. "Tell me what to do."

"Stop talking."

The heel of his palm skidded down her sweaty spine like the teeth of a zipper. With his other hand, he grasped the bottom of her braid and wound it around his palm, once, twice, three times. Each twist drew her head further and further backward. Her back arched, lifting her breasts right to his mouth. He pressed his lips against an urgently hard nipple, dragging it tight with suction and teeth. Temperance lifted high on her knees, pressing her pelvis into his belly, scoring fingernails across his shoulders.

His mouth went soft and hot, easing the ache with an indulgent drag of his tongue.

"*Tell* me," Duncan demanded. He let her braid unravel and tipped his head back to meet her eyes.

Outside, the hazard lights marked time to the rhythm of the rain. *Tick, tock, tick.*

Fluid looseness seeped into her muscles. Her hip joints felt heavy and weak. Busted hinges, desperate to drop her thighs wide. "Touch me."

His rough palms settled against her knees. So gentle. Tentative.

"Touch me, damn it." She clapped her hands down over his and pressed down hard, guiding them beneath her dress. "I'm not going to break."

At the bend of her hips, Duncan verged both big thumbs downward, pressing tight against her pubic bone, tracing the vee of her bikini line. Temperance arched against him, taut as a bowstring, aching for release.

She was beyond turned on. She was turned all the way up. Packed to the top with tension, filled to bursting.

Between her legs, two big fingers tugged elastic aside. Her panties had to be soaked.

"Oh, god," Duncan sighed. He dropped his forehead to her collarbone.

For a moment, the wind and rain hushed, like the storm itself paused to pay attention.

Tick, tock, tick.

"Do you have a condom?" Temperance whispered.

"No," he breathed into her skin.

"No?"

He met her eyes. "I'm not in the habit of fucking people in my truck, Temperance."

She started to sit back. "I—"

"We're not done yet," he said. His right hand palmed the cheek of her ass to anchor her in place.

Between her legs, Duncan twisted his wrist to slide two fingers inside her in one aching, fluid motion. Out again, with that slippery back-and-forth tug he knew she loved. The perfect pattern of thrust and rhythm and friction.

It didn't take long.

Temperance gripped the seat behind his head for leverage, slapping her other hand hard against the window. She came apart with an orgasm that bent her backward. It bloomed upward into her belly, pounded along the backs of her thighs. She collapsed downward, momentarily pinning Duncan's fingers inside her. In one slick movement, he repositioned, splaying his free hand against the small of her back. The other gripped the bend of her hip, fastening her down against the straining bulge inside his jeans. She was shameless, grinding out the rest of the sensation against that telltale heat.

Duncan's own hips rocked in an instinctive echo of hers, and his jaw was clenched tight. A tremor went through his hips and thighs. His eyes squeezed shut and his head tipped back. Through bared teeth, he panted her name like he was in pain.

Temperance *knew* those sounds he made. That agonized, whisper-soft *mmmmh fuck* growl and the quiet *ahhh god* exhale that followed it. The way his legs shuddered between her own.

Duncan Brady just came in his jeans.

When he stilled, she folded forward and pressed her forehead into the seat behind him. Her arms hung limp, her braid slithered down his shoulder. For a few moments, she simply breathed against him, riding the rapid rise and fall of his chest. His mouth was wide open and hot against her shoulder.

On one of the distant county roads, a siren wailed. The sound was as desolate and desperate as the sudden ache in her chest. How naive she'd been, to think she was safe as long as he didn't speak or kiss her on the mouth. Like always, he'd respected every one of her demands. But it hadn't mattered.

He'd used body and breath to paint emotion on her like a canvas. For Duncan Brady, words and kisses were amateur hour.

"Temperance."

Don't look up.

Don't.

She did.

"I am"—he blew out a sharp breath—"obsessed with you. And I hate it."

Colors suddenly flashed through the back window of the truck. Red, blue, red, blue. High-beam headlights flooded the interior of the cab.

"Oh my *god*," she groaned. She launched herself off Duncan's lap, tugging up her bra, smoothing her hair, yanking her skirt down her legs. "Shit, shit! Where's my top?"

Duncan twisted around to reach into the truck's narrow back seat. He flung the tank at her and snagged a flannel to throw across the dark stain in his lap.

"Well. This should be fun," he drawled.

Temperance barely had her second arm through her tank top when the deputy appeared at the driver's-side door with his flashlight. She lowered the window.

"Evening," the officer said. He was wiry and serious looking, with more hair in his mustache than on his head. "Everything okay here?"

"Doing fine, thanks." Temperance gave him a tight smile. "We were just waiting out the storm."

The deputy swung the beam of the flashlight up to the night sky, as if he was searching for rain to confirm her claim. "Looks to be about done." Then he shone it on Duncan.

Squinting, Duncan nodded and said, "Howdy."

The deputy shone the light in the footwell of the driver's seat. "Where are your shoes, ma'am?"

Temperance's bare toes curled. "They're—ah, in the truck bed. Back there."

The flashlight beam swung away as the deputy confirmed. He returned with a tight smile. "Why's that?"

"It's a long story."

"You folks been drinking tonight?"

"I have not," Temperance said.

"Few hours ago," Duncan said. "That's why she's driving."

Again, the deputy moved his flashlight between them. His face gave Temperance a little tickle of recognition, but she couldn't place him. "I saw quite a bit of movement through the rear window as I pulled up. You two do a driver's-seat switcheroo on me?"

"No, sir," Duncan said.

"Absolutely not," said Temperance at the same time.

"Huh." The deputy's mustache twitched. "What was I seeing, then?"

Temperance looked over at Duncan. Expressionless, he inclined his head ever so slightly.

"I was—" She sighed. "On his lap."

The flashlight beam returned to Temperance. "Is that right?"

"Look, man—check the seat, check the mirrors. They're obviously adjusted for her, she's half my size—"

The deputy moved the light to Duncan. "So, we're talking about lewd conduct instead of driving under the influence, is that what you're saying, sir?"

"Neither, Deputy," Temperance quickly said.

"Can I see your license and registration, ma'am? Yours, too, sir."

They both complied.

"Madigan." The deputy sucked his teeth. He came closer to the window and shone the flashlight into the cab at a gentler angle instead of in their faces. "Temperance. Temperance Madigan. I'll be damned. I'm Nolan Doyle—I dated your sister all through high school. You probably don't remember me; you were so young—"

"Nolan, oh my gosh, yes." Temperance had to grind her teeth to keep in the hysterical cackle that climbed up the back of her throat. This kept getting worse and worse.

The deputy shone his flashlight on his head. "Had a lot more hair back then." His mustache tipped like a seesaw when he smiled.

Deputy Doyle looked at Duncan's ID. "Brady—well, hell, there's another name I recognize. Your brother is the guy Maren married, isn't he?" He grinned and handed their licenses back through the window.

Duncan nodded. "He is indeed."

"Lucky bastard. You two—ah, keeping it in the family?"

"No, no—we're just—"

"We're friends."

"Friends."

"Well." The deputy winked, then thumped the side of the truck with his hand. "You two be safe tonight. You need help getting off the shoulder? I can call it in—"

"I think we're fine. Thank you, Nolan. Good to see you."

"We'll tell Maren you said hello," Duncan called after him.

Temperance slumped in the seat as he walked away. Her heart was a medicine ball between her ribs, so heavy it was a wonder it could still beat at all. The tag of her tank top grazed her chin.

Great.

"Remind me to thank Maren tomorrow." Duncan got out of the truck and came around to her side once the deputy was out of sight.

"I hope you're joking," Temperance said as he swung her door open.

Clouds had cleared and the rain turned to mist, catching moonlight and falling around him like glitter. He gripped the upper arch of the doorway and leaned into her face. "Move over. I'm driving."

"Duncan. Promise me you won't say anything to Maren about this."

"*Now.*"

She scooted across the seat and yanked her seat belt across her waist.

"I won't tell Maren about this. I can't guarantee Deputy Mustache won't be in her DMs tonight, though."

"Oh my god."

"Why does it matter? We're consenting adults."

Temperance pressed the heels of her palms into her eyes and laughed. She sounded as unhinged as she felt. "This isn't me, Duncan."

Liar.

This was exactly who she was. Daring and unbound and utterly his. To the center of her bones, she knew.

"Then who are you, Temperance?"

"We're permanently linked, whether we want to be or not. We didn't choose that—our siblings did. And now Rowan and Harry."

"Why the hell does that matter?"

"Duncan. If—*when*—we end it, even if it's friendly, we still have to be around each other. Forever. Imagine, someday, we're at Alice or Grey's birthday party, or one of a thousand other family gatherings Maren and Nate or Rowan and Harry want us present for. You introduce your wife to me. 'Hey, sweetie, this is Temperance. She's kind of an in-law through marriage, but not really, and thank god for that because I used to rail her in my parents' coat closet and go down on her in the bed of my truck. More charcuterie, honey?'"

Temperance tipped her face into her hands to smother a frantic laugh.

Now, rain on the roof whispered like a rumor.

"We have to do better, Duncan. This tension between us—" She met his eyes. "We have to try to be friends. It's the only thing we've never tried."

"You and I are not friends." The emphasis he put on *friends* made the word sound profane.

"Don't you think it would be easier?"

"Easier." His voice fell flat. "For fucking *whom*?"

"We have to try. For peace. At least until the wedding is over."

Temperance hesitated. "For Rowan and Harry—they've been through so much—"

"Wait." Duncan went still. "What did you just say?"

"I said we need to try to be friends until the wedding is over," she repeated.

Something odd passed over his features then, but whether it was the darkness or the shadows of rain on his skin, Temperance couldn't decipher it. Whatever it was, though—it was the visual manifestation of Duncan Brady making up his mind.

"Okay, then," he said, simply.

He didn't look at her again until they got back to Cloud Tide.

CHAPTER SIXTEEN

Temperance

Temperance woke up feeling unhitched from reality.

She rolled over and stared at the ceiling to get her bearings. She was in Duncan's cabin. In his bed. She ran her hands over her face, her arms, the tangle of her hair. The clock on the bedside table read 7:10 A.M. She hadn't slept this late in years.

Long ago, in one of her earliest conversations with Rowan, Rowan had mused about how a caterpillar had no idea why it made a chrysalis, let alone that it would become a butterfly inside it. At the time, Temperance had found this to be both very weird and very earnest, while Frankie had countered by wondering whether caterpillars and butterflies actually had any ideas at all.

In that moment, splayed out on Duncan Brady's bed in a ripped bra and a still-damp pair of panties, Temperance imagined she knew exactly how one of those emerging butterflies felt. A little bewildered, sore in confusing parts of her anatomy, and desperately, desperately hungry.

She sat up. "Duncan?"

Silence.

They'd managed to get the truck back onto the road just after midnight. When they'd approached Cloud Tide, the property was entirely dark—not even the ever-burning standing lamplights at the base of the drive were lit. The bottom of the hill was a fluid slide of mud and debris that not even the truck could navigate. It had slid backward and sideways as Duncan revved the engine—he'd tried three times before he'd slammed it into reverse and diverted down the lake access road to the cabin, fishtailing and cursing the whole way.

Once they made it to the cabin, Duncan had showered off the mud from pushing the truck off the shoulder. There wasn't a door between the bedroom and the bathroom, so Temperance had sat in the tiny den in the dark, waiting for him to finish. He'd insisted she sleep in his bed.

She had no idea where he'd slept, but it hadn't been with her.

At the foot of the bed sat her overnight bag from up at the house. His keys were on the bedside table beside a note.

Duncan's writing was as perfect as a digital font, with minimalist letters and uniformly spaced words. Each *s* had a slight inward curl on the upstroke, and each *i* was capped with a short slash instead of a dot. The note read:

> T—
>
> It's 6:00, don't want to wake you. Headed up the hill.
> The access road is safe now. Take my truck.
>
> —D

Temperance lay flat on her back and held the keys above her, dangling them like a dream catcher. Along with the fob for his truck, there were at least ten keys for the buildings around Cloud Tide, and a handful of smaller keys for miscellaneous padlocks and the Gator. There was a scratched and weathered metal heart that read DARWIN, the tag of the family dog he'd grown up with. Another aluminum disc was stamped BRADY, with an off-center heart beneath it. Temperance had a matching one on her own set of keys. Years ago, Alice had made them for everyone using a jewelry-stamping kit she'd gotten for her birthday, and she'd been too young to understand that even though Temperance was her family, she didn't share the same last name.

She left the bedroom. The cabin was a cozy rectangular space, smelling of sweet pipe tobacco and the faintest whiff of dry dust that was characteristic of old places, though every surface was tidy and clean. The ceiling and walls were exposed cedar, and a springy but faded rug covered the wide-plank wood floor. Temperance recognized the couch and a few other pieces of furniture from the carriage house where Rowan and Harry lived. To the left was the narrow galley kitchen behind two swinging saloon-style doors. They squeaked rhythmically on their hinges when she passed through.

The vertical molding around the kitchen entryway had horizontal lines etched into the wood. Beside each were names and dates. The handwriting was mostly the same on all of them, with a few exceptions. She ran her fingertip along them and whispered the names aloud. There were a few recurring names starting very low, reaching to about a foot taller than Temperance. This place had probably belonged to the same family until Duncan bought it earlier that year.

A long countertop and sink sat along the front-facing wall in the kitchen. Above the sink, filmy white curtains fluttered at the open windows. Hung from a small hook was a kitchen towel printed with faded vintage roosters and repetitions of the word "cocky" all over it.

There was something viscerally lonesome about the solitary coffee mug and single plate and fork that sat on the small drying rack on the countertop.

On a little breakfast table next to another window sat a closed laptop and a notebook with several dull pencils on top. Each one had its eraser worn down to a nub. Temperance lifted an empty mug to her nose. A faint but familiar hint of clove and spice clung to the tea bag at the bottom. Duncan had looped the string over the top of the handle and tucked the tiny paper label through, so it wouldn't fall down into the mug.

The box of condoms sat on the table as well.

"Ask Mal sometime what's in that box."

Temperance hooked a finger in the lid to lift it open for a peek. A combination of surprise and runaway tenderness made her breath catch in her throat.

A first-aid kit.

It was so very Duncan. Unexpected. A little irreverent. Practical.

She slid the lid back into place and went to the covered porch. The old screen door squealed and rattled as it banged closed behind her.

Outside, she was greeted by the melancholy coo of a mourning dove. Lake Vesper reflected the iridescent pink of a cracked-opal sky. The entire basin was otherworldly in the milky morning light, the air thick with woodsmoke and the luminous fog spilling down the Chardonnay rows to the east. The banks had flooded in the night, submerging the dock and overflowing into the flat grassy area between the shore and the cabin. Where they'd chased each other with water balloons last weekend, a small family of ducks floated by, lazily dabbling for breakfast.

Duncan's truck was parked under the carport, covered with sprays of dried mud. The tires were caked with the same, and the way the morning sun hit the passenger's-side window illuminated streaky impressions of her handprint.

This was going to be a long day.

A green tarp rustled in the breeze around the side of the cabin. Barefoot, Temperance went to look.

Beneath the covering, twelve antique barn boards stood propped against the side of the cabin with their long edges roughly aligned. Together, the pieces created a mural of a stylized honeybee with hexagonal honeycomb patterns on each wing. Each cell of the honeycomb appeared three-dimensional—some were deep wells, shadowed with deep purples and blues. Others appeared so convex they seemed to burst forth from the wood. Tiny sweeps of black and brown and burgundy paint on the bee's body were so finely rendered, the old wood panels might actually be soft and fuzzy to the touch.

Temperance absently rubbed her thumb over the tiny bee tattoo on the inside of her ring finger. She carefully covered the boards again and went back inside.

Amidst the spartan tidiness of the rest of the space, Duncan's bookcases were a joyfully haphazard collection of titles that ranged from graphic novels and high-fantasy epics to Rachel Carson's *Si-lent Spring* and several editions of Thoreau's *Walden*. A few books on environmentally sustainable design had dozens of tattered Post-it Notes poking out the tops. Malcolm's hardback thrillers had two entire sections of their own, every one of them still in their shiny dust jackets. Temperance tipped one out to peek inside the title page. The assertive scrawl of Mal's autograph was there. No doubt Duncan asked him to sign every one of them. In the small space left at the end of the row of Mal's books was a book about native mid-Atlantic ornamental plants that must have come from Rowan and a spiral-bound book of recipes Will had printed at the office supply store to gift to everyone at Christmas the year before.

Temperance ran her finger along the spines. This man loved his family.

On most of the shelves, notebooks and folders and loose papers were stuffed horizontally over the rows of books. There were several wallet-style folders clustered together near the top. When she stood on tiptoes and slid them down, a wisp of something small fluttered to the ground.

Temperance recognized it immediately.

The photo booth had kicked out two copies that day. They were both eighteen and beautiful in that high-gloss, full-spectrum sort of way. Ripe and impermanent as summer fruit. Duncan's skin was tanned tawny, hair burnished chestnut at the tips from sun. His full bottom lip was shiny where her strawberry balm had trans-ferred. Temperance barely recognized herself, a young woman well-accustomed to the closeness of the beautiful man who held her.

They'd gotten wasted on each other and assumed time would be a chaser.

She'd thrown her own copy of the photo strip in the trash that same winter. She went back to retrieve it later that day and sobbed for an hour when she learned Frankie had cleaned their room and emptied the bin into the residence hall dumpster.

How often did he look at this? Would he miss it if it disappeared?

Reluctantly, she tucked the photo back where it came from.

In another folder, each page was filled with architectural concept sketches and renderings of noteworthy buildings around the valley. The historic jewel-box-style bank in Linden and the old carhop diner in Shelby. A sketch of the historic Tudor-style library in Chapel Ford was so finely illustrated, it could have been a black-and-white photograph if not for the telltale smudge along the left edge. Scattered amongst the buildings were still-life sketches of everyday objects and a few pieces that looked remarkably similar to some of his tattoos.

One of the buildings was the Cloud Tide bank barn, but it was fanciful and idealized, with a few extra cupolas on the roof, and an all-glass sunroom extension off the tasting room. An exquisitely detailed sketch of the Bradys' Georgian Colonial included the gnarled old weeping cherry at the western corner of the house, which meant Duncan would have had to have drawn it within the first few months after his parents bought the place. That tree had come down in a storm later that first winter. Another sketch of the house showed snow on the roof and a wreath on the door. There were half a dozen more, and Temperance's pulse sped up with the later sketches she flipped to. In the more recent ones, the window to *her* room—the Primrose room—seemed to glow on the paper. How Duncan managed to accomplish it with simple pencil strokes wasn't a thing she could understand, but there it was.

There it was.

* * *

TEMPERANCE parked Duncan's truck in front of the Brady house and hiked up to the Cabernet Franc. Everything was wet and vibrant, and the air had a clean weightlessness that came only after a storm. Everywhere she walked, downed tree branches and debris from the vineyards cracked like tiny bones under her feet.

She found Rowan at the outer perimeter of the vineyard, tying vines back to the trellises and trimming away what was broken. She wore old denim overalls and a pair of gardening gloves with dirt-blackened fingers, and her hair was swirled into a big ginger bun as tangled as the grapevines.

She gave Temperance a quick once-over and said, "Nice shirt."

"Yep." It was an old Death Cab for Cutie concert T-shirt from Duncan's bottom dresser drawer. In the center of it, a crow was twisted in a red thread. The shirt fit her like a dress, so she'd had to tie it in a knot at the hem.

"Rough night?" Rowan removed her gloves to put her hair back up. Her engagement ring glittered in the sunshine.

"I always look tired." Temperance fiddled with a thumb-sized bundle of tiny baby grapes.

"Fair."

To the west, Duncan had his back to them, hurling huge pieces of lumber into a flatbed trailer. Every toss was followed by an explosive grunt of exertion she could hear even a hundred yards away.

Rowan had a thoughtful crease between her brows. She tugged her gloves back on and used the tip of her pruners to point to the vine in front of her. A sad-looking shoot was frayed at the end, and a leaf was shredded in half.

"See these?" Rowan said. "Right now, the priority is to get the damaged parts removed to reduce the chance of disease. I don't think there was enough damage to destroy the crop this year, but we won't know for sure until a little later in the summer."

From Duncan's direction, more guttural sounds of satisfaction. Temperance couldn't not look.

"Did you know grapes have secondary buds that only come through if the first ones are lost?" Rowan said. Her expression was entirely without guile. "A second chance."

Temperance rubbed the middle of her forehead and closed her eyes.

"They have a tertiary bud, too," Rowan said. "A *second* second chance. Isn't nature great?"

Yeah. This was definitely going to be a long day.

Rowan snipped a few frayed shoots with surgical precision. "So how are things between you and Duncan?"

Temperance's tongue stuck to the roof of her mouth. "I'm sorry, what?"

"Your armistice. Being friends."

"Oh. Great. Super. We're very good at it."

Harry arrived, streaked with mud and carrying two freshly filled carafes of water. With his hair in a low knobby ponytail, he looked like he belonged in the vineyard with Rowan as much as he belonged at his clinic with patients.

"Hey, T-Bird," Harry said. "You here to work?"

Temperance nodded. "I bet this is exactly how you'd planned to spend the weekend before Rowan leaves for Spain."

He chuckled and handed water to Rowan. Their movements mirrored each other's as they both took a drink. "I knew what I was signing up for." He picked a piece of grape leaf out of her bun and nudged a few sweaty curls off her forehead.

Temperance's heart gave an affectionate squeeze. These two were halves of a whole in a way she and Duncan could never be. There might be too much missing from them both to be able to fill each other's empty spaces.

"Harry and I have things covered here," Rowan said. "Why don't you go see what Duncan needs help with?"

* * *

PROTESTING would have just made Rowan more curious than she obviously already was, so Temperance went to help Duncan. She approached slowly, partly to delay the inevitable awkward conversation, partly to fully take in what she was seeing.

With a breathy grunt, Duncan lifted a log as big around as his waist onto a low stump, then raised the hem of his shirt to swipe his face. He turned, just enough that she got an eyeful of sweat-damp swirls of hair on a toned belly. A belt was threaded through the loops of his jeans, but it seemed a miracle of physics how they could hang so low on his hips without revealing the full extent of what he was packing beneath the button fly. When he turned away again, the back of his shirt rode up to reveal twin dimples in the columns of muscle along his spine.

He adjusted his ball cap, took a step back, and planted his feet shoulder-width apart. Lifting up on tiptoes for more momentum in the downward swing, he arced a block splitter high over his head. When the splitter made contact, the wood cracked like a starter pistol.

Duncan's throaty, explosive exhale followed.

The gray T-shirt he wore was parchment thin, clinging to the swell and thrust of his shoulder blades as he worked. Another swift intake of air past clenched teeth. Another swing of the splitter—*snap*—and another forceful burst of breath at the finish.

For a moment, she paused under the shade of a big maple. Really, she could watch this all day.

Back still to her, he rested the splitter on the ground and called out, "You going to watch me, or you going to come make some polite conversation?"

She had the sudden impulse to inch around the trunk of the tree and hide behind it like a cartoon character.

"Temperance, I know you're there." Another powerful windup. The burst of downward motion. The break. Duncan's deep, gratified growl.

God.

She gave him a wide berth as she came around in front of him. Lightly, she said, "Are you chopping this wood, or are you fucking it?"

Duncan looked up, smiled his canny side-slung smile, and raised the tattered bill of his ball cap to sweep his hair back beneath it.

His beard was gone.

Temperance's legs turned to warm taffy.

A beard might make a mediocre face more attractive than it actually was, but that wasn't the case with Duncan Brady. He was startlingly hot with it *and* without it. Seeing the entire lower half of his face here in the plain light of day felt intensely private, almost verging on obscene. Like walking in on someone naked and getting a glimpse of way more skin than you'd been prepared for. His lips were just—*there*—with nothing to divert attention from them.

His very bare mouth lifted at one corner. "Enjoy watching me?"

"Enjoy being watched?" she volleyed back.

His crooked smile turned into a full-on grin. "You know my answer to that."

"How did you know it was me?"

No reply, just an acrobatic lift of a single eyebrow.

"Seriously." She put her hands on her hips. "I made no noise."

"I'm very familiar with the sound of your breathing when your heart rate's up, Temperance."

She gave him a prim glare and tightened her ponytail. "What are you doing?"

"Oh, this?" He gave the splitter an acrobatic twist, then propped it against the cut wood. "This is all an elaborate thirst trap with absolutely no functional purpose. Just for you. How'd I do?"

Eleven out of ten. Possibly twelve.

He had no business looking as good as he did. His pale blue jeans were shredded at the knees and frayed at the hems. A retro-looking sailboat logo on his T-shirt declared BEST IN THE WET.

"Mmm. I give it a six out of ten. Jeans aren't tight enough. You lose points for not being shirtless, and you're barely glistening."

He breathed out a little laugh.

"Why not use a chain saw?"

"Ah, chain saws lean more menacing than sexy, don't you think?" He cupped a hand over the back of his neck, and the muscles in his upper arm flexed.

Temperance waved a finger at his bulging arm. "You do that on purpose."

"Do what?"

"That—thing." She pushed up her glasses and pointed again. "The thing where you lift your arm and flex. You've always done it."

"What, this?" He passed his hand over his hair. The movement made his biceps pulse like a heartbeat. The sleeve of his T-shirt rode up, revealing a dark, damp tuft beneath his arm.

Jesus. Everything about him simultaneously offended and aroused.

"Yes."

Duncan laughed and swung his arm down to his side. "I'll be more considerate about where I touch myself when you're around." With one of his canines, he ripped a short piece of duct tape from a roll that sat on one of the bigger logs. "Rowan's with Harry in the Cab Franc. I'm sure she'll have something for you to do."

"I just came from there. I'm here to help you."

He slapped the tape into a rip in the palm of his work gloves. "Help *me*?"

"I'm stronger than I look."

Duncan paused with a flask of water halfway to his mouth. "I'm more concerned about your willingness to follow instructions." He tilted his head to the side. "I go pretty hard, Temperance."

She lifted her chin and matched his tone. "I can handle whatever you give me, Duncan."

His throat pulsed rhythmically as he sucked hard on the flask. A few tiny fresh razor nicks marked skin glossy with sweat, and he had a faint tan line where the upper edge of his beard had been. Temperance's thumb used to fit perfectly in that deep dimple in his left cheek.

I know you.

It was silly, really, this sensation that she somehow knew the person who stood before her now better than the person he'd been only hours before. The beard, the tattoos—it was like he'd intentionally disguised the boy he'd been when he'd loved her. He'd been hiding in plain sight.

Temperance lobbed his keys at him with an underhand throw.

Her toss went wide, but Duncan snatched them out of the air without taking his eyes off her face.

"I thought nobody drove your truck?" she said.

"You're not nobody."

Warmth bloomed through her like a late spring peony, but she kept her tone light. "Why did you shave your beard? You look like you're eighteen."

"I thought you hated my beard." He scratched his jaw and glanced at his hand with curiosity, like the feel of his own face was foreign to him.

"*Hate* is a very strong word."

"What happened to *beards are dirty*?"

"I might have been"—she crossed and uncrossed her arms over her chest—"misinformed."

"Dr. Temperance Jean Madigan, changing her mind? *Pfff*."

"Duncan, your beard isn't why I won't let you kiss me. Is that why you shaved it?"

His eyes sparkled, but his expression quickly turned serious. He touched a fingertip to the side of her neck. "I hurt you."

She waved a dismissive hand. "It stung a little when I put sunscreen on. It's fine."

"It's not." A big breath rose his chest high under the thin shirt. "I never want to hurt you."

"Oh, god." Temperance cupped a hand over the beard burn. "*This* is why you shaved?"

A clattering bang came from inside the equipment garage up the hill. Will Brady howled, "Fecking *balls*."

"Language," sang Gia from somewhere deeper inside.

Duncan cast a distracted look in that direction. He took an impatient step closer. "I want to talk to you." His voice was heavy, like the words themselves had weight.

She blinked. "We're talking right now."

"Somewhere else. Later." He cut his eyes sideways and waved distractedly to the vineyard crew heading toward the gardener's cottage for a break. Then, toward where Rowan and Harry worked in the north vineyard. "*Please*."

Something urgent and aching swelled inside her. A metamorphic sort of fullness that could have been longing or lust or love or some inescapable fusion of the three. The heart of the boy she'd fallen in love with was still inside Duncan Brady, and the sum and substance of the man he'd become was more compelling than eighteen-year-old Temperance had had the capacity to imagine.

How cruel, for everything you'd ever wanted to be wrapped up in the one person who'd cut you the deepest.

"Temperance." He waited until she looked up at him. His cheeks were flushed. "I'm trying to bend here. But you're not doing enough reaching. We're never going to meet halfway."

The words were unexpected, but unsurprising. They were salt and sunscreen lingering in a beloved old beach towel, months into winter.

Longing nearly bent her in half.

She took a bracing breath. "Okay."

"Okay?" He held her eyes for a moment, then exhaled a relieved little laugh through his nose. "Well. We'd better get started then."

CHAPTER SEVENTEEN

Duncan

*D*uncan had been fully sober by the time he'd pulled his truck off the shoulder of County Road 25 eight hours ago, but he still had a skull-cramp headache from Florence Holley's damned mead.

It had been almost fourteen months since he'd heard Temperance's husky sighs and shuddery breaths when he sent her over the edge. Now he didn't want to go another fourteen hours without hearing them again.

Last night when they reached the cabin, he'd put three doors between them. The bedroom door, the cabin's front door, and the door to his truck. He'd slept crammed into the front bench seat, determined to not fall back into the same messy pattern with her before they had an actual conversation.

It was the same every time. Right as he'd manage to convince himself she was never coming to him again, she would. Sometimes it would be a few months between, sometimes a year. He'd let her climb inside the Goldbergian scaffolding he'd built around his heart, and she'd bang around in there for a few hours. But she'd never stay. And he couldn't ever be mad about it, either. He was a lovesick scarecrow handing a box of matches to a careless bystander, no right to be surprised when he was burned to ash.

Telling her no was the only thing as miserable as not having her at all. But at least that was something he had full control over. One of these days, it really would be the last time she came to him. She'd finally meet someone worthy of her—another doctor who could care for her like she cared for him, or some well-dressed attorney with soft hands who'd never gotten a sunburn on the back of his neck or broken off his own thumbnail with a fucking hammer.

That morning, he'd snuck in before dawn to grab some clothes and brush his teeth. The bathroom light had a built-in fan that chattered loudly when it ran, so he'd done everything by the light of a battery-powered lantern. Temperance hadn't stirred—she'd been starfished on his bed with her palms to the ceiling and her head tipped sideways on his pillow. Angry red marched up the side of her neck where he'd buried his face against her skin hours earlier in the truck. He hated himself a little for marking her.

So, he lost the beard by the light of that little lantern.

It wasn't rational, really. The initial swipe of the razor was impulsive, and maybe a bit of self-flagellation for daring to damage her. But the more of his face he revealed in the mirror, the more it felt like an excavation. He was still the same damned person without the beard as he was with it, but growing it in the first place had been because of her. Getting rid of it now felt symbolic somehow.

The scope of what he had to get done today to recover from last night's storm would have been daunting even at a time when he wasn't already juggling a truly alarming number of other things. He'd wanted to replace some of the trellis end posts in the Chardonnay vineyard for a while, but they hadn't been in bad enough shape to justify the time to fix them when so much else was more urgent. The only good thing about the storm wreaking havoc was that it gave him a reason to deal with some of the things he'd been putting off. An excuse to rebuild them better.

Last night in the truck, Duncan had been baffled to realize that Rowan and Harry were playing them. Sure, there was a chance it was coincidence that they'd used near-identical phrasing with both him and Temperance when they'd had their *try to be friends* conversations. A damned slim chance.

Peace for the wedding.

It would mean a lot to Rowan.

It would mean a lot to Harry.

Hell.

He wasn't sure what to make of it yet. Best to wait to see how it played out.

When Temperance first joined him that morning, he'd rattled off a long list of the tasks they needed to tackle. A few of the older trees on the property had fallen, and shingles had flown from the roof of the house by the dozen. The wicker cabana at the pool was blown half over. When some of Rowan's field crew came around offering to help, Duncan waved them off and told them they had it under control.

Maybe he was punishing her a little for what she did to his truck last night.

Maybe he just wanted an afternoon alone with her.

Maybe both.

Four hours in, Temperance struggled to get through a snapped cedar post with a small battery-powered reciprocating saw. She pressed the vibrating blade into the wood, screeching in frustration when it seized up for a third time instead of slicing through.

"Whoa, whoa, whoa—stop, *stop*—" Duncan approached with hands raised.

She released the trigger and sank to her knees, then sat back on her heels. "I hate this."

He lifted the saw out of her hands. "You're making it harder than it needs to be. You have to let the tool do the work, baby."

Temperance swung her head up. "What did you just say?"

Duncan's heart thudded into his gut when he realized the linguistic misfire. He'd lost the right to call her that more than a decade ago. "I said—" He kept his voice steady. "You gotta let the tool do the work, lady."

She studied him through narrowed eyes, but she didn't push back.

Sweat ran freely down his temples, bypassing his brows to sting the outer corners of his eyes. He lifted his ball cap and dragged the back of his bare hand across his forehead. Little pieces of grit bit into his skin.

Temperance's face was flushed, and strands of her hair were stuck to her forehead and cheekbones in a sheen of sweat.

"You doing okay?" Duncan pulled a clean white bandana from the back pocket of his jeans. He waved it in front of her face.

"White flag, hmm?" Temperance chuckled and took it from him to dab her forehead and the bridge of her nose. She laughed low. "You surrendering?"

Yes. For weeks.

He picked up her tumbler of water and extended a hand down to her. "I think we need a break."

* * *

THEY sat in the shade of Cloud Tide's old beech tree near the pond. By the size of it, it was at least a hundred years old. Decades ago, someone had carved the initials RJ + BS into its massive trunk. Late last fall, Duncan had hung a simple swing made from a wide slat of reclaimed barnwood and some leftover hemp rope. Temperance sat on it, and Duncan lowered himself to the grass beside her. He ached from his shoulders to the beds of his fingernails.

Alice, Grey, and Charlotte stood at the end of the pond's floating dock. Little Grey wore a life jacket faded to a sad grayish pink by the sun. In the shade of another nearby tree, Malcolm sat jotting in a notebook. He greeted them with a simple raise of his palm and a tight smile, then he returned his attention back to his writing.

The world felt slow-motion—even the birdsong overhead seemed to play at half speed, and there was no breeze. The humid air was as still as cold honey.

Temperance let go of the swing's ropes. She winced as she took off her work gloves. Duncan got to his knees in front of her and cupped her right hand in both of his, raising it to look more closely. Matching oval blisters had formed on her middle fingers, just above the first knuckle of each.

"Hang on." He removed his own gloves and pulled out his pocket first-aid kit—a sealed plastic baggie with a few adhesive bandages, alcohol wipes, and a twisted, nearly empty tube of antibiotic cream inside.

She let him tend to her hands, and her attention stayed locked on his face as he worked. When he finished, he rubbed sweat from his cheek with a quick lift of his shoulder.

"Not perfect. Should help cushion the blisters, at least. Make sure to wash with soap and water later, and try to leave them alone—"

Temperance had her lips rolled between her teeth to pin down a smile, and her eyes were soft.

"Shit." Duncan chuckled and tucked the baggie into his back pocket. "I'm giving basic first-aid advice to a doctor."

"Your bedside manner is impeccable."

"Yeah, yeah," he growled.

"Really. Thank you." A drop of sweat caught and hovered on the high arch of her cheekbone. It streaked like a tear down her jawline.

Temperance reached down to lift his hands. She rubbed her thumbs gently over the stained calluses at the base of his fingers. Compared to the willowy softness of her hands, his looked like bear paws. A fresh scrape arced across the heel of his palm—not enough to bleed, but enough to make his skin sandpapery. There was a black bruise under the fingernail of his left thumb where he'd glanced it with a framing hammer.

"You abuse your hands," she said.

"I work hard. Can't help it."

Another gentle swipe with the pads of her thumbs. "You should be more careful."

He tilted his right hand. The scar along the outer edge was silvery pink. "Remember this? We were fifteen, I think?"

She let his hands go and stood from the swing. "Oh god."

"That gnarly old fence at Maren and Nate's. You marched me into the house—"

She tightened her ponytail. "Don't say it."

"And you got that stuff out of the cabinet under the sink in the bathroom—"

Temperance sat beside him in the grass and put both hands over her face. "You are the *worst*."

"Poured it on—"

"No," she moaned.

"You used nail polish remover"—Duncan paused for dramatic effect—"on my open wound."

"I panicked. I thought it was peroxide—"

"Christ, I almost passed out from the pain."

"You screamed so loud, Harry and your dad both came running—"

"Then *you* started crying—"

"I felt horrible, Duncan."

"Clearly, you've always had the instincts of a medical professional."

"Yeah, yeah." She echoed his dissembling from moments ago.

Quieter, Duncan said, "I mean it, Temperance. You are the best person I know."

Bees drifted between clover blossoms tucked into the grass, and other bugs zinged through filmy rays of sun like tiny shooting stars. They sat in silence for a long time. Now that he'd loaded the conversation with something heavier than silly teenage nostalgia, neither of them was sure how to carry it forward.

"Uncle Duncan!" Grey waved from the dock with both little hands.

Grateful for the distraction, Duncan left Temperance in the shade and went to greet the kids. When he crouched to their level, they wiggled around him like tadpoles. From his pocket, he pulled out a second small plastic baggie, this one filled with leftover breakfast sausage for the kids to use as bait.

Seconds after he plunked his hook into the water, Grey reeled in a big bluegill. The fish swung through the air, thrashing at the end of the line. Alice squealed when it smacked her in the back of her head, and Grey's excitement quickly turned to horror when the gravity of the situation hit him. There was an *animal* swaying in front of his face—spiny and cold, its eyes bulging open in a permanent expression of surprise.

Grey screamed.

The fish flailed itself free, dropping back into the pond with a graceful *plonk*.

Duncan kneeled beside Grey. His fingers spanned the entire breadth of the little boy's back.

"Hey, buddy, look. He was fine. Just needed to get back in the water. Fish breathe different from us."

Alice looked on, scowling after the unexpected bluegill assault. She'd be grumpy the rest of the afternoon if he didn't distract her out of it. "Hey, Ace," Duncan said. "What do you call a boomerang that doesn't come back?"

Alice looked at him suspiciously, but her posture softened. "What?"

"A boomerwrong."

She cracked the tiniest grin and returned to fishing.

Duncan could feel Temperance's attention on him the whole time. He smiled up at her, and she smiled back. The moment felt uncomplicated and easy, but their eye contact held a little longer than it needed to.

He turned his attention back to Grey. The little boy sniffed and took a shuddery breath. "He was so scared."

"Nah. He was excited. I do that same dance every time I see you for the first time each day. You've just never noticed." Duncan shimmied his upper body and wiggled his eyebrows. Grey smiled a little. "Hey. You wanna go back to fishing without a hook?"

Grey nodded and sniffed again. Duncan picked up a net and led the little boy to the opposite end of the dock from the girls. He lay on his belly to show him a better technique for catching minnows, and left the little boy to swipe haphazardly through the water, catching more bubbles than fish.

Duncan rejoined Temperance under the tree. He sighed. "I'll need to remember to dance every time he sees me now."

"You're a good uncle." An enormous dragonfly with wings like miniature stained-glass windows landed on her wrist. She blew gently on it, and it flickered away.

"Eh." He cracked his knuckles. "I lied to him."

"He's eight," she said. "You didn't lie, you softened the truth."

"Same thing. Eight is plenty old enough to learn that if you're not ready to deal with a hooked fish, you shouldn't bait a line."

"Wow. When did you get so philosophical?"

"That's not philosophy, that's fact. Maybe I have hidden depths you've never seen before."

Softly, she said, "I guess there's a lot about each other we don't know." She cleared her throat and gestured to the pocket he'd pulled the baggie from. "Case in point—when did you start to carry leftover sausage in your pocket?"

Duncan smiled. "Can't use worms. It upsets the kids to hook 'em."

"See? Good uncle."

"Did you know Maren tried to get them to call me *Duncle*? One word. Like Usher, or Adele." He cut his eyes over to her. "But cooler. Obviously."

"Obviously." Temperance matched his earnest tone, but her lips twitched in a small smile.

The dragonfly was back. This time, it landed on Duncan's forearm, its colorful body camouflaged against his ink. He waved it away and squinted against the glare of late-day sun on the water.

"Your dad jokes are top tier, by the way."

Duncan's hand was close enough to hers in the grass that he felt the heat from her skin. "It's a little-known fact that uncle jokes are superior to dad jokes." He laughed low and picked a blade of grass. "You still want to have kids? Someday?"

"Yeah. You?"

"A dozen," he said. "At least."

"Always figured I would've by now." She twisted his bandana around her hand.

So did I.

"Temperance—"

"Uncle Duncan!" Charlie cried. "Come see!"

In unison, they both swiveled their attention to the kids. Duncan hung his head for a moment and blew a frustrated laugh through his nose. He stood and looked down at Temperance. "We're not done yet," he said.

He hustled back to the dock as Alice reeled in a long glob of stringy green algae. Charlie squealed out a protracted *"Yeewww."*

Duncan took the pole and laid it on the dock. He sank again into a squat. "Ah, my friends, this is a prize catch here." Strand by slimy strand, he removed algae from the hook.

All three kids looked at him with a healthy dose of skepticism. Under the tree, Mal set aside his notebook and tipped his sunglasses down his nose to watch. Duncan felt Temperance's eyes on him, too.

"Listen, *this* is the rare and mystical grass bass, and we are very lucky to be in its presence," he said.

"Ohh," Grey said.

Duncan pulled more strands away. "You each get a wish."

Charlie scoffed. "That's not true."

Duncan put on an exaggerated academic-sounding accent. "Says *whom?*"

"Uncle Duncan." Charlie made a frustrated sound in the back of her throat. "That's not even a fish."

Unlike his cousin, Grey was eager to believe in the magic of the mystical grass bass. "I wish for a puppy!"

Alice spoke in a rush. "I wish for Anthony Roanhouse to fart in social studies, and everyone hears it, and he's embarrassed forever and ever, amen."

Charlie gave her an odd look. "You don't say 'amen' after you make a wish, Ace."

Duncan waved a hand. "It's fine. The grass bass isn't very particular about phrasing formalities." He lowered his voice, and the kids leaned in toward him to hear. "Sometimes, it can even grant wishes you've only said inside your head. You don't even have to say them out loud."

"I want a mom," Charlie blurted. She flicked her eyes to where her dad sat under the tree. Then she looked at Alice and muttered, "Amen."

"Huh." Duncan's heart grew a size and broke clean in two. "I'm not sure moms are within the grass bass's magical purview, sweetheart."

"What's your wish, Uncle Duncan?" Alice said.

The kids looked at him in anticipation. Beneath the tree, Temperance sat cross-legged, watching. She leaned forward, elbows on knees. Mouth soft, eyes like a summer sky. He stared back at her so long, her smile slipped, and she looked down at the limp white bandana in her hands.

White flag.

"It's okay, Uncle Duncan." Grey patted him between the shoulders with a tiny hand, the same way Duncan had soothed him earlier. "You don't have to say it out loud for it to count."

"Ah, well." He knuckled his jaw and looked back to the kids. "We already used up all the wishes anyway. That's all we get, friends."

A collective *aww* of disappointment rippled through his tiny audience. Duncan hopped to his feet, effortlessly switching back to fun-uncle mode. He held some of the green stuff above his open mouth like spaghetti. The kids screamed with laughter.

After he sat back down under the tree, Temperance put a bit of extra distance between them by inching sideways in the grass. "You shouldn't sit so close. I smell awful. Weapons-grade."

"Come on, don't you run marathons in ninety-degree heat?" Duncan made a half-assed attempt to grab her.

She leaned away, laughing. "I never want anyone to know my body is capable of this."

"'Never' is for cowards."

"Listen, sometimes 'never' is very necessary."

"Like, never fry bacon while naked?"

She plucked a clover blossom and twirled it under her nose. "Never use the ass-end of a towel to dry your face."

When he advanced again, Temperance squealed and swatted him with the sweaty bandana. She tried to scuttle backward, but he crawled to her on hands and knees, caught her ankle, and surged over her.

Her fingernails dug into the fabric of his damp T-shirt. Whether she realized it or not, she subtly tugged him toward her instead of pushing him away. "You'll regret this."

"Doubtful."

He snagged her opposite wrist to lift her arm high. Temperance writhed and screamed with laughter, tipping her head back in the grass. The hand that grabbed his shirt pulled tighter, lifting the cotton right out of the waistband of his jeans.

Duncan made his way up her body. He pressed his face to her ribs, the bend of her elbow, her armpit. "Mmmm. This is artisanal," he moaned against the side of her neck.

There was something musky and primal about her after last night in the truck. His scent was all over her.

She smelled *marked*.

Duncan released her wrist and rose up over her. Laughter faded, and her arm fell gently down, draping loose around the back of his neck. Her hair was a thistle gone to seed, strands of it threaded through the grass around her. Her glasses were foggy along the bottom edge from the heat of her body, and her pupils spread into the blue of her eyes.

He was hard against her leg. Conspicuously so.

Hell.

Duncan rolled sideways and shot to his feet. He extended a hand down to help her up. Then he bent to retrieve his ball cap, setting it on her head instead of his own. Her cheeks were lit with a heat that had little to do with the ambient temperature. Other parts of her body flushed that very same color when she—

"You drink tea," she said out of nowhere. She glanced up at the bill of the hat, but she left it on.

Interesting pivot. He rubbed the back of his neck where her hand had been. "I do. Why?"

"It's just—something I didn't know about you." She brushed blades of dry grass from her shoulders. "We've known each other for so long, it just feels like we should already know everything about each other. But we don't."

"But we don't," he echoed.

"It's what made your beard smell like cloves, isn't it?"

Duncan nodded once. "Mal calls it my granny tea. It's, ah—faster and more consistent than coffee in the mornings."

"You planning to grow the beard back, granny?" Her eyes twinkled.

He chuckled. "Haven't decided yet."

They both turned their attention back to the kids on the dock. Softly, Temperance said, "Sometimes it feels like you and I could actually be friends."

"No." The single word came out harsher than he intended. It dropped like a stone between them.

"Why?"

"Look at me. Look me in the eyes, Temperance, and tell me we can be friends."

"We have to. We can't get back to a place we burned the bridge to."

"I build things—I fix things, damn it. It's what I *do*—"

"Duncan—"

"And if it's too broken to fix, I figure out how to build it new—"

Suddenly, raindrops poured down on them, even though the sky was as bright and blue and cloudless as it had been moments before. They both looked up, squinting into the overhead branches of the tree.

Everything happened faster than Duncan could process in the moment, though he would replay it in his mind countless times in the following days.

Branches above shuddered and sent down dozens of burgundy beech leaves to join the fall of water. Then, an abrupt crack of sound. An eerie *whoosh* of something massive moving faster than physics should allow.

A dead limb the size of a canoe broke loose high in the tree—and it swung straight for Temperance.

Part Three

CHAPTER EIGHTEEN

Temperance

*W*hen you're eighteen, you don't fret about time. Your metaphorical pockets are lined with it, and you throw it away by the handful, saying "There's more where that came from!" because you truly believe there is. Your concept of time is that it acts *for* you, not *on* you.

The front seat of his old truck was where she'd kissed him for the first time. Last time, too. She'd had more than three years to obsess about the first, but the thing about last times is that you usually don't even know they're happening until later. And when you're eighteen, there's no such thing as a last time. There's only forever, because that's how much time you feel like you have.

They knew the darkest spot in every parking lot in Vesper Valley that summer, but their favorite place was the old drive-in on County Road 25. It was a Wednesday, and Linden's classic rock station played "Just Like Heaven" by the Cure through the speaker on the passenger's-side dash. The speaker on the driver's side hadn't ever worked, and she knew the only reason it stayed broken was because he hadn't actually tried to repair it yet.

That was back when she believed there wasn't anything he couldn't fix.

It was the same kind of kiss they'd shared hundreds of times that summer. She sat in his lap, facing him. Her knees squeezed his hips, and his hands squeezed her thighs. Sometimes he'd forget to breathe when they kissed, and when he remembered to, he'd exhale *hard and hot across her cheek. It always gave her goosebumps when he did that.*

Maybe she'd have kissed him differently that night if she'd known it would be the last time. Goodbye kisses had to be different than hello kisses, didn't they?

The kiss ended because of a nosebleed, and she fretted when the blood got on the front of his shirt. It had happened a few other times in the past few weeks, but they never lasted that long. There were also more bruises than usual on her legs and arms, but she'd just assumed she was clumsier lately because she was tired. She was tired because she spent all her spare time in dark parking lots with him. She needed him more than she needed sleep.

"Do they usually last this long?" he'd asked after she bled through all the Dairy Bar napkins in his glove box. When the bleeding didn't stop, she had to use the flannel he always kept in the truck for her in case she got cold.

Then he saw the big bruises on the tops of her thighs. They were the shape of his hands. His big, gentle hands.

He cried during the drive to the hospital in Linden.

In the parking lot, she'd held the flannel to her nose and stretched out her other hand so he could take off the little turtle mood ring he'd given her just weeks before.

She'd said, "Just in case." There was a line on her skin where the ring had been. Pale, vaguely green.

He'd slipped it down to the first knuckle of his pinkie and said, "This way I get to give it to you all over again."

It wasn't something someone said if they knew it was the last time.

CHAPTER NINETEEN

Temperance

On the built-in bookshelves across from the bed in the Primrose room, there were three new framed photos since the last time Temperance had stayed there. It brought the total count to eleven, and Duncan's face was in nearly every one of them.

Gia definitely did it on purpose.

Temperance had come to think of the Primrose room as hers, though she'd probably never get to stay in it once the place officially opened as a bed-and-breakfast. It had satiny wood floors that always seemed warm underfoot. A fleecy cream-colored area rug brightened the room, and the ceiling was painted a soft robin's-egg blue. The floor vents brought kitchen smells and muffled voices from directly below. You could almost set a clock by the volume and energy of conversation, and the scent of whatever was being baked or cooked.

Temperance had a nasty bruise in the crook of her arm from the IV during her overnight hospital stay. With her history of a blood platelet disorder, she'd needed to stay for observation to ensure there hadn't been any internal bleeding.

There hadn't.

Another Technicolor bruise in the shape of the tree limb darkened her belly. Her left wrist was badly sprained from where she'd tried to break her fall, her tailbone hurt like hell, and she had a mild concussion from where her head had connected with the ground. Most of yesterday, she'd felt buzzy in the brain and nauseous in the guts, but now, the worst part of it all was a bad case of positional vertigo.

Earlier that morning, she'd tried a solo trip to the bathroom to pee, and had barely made it to the toilet to throw up from the spinning behind her eyes. On the way back to bed, she'd crunched her pinkie toe against a side table and sobbed for ten minutes face-down on the mattress, even though the pain of it faded after five.

Three brisk but quiet knocks sounded at the door.

"I'm awake," Temperance said.

That morning, Rowan and Gia were busy packing last-minute for a week in Spain, so she knew it probably wasn't either of them. The knock was distinctly not-Harry and not-Frankie. Maren was on an overnight camping trip with Alice's Girl Scout Troop, so there were only a few people it could be. But even after Temperance did the brief mental math, when the door cracked slowly open, it revealed the ab-solute last person she would have expected to pay her a sickbed visit.

Malcolm Brady ducked his head as he entered the room, like he was trying to make himself smaller. Sinewy and stiff-legged, he didn't have his cane. A crescent of dark hair was loose from the short pony-tail at the back of his neck, curved along the edge of a sharp jaw. Tucking it back, Mal exhaled and squared his shoulders, as if he had to brace for conversation.

"Do you need anything?" he said.

Temperance blinked. She couldn't have been more surprised if he'd belted show tunes. "I'm okay. Just can't move my head to the side too fast. Got anything for that?"

Mal shook his head once but stayed silent. He'd always been a little unsettling to be around. Taller and leaner than all his broth-ers, heavy brows pulled into a perpetual scowl. His wardrobe con-sisted exclusively of fitted black T-shirts and slim black jeans, and he had one of those deep baritone voices that made whatever he said seem more intense and edgy than it actually was. By the time Temperance had started staying with the Bradys in the summers, Mal was already off doing adult things in New York City, so she'd never gotten to know him the same way she knew Duncan and Harry.

But in the past year, she'd seen him more than she had the entire time she'd known the Bradys. Watching him with his daughter, Charlotte, had softened her a bit. The pediatrician in her recognized an objectively good parent and a physiologically, mentally, and emotionally thriving child when she saw one.

Temperance felt the need to fill the silence. "Thank you, though."

For someone who made a lucrative living by arranging words in compelling ways, Malcolm Brady certainly had a hard time verbalizing them. He cleared his throat, moved back to the doorway, and hesitated. He leaned on the doorjamb, subtly shifting his weight off his weaker leg.

"I know what it's like," he finally said. "To feel out of control of your own body."

Temperance pinched her lips between her teeth and raised her eyebrows. If she opened her mouth to speak, there was a fifty-fifty chance that a sob would burst free instead.

For several awkward seconds, they looked at each other across the room.

"That's it." Another long exhale, like the effort had cost him something. "I just wanted to say that it sucks, and it's okay to feel mad about it. I wish someone had said that to me. After my accident."

"Thank you."

He flexed two fists, then splayed open his fingers. "And even if you're not ready to *ask* for help, just—ah, try to accept it when it's offered. It makes it suck less." Mal nodded once. When he turned to leave, he plowed full-bodied into Frankie. He grunted with an explosive *unf* and wavered backward, catching himself with hands flung outward to grip the doorjamb.

Frankie chirped in surprise.

Temperance sat up so fast it made her vision swim.

The warm amber spice of Frankie's perfume preceded her into the room. Malcolm's nostrils flared, his chest rose in a big inhale, and Temperance was positive she saw his eyes glaze over. He froze with his back to the jamb to let her pass, but Frankie stood her ground and looked him straight in the face. "You shouldn't lurk in doorways," she said.

Mal stepped sideways into the hall and stalked away, muttering under his breath.

Rowan slid past Frankie into the room. She wore a remarkably clean sundress decorated with watercolor oranges. "Yikes." She glanced over her shoulder.

"Wow, what's his problem?" Temperance said.

Frankie closed the door behind them and came over to the bed. She dropped a pale floral canvas tote at Temperance's feet. Casually, she said, "I kissed him at the Honey Moon. Now he hates me even more."

"Oh my god. *Why*?"

"I felt like it." Frankie shrugged. "He's an incredible kisser. Smooth as hell. Made this low growly sound, pulled my hair a little. Total tingler."

"*Frances,*" Rowan groaned.

Temperance massaged the middle of her forehead. "My brain is breaking right now."

"*Shhh*. It's fine." From the tote, Frankie withdrew a pillow covered in a cream satin pillowcase, Temperance's favorite slippers, a plush lavender sleep mask, and a brand-new tube of her favorite buttercream lip balm. "I thought you might want some comforts from home. This was all I could find in the moving boxes."

Temperance gathered the pillow to her chest and propped her chin on it. "I love you."

"I know." Frankie smiled. She'd also brought a few theater-sized boxes of Hot Tamales candy and several paperback historical romances. Their spines were well-lined, the corners of the covers frayed with age.

"You have to promise us you'll rest." Rowan climbed onto the bed and sat at Temperance's feet.

"I'm going to be okay."

"Says the queen of performative okayness," Frankie said.

"I'm just tired."

Rowan persisted. "You don't have to pretend—"

"I don't *pretend* anything," Temperance said.

Frankie gave her a long look. "What about that time you got the world's worst case of food poisoning from Barrett's Chicken Shack, and you still took that—that *whatever* exam in med school—"

Temperance groaned and put a hand over her face. "It wasn't that bad."

"T.J.," Frankie said. "You wore a diaper to the exam in case you—you know."

"She *what*—" Rowan cut in.

"I never should have told you." Temperance closed her eyes and sank into the pillows.

Frankie pressed on. "There's nothing virtuous about pushing yourself until you collapse. Or poop your pants."

"Let the record show"—Temperance held up a finger—"I did not poop my pants that day."

"*That day?*" Rowan chimed in again.

Frankie's tone was still serious. "The fact that you even felt compelled to do that when you were so sick—god, honey."

"You've been burning your candle at both ends for so long, you're basically a lump of melted wax and burnt hair," Rowan said.

"You're both gross, you know that?" Temperance took off her glasses and rubbed her closed eyes.

"You love us." Rowan hopped up from the bed and gave her a kiss on the forehead. "Gotta run. I'm way behind on packing."

After Rowan left, Frankie said, "Did you ever think there'd be a reality where Rowan McKinnon would be packing to go to Spain with her future mother-in-law?" She tidied the bedside table and opened the blinds. "Always thought you'd be the only one of us to put a ring on it."

Temperance sighed. "Don't start, Frank."

From the bookshelf built into the adjacent wall, Frankie picked up one of the framed photos. "Duncan is giving early-2000s Josh Hartnett vibes here." She bobbed her eyebrows.

Temperance cracked her eyes open, just enough to see which photo Frankie held.

Harry and Duncan were both young and lanky and messy-haired, their skin gilded golden by early-summer sunshine. They smiled the same open-mouthed sideways smile with arms slung around each other's shoulders. Duncan was clean-shaven, and his features were a gentler iteration of what they were now. There was a deep dimple in his left cheek and a shallower dimple in his chin.

Until two days ago, Temperance hadn't seen those dimples in at least seven years.

The photo was old, from the evening of Harry's undergrad graduation party. That day had been the first time she and Duncan had been in the same space after they'd broken up. They hadn't spoken a word to each other, but anytime Duncan had been in her periphery, she'd felt his attention on her. On the drive back to Philadelphia that night, she'd felt him all over her skin, as if his gaze had been a palpable thing.

Frankie picked up another photo, this one a professional shot of Malcolm, Harry, and Duncan at the reception for Harry's first marriage, to Nicola Baldwin. All three men stood with hands in the pockets of sleek black tuxedos. They smoldered at the camera. During one of her trips to the bathroom yesterday, Temperance had stuck an oval produce sticker on the glass to cover Duncan's face.

Frankie peeled it off and held it out on the end of her finger. "You do this?" She side-eyed the bunch of bananas on the bedside table.

Temperance closed her eyes again and sank further down in the pillows. "I made some poor choices that night. I don't want the reminder staring back at me."

By then, they'd hooked up a few times in the years since they'd ended, but it was always fast and soulless. That night had been different. Equipped with a handful of condoms from the hotel front desk and an ironclad set of rules, she'd showed up at Duncan's hotel room door. No conversation, no expectations, no implications. Duncan had been frozen in place, wearing only a pair of navy-blue boxers, with one arm high on the jamb and the other holding the door open. His cheeks flushed fast and hot when she made her proposition, and for a horrifying moment Temperance realized he might *already* have someone in the room with him. But his hesitation had been short-lived. He'd hauled her into the room by her waist, hungry hands shearing off some of the tiny beadwork on the bodice of her dress. They hadn't even made it to the bed the first time— he'd flipped her around and taken her against the hotel room door. They'd always had incredibly short fuses with each other, but what they lacked in stamina had always been doubly compensated for with volume.

Duncan Brady had a remarkable refractory period.

Sometime around hour three of wall-banging, soul-bruising sex, dawn came bloodred through a crack in the curtains. With his face against her neck, he told her he still loved her. Temperance had felt the heat of his tears on her skin.

Then she cried, too.

He'd lifted her against him, frantically skimming his hands over her legs and arms, terrified he'd hurt her, even though, that night, *he* was the one who'd been marked. Streaky welts where her fingernails had scored his shoulders, love bites blooming wicked pink up the sides of his neck. She'd even bitten his lip.

Frankie's voice broke through the memory. "T.J."

"Sorry. I'm just tired."

Frankie put the frame back. "You'll need his help over the next few days. It's either him, or Big Will. I can't come back until Monday. Apparently, I have bats living in the ceiling at the new studio, and I've got a furniture delivery to the apartment on Saturday morning."

"I'll be fine, honey."

Frankie lifted a photo of Duncan and Mal on the day after Charlotte was born. She was swaddled in a blanket covered in pastel elephants, tucked into the crook of Duncan's arm. He wore an incandescent grin, and the outer edge of his forearm was still tattoo-free. A blank canvas.

Mal looked genuinely happy in that one, too.

"I guess Malcolm could help . . ." Frankie said. The hazy softness in her big brown eyes when she looked down at the photo was alarming.

"Frances," Temperance said. "He probably has the bedside manner of Annie Wilkes."

"Disagree." Frankie tapped a manicured nail against the frame. "He's a crème brûlée. Crackly outside, gooey inside."

"Gross," Temperance said.

Frankie held the frame to her chest. "You don't like crème brûlée?"

"Crème brûlée is fine. I'm trying not to think about Malcolm Brady's creamy center."

"Gross," said Frankie.

"See?"

"I said gooey, though. Not *creamy*."

"Crème brûlée is inherently creamy," Temperance said.

"I don't care what anyone says." Frankie replaced the photo on the shelf. "It's the worst word."

"Malcolm isn't a project for you, honey. Those red flags are so complex, they've become self-aware and started waving themselves."

"You're insufferable, and I love you." Frankie pulled a few envelopes out of her purse. "I almost forgot—you had some mail. Want me to open it?"

"Please."

Two of the envelopes were junk. The third was a letter from one of the banks where she'd applied for a loan for the clinic. Frankie began to read. "Dear Dr. Madigan. Regretfully—"

Temperance snatched the paper out of Frankie's hands and crumpled it into a tight ball. She chucked it across the room and put her arm over her eyes. "Damn it."

Strike five.

"I'm sorry, T.J." Frankie put her hand on her knee.

She hadn't felt this helpless since she was eighteen. Her whole body felt like an old seashell. Hollow and brittle.

This one had been for a medical practice acquisition loan from a healthcare-specific lender, and it had been the one she'd held out the most hope for. Two of the others had approved her, but one had an interest rate too high to even consider, and the other only approved her for ten thousand dollars, which was laughable.

God, she needed to run until she blacked out. But she couldn't even make it to the bathroom to pee without barfing in the sink.

Frankie curled up on the bed next to her and stayed for a while. After an hour, she slipped out to leave Temperance to doze.

This place was usually filled with sound. Music, laughter, conversation. The thump of old pipes in the walls and the creaky floors. Now, it was silent.

God, she hated this stupid room.

She hated all four hundred and fifty-one beads in the stupid crown molding on the wall opposite the bed, and she hated the stupid robin's-egg-blue ceiling. She hated how the air blowing through the floor vent somehow carried the same comforting smells the Brady household had always had, even though this wasn't the same stupid house she'd spent all those summers in.

And she hated Duncan Brady's gorgeous face staring back at her from all the photos across the room.

Temperance threw back the sheets and lurched over to the bookshelves. She clung to the edge of the bed for balance, then the footboard, then the shelves themselves. One by one, she laid the frames face-down.

Her and Harry, hugging belly to belly, both of them fresh-faced with the rangy awkwardness of youth. Duncan stood a bit off to the side, leaning toward them but closed-off in every other way. His smile was tight, his arms were crossed. That was the first year Harry'd stayed at Brown for summer break, but he'd come home for the Brady family vacation. They'd gone to Virginia Beach, and on the five-hour drive back home, she'd fallen asleep on Duncan in the back seat of the Bradys' old minivan. To this day, she could *swear* he'd kissed her forehead as she drifted off.

Another. This one was a group shot of the Bradys and eighteen-year-old Temperance. They all smiled in front of a confectionery-colored sunset over Lake Erie. Everyone was windblown and sunburned, clustered together in a row. Arms slung around waists and heads tipped against shoulders. Bright smiles and tired eyes. Other than the photo booth strip Duncan had saved, it was the only photo that still existed of them when they'd been *together* together, even though the image didn't explicitly reveal it. Behind their backs, their hands clasped tight where nobody else could see. He'd slipped a silly little souvenir shop mood ring on her finger the day before, and she'd worn it the rest of the summer.

Duncan had used it to measure the size of her ring finger, for something far more permanent.

The knot in her throat was impossibly heavy, aching all the way down to her collarbones. But she couldn't cry to dislodge it. This family had always treated her like one of their own, even though she'd always tried to hold herself to the emotional periphery. They were *Maren's* people, not really hers. She'd always felt like she existed in a state of half-belonging—not really a Brady, but not *not* part of the family, either. A little like a stray.

Now here she was, in her thirties, once again stuck between the family whose validation she couldn't manage to stop craving and the one who loved her without reservation even though she'd never given them any real reason to.

She'd never fully belong here, because she and Duncan would never be able to peacefully coexist.

Temperance laid down the last photo. Dizziness spun her like a top when she turned away too quickly, and she had to hold on to the bookshelves to lower herself to the rug. She cried until she fell asleep.

* * *

THE room was dark and still when she awakened in the bed. Someone had lifted her from the floor and tucked her in. She knew it had been Duncan, because he'd kissed her on the forehead before quietly leaving.

CHAPTER TWENTY

Duncan

*D*uncan lingered in the doorway to the Primrose bedroom with lungs like lead balloons.

Temperance had been asleep for nearly eighteen hours. That afternoon, he'd checked on her once an hour to make sure she was still breathing, indulging a little in the chance to look at her without worrying who noticed. On a normal day, she was in constant motion, and now that she was at rest, she almost looked like a different person. Her face was a visual poem—eyebrows arched like winter rye, the faintest scatter of pale freckles along the bridge of her nose. The sunshine flooding the room accentuated the lavender shadows under her lashes, and her eyelids were pink, like she'd been crying in her sleep. Her braid lay beside her, long and limp as a mooring rope snapped from a ship in a storm.

She looked *terrible*.

She was *perfect*.

The crack and whoosh of that tree limb as it swung through the air would haunt him for the rest of his life. It was surreal, a thing that massive moving so, so quickly.

And the sound of Temperance's breath rushing out of her lungs. And the way his ball cap seemed to sail off her head in slow motion.

Her little whimper as he lifted her into the back seat of Harry and Rowan's car.

He'd tailed them in his truck on the way to the hospital, barely keeping his shit together. His brain was overrun with the memory of how he'd sped down that same county road to get her to the hospital fourteen years earlier. It was a dark mark in his subconscious. Permanent ink bled through paper to stain the surface beneath. That night fourteen years ago, they'd triaged her to the ICU, and he hadn't been able to go with her in case her immune system was suppressed. For days after, Duncan convinced himself he'd never see her again, and he would try to remember the way she looked before they wheeled her away. But the only thing his brain could manage was a memory of the blood-burgundy color of the nurse's scrubs.

He didn't see her again until weeks later.

He should have noticed the fucking tree limb. This property was his responsibility, and he should have hired someone sooner to prune away all the weak and dead wood from the bigger trees. If she'd been standing just a few inches to the right, a single step forward—

Goddamn it.

On the bedside table, her tortoiseshell glasses sat next to lip balm and a stack of empty Styrofoam cups from Nelson's. A hairbrush threaded with a few strands of pale gold had fallen to the floor, along with a romance book with a colorful cover. He crouched to pick everything up.

"Duncan," she said above him. Her voice was creaky.

The clock on the wall ticktocked a few times before he spoke. "How'd you know it was me?"

She didn't open her eyes. "You sound large."

"I have something for you. Hold out your hands."

He gave her a new cup of Nelson's ice, and she cradled it to her chest. "You're the one who's been bringing me this?"

"I know you," he said, gently. "We'll have to get rid of all this Styrofoam before Rowan gets home, though."

"I had one of their refillable Whistle Wetter mugs. Last I saw, Grey was using it to catch tadpoles."

Duncan dragged the wooden desk chair next to the bed and sat. The joints creaked under his weight. "What have you eaten today?"

She pointed to an empty Dr Pepper bottle on the bedside table.

"Glad to see you learned how to take care of a human body in all those years of med school and residency."

Her smile was weak, but it was there. "Shut up."

They sat in silence for a while. The air-conditioning unit outside kicked on with a loud hum. A warm malty scent from the floor vents rose from the kitchen below. It smelled like autumn, even though it was barely a week into June.

Temperance spoke again, just as he thought she'd fallen back to sleep. "You know what I always loved about your parents' house when I would come to stay for the summers?"

"Tell me."

"It always smelled like food."

Duncan chuckled. "Really?"

"Those chocolate coconut cookies of your mom's—"

"Christ, I hate those cookies."

"—or your dad's pineapple upside-down-cake pancakes—"

"Oh, god." He groaned and sat back in the chair. "I'd forgotten about those. He hasn't made 'em in years."

"The Spanish ham croquettes, or that cheesy potato casserole Nate makes—"

Duncan dragged his hand over his mouth. "You'd better stop. I haven't had lunch."

"The lilacs, too. The way the whole house would smell like lilacs for a few minutes after someone came in the front door." Quieter, she said, "I couldn't even tell you what my parents' house smelled like when I was growing up."

"Ambition," he said, and they both laughed.

Her belly growled.

"Dad's testing toffee pudding recipes downstairs. I can bring you some—"

"No, no. It's fine. And you don't need to stay here with me, Duncan. I'm okay being alone."

"Well. Maybe I'm not." He laid his hand on the bed next to where her thigh rested under the blankets, careful not to touch her. Just enough to let her feel he was there.

She moved her pinkie alongside his. Duncan nudged a tentative finger under her palm and held his breath. She slid her own fingers through his, then they both squeezed and squeezed until his bones ached.

"Can you look at me?" he said.

She tugged at her bottom lip with her teeth and leaned her head sideways on the pillow, just barely. When she opened her eyes, the pale blue of her irises jerked sideways over and over again, as if tugged by an invisible string. She lowered her lashes quickly, making a frustrated sound in the back of her throat.

Duncan frowned. "What's happening?"

"Hitting my head knocked some stuff around in my inner ear. My brain is getting weird signals about my equilibrium, so my eyes are trying to compensate." Pointing to her face, she said, "Wild, right?"

"Does it hurt?"

"No, but it makes me nauseous."

"You look like one of those scary vintage baby dolls with the googly eyes."

Temperance laughed softly.

"How long will it be like this?"

"A day or two? A few weeks? Months?" Abruptly, she let go of his hand and sat up. She flipped back the sheets and lifted her legs over the edge of the bed. Her head hung between her shoulders. She clutched the quilt at her sides. The veins along the backs of her hands were ashen blue, her knuckles so white they were almost pearlescent. Her bare shins brushed against his jeans. "I'm disgusting. I've barely left this bed for two days."

He scooted back in the chair to give her space. "Let me help you."

For all that his identity was caught up in his ability to fix things, hers was rooted in the fact that she never needed fixing. This Temperance, though—she was small and brittle, and Duncan knew better than most that it was the fate of brittle things to break.

Like hell he'd let her push him away.

Eyes still closed, she stood and took small shuffling steps forward, and she wobbled sideways barely a foot from the bed. Duncan shot to his feet to steady her with hands around her rib cage, planting his feet wide for balance. When he adjusted his grip, his thumb brushed the underside of her breast through the thin cotton of her pajamas. Her hands clamped down on his forearms. They both froze.

"It's okay. I can do this—"

"Let me help you, damn it," he repeated. "Pretend I'm someone else if you have to—"

"Pedro Pascal?"

Duncan chuckled. "Wow, you jumped on that opportunity *real* quick."

Her laugh was soggy and sad. She let her forehead rest against his sternum. "Okay."

Relief made him lightheaded. Duncan led her to the bathroom with an arm around her back. While she brushed her teeth with one hand gripping the sink, he hung a towel and a washcloth within reach, and sat an assortment of shampoos and body washes on the floor of the walk-in shower.

She turned around slowly, drying her mouth on a towel. Temperance squinted at the wide-seated shower stool he situated in the center of the shower. "Where in the world did you get that?"

"You'd be amazed at the stuff we've found in that equipment garage."

She twisted the end of her braid around her fingers. "Is it safe?"

Duncan stepped into the shower and sat down on the stool, hard. Then he gripped the handlebars. "Solid."

Her eyes narrowed.

The stool didn't budge when he wiggled his ass vigorously back and forth. The joints didn't make a sound. "Hell, we could probably hop on this thing together and—"

"Duncan." She pressed her lips tight.

"Sorry."

She squeezed her eyes shut and tipped her head to the ceiling. "*Please* don't say you're sorry."

He swallowed the next *sorry*.

She turned to hold on to the sink again and tried to undo her braid one-handed. Duncan moved behind her, gently lowering her hand away from her hair. "The whole point of me helping is for you to actually let me help."

Temperance dropped her other hand to grip the sink, and Duncan got to work on the braid. It was a mess. A combination of restless sleep and sweat and sunscreen had felted the fine strands together in places, and in others, it was tangled and looped.

Every move they made echoed in the silent space of the bathroom. The snap of her hair elastic against his fingers. The scrape of his boots on tile as he shifted to support her. A faint squeak of her sweaty palms against the edges of the sink.

It took almost ten minutes to get the braid out. Free of the plait, her hair hung like rain-damp hay down her back. Duncan drifted his fingertips over the bump on the back of her head. Their eyes met briefly in the mirror over the sink, and her lips parted in a silent sigh. She went slack against him, and Duncan didn't breathe. Her elbows socketed gently into the bends of his own arms, and the soft contour of her butt skimmed his upper thighs.

Every muscle in his body felt like it'd come loose from his bones.

"Hold on to the sink again." He pressed a hand to her back. "I'm going to turn on the shower."

The flow of water in the glass-walled space sounded like summer rain on a window. Steam swirled down from the ceiling and churned up from the floor.

Then she fidgeted with the hem of her tank top. "Close your eyes."

"Temperance, I could sketch your nipples from memory, to scale—"

"*Shhhh.*"

"We're alone. There's no way Dad's coming up here."

"Malcolm is here."

"He's probably sleeping. That's what vampires do during the day."

"Ha ha."

"Look." He softened. "If I can't see, how can I catch you if you start to fall?"

She grumbled, working at her bottom lip with the edges of her teeth. "Fine. But don't take your eyes off my face."

"Promise."

Holding the sink with one hand, she bent sideways to push down her sleep shorts and underwear. They tangled a bit around her ankles when she tried to slip her feet free. Duncan caught her by her arm, and again, she met his gaze in the mirror as she kicked the clothes away. Stripes of pink lit her cheeks when she shucked the tank top over her head.

Duncan opened the shower door, and she stepped carefully inside, gripping the handles of the stool for stability before she sat down.

"Can you reach everything?" he said.

Her sigh sounded like she'd emptied herself from her lungs all the way to the ends of her toes. "Haven't tried yet. Just enjoying for a moment."

Duncan sat on the floor beside the sink with his arms hooked over his knees. A very lacy strip of underwear peeked out from the waistband of her sleep shorts.

He hadn't made any promises to not look at *those*.

From the shower, another long sigh of pleasure.

He smiled. "Temperature good?"

"It's perfect." She swiped her hand through the condensation on the glass and opened her eyes just long enough to meet his. "I live here now." A blob of bubbles was caught in her eyebrow, and another tracked down her jaw. She gave him a weak smile as the glass clouded over again.

Then she talked as she worked the shampoo through her long hair.

"In my last year of undergrad, I had to write a research paper for my history of medicine class. One of my great-great-grandmother's contemporaries was named Jennie Smillie Robertson—she was Canada's first woman surgeon. Her first love was a boy named Alex, but she chose medicine instead of a life with him. Didn't think she could have both. Then when she retired in her seventies, she found him again. She married Alex."

"That's really sweet."

The splash of water echoed off the tile as she squeezed out her hair.

"It's not, Duncan. They only had ten years together before he died." Her voice had a hard edge. She made another clear spot on the glass and exhaled a shuddery breath. "Ten years wouldn't be enough for me."

She closed her eyes, and her streaky little window fogged over again. Her body was a peachy blur. The curve of her back seemed the geometry of defeat.

After a while, Duncan left her to put clean sheets and pillow-cases on the bed. She stayed in the shower until the water ran cold. He opened a towel for her, plush as a sweater and big enough that it wrapped around her twice. Temperance clutched it tight between her collarbones and turned to look up at him, pressing her back against the outer wall of the shower to keep her balance.

"Thank you."

"What are friends for?" he said.

Her eyes flooded. When she pressed them shut, tears squeezed free and raced down her cheeks. The corners of her mouth turned all the way down, and her chin went wobbly. She bent at the waist and crumpled to the floor.

Duncan followed her down. He sat on his knees in front of her, vibrating with the restraint it took to not touch her. A sob made her shoulders heave. "I hate this," she said.

Blood pounded in his ears, but he kept his tone gentle. "I'm going to hold you now, okay?"

When she nodded, Duncan leaned forward and cupped his hands under her elbows, tugging her gently toward him. She wept in his lap there on the bathroom floor, her tears and the wet of her hair soaking his shirt. She pressed her face into his collarbone, pounding the sides of her fist against his chest.

"Take what you need," he murmured into her hair. *It's yours. All of it.*

"This feels like when I got sick." She sniffed—a wet, awful sound. "I lost control of my body, I lost you. It was my fault."

"It wasn't."

"Would we have ended if I hadn't gotten sick?"

He hesitated. "Probably not." His thumb skimmed over the back of her hand.

"See? It's my fault."

"No. I have *never* blamed you. And thank god for that, because I'd have hated myself even more if I had."

Her body jerked against his as she cried herself dry. After a while, she exhaled a steamy breath against his neck. Her body went lax and still in his arms.

"Hold on to me," Duncan said.

She sagged into him, but her arms went tight around his neck.

"Good girl," he whispered against her temple. He got to his feet, lifting her easily.

In the bedroom, he brought her clean clothes and turned his back while she got dressed on the bed. Then he tucked her in and kissed her forehead.

When she spoke again, her voice was small. "Maren and Nate made it. We could've."

Duncan sank to his knees beside the bed. He carefully considered his words. This was it. This was the start of the conversation he'd ached to have with her for months, and as it always seemed to be for them, the timing was absolute shit. They couldn't do this now, not with her at less than a hundred percent. Not when she might regret it or play it off later as a moment of weakness—to herself or to him. He'd waited too damned long to chance it not being perfect.

"They were ten years older than we were," Duncan said. "They had degrees, they had jobs, they had resources. We had *nothing*."

"We had each other."

"What about when your parents inevitably found out about us, and cut you off? Either you wouldn't have become a doctor, or we'd have started our lives together with half a million dollars in student loan debt. I couldn't do that to you."

"We'd have figured it out," she said.

"'Figuring it out' is not a plan. It's *stalling*. Love is delusional at eighteen. It feels eternal because the eighteen-year-old brain is *incapable* of actually seeing that far ahead."

"I'm a pediatrician, Duncan. I know how adolescent brains work." She laid her hands over her eyes. "You decided for us. You stripped away my agency at a time when it was the only thing I had. You didn't even give us a chance."

"I tried to fix it—you didn't let me fix it—"

She didn't let him finish. "Have you ever wondered why I started doing all those wild things? The skydiving, the marathons, all the other crap I'm supposed to be too fragile for?" Her bottom lip was tucked tight against her teeth. "I get to be reckless and chaotic and messy, and people fucking *congratulate* me for it. It's *mine*. Nobody else gets to decide."

Finally, some fire in her.

"You're none of those things," Duncan said.

"Yes. Yes, I am. I am *all* of those things sometimes. I wonder if you've ever really seen me like I thought you did. If it was really me you loved, or if I'd gotten so good at pretending to be perfect for my parents that it bled over into how I behaved with you."

Duncan drifted his thumb over the back of her hand. "I've always seen you, Temperance. Maybe what you see as reckless and messy—I see it as brave. And real."

"Don't." A sob slipped loose. "It's easier when we're mean to each other. You, me, like this—I never wanted to feel like this again."

"Never is for cowards."

"I'm okay with being a coward." Her voice was hoarse.

"Says the woman who skydives out of hot-air balloons."

Her chin quivered. She started to speak again, then turned away. Tears came faster now, streaking from the corners of her closed eyes.

"Tell me," Duncan said. He held his breath until she spoke again.

"One of my early jumps, my chute lines were twisted. It's pretty common, but some are harder to fix than others. Some, you have to cut your chute away and use the backup. But I panicked. I forgot everything I knew, and a few seconds passed where I actually thought I was going to die."

Duncan couldn't breathe.

She met his eyes. This time, they didn't waver. "It was you, Duncan. You were the only thing in my mind when I was falling. And you're still who I want whenever I'm scared or sad. When I do something special, or accomplish something hard, you're always the first person I want to tell. It's always you."

CHAPTER TWENTY-ONE

Duncan

*T*emperance tasted like Fireball Whisky.

Duncan wasn't sure what was hotter—the cinnamon blaze of her tongue, or how efficiently she'd dropped his pants *and* his boxers without disengaging her mouth from his. Once he was bare-assed, she shoved his tuxedo coat down his shoulders and ripped his dress shirt open with savage enthusiasm. The buttons popped off like miniature champagne corks, landing on the floor of the hotel room with cartoonish high-pitched *ping!* sounds.

His singular remaining brain cell was aware of two things—he definitely wasn't getting his deposit back for the tux rental, and how the hell had the buttons made that sound when they'd landed on *carpet*?

Like a spliced film reel, they were on the bed in the next blink, and Temperance was magnificently naked, clutching at him, clamping every centimeter of her body against his. Then he was plunging into her, and it felt like free-falling from space, or falling in love, or both at the same time.

He was still wearing his bow tie. *Only* the bow tie.

With every one of his thrusts, the pulse in his skull beat out a pounding rhythm. It had a voice, chanting, *It's happening—this is happening—it's happening*. He fucked her up the mattress, slapping a palm to the cushioned headboard for more leverage once they got there.

He forgot to breathe and nearly blacked out, losing himself in the body of the woman who owned his every molecule.

It's happening—this is happening—it's happening—

Then Temperance began to cry.

"Don't stop," she demanded through the tears, and he wanted to tell her he'd give her anything, everything she'd ever wanted, but his mind was so overclocked all he could manage was an incoherent, heaving growl of assent into the hot skin of her temple.

Instead of streaking down her face and to the pillow beneath her, her tears defied gravity and moved *upward*, leaking into the corners of his mouth, climbing his cheeks, drifting past his ears. Drenching him with her salt. The tears moved beyond him, trembling skyward in slow motion—*what the fuck?*—like rain in reverse. Her body shuddered with the force of her sobs, but she clung to him. Frantic. Gouging fingertips like masonry nails into his scalp, into the bunched muscles of his shoulders, his back, his ass, his thighs—*god, how did she have so many hands?*—and her legs were locked so supernaturally tight around his hips, churning him into her so hard he couldn't have relented even if he'd wanted to.

"Don't ever stop," she said.

It's happening—this is happening—it's happening—

Don't stop.

He came with a terrible roar, hating himself for rutting so relentlessly while she cried, and loving her at the same time—*god, he loved her*. He threw his head back with the ecstasy of it, baring his teeth at the ceiling—

An ocean.

There was an *actual ocean* on the ceiling. Roiling and turbulent, impossibly vast. The walls of the hotel room fell away like a set on a theater stage, and Duncan could *feel* the misty spray of the crashing waves above him. Brine stung his eyes, puckered his tongue, dripped down the back of his throat. And that roaring—it hadn't been *him*. It was Temperance's ocean of tears, in all its enormous, terrifying power.

In another rapid splice of the film reel, he was sitting naked in damp, cold sand on a monochromatic beach—grit in his hair, between his bare toes, in the crack of his ass—and Temperance was gone. The bed was gone, the hotel room was gone. The ocean rose up and came for him with sentient purpose, and he knew—*he knew*—he wouldn't survive it.

He started to scream.

* * *

"FUCK!" Duncan vaulted out of bed and fired his pillow across the room with a vicious swing of his arm. The sheet around his waist and thighs was as twisted as seaweed, nearly tripping him to the ground. He yanked it off and tossed it away, stumbling toward the bathroom.

He was wet from temples to toes, but it wasn't ocean water that soaked him, or Temperance's tears. It was the thick, stinking sweat of a nightmare.

Duncan looked down. His dick curved gleefully outward, raging hard and flushed, slick at the tip. His balls felt so heavy they might have contained that same ocean from the dream. His privates clearly missed the signals of terror his dream brain had sent to the rest of his anatomy.

The ones that were simultaneously horny *and* horrifying were a truly diabolical joke of his subconscious.

He shoved sweaty hair out of his face. God*damn* it.

He cranked the shower and stepped in before the water got hot. The icy spray hit the back of his neck and shoulders, drawing goosebumps across his skin, tightening his groin. He pressed his back to the cold tile wall and took himself in hand, sucking a breath through his teeth against the cold. Squeezing his eyes shut, he tried to summon Temperance from the earlier part of the dream. Before it had turned into a fucked-up Christopher Nolan flick.

He couldn't find her.

The shower got hot fast, inciting the furious heat between his legs, in his gut, in his chest. He planted his feet wide and clenched the cheeks of his ass as familiar explosive tension coalesced at the base of his spine and deep in his balls. Sixty seconds was all it took, primed as he was from the dream. His knees buckled, and he slid down the wall, riding the eruption all the way to the shower floor.

He came so hard he felt nauseous.

His hand hung loose between his legs as he gasped and seethed at himself for being so pathetic. Hot water beat against his scalp, running into his eyes, into the corners of his mouth.

There wasn't any denying it. The Temperance-shaped place inside him that he'd kept meticulously hollow for more than a decade was filling up again, and like a tipped hourglass, there was no stopping it.

CHAPTER TWENTY-TWO

Temperance

A breath of record heat blew into Vesper Valley.

The electricity had been out at the house since two o'clock that afternoon, a result of the rural power grid being overloaded by wheezing air conditioners. Temperance had a mild headache that day, but it was related more to the unrelenting high temperatures than her head injury. She hadn't gotten dizzy in a few days, and the pain in her wrist was mostly gone. The bruise on her belly had already begun to fade to a pale olive green around the edges.

She slid on her glasses and blinked at the wall. When she'd set them on the bedside table before her nap a few hours ago, the lenses had been streaked with the tracks of salty tears. Now, they were clear and clean. Her carafe was also full of fresh ice from Nelson's.

Frankie hadn't been there to see her since the first day, too busy moving into her new photography studio and apartment in Linden. Harry dropped in a few times throughout the week, but with Rowan away in Spain, he picked up extra per diem shifts to fill the time. Mal spent most of his days battering the keys of an old laptop while he watched the kids. Maren and Nate were working ten-hour days running the business side of Cloud Tide, and Will rarely left his kitchen during daylight hours.

By far, the most constant presence was Duncan.

The one essential thing that Frankie hadn't been able to find in the boxes of her belongings was the dental night guard Temperance wore to protect her teeth. She clenched her jaw so badly when she slept that she ground holes through her custom-fit guards every few months. After only one night without one, she'd woken up with a stiff neck and a tension headache that had her in tears.

Temperance did a lot of crying these days.

Later that same afternoon, Duncan brought her five different brands of over-the-counter night guards—one that was actually a mouth guard for athletes. He dumped them out of a plastic pharmacy bag in the middle of the bed and helped her open the boxes for each, giving himself a paper cut in the process. One of them fit, and she hadn't had any more morning headaches since.

On the third day, he'd noticed how broken some of her fingernails were from the work in the vineyard before her accident. So, he'd given her an impromptu bedside manicure, complete with hand massage. He'd kissed her knuckles after.

Five nights in, Duncan and Mal had set up an outdoor movie for the kids. They'd daisy-chained extension cords to power a DVD projector, using the solid stucco wall of the west wing of the house as the screen. In a tent with the front zipped open, the kids lay on sleeping bags, and Mal lounged in a hammock strung between two big oaks. In the back of his truck, Duncan made a comfortable nest with an air mattress and blankets and pillows. Gia had off-loaded most of their DVDs to the thrift store when they'd moved a few years ago, and *Twister* was the only one they could find. Temperance died a little inside when Ace declared it a movie "from the old days."

"Old days" notwithstanding, the kids had been hooked by the end of the opening scene. Temperance joined them with a little help from Duncan, but she'd barely made it to the midpoint of the movie. Fatigue swirled around her, and with Duncan as her anchor, she'd let herself drift. When she'd awakened, her head was nestled in the dip of his shoulder, and one leg was flung over his thigh. The night was utterly still and silent around them, too late even for crickets and fireflies and the wind in the trees.

He'd carried her inside sometime before dawn. She found twelve mosquito bites on her legs the next morning.

This week was the longest she'd gone without running since

she was eighteen. Once she was able to safely navigate the stairs, she'd spend a few hours in the mornings on the sun-warmed wicker chaise on the porch with one of the romance books that Frankie had brought. Once it grew too hot in the afternoons, she'd retreat inside and spend a few hours on the phone with Coleman and others about the state and fate of the clinic. Her parents hadn't called at all, thankfully.

From the recessed window seat in her room, or the wicker chaise on the porch, Temperance learned the rhythm and routine of Duncan's workdays. Every morning, he'd arrive an hour or so after sunrise and chat with Nate and Will in the kitchen below the Primrose room. She couldn't ever make out the details of their conversations, but the timbre of his voice and the resonant lilt of his laugh were as familiar to her as her own inner monologue. Then he'd leave again and return just after noon. Temperance knew he was coming from Linden because he brought her a fresh cup of Nelson's ice every day.

Whenever he came to her, he smelled like the rosemary-mint hand soap from the kitchen, and the practical sweetness of wanting to be clean for her made her flush with warmth.

Last night, she'd gone downstairs to get a drink around three o'clock in the morning and found him asleep at the table in the dining room, slumped over an open notepad with his head resting on his upper arm. A laptop was open beside him, the screen saver casting a glow of slowly shifting colors onto his face. A full mug of tea sat untouched just beyond his outstretched hand, like he'd tried and failed to reach it before he'd surrendered to sleep.

Temperance tugged the pull chain on the bedside table lamp. Still no electricity.

After seven days, she could judge the time of day by the way the sun shone into the window. Now, the glow that painted the room was apricot and rose, and shadows stretched long. About an hour before dusk, then.

There wasn't enough light in the room to read by, and her phone battery was at twenty percent, so listening to a podcast or mindlessly scrolling social media were both out. The waistband of her pajama shorts was damp with sweat, as was the pillow behind her neck. At the open windows, the sheer curtains hung as straight and still as the walls beside them. The ceiling fan was motionless. Her attempt at yoga on the bedroom floor lasted approximately three minutes before she rolled sideways and groaned from boredom. After brushing her teeth and re-braiding her hair, Temperance went downstairs. The grandfather clock in the foyer ticktocked, but without the hum of appliances and music, the house seemed unnaturally silent.

Outside, the day was fading, but the heat was still oppressive. On the glass-topped wicker coffee table sat three open pints of ice cream and a tub of raspberry sherbet, each with four teaspoons sunk down inside. Duncan was there at the porch stairs, waving goodbye to a minivan that pulled down the driveway.

He turned, licking vanilla ice cream off the back of a spoon. The fabric of a slate-colored button-down puckered where it was snug around his biceps. A pair of buff chinos did the same around his quads, but they fit so perfectly otherwise they could have been stitched onto him in place. The way the flat front hugged his hips made them the business-casual equivalent of gray sweatpants.

With one last swipe of his tongue across the back of the spoon, Duncan gave her a slow head-to-toe once-over. His cheeks flooded with ruddy color, and his eyes went a little glassy.

"Why are you looking at me like that?" Temperance said.

Duncan cleared his throat and lowered the spoon. "Ah—weird dream last night. You were in it."

"Oh?"

"We were at the beach."

"Doesn't sound weird."

His answering laugh was dark.

"What happened here?" Temperance asked.

"Just missed it. Freezer-clearing party. Couldn't let these go to waste." He spooned out another curl of ice cream and held it out to her. When she shook her head, he brought it to his mouth and made most of it disappear with a hedonistic swirl of his tongue.

The taillights of the van disappeared down the hill. "Is that Maren and Nate?"

Duncan nodded. "Dad and Mal, too. They're taking the kids to Linden to see a movie tonight. Mostly for the air-conditioning, I think. You want to go? I can call them, tell them to turn around—"

Temperance laughed softly. "No, no." She perched on the edge of one of the cushioned wicker chairs and stared out over the lawn.

Duncan studied her for a moment, licking the last of the ice cream off his spoon. His mouth lifted in a smug little smile. "You're bored, aren't you?"

She groaned and collapsed theatrically into the chair behind her. "Oh my god, Duncan. I am so bored."

"Go put on some shoes. Let's go for a ride."

* * *

DUNCAN thumped a hand on the green hood of the Gator. Today, the dune flag that projected off the back had a little cartoon bee wearing a cowboy hat, and BEE-HAW printed underneath.

It was an open-topped and doorless utility vehicle, with two seats in the front and a small flatbed in the back. At any moment of the day, there was usually someone zipping around the Brady property on it.

Every flat outer surface of the Gator was covered in stickers. LOVE YOUR MOTHER with a graphic of a smiling earth. BABY ON BOARD and I'M ONLY SPEEDING BECAUSE I HAVE TO PEE. The Linden Community College leopard. Pride flags, racing flags, flags from a dozen different countries. Several versions of the GREETINGS FROM VESPER VALLEY sticker from the Vesper County tourism board. Vinyl logos of everything from Vans to Esso to LEGO.

Like the Gator was a horse-drawn curricle and she was an Austen heroine, Duncan took her hand and helped her into the little bucket-style passenger seat. He had to wedge his big frame into the driver's side and spread his legs wide around the steering wheel. His thigh settled alongside hers in the tight space.

The Gator rumbled to life. "What's with all the stickers?"

"There were a few already on the back when I bought it at the farm auction in Linden. A few old political campaign stickers, a few agricultural brand logos. One day last year, there was a new sticker on the hood. It said, TGIF: THIS GRANDPA IS FABULOUS. Over the next few weeks, more kept showing up. Stuck in different places."

Duncan glanced over at her and smiled. She smiled back.

"Anyway. Pretty sure Rowan started it. Then it just escalated. I think everyone does it now. Vineyard folks, my crew. I find a new one about once a week. I watched Mercy add the one of the rubber duck wearing sunglasses a few days ago," he said. "Even she's calling me Ducky now."

Temperance chuckled. "Where are you taking me?"

"I usually take a spin around at the end of the day to check in before everyone goes home. Hang on." Duncan pulled away from the house, extending a forearm across her body when the Gator lurched forward. Each knuckle at the base of his fingers was scraped, and his fingernails were freshly bitten since she'd seen him last night.

"Rowan told me about your little rivalry. She said she has to fight you to use this thing every day," Temperance said. "Why don't you just get a second Gator?"

"Eh, that's no fun." A brow lifted. "She ever tell you about the prank war she started?"

"No, but now I have to know."

"She left it parked in the vineyard one night last fall. I couldn't find it that morning when I needed to haul a bunch of stuff down from the equipment garage, so I gave her hell about it. When she brought it back later that morning, she'd left a rubber snake on the floor." He pointed down between his feet. "Nearly pissed myself."

"If you'd fussed at her, it's what you deserve."

"Probably." Duncan glanced over with a quick smile. "Things devolved from there. We'd go back and forth—a whoopee cushion under the seat. Raw trout under the hood. She put tasseled nipple pasties on the headlights once." He shook his head and sighed. "I can't win. It's like being in an ass-sniffing contest with a Doberman."

"Rowan definitely doesn't like to lose."

Despite keeping her entire lower body in a controlled clench that would've made her Pilates teacher proud, Temperance's sweat-slick thigh rocked lengthwise against Duncan's with every sway of the Gator. It growled down the hill to the west pasture barn, where Rowan's Katahdin sheep lived with their notoriously overprotective bodyguard—the donkey with an inexplicable dislike of Duncan. Asparagus.

As they pulled up and parked, the sheep crept like synchronized swimmers along the outer fence of the Chardonnay vineyard nearby. The donkey followed close behind, nibbling clover.

Temperance stayed in the parked Gator while Duncan chatted with the two men who'd finished the new metal roof on the barn. There were lots of nods, lots of laughter, and at least one "I'll be damned" from Duncan. As he left, his hip knocked into the tin bucket hung on a fence post. The Bradys didn't have a sheepdog, so Rowan had trained the flock to come when she rattled treats in the bucket every evening. A chorus of excited bleats went up in the distance, and the little flock rumbled toward them. The donkey trotted close behind.

"Ah, shit," Duncan muttered. He did an about-face and disappeared into the barn.

Temperance hopped out of the Gator and hustled to the open double doorway of the barn as the sheep arrived, nudging around her legs to get to Duncan. She put herself bodily in the donkey's way, splaying her arms wide and making what she hoped was a threatening hissing noise in the animal's face.

"No," she shouted when the donkey tried to push past her.

Asparagus stopped and flicked her ears forward and back, then blew a bored breath out of her big nostrils. It was warm, smelling of grass and grain.

Over her shoulder, she warned, "Duncan. Your friend is here."

Then he was behind her, his body warm against her back. He settled his hands on her shoulders, and she dropped her arms. Against her ear, he whispered, "Don't move. She smells fear."

A few tense seconds passed. Asparagus swished her tail and took a slow step closer, and Temperance planted her feet wider. Duncan's hands slid down to her elbows, holding her gently against him.

The donkey raised her head and let out a squeaky vibrato *heeee* right in Temperance's face.

Duncan laughed.

Temperance made an annoyed sound. She tugged her arms free and whirled on him.

Still laughing, Duncan gave her a quick pat on the ass and moved out from behind her. Asparagus made little wheeze-whistle sounds of donkey joy as he took her blocky head in his hands. "Were you"—he looked back at Temperance over his shoulder—"*protecting* me?"

"You're a jerk." She shoved him in the arm.

His laughter faded. "I'm sorry. You were so ferocious. I've never seen anything more terrifying." He rubbed the donkey's cheeks and pressed his forehead between her eyes, and she made a contented snuffling sound. "Asparagus and I are buddies now. Must have been the beard she hated."

Temperance crossed her arms over her chest. "So what happens when it grows back all the way?"

"Maybe I won't let it." Duncan turned away from the donkey and rubbed the dark shadow on his jaw.

"I thought you had reasons"—she used her fingers to curl air quotes around *reasons*—"for the beard?"

His attention dipped to her neck. "I've got reasons to leave it off, too."

*   *   *

THEY were waved down several times on their way to their next stop, by people wanting to chat with Duncan before they left for the day. Each person he encountered was genuinely pleased to see him, and everyone got at least a few minutes of his full attention. One of the guys from his maintenance crew planned to propose to his girlfriend tomorrow, and Duncan asked about her by name. He even checked in with one of the vineyard workers about her dog—a mastiff named Gravy who struggled with seasonal allergies. By the way the young woman's eyes and posture softened—and by the way she gnawed the inside of her lip when she glanced at Temperance—she had a devastating crush on Duncan Brady.

Temperance couldn't blame her.

Their next stop was south, down the hill to the bank barn.

A crew from a landscaping contractor in Linden was on day two of laying pavers for the firepit patio adjacent to the winery's tasting room. An electrician was there, too, plotting placement for two electric vehicle charging stations in the parking area. Temperance remained with the Gator while Duncan jogged over to socialize and get a recap of the day.

Finally, they went north to a pasture of gently rolling hills. The far side of the field looked like a lumberyard now, with massive wooden beams, planks, and boards arranged on the ground in parallel stacks next to the post-and-beam skeleton of the former barn.

Duncan barely had time to cut the power to the Gator before five people converged on him. Handshakes were passed, then he stood with his hands on his hips, listening intently while the others spoke and pointed to the lumber stacks. An elderly man in denim overalls and an ancient Eagles ball cap said something while he gestured to where Temperance sat. She raised her hand to wave, and Duncan turned. He gave her a long look, then said something that made the other man give him a few hearty thumps on his back, laughing.

He made his way back to her ten minutes later, haloed by the disappearing sun. She'd always loved the way he walked. Loose-limbed and confident, but without the pretense of a swagger. The moment felt very Mr. Darcy striding across the moors.

The shape of his shoulders was a bit more bent now, and the sleeves of his button-down were rolled up to his biceps. He wore fatigue like an extra layer of clothing. She recognized that quiet vulnerability, the invisible load he carried. They were both people-pleasers, driven by a genuine desire to *do* for others. Her own need to please had externalized as academic ambition so she could fit the

Talbot-Madigan family paradigm. She'd always assumed Duncan had chosen to stay in the valley to work for his family, with no personal ambition at all.

Until today, she'd had no idea how wrong she'd really been.

This man was hardworking, but for the right reasons. Assertive but compassionate, and resilient without being hard. Imaginative and funny and gentle and—

He could be mine.

The thought was so abrupt and intrusive, her chest and neck flushed with heat. She pinched and lifted the front of her tank top to fluff air against her chest.

Duncan breathed out a rumbly sigh as he sat down in the driver's seat. He sat there for a moment with his hands on the steering wheel. "Sounds like most of the wood here is American chestnut and white oak."

"Is that good?"

"Yeah. Real good." He rubbed the back of his hand across his forehead, looking a bit dazed. "Like—five-figures-of-profit good."

"Whoa. How?"

"Lumber like that doesn't exist anymore. Some of those big beams were from trees that would have been hundreds of years old when they were harvested, even back in the early 1900s. Valuable."

"What did the man in the Eagles hat say to you?"

Duncan knuckled his jaw. "That's Hugo. He's got a timber-testing lab in Chapel Ford."

"He said something that made you turn around to look at me."

"He said—" Duncan hesitated. He had a far-off look in his eyes when he breathed out a laugh and shook his head. "Ah, hell, Teacup."

"Tell me." She laughed.

"He said that maybe with all that money, I'll be able to afford an actual car to drive my wife around, instead of a shit-kicking old John Deere." Duncan looked her right in the eyes. "I told him I'd have to ask you to marry me again first."

"Ah." Temperance pressed her lips between her teeth and

straightened in the seat. She clenched her knees together in the little footwell in front of her.

Duncan shrugged and gave her an amused smile. "You asked." He hit the gas.

She braced a hand against the dashboard as the Gator pitched forward.

In a span of forty-five minutes, Duncan had interacted with nearly thirty people. They all received a hearty handshake, a squeeze on the shoulder, and the full force of his incandescent smile. He knew everyone by name, what they'd worked on that day, what they needed from him, and who they'd go home to that evening. He brought his entire self to each interaction, and left people better than they were before. He gave all of himself away, every day.

Then he got up the next morning and did it all over again.

"You still feel okay?" he asked.

"Yeah. Just hot."

The sun dipped behind the tree line to the west, and the world dimmed.

"You want in on a secret before it gets fully dark?"

"Always. It's getting late, though—"

"I have time for this," he said, quickly. "I mean, if you do."

Temperance's belly thumped. "Okay."

He drove them to the equipment garage at the top of the hill, on the opposite side of the property from the greenhouse. It was a sprawling four-bay building with red-paneled siding. When the Bradys first bought the property, Duncan had lived in the second-floor apartment above it for a while, but now the family used the entire loft as an office space.

Duncan gave her a wide-beam flashlight and kept a smaller one for himself. They entered from a side door, into a bay that seemed to have served as a dumping ground for orphaned household items from the previous owners. Temperance waited in the doorway while Duncan unlatched and manually opened the huge garage doors to let in the remains of natural daylight.

She lifted the lid of the cardboard storage box closest to her and shone the beam of her flashlight inside. It was full of plates and saucers with a vintage floral pattern around the edges. Her heart ached a little. She imagined this very dishware at a fully set table, and the family around it. Sharing each other's company. She imagined the person who had carefully packed this box. Surely they wouldn't have intended for it to have been forgotten in this dark old space.

"Ma means to go through all the boxes in here, someday. You could help."

"Maybe." She gave him a small smile and traced a fingertip through the dust on a box marked CHRISTMAS in faded red ink. Why would a family leave all this behind?

The back half of the bay was tidy and more open, and there was something big beneath old beige drop cloths. A foot or so taller than Duncan's six foot three, and half again as wide. The covering billowed gently as he pulled it down.

Temperance gasped. She approached and whispered, *"Duncan."*

"This is the only place on the whole property Rowan never goes. I had to scream and pretend I saw a spider to chase Harry out of here a few weeks ago when he snooped around for a watering can."

It was a wooden arbor. A lattice of grapevine canes embellished the inner corners where the vertical beam at the top met the horizontal ones at the sides. No hardware was visible—each piece notched into its adjacent pieces with such precision it might have grown out of the ground exactly as it was. The craftsmanship was remarkable.

She stepped beneath it, reaching up to run a finger along the underside. "You made this."

"Yeah." He looked down and toed an old tennis ball.

"For the wedding," she said.

"Something new from something old, you know? It's reclaimed wood from the barn we just came from. I took it when they first started demolition a few weeks ago. Those grapevine canes are the ones we used to decorate the greenhouse for Harry's proposal."

"Duncan. This is *art*."

He could be mine.

The tennis ball rolled to her, and she nudged it back toward him. "You said it was a secret?"

"They don't know about it." Duncan recaptured the little ball under his foot. "Ah—they didn't *ask* for it, either. I hope they like it."

Temperance's heart squeezed. "I think when you know someone well enough, you can usually predict how a surprise will land."

"No idea how we'll get it into the vineyard the morning of the wedding without them noticing, though."

"You'll figure it out."

"Usually do."

Temperance smiled, and they shared a long look.

"It'll still be hot in the house," Duncan said. "Let's make one more stop."

CHAPTER TWENTY-THREE

Temperance

There were no lights from outbuildings or porches, and the last of the brake lights from the contractors' vehicles disappeared out of Cloud Tide. Temperance let herself be lulled by the rugged purr of the Gator's engine as they drove down the hill. Fireflies were out in force, hovering and flashing all around them. It felt like driving through a star field.

A tall hedge surrounded the pool, dense enough that it seemed to contain the muted blue shine of the solar lamps beneath the water. Even though the sun was gone, the air was still syrupy, heavy with the scents of chlorine and the poet's jasmine that meandered up the south side of the little pool house.

Temperance kicked off her sandals and sat at the edge of the pool. She submerged her legs from the knees down. The painted concrete was warm through the thin cotton of her shorts.

Duncan went to the outdoor closet for one final project. Using his teeth to aim his small flashlight, he tightened screws on the strike plate in the doorjamb, then opened and closed the door a few times to test the fix. He made a satisfied little sound in his throat when he finished.

"You can't stop, can you?" Temperance said.

"That's been on my to-do list for weeks, but I haven't been able to prioritize it." He linked his fingers behind his head and stretched, canting his hips forward and boosting high on his toes. He grimaced and rolled his shoulders. "I was here, so I did it."

Temperance scooped water up onto her legs. "I could have held the light for you."

"Nah." He pulled the hem of his shirt free from his pants and unbuttoned it. "Still feel okay?"

"Tired, that's all."

"No more googly eyes?"

"None today, at least."

Duncan toed off his oxfords and lifted his white undershirt over his head in the same smooth motion. Then he undid the buckle of his belt and flicked open the top button of his pants.

"Oh, no—don't even think about taking those off," Temperance warned.

His hands hesitated over his fly. For a moment, he studied her, then without taking his eyes off hers, he began to empty his pockets onto the little glass table beside the wicker cabana. His phone and a small pocketknife came out of one. From the other, a large pocketknife, a handful of coins, his plastic baggie first-aid kit, and—inexplicably—a twenty-sided gaming die. From the rear, he withdrew his wallet. Then he yanked the belt free of its loops and laid it on top of everything.

He pulled off his socks, and in three strides, he was lowering himself into the pool.

With his pants still on.

Bands of muscle in his neck pulled tight. "*Jeeeesus elder millennial Christ*, it's cold." He sucked a breath through clamped teeth.

"What the hell is wrong with you?" Temperance laughed.

"You told me not to take off the pants. I'm a good listener."

He swam up beside where she sat and propped his forearms on the edge of the pool. An owl's haunting call came down from one of the nearby trees. A few moments later, another answered.

She skimmed a fingertip across the back of his left hand. "This one's new. What happened?"

He lifted his hand to look more closely at the half-healed scrape. "Pulled a board out of a stack of lumber I should've put away better. This one's Past Duncan's fault. I fucking hate that guy sometimes."

"Hmm. You should be kinder to him."

Duncan grunted and rested his chin on his forearm. "He's caused me a hell of a lot of problems."

"Seems unfair to hold him accountable when he can't be here to defend himself, though."

"I'm still the same guy, Temperance."

"Are you, though?"

Duncan drifted away from the wall and floated in front of her. He stayed close enough she could feel the little zone of ambient heat his body created in the water. "All right. Enough stalling." He swiped water from his jaw with the back of his wrist and nudged his chin toward her. "Get in."

"You're funny." With a pointed foot, she pushed against his collarbone.

His hand closed around her ankle, middle finger meeting thumb. He swung wet hair out of his eyes and quirked a brow. "Funny." His expression was anything but. "Is that what I am?"

With her free foot, she pushed against his shoulder. She might as well have pushed a stone wall.

Duncan snagged that ankle, too. A wide callus at the base of his fingers was coarse against her skin. A droplet of water glimmered on his bottom lip. He blew it away.

God.

Temperance had to lean back and brace herself on her hands to stay upright. Duncan's attention diverted downward with a single flick of his lashes. Her nipples stiffened beneath the thin cotton tank.

"I want you in." He tugged gently at her ankles.

An old memory flooded in, urgent and oversaturated. Maren and Nate's basement. Duncan hunched over her on a couch too small for him to fit on, one big leg planted firmly on the floor for leverage. Their laughter when he propelled the couch into the side table and knocked over the lamp. Her, clamped against his body, as if *she* could somehow be the one inside *him.*

She swallowed hard. "We don't have towels."

Another tug. Her butt slipped against the painted concrete. It brought her alarmingly close to the edge. He squeezed her ankles tighter, and his playful rumble of mock frustration vibrated through his hands. "It's so goddamned hot, we'll be dry before we even get back to the house."

His pants were a dark blur beneath the water. The absurdity of it was too much. "You have absolutely lost your mind."

"I think you're absolutely right." He moved fast. He slid his hands up her calves, along the backs of her thighs. Water sloshed over the rim of the pool as he surged toward her, lifting her with two hands cupping her ass. She screech-laughed, pushing away with her knees against his chest. His laughter joined hers, and the night went silent around them.

"Wait!" she screamed. "Wait, wait."

Duncan's eyes narrowed.

"I have, ah—a very expensive lingerie habit. Okay?"

All the levity disappeared. He lowered her back to the concrete.

"You've already ruined one of my bras." She nipped the inside of her bottom lip, considering. "I'll get in, but you have to stay over there." She pointed to the far end of the pool. "With your back turned."

Duncan released her and floated backward. His eyes stayed on hers.

"Turn around," she said.

He disappeared beneath the water and surfaced a few seconds later at the far end. Temperance stripped quickly, leaving her clothes in a warm little pile next to the pool. The water was chilly enough to steal her breath.

"Talk to me," Duncan said after a while. He was so low in the water, his voice echoed around the inner edge of the pool.

"About what?"

"Anything. I like your voice."

"Hmm." Temperance floated on her back. "I talked to Coleman today. Someone paid for us to use the community room at Linden CC for the clinic for the next few months. Bought us some time."

"Ah. That's great." Lightly, he added, "They mention who it was?"

"No, but we hadn't told the public about the clinic's closure until the Honey Moon. Whoever it was worked fast."

An airplane passed overhead, its intermittent lights tiny but unmistakable in the night sky. A long time ago, on a summer night like this, Temperance and Duncan had stargazed from his truck bed, and they'd seen a plane cross the sky. *"There's people up there,"* she'd mused, and it had struck them both as so absurdly funny they'd both laughed until they cried.

Temperance drifted for a while, reveling in the coolness of the water against her back, the heavy warmth of the summer air on her belly and breasts.

He'd been right to bring them here. She'd needed this.

When she looked over again, Duncan still faced away from her. He was submerged all the way to his chin, a dark shape in the water.

Temperance lowered her toes to the concrete bottom. "I can't believe how many things you handle every day, Duncan."

"Nah. I just like to under-promise and over-deliver. Makes me look good."

"Not true. You do too much."

A soft laugh. "Christ, woman. I could say the same about you."

"I guess—when you're already overwhelmed, it's easy to just pile on one more thing, you know? Adding one more plate on the stack probably won't bring the whole thing down. What's one more, when you're already spinning twenty?"

"Ever think about *why* you do it, though?" Duncan said.

Temperance tipped her head in the water to smooth back her hair. "It's just—who I am."

"Is it, though?"

Her laugh was dry. "Okay, since you know so much about me, *you* tell me why I do it."

"I just think—if pushing ourselves like we do was going to work, by now it would have."

She'd drifted close enough to him now that she could extend a leg and touch his back with her toes if she wanted to. "What do you mean, *going to work*? Work on what?"

"You're smart, Teacup. You'll figure it out." He squeezed water back from his hair. His tone shifted a shade darker. "I want to see your face."

Temperance bobbed there for a moment with her arms wrapped around her middle. Her braid arced out around her. "Turn around, then."

He did. Once he faced her, he was motionless. She couldn't even tell if he was breathing.

She let herself float toward him. He cupped her elbows to pull her close. Her knees bobbed gently against his thighs.

Their hands moved in unison—hers to settle where his neck met his shoulders, his to lightly support her waist. Her legs floated forward, instinctively bending to wrap around his middle. His thumbs passed over the soft skin of her hip bones, once, twice, before reaching around to cup the cheeks of her ass in both hands.

Temperance rested her forehead against his. Between her thighs, the ridges of his ribs stopped their rise and fall. He *was* holding his breath.

A swell of water rocked their bodies in a rhythm that was so much like slow, dreamy sex, she had to consciously resist echoing the sway of it with her hips. The space between them became a tiny echo chamber, magnifying the sounds of their breath and the *drip, drip, drip* of water from their hair.

She ran her thumb across his Adam's apple. Watched his nipples tighten. Dark brows snapped together, and his fingertips dug into the soft spot where the lower curve of her ass met her inner thigh.

Duncan caught a droplet of water on his lip with the edge of his tongue, then dragged his bottom lip through his teeth, leaving it dark and wet in the low light. "Everyone's coming home tomorrow."

"Yeah."

"This will change again, won't it?" he said. "We'll go back to being assholes to each other."

"I don't know."

His rib cage jerked hard between her thighs.

Hiccup.

Temperance let her nose graze the ridge of his cheekbone when she tilted her head to meet his eyes. Her heart stuttered in her chest. "I thought you said you didn't get hiccups anymore when you're nervous?"

"I'm not nervous."

"Cold?"

"No."

"Worked up?"

Underlit by the pool's eerie glow, Duncan's eyes turned quicksilver. "Slide your body down and find out."

The tiny hairs at her nape rose in response to his words. An aggressive trail of goosebumps shot down her arms. She let her knees fall away from him and drifted backward like an untethered canoe.

He didn't pursue. "You promised me a conversation, Temperance. About the night of the festival. What happened in the truck."

I'm trying to bend here, he'd said the morning after in the vineyard. *But you're not doing enough reaching.*

Temperance swallowed hard. Hesitated. "There's this— inevitability to a storm. The power of it. The weather always wins. It frees you from even trying to fight it. All I could think about was how badly I wanted to be out there in it. The enormity of it. The wildness. Something's broken in me, Duncan. But I shouldn't pull others into that. I'm sorry if I scared you. I never want to hurt anyone."

A vein throbbed visibly in his neck. "Is that why you come to me sometimes? Because it feels dangerous?"

"Maybe. In those first few years after we broke up."

His lashes clumped around haunted eyes and cast spiky shadows. "What about now?"

The quiet ache in his expression brought her heartbeat into her throat. They'd arrived at the pivot point they'd been heading toward for the last week, but now that they were there, they circled it like a Maypole. Unable to move forward in a unified direction.

Vehicle headlights shone through the hedge. The other Bradys were home from the movies. Duncan hung his head and swore under his breath, and Temperance swam as fast as she could for her clothes.

* * *

THE electric service returned just before one o'clock in the morning.

Temperance sat in the window seat of the Primrose room in fresh pajamas, untangling long strands of hair with her fingers. A bright spot to the west caught her eye. Work lights were on down at the bank barn, and the Gator was parked out front. The huge sliding doors were open, and she could see all the way to the loft at the rear. Duncan was there. It was too far to make out features, but the way he moved was unmistakable. She knew the shape of him by heart.

He sliced open a cardboard shipping box half again as tall as he was and pulled out what looked like panels for Rowan and Harry's reception photo booth. Then he grabbed something from his tool bag and began to work.

"*I have time for this,*" he'd told her. That was two hours ago.

God, he had to be so tired.

Temperance didn't really know what a soul was. It couldn't be labeled on an anatomical chart, and a damaged one couldn't be treated by anything she'd learned in medical school. But she unequivocally believed in its existence, because the thing inside her that ached for Duncan Brady was bigger than her body could contain, and stronger than any logic her mind could throw at it.

She was in trouble.

CHAPTER TWENTY-FOUR

Duncan

Set back from the road on a quarter-mile lane bordered by feathery white pines, the Madigan home was a sprawling mid-century modern ranch built in the late 1950s. Deceptively modest from the front, it had a white brick façade and low-sloped roof, and an open courtyard with beautifully sculpted conifers and ornamental grasses. The true magnitude of the U-shaped house was obscured from view—the sides of the house plunged deep into the woods around it, with wall after wall of windows that provided an unobstructed view of nature.

Architecturally speaking, it was a gem.

Duncan hated it.

He parked his truck in the circular driveway next to Temperance's little car. Approaching the recessed entryway made him nauseous, like he was a fucking teenager again.

This was only the third time he'd been there, but he could have sketched the place from memory. The first time, he'd been fourteen years old, tagging along with Nate and Maren to pick up some of Maren's things. Corbin Madigan had answered the door that day, and when he'd slid the moving boxes onto the porch, he'd told them Laine wasn't feeling well, and she sent her regards. Maren had cried in the car on the way back to Westfall, and Nate drove the whole way with one hand on the steering wheel, the other on her leg.

The second time was the afternoon he tried to fix things with Temperance when she was home from college for the weekend.

He'd stood there for ten full minutes that day trying to churn up the nerve. Shame and anxiety had saturated him like sweat. But he'd knocked. And she'd told him to go to hell.

Duncan ignored the massive brass knocker shaped like a caduceus. He rang the doorbell instead.

When Temperance answered, she was surprised to see him, but she hid it well. "Whatever you're selling, we've already got one." She wore her contact lenses instead of her glasses, and her hair hung loose, silvery bright as noon in January. The ends drifted around her elbows as she leaned out the doorway to look past him. "Where's Rowan?"

Earlier that afternoon, Rowan had conscripted him to do today's pre-wedding flower pickup from a CSA in Linden. She'd asked Duncan to pick Temperance up, as if it was an afterthought. "*She knows her way around Linden*," Rowan had said. "*So does my GPS*," Duncan had muttered to himself on his way out the door.

"There was a misunderstanding," Duncan said.

"We were going to have Tiffany mimosas and turmeric facials at Terra today."

"Say that ten times fast."

Temperance rolled her eyes, but she laughed.

"Rowan assumed she could use my truck for the flower pickup after your turmeric mimosas, or whatever."

"I'm not seeing the problem."

"Nobody drives my truck, Teacup."

She looked smug. "I did."

"How did that work out for us?"

A dainty lift of her shoulder. "Fair."

Quieter, Duncan said, "You're also not nobody."

A tiny line appeared between her brows. "She could have driven her car, though."

"Do you have any idea how many flowers will be at this wedding? Imagine a practical number of flowers for a wedding, then abandon all reason and restraint, and you might come close. We might have to make two trips, even with my truck."

Temperance stepped back from the door to let him in. "I need to put some shoes on." As she walked away, her bare feet made fleeting impressions on the gleaming teak floors. In a white sundress that hit the back of her knees, she looked like a lonesome little ghost.

Immediately inside the foyer were several totes and cardboard boxes of her things. The air was still and sterile.

"I assumed your parents would sell this place when they moved to New York."

"They'll never sell this place." Her voice echoed from deeper in the house. "I don't think the stipulations of my dad's family trust would allow it even if they wanted to."

There were large photos on the walls in brushed metal frames. It was strange, though. Each one featured Laine and Corbin at different ages—together, more often than not—but there were none of Temperance or Maren. The closest thing to a baby photo of either one of them was one of Laine Talbot-Madigan, her very pregnant belly poking out of a white lab coat as she held a stethoscope to the chest of a blurred figure in the photo's foreground.

Who the hell framed photos of themselves at work to display in their home?

Duncan passed the kitchen. The materials and finishes there alone were likely worth more than the house where he'd grown up in Westfall. Countertops and a cooktop island of high-end black marble. White marble underfoot. It was bleak and unimaginative, nothing like the warm and bustling kitchen his parents kept. A bottle of hand soap sat by the sink with a black towel—the only sign that anyone existed there at all.

In the main living room, the vaulted ceiling followed the clean geometry of the roofline, tapering toward the walls into flat soffits with recessed lighting. Floor-to-ceiling glass covered the entire south-facing wall, and all of the other walls were crowned with broad clerestory windows that allowed ever-shifting beams of sun to flood the space through the surrounding woods outside.

A huge skylight was strategically positioned to accentuate the statement fireplace—a low, sprawly fixture of whitewashed brick, flanked by built-in bookshelves and luxurious banquette seating. All the other furniture in the room was covered in pale dustcloths, but Duncan had no doubt all of it was expensive. And probably white.

He had a vivid memory of staying home sick in fourth grade. Ma had made him a mug of vegetable soup to eat—the kind from a can, of course, one of the only ways he'd eat veggies at that age—while he'd watched *The Price Is Right* from a nest of blankets on the couch. He'd spilled a generous splash of it on the beige carpet when he reached for his SunnyD on the side table. Rather than fussing at him, Ma had cleaned it up, reminded him to be more careful, and asked if he wanted her to heat up another can. A shadow of that stain had remained on the carpet until they replaced it with new Berber a decade later.

Duncan couldn't imagine Temperance being allowed to eat vegetable soup in this room. Hell, he couldn't even imagine her being allowed to be ill.

The bones of this place made it an architectural dream. But it was the equivalent of art rendered with AI. Objectively gorgeous, entirely soulless.

There was something eerie about it, too, but he hadn't been able to pin it down until he passed the bank of sleek electronics in the recessed entertainment center. Not a single one had a glowing LED standby light or time display. No lamps or ceiling fixtures were lit, there were no ticking clocks. It was a space in total stasis.

"All right. Let's get going," Temperance said behind him.

Duncan jumped and whirled around. "Jesus."

Temperance frowned, then smirked. "What?"

"This house is a fucking museum." He side-eyed a painting of a woman in a white shirt. It was faceless, featureless—but it seemed to stare straight into his soul. "Why don't you just come stay with us while you look for a new place?"

She made a dubious noise in her throat and moved past him, gathering her hair over her shoulder to braid it. The cool floral sweetness of her shampoo lingered behind her.

Duncan followed her to the front door, where she armed the security system from a panel on the wall.

"Are you even allowed to have lights on when you stay here?"

"I try to keep a low profile. I left a used tea bag in the sink a few years ago and got a strongly worded email from Ms. Eccleston about 'drawing vermin.'"

"Who is Ms. Eccleston?"

"Housekeeper, gardener. Security guard. She keeps the property ready for whenever my mom and dad are in the area. The only time they ever leave New York anymore is for their annual gala, though. And they always stay in Philly that weekend, anyway."

Outside, he jogged ahead to beat her to the passenger's-side door of his truck. He was surprised when she let him open it for her. "You, ah—ever go to that? The gala?"

She grabbed the handle above the window to boost up into the seat. "Why would I spend a thousand dollars on a ticket to go disappoint them in a fancy dress and uncomfortable shoes? I get to do that every day for free."

*　*　*

THE CSA Rowan had sourced her wedding flowers from was a mile or so outside the Linden town limits, so they stopped there first. It took Duncan and Temperance an hour to load all the live potted perennials into the truck. By the time they finished, the bed was packed corner to corner, a pointillist canvas of color.

Even though they arrived at Fortuna's in Linden just before they closed, the whole block still smelled like hot sugar and dough. Fortuna's had been a Linden staple for decades, famed for their biscotti and pistachio cannoli. They also had their own take on fortune cookies, with a message printed on the bottom of the paper liners of their cupcakes.

The glass front door to the bakery was propped open, and Duncan's head nudged the little bell that hung above it when he followed Temperance through.

Two women turned away from the checkout counter and headed for the door as they entered.

Millie.

And her mother, Nina.

Millie carried a stack of boxes so tall her eyes barely peeped over the top. Nina looked more tired than when Duncan had seen her a few weeks ago, but when she saw him, her narrow shoulders straightened, and her eyes lit with fondness. Her expression turned to confusion when she looked past him to see Temperance.

"Duncan, hey!" Millie bent her knees to slide the boxes onto a table. She put her hands on his forearms and gave him a sweet kiss on the cheek.

"Hey, Mills," he said. "Hi, Mrs. Bristow."

"Hello, honey," Nina said. Again, her eyes flicked to Temperance.

The next few moments were a choreography of subtle glances. Nina assessed Temperance from head to toe, while Millie cut her eyes from her mother to Duncan. Duncan's attention skipped from Nina to Millie to Temperance, and Temperance glanced at Millie before looking to Nina.

Then, all three women looked at *him*.

"Ah—Mrs. Bristow, this is Temperance Madigan," Duncan began. "My, uh—"

What the hell did he say?

Temperance stepped forward with a warm smile and reached out to shake Nina's hand. "I'm a friend of the Brady family. We're here to pick up wedding cupcakes—my best friend is marrying Duncan's brother tomorrow."

"I'll be there!" Millie clasped her hands together and rocked on her heels. "I hope the rain holds off."

"Me, too," said Temperance. If she was rattled, it didn't show.

Then, a few beats of silence. Behind the counter, the swinging door to the kitchen squeaked rhythmically as the baker disappeared to the back.

Millie turned to her mother. "Mama, Temperance's sister, Maren, is married to Nathan, one of the twins. So they're practically family."

"That's the one." Duncan snapped his fingers.

Nina Bristow's eyes were kind. "Such a nice family."

"Maren is the sweetest," Millie went on. "Loaned me a pair of jeans and some wool socks last winter after I—"

Duncan coughed into his hand.

Millie pressed her lips together for a moment, then smiled. She lifted the boxes again. To Temperance, she said, "Brioche buns. For the barbecue truck. We need to run."

"Yum," Temperance said.

Millie said, "I'll see you tomorrow, Duncan."

Once they were gone, Temperance said, "She's really cute."

Duncan grunted and followed her to the bakery counter.

A small young woman with deep brown skin and short curls dyed bronze came out from the kitchen again, wiping her hands on a towel. "Hey, what can I do for you?" Her name tag said AUDRA.

"Hi," Temperance said, "we're here to pick up wedding cupcakes. Last name is Brady."

"Sure thing. Back in a sec."

The baker returned with three huge boxes in her arms. She carefully slid them onto the counter and lifted the lids for inspection. The miniature cupcakes inside were all nestled in their own cardboard pocket, decorated with realistic-looking wildflowers made from piped frosting. Each flower was airbrushed and shaded with food coloring. Rowan would ascend into orbit when she saw them.

When neither Duncan nor Temperance spoke, the baker leaned forward and said, "Are they okay?" with a little notch of concern on her forehead.

Temperance looked up. "Oh. Oh, yes. They're stunning."

"Perfect," Duncan said.

The baker said, "Y'all make a really beautiful couple. You must be so excited."

"Oh, he's—" Temperance began.

Duncan chuckled and leaned into her. "Oh yes, we're *so* excited, aren't we, Mrs. B?"

Temperance pressed a hand flat against Duncan's arm and gave the baker a patient smile. "He's joking. These aren't for us."

"I'm so sorry. Y'all had the look." Audra pushed a clear plastic clamshell across the counter. Inside were two cupcakes with butter-cream frosting. "For you two. On the house."

Duncan withdrew a fifty-dollar bill from his wallet. He insisted on paying for them, but the baker said, "No need. We donate everything we have left at the end of the day to the Lillian Center in Chapel Ford. They actually prefer it when we send fewer sweets."

After Audra thanked them and returned to the kitchen, he tucked the fifty into the tip jar instead.

"Wow, big spender," Temperance teased.

Duncan cracked open the clamshell container and handed her a cupcake. He peeled back the wrapper on his and ate most of it in one bite. "That was all I had on me."

"She said they were free, though."

He chuckled. "Yep, but so is the guilt."

Temperance unwrapped her cupcake entirely, gently pinched off the bottom half, and stuck it upside down on the frosting, like a sandwich. When she took a bite, not a crumb was lost, and her lips remained frosting-free.

Duncan licked a glob of buttercream from his upper lip. "That's genius."

"I know," she mumbled around her mouthful. She took a final dainty bite, tipping a stray crumb into her mouth with the edge of her pinkie. When she read the fortune printed in the wrapper, she paled and paused mid-chew.

Duncan frowned. "You okay?"

"Mm-hmm."

He looked down and read his own fortune. He huffed a quiet laugh and folded it into a little square. "I'll tell you mine if you tell me yours."

"Mine—" Her eyes darted to the side, then back to him. "It's blank."

"Really? That seems ominous."

"We should get going. The flowers in the truck—um, it's hot—" She crumpled the paper liner between her fingers and pushed it into the trash, but she was so focused on getting out the door she didn't notice when the bin's swinging panel kicked it back out onto the floor. By the time Duncan crouched to pick it up, she was on the sidewalk outside. Her dress billowed around her legs as she headed for the truck.

He unfolded the crumpled liner and read it. He shook his head, stuffed it in his pocket with his own fortune, and picked up the boxes of cupcakes to follow her out.

* * *

WARM summer air buffeted them both through open windows. Waves of Duncan's hair lifted and tossed in unison with the whipping tendrils of Temperance's.

He hadn't been on this road in years. The deer were dangerous at dusk. Almost as dangerous as the memories.

The truck dipped down a small hill before the road became a flat stretch of weathered asphalt bracketed by tall forest on either side. Late-afternoon sunshine flooded the cab like sun tea in a Mason jar.

"Millie's mom," Temperance said after a while. "She's sick, isn't she?"

Duncan hesitated before he replied. "Why do you ask?"

"I already know the answer, Duncan. I saw her medical alert bracelet when I shook her hand." She clamped the tip of her thumbnail in her teeth. "Addison's disease?"

"Yeah."

"Is she in treatment?"

"It's early, but yes. She's stable." Duncan glanced across the seat, then back to the road. "Millie, ah—takes really good care of her."

"I can tell."

"She's a really good person."

"I can tell," Temperance said again.

In the distance, an ancient sign poked out from the otherwise unrelieved expanse of woodland. THE BOONIES, it read in classic 1960s script, with a massive arcing arrow pointing into the trees.

On weekend nights during the drive-in's prime, cars would line up for admission on the gravel shoulder as far as one could see, lighting up the trees with an eerie red glow.

They drove past the entrance. The huge marquee that had once announced the upcoming shows now read WE ARE GIVING UP in crooked track lettering. The former owners had tried in vain to keep the place alive with fundraisers and special weeknight events, and back then, the marquee had read WE AREN'T GIVING UP. Time had completely changed the meaning of the phrase by dropping just a few tiles.

Before he could overthink it, Duncan hit the brakes in the middle of the road, hooked his arm over the seat back, and put the truck in reverse.

"What the hell are you doing?" Temperance sat up straighter in her seat.

"We've got some unfinished business."

A high metal gate with flaking red paint spanned the drive-in entrance, harnessed together with an ancient chain and padlock. Duncan pulled the truck around it, following a path of rutted tire tracks made by more than a decade of trespassers.

When he'd been here last, the trees were copper and red, and in a sky as dull gray as soapstone, thousands of starlings had moved overhead like a cloud of ash. Crows as big as stray cats had picked through muddy popcorn buckets and candy wrappers faded by months of summer heat.

Now, sunbeams shot through the trees, illuminating a thick haze of dust kicked up by wheels grinding gravel. In the distance, between a circular thicket of Pennsylvania hardwoods, a ghostly white screen loomed behind row after row of skeletal pole speakers.

Duncan aimed the truck for the back left corner. The spot farthest from the squat cinder block concessions building, farthest from the screen. Speaker 492.

Their spot.

He shoved the gearshift into park and killed the engine. After the rumble along the rural road, the silence inside the cab made his ears feel stuffed with cotton.

Duncan got out of the truck and moved around the front. When Temperance didn't get out, he opened her door and simply said, "Please," with an outstretched hand.

He was surprised when she took it.

The evening woods were wild around them, a solid wall of noise. Nostalgia was potent. Duncan could almost smell the popcorn and the cotton candy. Hot tires, cut grass, and the scent of faded Little Trees air fresheners through all the open windows. Someone would be smoking a Swisher Sweets cigarillo, and someone would be smoking weed, and some asshole would inevitably leave their car running for too long before killing the engine, filling the air with exhaust fumes.

Temperance approached the speaker pole like it was a casket at a funeral. She touched a finger to the letters etched into the metal casing: TJ + D 4E.

How naive. How bold, to be only eighteen and engrave "forever" into something as eternal as metal.

"Second chances are for when you weren't ready for the first," Duncan said behind her.

She whirled on him.

"It wasn't blank. Mine said the same thing."

Her face paled. "They make them in batches, they probably all say the same thing—"

The wrappers rained crumbs when he held them up for her to see. "What about this phrase feels threatening to you?"

"We have to be civil. The wedding—"

He laughed through clamped teeth and rubbed the bridge of his nose. "Cut the shit, Temperance. We're not friends. We are never going to be friends." He tucked the cupcake wrappers back into his pocket.

"We have to try."

"If we could, don't you think we'd have done it already?"

"Rowan and Harry don't deserve to be caught up in our mess right now—"

Duncan pinched his fingers to his thumbs and thrust both hands in front of her face, like he was trying to conjure clarity for her out of thin air. "They're *playing* us."

"What?"

"Tell me again what Rowan said to you. Do you remember?"

"Something about peace, for the wedding." She shrugged. "And that it would—"

"—mean a lot to Harry?" he finished for her.

She narrowed her eyes. "Yes."

"Harry gave me the same line. Said it would mean a lot to Rowan."

"That doesn't mean anything—"

His patience started to fray. "Oh. Really? How about how Harry put us together to decorate the greenhouse for his proposal? How Rowan stuck us together to clean up the vineyard after the storm? Harry being a literal doctor and being mostly MIA while you were stuck in bed? Sending us on these fucking errands together? Rowan told me to bring you today because you"—he curled his fingers in air quotes—"knew your way around Linden."

Temperance rolled her eyes. "So does your GPS."

Duncan threw his hands up. "*Thank* you."

Fireflies flickered in the high grass like sparks from some phantom fire. Temperance twisted the end of her braid around her fingers. She wouldn't look at him.

"How long have you known?" she said.

"A while. A month, maybe."

"So you let me go"—she paused—"for a month"—another angry pause—"thinking we were trying to be friends. But it was a fucking *game* to you?"

"I'm sorry," he shot back, "but what part of *literally anything* that's happened between us in the last few weeks has given you the impression that I want to be your friend?"

"What's your angle, Duncan? Did you think you were winning at your own game, pretending we could be friends, then you found *yourself* having feelings again?"

"It's cute that you think I ever stopped."

"Don't."

"Part of me wanted to find out if we could do it. You said it would be easier, and I wanted to believe it." Duncan took a step toward her. "I thought—if you really believed it, it would help me believe it, too."

She blazed up at him like a little ember.

Softer, he said, "I miss you."

Temperance crossed her arms. "How can you miss me? You don't even know me anymore."

His laugh was bleak. "*Know* you? I've never had a chance to *not* know you, Temperance. You are *everywhere* for me. Everything." He shook his head, swept his arms wide. "All the time."

"Don't."

"Don't what? Tell you how I feel? I will never get over you. I've spent the past fourteen years under you."

Temperance got loud. "*You're* the one who ended things."

Duncan buried his fingers in the front of his hair. "I tried to come back and fix it—"

"I knew about Millie by then, Duncan." Her chin trembled.

He groaned. "She was a friend back then, and she's a friend now."

"So you've never slept with her."

Duncan hesitated. He sheared off a hangnail with his teeth, welcoming the sting. "I didn't say that. But it was months, *months* after—"

"Samara Mooney, Eden Liang, Florence Holley, all the others over the years? Were they your *friends*, too?"

His eyes went wide. "Are you slut-shaming me? I know you're not that small-minded—"

"Duncan, I don't care if your body count is in the hundreds. The point is that you've spent the last fourteen years disappearing into other people to feel whole."

Now he was pissed off. "You've always seemed to be fine with it when you're the one unzipping my pants," he snapped.

"*Excuse* me?"

"You've been breaking off pieces of me for years. Using them to fill up the empty spaces inside you."

Temperance spun away. She pressed the heels of her palms to her temples. "Oh, my god—is that what this has been about?" She whirled on him again. "You've always been able to say no."

Duncan's voice rose. "I don't *want* to say no to you."

"Then that's on you for not using your words."

"Don't use your pediatrician voice on me, Temperance."

"So everyone's either a throwaway hookup or propped up on a pedestal? Is that how it works?" She got in his face. "The funny thing about pedestals is that the people we elevate never deserve to be there. I put my parents on a pedestal for the first half of my life, Duncan. I know what it looks like."

Temperance was as mad as he'd ever seen her. Her eyes blazed like a gas flame, and her lips were tucked tight against her teeth. She hadn't run yet, though. That was something.

Quietly, Duncan said, "I love you, Temperance. I'm tired of pretending I don't."

Her breath caught, and her chin wobbled again, but her jaw clenched tight. "No. That's not fair." She shoved past him and stalked back to the truck.

"There's something I need you to know—"

"We're done, Duncan. I'm not doing this here."

He shouted after her, "Whatever is happening between us—I'm calling it. I won't be your drop-in fuckbuddy, then go back to not speaking to you for months at a time."

She got to the truck and yanked the passenger's-side door open, turning to face him again before she climbed inside. "An ultimatum? Really?"

"No. It's a boundary. I'm using my words, Dr. Madigan. Not my problem if they aren't the ones you want to hear."

CHAPTER TWENTY-FIVE

Temperance

Temperance found Rowan in the greenhouse on the morning of her summer solstice wedding day, stinking of sulfur and covered with enough dirt to pot up a peony.

"I can't believe you're doing this today," Temperance said.

"Have to. I'll be busy over the next few days." Rowan looked up from a tray of chives, eyes sparkling.

She was near the back, at a table covered corner to corner in flats of herb seedlings. Parsley, basil, fennel, dill, a few others Temperance didn't recognize—all at different stages of growth, from just poking out of the soil to fully leafed. Temperance had known Rowan for a decade, but she'd learned more about plants from her in the past year than the entire time she'd known her. Nowadays, she rarely passed a plant without touching its leaves to feel the texture or experience the scent of the foliage. Rowan was eternally pinching leaves and sniffing them. She was the only person Temperance knew who could get away with relentlessly inviting people to smell her fingers.

There were more flats of cilantro than any other herb. Temperance ran her hand over the lacy leaves as she roamed past, releasing their citrusy floral odor. "Why's there so much cilantro?"

"Gia loves it. She makes pesto from it. And cilantro tea! Can you imagine?" She aimed a gentle stream of water into a tray beneath basil seedlings and waved a gloved hand at the expanse of green beside her. "Everything on these tables is cut-and-come-again, but cilantro can be fussy. Harvest too much at one time and it won't grow back very well. Also does terrible in the heat. So I grow a lot, as a buffer."

"Rumor has it, Wegmans always has fresh cilantro available," Temperance teased. "You could just skip all this, and Gia could—"

"Not on my watch," said Rowan.

Temperance laughed and moved in beside her.

Rowan looked up. The panes of glass overhead reflected in her unusual amber eyes, and her expression was exquisitely unburdened. Fairy lights were still strung along the ceiling just as they had been when Temperance and Duncan hung them in May. When Harry and Duncan had tried to take them down a few days after the proposal, Rowan chased them out of the greenhouse with a broom handle.

Cut the shit, Temperance.

We're not friends.

We are never going to be friends.

In that moment, Temperance felt no regrets for the tension with Duncan over the past few weeks. The love she had for Rowan McKinnon and Harry Brady was obviously different than what she felt for Duncan, but it was of equal magnitude and importance.

"You ready for today, honey?" Temperance said.

"In those early days, after everyone found out we were together, I didn't recognize the person I'd become. Happy, protected. Nourished. I *liked* that new Rowan when I looked in the mirror, but it kind of felt like I was wearing someone else's life." She ran her fingers through lacy stems of lemon thyme. "Now, it's the old me that's unrecognizable. I wish everyone could have this, T.J."

Temperance squeezed Rowan's filthy hand. Outside, Will buzzed past on the Gator. Someone had mounted the flag from the Honey Moon 5K on the back. Rowan's smiling face and ROWAN KEEP GOIN' bounced and twitched in the wind on a long flexible rod.

They looked at each other and laughed.

For a while, they worked together in silence. Rowan showed Temperance where to snip early flower buds from oregano and basil, then she began shaping woodier rosemary and lavender in terra-cotta pots. The air bloomed with the holographic green scent of herbs.

"I need to ask you something, and I need you to tell me the truth," Temperance said. "Not that you would ever lie, but I don't even want you to try to tie a pretty bow on your answers, okay?"

"Yes," Rowan said without looking up from the rosemary.

Temperance blinked. "I haven't even asked the question yet."

"I already know what you're going to ask me, and the answer is yes."

"How could you possibly know?"

"I'm good at romance now, remember?" Rowan tapped her temple with a dirt-dusted finger.

Temperance laughed and looked down to pick at a loose thread on the hem of her running shorts. She felt Rowan watching her.

"Remember after Harry left last year, and you said people in medicine don't want to wait on forever?" Rowan said. "The impermanence of life, or something like that?"

Temperance cringed. She met her friend's gaze. "Sounds vaguely familiar."

Rowan had an eerily perceptive look in her eyes. "Was that a boatload of bullshit from the captain of the USS *No Bullshit*?"

"You and Harry don't really want Duncan and I to be friends."

"Do you and Duncan *want* to be friends?" Rowan said.

"You know the answer to that."

"So do you, T.J. Your chemistry with Duncan is not platonic. It's cosmic."

"He told me he loved me yesterday."

"That monster," Rowan deadpanned.

Temperance laughed. "God, you're smug. You giving me relationship advice was never something I'd have imagined on my bingo card for this year."

"Listen, you and Frankie had a Cheesesteak Friday bet about Harry and I." Rowan glanced up with an indulgent smile. "We're even now."

Temperance chuckled. "So what's payback for Frankie going to be?"

Rowan pinched her lips between her teeth. "Hm. That one's still marinating."

"Oh my god, wait—was Frankie in on this, too?"

Rowan's cheeks pinkened. "Let's just say—she didn't have as many photo shoots as she said she did while you were bedridden a few weeks ago."

Temperance pinched her lips together. "Risky, though. Don't you think?"

"You take a risk every time you light a fire, T.J. The important thing is knowing how it's going to burn."

Behind them, the greenhouse door creaked on its hinges as it opened. It was Harry, looking fresh and handsome in lightweight khaki shorts and a pale pink polo. "Am I interrupting?"

Rowan virtually levitated to get to him. Temperance turned to give them a moment, but she could still see their reflection in the glass. Rowan's arms stayed loose at her sides so she didn't get soil on him, while Harry had her face cupped in his hands, kissing her with back-arching thoroughness.

"Hi there, Dr. Brady," Rowan purred.

"Well hello, Dr. Brady," said Harry.

"Not for another eight hours."

Harry murmured something inaudible, and Rowan giggled. She honest-to-god *giggled*.

"I'm still here," Temperance sang.

Harry laughed. "Hey, T.J. You can turn around."

"Are you two still clothed?" Temperance teased. "Do you have anything for me to decorate today, Harry? Maybe some errands that need running?"

Harry looked to Rowan, and Rowan laughed. "She knows," she said.

Temperance looked up at the fairy lights. "Harrison Brady, did you seriously leverage your own marriage proposal as an opportunity to meddle in other people's love lives?"

Rowan chuckled. "I'm sorry, have you *met* him?"

"I had enough data to figure it was worth the risk," Harry said.

"What if it doesn't work out, though?"

Harry and Rowan looked at each other. They both raised their eyebrows in mirrored miniature shrugs.

"Never occurred to us that it wouldn't," said Harry.

"I wish I had the same kind of faith," Temperance said.

"Well." Harry lifted a dried leaf out of Rowan's curls. "The great thing about faith is that there aren't any prerequisites. You can just . . . decide to have it." They stared at each other for so long, Temperance legitimately thought they'd forgotten she was there.

Rowan was the first to snap out of it. "Shoo, you." She swept her hand in front of her face. "Unless this is the way you want to marry me tonight. I have so much to get done."

Harry touched a fingertip to the streak of dirt on her cheekbone. "I'd marry you every way." He headed for the door. With his hand on the jamb, he turned and leaned into the open doorway. "Oh, T.J.?" He grinned. "You're welcome."

"Wow," Temperance said once he was gone. "He's seriously insufferable."

"I know." Rowan crinkled her nose, beaming. She grabbed a broom and began to sweep the floor. "Isn't he the best?"

"I almost asked if you two wanted me to give you a few minutes alone."

Rowan hummed a quiet little sound. She pinched her lips together and moved away, brushing some potting soil off a table into her hand. She let it rain down into a bin by the door. Her ears were crimson.

"Rowan," Temperance breathed. "You and Harry did it in *here*?"

Her cheeks and neck blotched with red. "Well, '*did it*' implies—ah, a singular instance." She picked up a broom. "The first time was a turning point for us. He was so angry with me, T.J. He'd been holding back an entire side of himself."

Temperance frowned. "He didn't—hurt you, did he?"

"Oh my god, no, no. He just—*unleashed* all of his frustration. It was—" She paused with a faraway look in her eyes. "It was really, really hot."

"Okay, okay." Temperance laughed. "I don't need specifics."

"The point is—when Harry let me see his mess, it made it easier for me to show him mine. Real love can be messy, T.J. Anyone who says otherwise is either doing it wrong, or they just haven't gotten down to the bones of it yet." In one hand, Rowan picked up a tiny plastic pot filled with fluffy black soil. In the other was a little round seed. She tucked it down into the dirt and smiled softly. "In the dark is where the growth begins."

* * *

SINCE Rowan had moved into the carriage house with Harry in the fall, the gardener's cottage next to the greenhouse had served as the break room for Cloud Tide's vineyard crew, air-conditioned in the summer and heated in the winter. Several times a week, Will Brady would drop off a plate or two of his bed-and-breakfast menu experiments, and everyone could leave anonymous feedback in a wooden box with a slot cut in the top. He had some of the more complimentary notes pinned on a corkboard in the butler's pantry at the house. It was one of the sweetest things Temperance had ever seen.

Today, the gardener's cottage was repurposed as Rowan's bridal suite.

The ceremony was due to begin in about an hour, and Temperance was tasked with keeping Rowan out of the tiny bedroom at the back of the cottage. The big picture window there would give a clear view of where Duncan and his brothers were setting up the arbor he'd built.

With rollers in her hair the size of soda cans, Maren sat on the bed, painting Mercy's nails a pearlescent pink.

Temperance's phone suddenly blasted the *Halloween* theme. It almost vibrated off the edge of the table. She pointed at her sister with the wand from her mascara. "Maren, is this your fault? Were you thinking about them?"

Maren laughed, then grimaced at the clamoring phone. "Not this time. Promise."

Mercy looked at them like they'd lost their minds.

"Our parents seem to call every time Maren mentions them. It's witchcraft," Temperance explained.

With her free hand, Mercy lobbed her phone to Maren on the bed. "Do Tom Hiddleston for me."

Temperance snorted.

"What is it with them now?" Maren said.

"I still haven't answered them about the DORA pediatrics program. Last time, I got the 'This is your chance to do more with your career than gen peds' line."

"Gross," Maren said. "That's as bad as 'We didn't spend six figures of Capewell-Talbot money so you could be a housewife and a stay-at-home mom.'"

"Listen." Temperance swept a thin layer of mascara on. "If they'd actually parented either of us, they'd know what a hard job it is. And you're incredible at it."

Mercy blew on her nails. "Your talent isn't a currency for them to spend, ladies."

"*Thank* you," Temperance and Maren said in unison.

Frankie slid into the room and quickly closed the door behind her. She went straight to the window and pulled back a sheer curtain to peek outside. Heavy clouds scrolled across the sky, temporarily blocking the sun.

"How's Rowan?" Temperance said.

"She's a goddess." Frankie's attention was still out the window. "Nary a speck of dirt under her fingernails. Astonishing, really."

"Sweet Jesus, Frankie," Mercy said. "What is that smell?"

"You smell it?" Frankie wafted her hand in front of her face. "Good, good. It's my insurance policy for tonight."

Temperance looked over her shoulder. "She ate most of a bulb of roasted garlic at lunch."

Maren made a face. "Are we expecting, ah, vampires on the guest list?"

"She kissed Mal earlier this month at the Honey Moon," Temperance said.

"Pardon?" said Mercy.

"I *knew* he was a vampire." Maren twisted the lid onto the nail polish.

"It was a hate-kiss," Frankie muttered.

"You're on the path to the dark side now. Hate-kissing leads to hate-sex," Maren said. "I don't make the rules."

Distracted, Frankie dropped the curtain and murmured, "I'll make sure to stock up on cranberry juice."

"The science on that is limited at best, Frances," Temperance said.

Arden plowed into the room in an oversized flannel and a pair of cutoffs so short it looked like she wasn't wearing any at all. Creases from a bed pillow still marked her left cheek, and she smelled like fresh toothpaste. She had to turn sideways to squeeze past where Frankie had set up to braid Temperance's hair.

"Oh my god, it's like a clown car in here," Arden said.

Everyone went silent.

After an awkward beat, Arden looked from Mercy to Maren to Frankie to Temperance. "Oh, please. If I had a dime for every time I overheard people talking about my brothers, I wouldn't be using loans to pay for college. Malcolm definitely needs a Frankie-shaped wake-up call, and *you*"—she pointed at Temperance and swirled her finger in the air—"you don't hide anything nearly as well as you think you do. Honestly, the way you and Ducky have always avoided each other is far more telling than anything you actually say or do."

Arden blithely stripped to her underthings in the center of the room, then wiggled into her dress for the wedding.

Mercy broke the silence with a bubbly laugh. "Thank *god* someone finally said it."

Frankie met Temperance's eyes in the mirror, and something inside her broke loose.

"We're in it again." Temperance closed her eyes. "It's like I'm looking into a clear lake, and I'm confident I know the depth, but after I dive in, the bottom isn't where I thought it was. So I sink. And sink, and sink. Then when I start to drown, I realize it wasn't a lake at all. It's an ocean, and I've already fallen so far in that I'm never getting out again, because it's so much bigger than me. Indifferent to my smallness. And I belong to it now, sinking forever until I'm just—" She swallowed hard and opened her eyes. "Bones."

"Holy shit," Maren said.

Arden said, "Is Duncan the ocean, or—?"

"I think it's a metaphor for love," Mercy said.

"Deep," said Frankie.

"Yeah," Temperance said. "So's my salty ocean of feelings."

"Do you want to know what I think?" Arden pulled a brush through her hair. When Temperance nodded, she said, "I think, when someone makes you feel those big feelings, that's your heart telling your brain to let them."

The door cracked open, and Gia poked her head through. Her eyes were dewy. "She's ready."

* * *

ROWAN stood in the little living room of the cottage, limned by gauzy evening sunshine through the windows. She wore a simple cream off-the-shoulder dress with flowy sleeves and a floor-skimming hem. Her burnished curls were crowned with a garland made of braided grapevine and wildflowers.

She was the most radiant bride Temperance had ever seen.

As the women filed out of the cottage for photos before the ceremony, Gia's ring snagged on the back of Temperance's dress. They hung back to untangle it.

"We'll catch up," Gia told the others.

Gia sat on the little painted yellow bench on the cottage porch while Temperance faced away. As far as she could see, the sloping lawns and vineyards of Cloud Tide were an embroidered tapestry of greens and yellows and reds.

"I expected you to marry one of my boys before a stranger did, you know," Gia said.

The muted music of a small string quartet came from the direction of the vineyard, accompanied by a chorus of familiar voices. Duncan's big, full-throated laugh resonated over the rest. Longing laid a heavy hand around Temperance's throat.

She deflected. "You didn't let Rowan stay a stranger for very long, Gia."

The sun emerged from behind the intermittent clouds, and for a moment, a mist too delicate to be called rain drifted over them. Like standing too close to an ocean breaker.

Gia hummed a curious sound. In Gallego, she quietly said, "O lobo está a casar co raposo."

"Hm?"

"It's a sun-shower. In Galicia, we say that the wolf is marrying the fox. My mother said it was always the most unexpected pairings that created the most beautiful unions. Salt and sugar. Sun and rain. Wolf and fox."

The story encapsulated everything Temperance loved about Gia Brady. Earnest and lovely and a little bit weird.

A cloud dimmed the sun again, and the mist was gone as quickly as it had come. Temperance hoped the rain held off long enough for the ceremony.

Over her shoulder, she said, "So who is the wolf, and who is the fox today?"

"I wasn't talking about Harry and Rowan, love." Gia stood and smoothed her hand over the lace of Temperance's dress. "All fine, now."

Temperance knotted her fingers together and turned. "Thank you," she murmured.

"My son—" Gia began, nodding in the direction of the laughter. "He defines his self-worth by his readiness to help people. How much of himself he can give away without disappearing entirely." Gia didn't specify which son she referred to. But she didn't need to.

She took one of Temperance's hands in her own. "And you, darling. You only feel worthy if you can be brave. To handle everything alone."

Temperance captured her bottom lip in her teeth to stop it from trembling.

"You two can't be those people all the time," Gia said. "When you can't be brave, be ready. But when you can't be ready, be brave."

Duncan's laughter came again, and for a few seconds, Temperance couldn't breathe. She steadied herself with two fingers against the back of the little porch bench.

"Did I ever tell you about my ring?" Gia held out her hand. The ring was dainty and old, with two clasping hands carved into the gold.

Notably, there were no rough surfaces or stones that could have possibly gotten caught on her dress to necessitate them staying behind. Gianna Brady was a wily one. Temperance swallowed and shook her head.

Gia looked fondly at her finger and twisted the ring off. The fit was a little snug over her knuckle. "William and I had been married for a few years before we could afford to get a ring. Victorian, the antiques jeweler told us. Found sewn into the sleeve of a wedding dress that had belonged to a woman's great-great-aunt, discovered over a century after she'd died. But the woman had never married." Gia handed the ring to Temperance. "See the engraving, though?"

It was smoothed by age, but still legible. Temperance turned it toward the sun and read it aloud. *"I will find you."* She met Gia's eyes and returned the ring. "They must not have found each other. That's so sad."

"I like to imagine that William and I gave a second chance to the love that this ring originally symbolized."

Gia slipped it back on, caressing the underside with her thumb.

"So you believe the story, Gia?" Temperance asked. "Have you ever had the ring dated?"

"We never bothered. An appraisal would have cost us money we didn't have." Gia gave her a tender smile. "Believing is free."

CHAPTER TWENTY-SIX

Duncan

Duncan didn't have many opinions about weddings, but there was one thing he was sure of: planning one outdoors was risky business. Especially in a year where storms had piggybacked through the valley with record frequency. Low-lying areas around Cloud Tide were still saturated from the previous weeks' rainfall, and the mosquitoes had been hell.

Thunder rumbled on the horizon, and the sky had grown dim enough that crickets sang in the grass around them. Beneath cottony white, the clouds were dusky and gravid with rain.

A few dozen mismatched wooden chairs sat in a semicircle at the edge of the vineyard. Trellis posts in either direction were draped in oblong wreaths of enormous creamy white chrysanthemums, and the perennials Duncan and Temperance had retrieved from Linden now sat everywhere in flower pots of ceramic and terra-cotta. Mercy and Maren had been gathering the pots from secondhand stores around the valley for the last few weeks.

Harry and his attendants lingered around the back side of the greenhouse, waiting for Rowan's attendants to finish with the photographer outside the gardener's cottage next door. Harry wore charcoal pants and a lighter gray houndstooth vest over a cream button-down, sleeves rolled to his elbows. A few sprigs of rosemary and lavender were tied together with twine and pinned to his vest's left lapel. And despite a wave of stoic tears after a conversation with Dad and another when he first saw the arbor Duncan had built, he was calm. A hell of a lot calmer than Duncan would have been in his shoes.

Duncan cuffed him affectionately on the arm. "You look damned good. For once, you're more handsome than me, and I'm not even mad about it."

The groomsmen wore chocolate-brown chinos and similar cream button-downs, sans vests. Duncan stretched his shoulders and popped his knuckles. His shirt was a bit too small, and the fabric whiskered outward around the buttons closest to the center of his chest.

At least he didn't have to wear a fucking bow tie.

The clouds temporarily cleared to reveal a hyacinth-blue sky. Beside Duncan, Mal leaned on his cane with a scowl and a long-suffering sigh. Charlie had decorated his cane with stick-on gemstones earlier in the day—"*To make it resplendent,*" she'd said in her serious little voice. The plastic jewels caught the sun, painting a rainbow of shifting, sparkling colors whenever Mal moved.

"Cheer up, buttercup," Duncan said to him. "You look resplendent."

Mal growled and held up a middle finger.

Movement and chatter erupted from around the opposite side of the greenhouse as Rowan's bridal party finished with the photographer. Arden was the first to appear. She skipped ahead of the rest of the crowd, wearing a dove-gray vintage lace dress, waving her small wildflower bouquet above her head.

Frankie and Maren and Mercy followed, each in a different vintage gown in shades of yellow and gold, holding small bouquets of wildflowers. Arden plowed into Harry with a hug that made him waver on his feet. "Your wife is back there, Harry. I hope you have tissues."

Harry pushed his hands into his pockets and swallowed hard. "My wife." Tears glittered in his eyes.

"Ah, Christ, Arden. Don't get him started again," Nate said.

"Poor dude's going to need electrolytes by nine P.M.," said Patrick.

Duncan laughed. Arden fixed him with a calculating look. She narrowed her eyes and pointed at his chest with her bouquet. "You are *especially* unprepared, Ducky."

"Fucking hell." Duncan sighed and cupped his hand around his forehead. "Not you, too."

As soon as the words were out of his mouth, Temperance appeared around the corner of the greenhouse.

He held his breath, but she stole it anyway.

Sunlight reflected from the glass panes of the greenhouse, setting pale fire to every elegant centimeter of her. She wore a buttery-yellow sheath dress with cap sleeves and a low square neckline, and her hair was in a thick side braid that curved long and loose over her shoulder. In her hands, she carried a small bouquet of creamy yellow wildflowers.

She was a sunbeam come to life.

She kept her attention downward as she approached, tiptoeing a bit on the still-soft earth. When she looked up, her gaze collided with Duncan's and held, and her bottom lip dropped into a tiny little *oh*.

Duncan widened his stance and curled his toes in his wingtips to keep from being tugged bodily into her orbit. He clasped his hands in front of his waist and fought the urge to crack his knuckles or push his fingers through his hair.

Arden took her place at the front of the lineup to prepare for the processional. Mercy and Maren kissed their husbands, and Frankie sidled up next to Mal, slipping her arm through his. Mal made a rumbly noise in the back of his throat, stabbing at the ground with his cane in his free hand. Frankie responded with an incandescent grin.

Temperance stood beside Duncan, and he lifted her arm by the wrist to link it through his for the walk down the aisle. It flopped like a cold noodle, so he squished it between his ribs and his forearm to keep it in place. He leaned closer and murmured, "Hey, bestie. Here we are again, at a wedding."

"Please don't," she whispered, keeping her eyes forward.

"Just making polite conversation."

Temperance squared her shoulders. "I know what you're doing." She had a white-knuckle grip on the little bouquet of flowers, and there was a visible flutter at the base of her neck when she swallowed.

Duncan lowered his mouth to her temple. "I know you're going to come to me tonight, Temperance. Maybe we should just plan it this time." The sun passed behind a bank of clouds, and for a moment, the world dimmed. The breeze was warm and warned of rain.

Temperance leaned forward and tapped Mal on the shoulder.

Mal turned and gave her such an imperious look down his nose, it was comical.

"Let's trade," Temperance said to him.

"I am *not*—" One of Mal's eyebrows lifted in synchrony with an upward curl of his lip. He looked to Duncan. "—walking down the aisle with *him*."

Frankie hooted a delighted laugh.

"Oh, for god's sake." Temperance bristled like a little pine cone. "You know what I mean."

Frankie turned then, without releasing her grip on Mal's arm. He grunted and planted his cane again for balance. "You two work this out." Her eyes danced between Duncan and Temperance. "Goth Rainbow Dash here is walking down the aisle with me. I'm his emotional support extrovert. Bride's orders."

Mal expelled a loud, long breath through his nose.

"Harry," Temperance leaned out and whispered loudly down the lineup. When Harry turned, she said, "Let me walk down the aisle with you."

"That's not how this works," Frankie hissed. "You can't walk down the aisle with the *groom*."

"What the hell is that smell?" Duncan said.

Bewildered, Harry said, "Huh?"

Maren and Mercy gave them all a hearty *shush*.

The violin trio began playing the processional music—an upbeat instrumental rendition of "You Are the Sunshine of My Life" by Stevie Wonder. In front of them, Frankie subtly swayed her ass.

"Stop moving." Mal's cane cast a shimmery rainbow in an arc around him.

"Can't help it. You're a human disco ball," Frankie said.

"You're a human wrecking ball," said Mal.

"Oh my *god*, you two." Temperance groaned.

Arden started the procession, and Harry followed. The rest of the wedding party proceeded slowly behind them, and Duncan and Temperance brought up the rear.

"Looks like you're stuck with me," Duncan said.

Temperance inhaled through her nose and blew it out through pursed lips, long and slow. The exhale smelled like peppermint and cream and the indescribable essence of *her*, and Duncan wondered in that moment if he'd actually ever get to kiss her again in this lifetime.

They disengaged to take their places on opposite sides of Harry. A ripple of thunder sounded in the distance. Clouds scudded in, heavy with the promise of rain. They blocked the sun at the same moment the string quartet eased into a gentle rendition of "Here Comes the Sun" by the Beatles. When Rowan rounded the corner of the greenhouse escorted by Ma and Dad, she brought her own kind of light with her.

Harry wavered on his feet when he saw her. Duncan pressed a hand lightly against his brother's back to anchor him, and Harry let out a shuddery breath and stood taller. Midway down the aisle, Rowan glanced from the arbor to Duncan, her eyes glossy with tears. *Thank you,* she mouthed, and Duncan inclined his head with a gentle nod.

Ma and Dad each gave her a hug when they reached the end of the aisle, then quickly sat down.

With little regard for patience or restraint in the name of tradition, Harry and Rowan both laughed out loud once they were face-to-face. He wrapped his arms around her waist and lifted her off the ground, kissing her without hesitation. The audience erupted in applause and laughter, and Colby Everett did a few looping trills of his loud two-finger whistle. The officiant—an extraordinarily tall friend of Rowan's named Aida—playfully waved the end of a colorful scarf at them and said it wasn't time for that yet. She welcomed everyone with a brief speech about how the union between two people was the cultivation of a new future. How real love itself was a force of nature as discernible as a storm or the tides.

Again, Harry and Rowan kissed prematurely, and the audience laughed.

They said their vows.

"You are my nourishment . . ."

"My wildness, and my weakness . . ."

Duncan leaned sideways and caught a glimpse of Temperance. Her jaw was set, and she blinked fast to hold back tears.

"I can't believe you're mine," Duncan heard Harry say. "I can," Rowan answered.

As they slid rings onto each other's fingers, the storm arrived.

Clouds brought premature nightfall in an instant. The leaves on the grapevines flapped in the rising wind, and a few cold globs of rain dashed against Duncan's shoulders so hard it felt like they'd been hurled intentionally from the sky. The audience murmured and shifted in their chairs. Temperance looked a little unsteady on her feet.

Dad popped up from the front row and cupped his hands around his mouth: "Husband, wife. Married! Done. Everyone to the barn!"

A long rumble of thunder, then the sky let loose.

Chairs tipped and feet slipped in the grass. Silk scarves were caught by the wind, whipped skyward like colorful birds. Excited screams and nervous laughter were punctuated by booming thunder. Duncan glanced around for Millie. She was already sprinting barefoot toward the bank barn with the other guests, her high-heeled shoes dangling from her hands by their straps. Good.

Everyone had sachets of dried lavender to toss at the newlyweds after the ceremony, and the wind caught those, too, scattering leaves and tiny purple petals into the air like fragrant snow. Duncan spit a few pieces out of his mouth and hung back with Nate to make sure everyone was on the way to the barn.

"Go!" he called to Nate over the howling wind. The change in air pressure made his voice sound muffled inside his head. Nate took off to catch up with Maren and the kids, and Duncan scanned the retreating crowd for Temperance.

Nearly two decades of practice made him good at finding her fast. She ran like a gazelle, effortlessly loping across the lawn, but she suddenly swerved. There was something confused and unnatural about the way she moved.

Was he fucking dreaming again?

He glanced upward. No sky-ocean.

Temperance *fell*.

Duncan was by her side in moments. "Are you okay?" he shouted, extending a hand. A grass stain slashed across the front of her dress where her knee had hit the ground.

"I'm fine," she yelled back. The wind whipped her braid into her face, and she shoved it away. When she got to her feet, she slumped to the ground again after a single step.

Duncan put his hands under her arms and lifted her to her feet. "What the hell is going on?"

She jerked away from him and fell again, pressing her hand to her ear. Raindrops pummeled them in earnest now. Everyone else had reached the barn. Lightning blew like enormous flashbulbs. The storm was right on top of them.

"Hell with this." Duncan scooped Temperance into a bridal carry, and ran.

A crowd had gathered in the wide doorway of the bank barn, watching them approach. Duncan bent at the knees to set Temperance down beneath the roof's overhang. She took a few lurching steps, dropped her bouquet, and bent at the waist to throw up.

CHAPTER TWENTY-SEVEN

Temperance

*O*nce Temperance found her balance, Frankie ushered her to the back of the bank barn's event space. In the partially finished kitchen, Maren had had the forethought to set up a makeshift dressing room for any of the wedding party who needed to freshen up after the ceremony. She needed more than freshening up. She needed an entirely new identity. But this would do.

Rowan was already there, bent over and using a pair of scissors to hack off her muddy wedding dress at the knees. She'd already ditched the wildflower garland from her head and wound her curls into an unruly bun. "You okay, T.J?"

"Eh." Temperance slumped in a wooden chair and pressed her fingers to her temples. "I've been trying for hours to figure out how to make your wedding day about me. How'd I do?"

Frankie buzzed around her like a bumblebee. She slipped off Temperance's shoes and handed her a dry hand towel, then got to work on the grass stain on her dress. "At least it was only dry heaves. Could've been worse."

"Pressure change from the storm, you think?" Rowan stepped away from the scraps of her wedding dress. "Still the vertigo?"

"I think so. I'm fine now. Not sure about my pride, though."

Frankie dried and rebraided her hair into the same elaborate fishtail braid she'd done earlier, and a few minutes with a hair dryer restored Temperance's shoes and dress to wearable.

"I'm sorry it's raining on your wedding day, honey," said Temperance.

"No, no. This is good. Rain like this means I won't have to water anything the rest of the weekend. It's a relief, really. I have more important things to do over the next few days." Rowan wiggled perfect auburn brows.

"Rowan Brady." A loud giggle bubbled up. Temperance's eyes filled with happy tears. "You're *married*."

Rowan's eyes went wide. "Oh my god, I *am*."

The three friends stood in the middle of the kitchen in a little cluster, foreheads tipped together, each with an arm around another's waist. Beyond the thin wall, music thundered louder than the storm overhead.

"I love you both. So much," Rowan said. They all smiled and hummed happy sounds of agreement. After a beat, Rowan stood back and said, "But oh my *god*, Frankie—the *garlic*."

They howled with laughter.

"Ooh," Frankie said. "Who did this?" On the granite countertop island in the center of the kitchen was a bottle of Dom Pérignon on ice, vintage 2010. There were three champagne flutes, waiting.

"I assumed it was one of you," Rowan said.

"Rosebud, this is a five-hundred-dollar bottle of champagne." Frankie laughed.

"Wasn't me," Temperance said. "André bubbs are more my budget."

"Is there a note?"

"No. Nothing." Frankie shook her head and popped the cork. "We'll figure it out later." She poured the bubbly into two flutes.

Temperance put a hand on Frankie's arm as she poured the third. "Just a little for me."

"You sure you're okay, T.J.?" Frankie frowned.

"Yes, yes—I just don't want to get dizzy."

When Frankie handed the champagne to her, Rowan said, "Sometimes I think about fate. Like, what I'd be doing in any given moment if I hadn't gone with you to the Brady party that night, T.J. Or if I hadn't gone to the greenhouse to hide during that game of Team Tag. Or if I hadn't played at all. What would I be doing right now, in this exact moment, if I'd never met Harry?"

"Mm. I think the odds are good that whatever it is would've involved cheese popcorn, bottom-shelf Cabernet, and some seed catalogs," Temperance teased.

Frankie took a sip of her wine. "It's funny—everyone assumes fate is on our side. Maybe we spend our whole lives fighting against it."

"It's kind of terrifying how an entire life is decided in such tiny little moments," Rowan said. "Coincidences."

"I like to think of coincidences as convenient opportunities," Frankie said.

"Well." Temperance held out her flute between them. "What should we toast to?"

Frankie said, "To fate and coincidences, obviously."

Outside, thunder shuddered along the roof of the barn.

Rowan raised her glass. Her eyes glittered like the champagne. "And to joy. Even when it storms."

* * *

THE sliding barn doors stayed open during the reception. As night fell, the storm opened up further, streaming hard from a gunmetal-gray sky. Rain squalled against the roof and overflowed the gutters, and some of the chairs from the ceremony blew across the lawn like doll furniture. But the atmosphere inside the barn was lively and loud. A year ago, this kind of rain would have sent Harry into a spiraling panic attack, but tonight, he barely seemed to notice.

For Harry, Rowan brought the sun wherever she went.

He spent the cocktail hour of the reception mingling and asking, *"Has anyone seen my wife?"* and *"Have you met my wife? Let me introduce you to my wife,"* even when Rowan stood at arm's length, or the people he spoke to had, most certainly, already met his wife.

After the meal, Duncan stood at the end of the wedding party table for the first toast of the night. He'd rolled the sleeves of his cream button-down halfway up his forearms, making the vivid ink on his skin seem even brighter. A champagne glass balanced lightly between his thumb and first two fingers, absurdly dainty in his big hand. Before he began, the deejay approached with a small wireless microphone. Duncan laughed and waved her off.

Everyone went quiet, turning in their chairs to face him.

"Really appreciate everyone being here this evening. I'm Duncan Brady—"

A crack of thunder interrupted. Duncan slowly looked to the ceiling, and the crowd chuckled. "Wetter than an otter teat out there," he muttered, and the crowd laughed louder.

He already had everyone in his palm, and he'd barely started.

When everyone quieted, Duncan began again.

"Everyone has a person in their life who stands out." The warm bass resonance of his voice filled the high-ceilinged space in spite of the noise from the rain. "There's something about that person that makes them—bigger, somehow. Smarter. Wiser. More charming. More everything." He paused and looked around the room. "This person becomes the standard you aspire to. You think, if you can be even a *little* bit like them, you're doing something right." He looked down into his champagne glass for a moment, then raised his head with a rakish grin. "But that's enough about me."

The crowd roared. Harry's chest shook with a silent laugh, but the emotion was plain on his face. Duncan was about to wreck him, and he knew it.

He indulged the murmuring crowd a moment longer before he continued. "When Harry and I were kids, we spent hours barefoot in the yard. It was a solid carpet of dandelions out there, just yellow, everywhere. I was probably seven or eight, and I stepped on a bee. It stung the shi—" Duncan cut his eyes to Gia. "Ah, the *heck* out of my foot. Harry carried me into the house that day, and I cried for an hour afterward." He waited a beat. "Haven't ever cried since, obviously."

Another low laugh from everyone.

Temperance indulged in the excuse to openly watch him. He was made for this. Charisma and emotional intelligence radiated from him like heat from a flame. An understated lift of his eyebrow here, a gesture with his golden glass of champagne there. And he was beautiful in a way that went beyond the obvious. It was the way he brought his full authentic self to everything he said and did, and made others feel like they could do the same. It was in the way he carried himself, and the way he looked at a person and made them feel seen in their entirety.

Duncan Brady would always stand out in all the best ways, no matter where he was, or who he was with. He was barrel-proof whisky at afternoon tea. A hot-air balloon in a field of plain paper kites.

He could be mine.

All the blood rushed out of her head and into her belly.

"For weeks after that, I refused to go out to play, even *with* shoes on. One day, Harry dragged me out onto the porch, and our little yard was completely clear of dandelions. A stretch of green, bee-free grass. There was a bucket on Ma's rocking chair, full to the top with the yellow flower heads. Harry'd picked them all. Had to have been hundreds."

A sentimental "*Awww*" went up through the audience.

Harry looked ruefully at Rowan, who gave him a teasing smile and a contrived look of disappointment.

Duncan turned his attention to Rowan. "Red, I debated whether I should tell this story tonight. I know how much you love dandelions. But then I realized—there's a connection here. Harry picked those dandelions back then because he loved me. Nowadays, the reason this entire family leaves them to grow is because of you. We love them because *you* love them. We love *you*."

Rowan hid her face behind her hands for a moment, and Harry kissed her temple. He bent his head to murmur against her ear, and she lit up like a star.

Duncan raised his champagne and waited for the crowd to follow suit.

Once all glasses were lifted, he said, "To Harry and Rowan Brady."

The crowd echoed the same, and someone catcalled loudly from the back. Another trill of Colby Everett's whistle.

Duncan held his glass even higher. With a subtle downward tilt of his chin, his eyes found Temperance's . . . and held. "And to finding your perfect match."

The reception crowd exploded into applause and cheers and pounded fists against tables. Duncan kept his gaze locked on Temperance as he tossed his champagne back like a shot. Then he sat down and leaned back in his chair, crossing an ankle over the opposite knee.

How the hell was she supposed to follow that?

Her mouth went dry, and her fingertips numbed. She stood.

Her turn.

"Good evening, everyone. Does anyone have any champagne left in their glasses?" Temperance's laugh wavered as she scanned the crowd. Everyone chuckled. The people-pleaser in her wanted to apologize for not being half as charming and fun to look at as Duncan Brady. "I'm Temperance Madigan. I'm, ah, not a Brady, but—"

The deejay trotted over again with a microphone, and she gladly took it. She tapped on the top, and it made a crackly noise over the speakers.

"Let's try this again. I'm incredibly lucky to call Harry and Rowan two of my soulmate friends. I've known them and loved them separately for more than a decade, and now—wow. They're married." Temperance pushed her knuckles against her lips for a moment before she continued. She turned to them. "There's, um—this Japanese phrase. Koi no yokan. It doesn't have an exact English translation. It's a feeling you get when you first meet someone. An intuition."

At the edge of her vision, Duncan shifted in his seat. He lowered the leg he'd just crossed and sat forward with his elbows on his thighs.

"It's this awareness that, someday, you're going to fall in love with them."

When she looked down into her champagne, Duncan was motionless in the periphery of her vision. Still enough that it was a distraction. A single unmoving tree while the forest around it swayed in the wind.

Don't look.

"You two are the embodiment of it." Temperance looked back to the newlyweds and took a deep breath, trying to cling to her script. "Rowan, I think *you* denied it for a long time"—that drew a genuine laugh from the crowd—"but Harry, I'm pretty sure you felt koi no yokan the first night you met her."

Everyone tapped silverware against the sides of their glasses, and the barn filled with chaotic, joyful tinkling. Temperance paused to take a baby sip of her own champagne while Rowan and Harry shared a kiss. Over the edge of her flute, she looked to Duncan.

The way he watched her was so heated it should have raised a trail of fire across the wood surface of the table. His chest rose and fell unnaturally fast beneath his shirt, and above the open vee of his collar, his throat convulsed in a painful-looking swallow. The force of his gaze made her feel hot and hollow.

He wasn't simply staring at her. He was staring *into* her.

Goosebumps pulled her skin tight across her arms. She gripped the microphone in both hands like it was a gravity anchor. The crowd quieted, and an anticipatory hush fell again as everyone waited for her to continue. She looked back to the newlyweds. "I really love you both."

* * *

BEYOND the toasts, Rowan and Harry had decided to forego any other wedding reception traditions and treat the evening like a big party. Everyone loved it.

Except Temperance.

For her, it meant staring down an entire night of unstructured socialization in an intimately lit, overtly romantic atmosphere where Duncan Brady could—and *would*—materialize at any moment.

After the toasts, the deejay invited everyone to the dance floor, opening with a pulse-pounding EDM track. Temperance danced with Frankie and Harry and Rowan, losing herself in the music—and a single shot of Fireball. On the other side of the dance floor, Duncan and Millie truly were dazzling together. Striking and unrestrained, somehow more vivid than the people around them. Like an artist had outlined them in high-contrast ink. Temperance felt faded and itchy in her grass-stained vintage lace.

As the song wound down, they took a few selfies, and when Millie lowered the phone, Duncan met Temperance's eyes across the crowd. He bent to say something in Millie's ear, and a new song started to play.

"Just Like Heaven."

"Oh, crap," Temperance mumbled under her breath. Louder, she made excuses to Frankie and Rowan, planning to slip away from the dance floor unnoticed.

When she looked in the direction she'd last seen Duncan, he was gone. And she knew it all the way down to her bones—he was on his way to her.

* * *

TEMPERANCE fled the dance floor, mumbling "*pardon me*" and "*sorry*" and "*right behind you.*" At the quieter end of the bank barn, the ramp to the barrel room was blocked with a sawhorse and a sign in Duncan's handwriting that read NOPE. The rain was still a solid drone of noise on the barn's roof, so she couldn't go outside, either.

If anyone were to ask in that moment, she couldn't have explained how she *felt* Duncan bearing down on her in the darkness. She didn't even really know why she was trying to get away. It wasn't fear—it wasn't even anxiety. It was an impulse pumped through her bloodstream with every beat of her heart. All she needed was five minutes. Five minutes to breathe, five minutes to tighten the bolts in her armor. Five minutes to quit shaking like a fucking tambourine.

The photographer was shooting the dancing, so the photo booth Duncan had built in the loft was still dark. Temperance scurried along the rear wall, then hiked up her dress to take the stairs two at a time. She stopped midway to yank off her heels. A table sat along the wall beside the booth, covered in novelty hats and sequined masks and feather boas. She knocked an oversized rainbow Stetson to the floor when she threw back the curtain and ducked inside. Breathing deep in through her nose, she released it in a tight stream between pursed lips.

The occasional strobe of the deejay's colored lights from below were the only illumination inside the booth. A disc-shaped flash sat dark and still at the front corner, and the back wall of the booth was covered corner to corner and ceiling to floor in fresh flowers. They were insanely fragrant. Provocative, somehow.

Sitting in front of the wall was the Victorian sofa she'd overheard Gia talking to Rowan about a few weeks ago. Duncan had found it at an estate sale in Philadelphia, specifically for the photo booth. The upholstery was velvet—dusky pink or a deep apricot, she couldn't tell in the darkness—and despite its strangely asymmetrical back, it was absolutely gorgeous. One of the historical romance books Frankie had brought her had a near-identical one on the cover.

Temperance sat, cradling her face in her hands.

The air moved at the entrance to the booth, and Duncan was there. White light streaked over his face, then disappeared. The heavy curtain rippled closed behind him.

She'd barely had thirty seconds.

Temperance shot to her feet. Her heart dashed itself against her ribs, a wild bird in a bone cage. She opened her mouth to speak, but he beat her to it.

"White flag," he said. "Whatever game we're playing, I concede. I can't do this anymore. I'm fucking miserable."

The words sank so deep, they entered her bloodstream.

He took a hesitant step toward her. "Just give me anything. And I swear it, Temperance—I'll give you everything."

"Where's Millie?" she said. It sounded weak and silly, even to her own ears.

He closed his eyes and sighed. "She's getting ready to go home. As soon as there's a lull in the rain."

Temperance blinked. "Why?"

"She got what she needed." Duncan moved closer, close enough that he wouldn't have to shout over the music. The backs of her calves hit the velvet chaise. He loomed over her, his attention riveted on her mouth. "The Millie thing is sorted between us. I've already told you—" He cut off like he'd been choked. His nostrils flared. "Have you been drinking Fireball?"

The sweet-hot cinnamon of the liquor on her breath was powerful in the enclosed space, even though she'd done only one shot. "Yes. So?"

Duncan groaned and spun away. "God*damn it.*"

"Why?"

He swiped a hand over his short new beard. "I want to kiss you." The words were sharp. Like an accusation.

"Well, you don't have to look so *mad* about it," Temperance fired back.

Then he was kissing her, open-mouthed and consuming. Kissing her so hard her head rocked back, his body following her down as she bent like a bow. It turned filthy fast, hot and wet and hair-pulling, the force of it jamming lips against teeth.

Duncan Brady kissed with his entire self. His mouth was just the messenger.

Without disengaging his lips from hers, he reached low and dragged her dress up her thighs. He straightened to his full height and lifted her against him in the same motion. She followed his lead, locking her ankles behind his waist. With one hand cupped around the back of her neck, he pinned his other arm beneath her ass and clamped that hand on her thigh.

He was *handling* her.

Everything went black.

The music cut off, followed by a moment of unnatural silence.

Temperance drew back. She searched up, down, around for any source of light. Duncan's hot exhale drifted warm across her forehead, down the slope of her nose. They could've been in a submarine a thousand meters under the sea, or the lone passengers of a derelict ship floating through space.

Thunder boomed. Gasps and chatter spread through the crowd. The storm beat a relentless incantation against the roof.

Duncan's hand closed around her jaw. He turned her head toward him to align her face with his in the darkness. Against her mouth, he growled, "We're not done yet," and the force of his lips spread hers wide. His fingers pressed tight into her cheeks where he gripped her chin. Her hands thrust upward and fisted into his hair, knuckles and nails pressing hard against bone.

Darkness amplified all her other senses. The buttery fabric of his shirt was still damp from the rain, and thin enough that she could feel the texture of the hair on his chest beneath it. The taste of him was achingly familiar on the back of her tongue, warm and dark and savory.

She wanted him. Here.

Her finger was in the rip cord. All she had to do was pull.

"Duncan," she whispered, dragging the edges of her teeth over his bottom lip. "*Please* tell me you have a—"

"Front pocket. Left side."

He swung them around to swap their positions so he could sit on the chaise. By the time his ass hit the sofa with her astride his lap, Temperance had already found the condom and had his belt buckle free. His pants were more challenging. Tight, strained over the prominent ridge in his lap. The buttons were impossible to open in the darkness. She made a little sound of frustration against his mouth. Gently, he took her by the wrists to move her hands away. In seconds, he'd opened the buttons and rocked side to side with her still on his lap. Temperance rose to her knees to give him room to get his pants down. The velvet fabric of the chaise dragged against her knees.

She took his erection in both hands. He was soaked at the tip. She gathered some of that wetness with a swirl of her thumb and pumped loose-wristed strokes along the length of him. Choking out an obscenity, he thrusted instinctively against her palm, before snatching her hand away.

Duncan gasped *"Please"* like a prayer.

She slid on the condom with a smooth pinch and roll. Duncan clamped his big hands at the bend between her hips and thighs, running his thumbs down her pubic bone and into the side seams of her panties. He slid them up the slick center of her.

"Oh, Madigan," he breathed, "you're as ready for this as I am."

The storm raged on the roof like a living thing. Temperance felt pinned between two forces of nature—one celestial, one urgently, achingly human.

The pitch blackness was starting to fuck with her head. Seeking an anchor, Temperance traced the pads of her fingers across Duncan's face. His brows were drawn tight. A flicker of muscle at his temple. His mouth found the center of her palm, kissing, tasting with his tongue.

Reflexively, her fingers curled into his beard. A caress. She found the thundering pulse at his neck. A tempest.

"You sure?" she whispered against his lips.

He groaned. "Temperance, I've been sure for over half my life—"

She pressed her fingers against his mouth. "Are you sure right *now*, in *this* moment?"

Hot breath blew down her forearm. His lips moved against her fingers. "Yes, for fuck's sake—it's always going to be yes for you—"

"Then stop *talking*."

Duncan *bit* the pads of her fingertips.

The heat of his erection was tangible, straining upward between her spread legs. Just centimeters from the hot center of her. Duncan tugged the crotch of her panties aside—she was *sure* she felt a seam bust—and he closed that tiny distance with an upward thrust of his hips and a downward tug on hers. They both exhaled through open mouths—his to her chest, hers to the infinite black above them.

Her insides were in free fall.

Temperance rose up, tilting her pelvis forward until only the tip of him remained inside her.

"What are you—" he began, but when she sank down again, he cut off with an agonized exhale.

She did it again and again, withdrawing and resheathing him bit by delicious bit, churning her hips in a slow, coiling curve. Heat hung low in her belly, unbearable pressure and friction mounting. Palming the cheeks of her ass, Duncan pistoned his hips beneath her, echoing the tempo she set.

Abruptly, his thighs pulled taut beneath her. Fingertips dug into her hips, halting her in place. "Don't move." The words were a steamy shot of breath across her collarbone. "This is going to be over real quick if you don't slow down."

"That's the point." She rolled into him, sinuous and slow.

He cupped a hand around her throat, cuff-like and featherlight, using his thumb again to turn and tilt her chin to bring her mouth to his. Temperance was desperate to focus on the determined slip of his tongue against hers. The eager throb between her legs. But Duncan downshifted the kiss from electric to tender before she could brace for it. His hand went loose and gentle around her jaw, cradling her like something rare and beloved and terrifyingly temporary. A sound of breaking and burning rumbled forth from him, and the same lonesome thing inside her answered.

Impossible heaviness dropped between her legs and swirled up her belly. Her nipples tightened; her breath hitched. Temperance's whole body began to shudder, and she bared her teeth in the darkness, panting like she was possessed. Her toes curled, cramping the arches of her feet. She lifted from his lap to taper some of the friction, but Duncan gripped her by the waist and pulled her back down tight.

"Stay *here*," he said through his teeth, punctuating with a hard upward jerk of his hips.

That did it.

The orgasm rampaged through her entire lower body. A sensory supernova in her belly, her thighs, her ass. She pressed her mouth to his temple, swallowing her moan. Duncan met her there at the top, his shuddering exhalation muffled by her hair. A convulsive breath of relief. He pressed his mouth to the curve of bone behind her ear and said something quiet and incomprehensible. Then, a low, rolling groan into her neck as he began to buck beneath her. Temperance wrapped her arms around his head, holding him tight to her.

For a long moment, they sat there in the endless black, each of them riding the tide of the other's breathing.

Temperance let her arms slide away. He pressed a kiss to her forehead. His mouth was warm and unimaginably soft.

"Why do you do that?" she whispered.

He didn't answer right away. "You know why."

She did know why. Maybe she'd asked simply because she wanted to hear him say it.

The power returned in a blaze of party lights and house music. Temperance could feel the rumble of the bass through Duncan's body beneath her.

It had barely been five minutes, and everything had changed.

Temperance lifted herself off him and stepped backward. The elastic in the crotch of her panties was definitely ruined. She smoothed the front and back of her dress. "I don't know what we say to each other now."

Duncan pulled a folded white bandana from his back pocket and used it to manage the condom. He stood to redo his buttons and belt. The buckle made a quiet tinkling sound. Blue and green lights from below strobed across his face when he gave her a tender side-slung smile.

He dropped a warm kiss on her mouth when he stood. "I think we just said everything."

Part Four

CHAPTER TWENTY-EIGHT

Temperance

The second week of July, the clinic in Linden closed. The university moved all the large equipment back to the school, with plans to redistribute it to the remaining open clinic closer to campus in Philadelphia. With Ike Elias's and Cole Bello's help, Temperance convinced the board to agree to cover insurance and the salaries of the few permanent staff members—herself included—through the end of August, so they'd have time for outreach from their temporary location at Linden Community College.

She still hadn't found an apartment, so she was still squatting at her parents' house in Linden. Frankie was fully moved into the apartment above her new photography studio in Linden, and Temperance still saw her nearly every day, even though they weren't roommates anymore. The building she lived in now had a green roof with nearly three thousand square feet of garden space.

Duncan would love it.

She missed him, but she hadn't been back to Cloud Tide since Rowan and Harry's wedding.

For the past week, she'd been at the clinic ten hours a day, packing the smaller items that the university left behind and cleaning the place to prepare for the lease end. It was also her responsibility to do all the needful operational sorts of things like canceling the utilities and redirecting mail. That bit of the whole situation seemed particularly cruel.

That morning, a package arrived for her just before she left for the clinic. She brought it inside without much of a glance, assuming it was an odd one-off meant for her parents. But as she tossed it onto the island in the kitchen, she saw that it was clearly addressed to her.

Inside the larger cardboard shipping box was another box—white with a black satin ribbon. Temperance gasped out loud when she opened it.

It was full of sumptuous Fleur du Mal lingerie. A blush-pink angel-sleeve robe, and a silk bodysuit with a lace cutout panel down the belly. Bras—balconettes, bustiers, a plunge demi with intricate embroidery. Several that were on the more practical side, but were still so soft and sexy Temperance couldn't resist rubbing them against her cheeks. There were matching panties for each bra—cheeky low-cuts, wisp-thin thongs, and lace high-waists that were just as luscious as the racier pieces.

This was *thousands* of dollars' worth of silk and lace, and every piece was her size.

There was no note, but she didn't need one to know who it was from.

* * *

TEMPERANCE had just finished loading the final box of supplies from the clinic into the trunk of her car when she ran bodily into Millie Bristow. She wore dusky-pink scrubs with a laminated ID badge clipped to the neckline.

"Dr. Madigan, oh my gosh, hi there."

"Hi, Millie—please, call me Temperance." An awkward few seconds passed. She had no idea what to say, and Millie simply stood there blinking her big, beautiful eyes like she was waiting to be dismissed. "You're in scrubs. Are you—?"

"I'm a CMA at the urgent care over on Bridgeview. After-work coffee run." Millie did a balletic little bob, and words rolled out of her like notes from an overcranked music box. "I'm starting school to be a midwife this fall. God, I'd have never made it through the math in physics 101 at LCC without Duncan. He's so smart, you know? Are you in town for his presentation tonight?" The way her eyes sparkled made it plain how fond of him she was.

"Presentation?" Temperance said.

Millie's smile sagged a bit. With narrowed eyes, she scanned Temperance's face. She pressed her lips together with a low *hmm*. For the first time ever, Temperance saw beneath the other woman's perky façade.

Millie Bristow had backbone beneath all those bubbles.

Slowly, Millie said, "What don't you know?"

Temperance suddenly felt very tired. Her eyes tingled, and all the emotion of the past few weeks coalesced into a knot low in her throat. She tried to swallow it down, but that only made it worse. "I think there's more that I don't know than I *do*."

Millie reached out to squeeze her arm. "Do you have a few minutes? We should talk."

* * *

TEMPERANCE walked with Millie to Binding and Bean, a dual coffee shop and secondhand bookstore in downtown Linden. The toasty fragrance of coffee beans mingled with the musty, sweet scent of old books. The building used to be a church, with a vaulted and coffered ceiling paneled with glossy blond wood. It retained the original arched stained-glass windows and the pendant lighting, and a few of the pews were converted into booth seating. Temperance and Millie sat in a small U-shaped nook beside one of the windows.

"Disclosure number one." Millie wiggled her butt back and forth to settle into her seat, like a kitten burrowing into a blanket. "He's going to be mad at both of us for this. But I warned him I'd tell you if he didn't. And that was last month. So, he's had his chance."

"Okay." Temperance sipped a perfectly frothed cortado.

"Disclosure number two. We were kind of a thing, ages ago. Duncan and me—we're built the same way. Neither of us put much stock in physical flings, and we just really *like* each other for all the best reasons." Millie stirred honey into an iced coffee. "God, this is *so* embarrassing—"

Temperance breathed out a quiet laugh. "It's okay, Millie. We're grown-ups."

"We hadn't seen each other in ages, until we were in a sociology class together at LCC two years ago." Millie withdrew her phone from her bag, swiped around on the screen a few times, then handed it to Temperance. It was her Instagram profile, filled corner to corner with pictures of her and Duncan together. All of them were selfie shots, and they spanned seasons.

A photo of Duncan with a swoop of hair falling down over his forehead, and Millie wearing his favorite ball cap backward. The leaves in the trees behind them were bold orange. Another, both of them in colorful knit caps with cold-reddened cheeks pressed together, and one of Millie riding piggyback with her arms around his neck. A photo from earlier this summer, when Millie had shown up at the cabin at the lake in her cute little truck. The two of them looked more vivid than life itself, with sun-kissed cheeks and big bright smiles, each with the impossibly thick and shiny hair of a shampoo commercial.

At first glance, they looked like a happy couple, but a scroll through the images didn't show any of them kissing, and all of them were taken in public spaces.

"Gavin, my ex-husband, is a real jerk. Harassing me online, showing up at events where we had the barbecue truck. Never anything serious enough that I could get a restraining order for, but enough to scare me. Enough to scare my mom."

Temperance looked up from Millie's phone. "I saw her bracelet at the bakery a few weeks ago. Stress is dangerous for people with Addison's."

Millie nodded solemnly. "So, last year, I shared a picture of Duncan and me together, just for fun. We were at the student organization fair at LCC. Gavin stopped contacting me after that, and it was one less thing for Mom to worry about."

There were a few photos in a series from Harry and Rowan's wedding. Millie looked radiant in her fire-engine-red dress, and the sheer volume of photos sold the romantic narrative. But Temperance knew that Millie had left barely an hour into the reception.

"*She got what she needed.*"

"Anyway, all fake." Millie tapped the glass screen with a fingernail and sat back in the booth. "It was Duncan's idea. Pretty smart, huh?"

"Oh, Duncan." Temperance sighed. Her eyes burned with tears.

Without pause or pretense, Millie asked, "How long have you known you were still in love with him?"

The power of the question was in its simplicity. "Long time," Temperance said.

"I'm heading to school in Michigan at the end of the month." Millie plunged her straw up and down in her drink, making the ice clatter against the sides. "I'll be at a safe distance from Gavin, and my mom won't have to worry anymore. I hate the thought that this has somehow kept you two apart—"

"Oh, no. We've got plenty of other issues." Temperance's laugh was sad. "Why didn't he want anyone to know about school?"

Millie lowered her coffee and shook her head. "I'm not sure. But that's not my story to tell, even if I did."

Temperance laughed softly. "Duncan used that same phrase when I asked him about you."

"Dr. Madigan—"

"Millie, you *have* to call me Temperance."

"Temperance. It doesn't seem right that I know more about how you two feel than either of you do. The way you love each other deserves to be more than a secret."

* * *

PRESENTATIONS had already begun by the time Temperance snuck into the back of the LCC auditorium and sat in the last row. On a brightly lit stage, a person in an indigo pantsuit talked about the sociological and environmental aspects of architecture in front of a projector screen. At the far end of the stage was a long table covered with architectural models made of white foam or 3D printed plastic.

She spotted Duncan immediately, seated in the front row between a woman in a mint-green hijab and a person with long blond hair even paler than Temperance's own. His shoulders rose high over the seat back. He was a black bear amidst tropical birds.

Duncan was the sixth person out of seven to present. To introduce his work, he presented a few case studies of adaptive reuse in agricultural settings, highlighting the long-term cost effectiveness of energy efficiency, the importance of reducing carbon emissions, and the imperative of employing materials and methods that were truly sustainable and not just "greenwashed."

The expressive bass of his voice filled her all the way up even at the very back of the room. The rest of the world smudged to a monochrome blur around him. He shepherded the audience's attention with purposeful movements of his body and hands. He paused for impact. When he used phrases like "driving force" and "main thrust" to describe what he'd set out to accomplish—god, who *was* this man?—Temperance squirmed a little in her seat. When he transitioned into the segment of his presentation about the work on his cabin and the Cloud Tide winery, the photos on the screen hit her with such a wallop of homesickness, she felt lightheaded.

I'm not at a place in my life where I pass up a chance to get something I want if I have the means to get it.

He used the cabin as a brief proof of concept, and based on what she'd seen in the other students' presentations, his choice to do so was a departure from how these things typically went. The slides began with amateurish photos of the cabin from earlier in the summer—the place was a mess. The "after" photos of the cabin were professional quality, crisp and as beautifully composed as a real-estate listing. They were paired with the schematics—or whatever architects called them—of the structural updates Duncan had made to the place. The new metal roof, the solar panels, the reclaimed barnwood planks on the front porch. Even a 3D rendering of how he'd installed radiant heat in the floors.

In the final part of his presentation, Duncan focused on the Cloud Tide winery renovation. He seamlessly wove together anecdotes and lessons learned, with a proposal for how he'd approach a brand-new sustainable winery design. He melded the architectural elements with his business savvy and years of contracting experience, dissembling a bit with a joke about how much older he was than his classmates.

Even as an outsider, it was clear to Temperance that his work was on an elevated level compared to that of his peers. Duncan was in his thirties, already balancing a staggering amount of operational and interpersonal responsibility, and he'd still chosen to take this on. Because he'd wanted it bad enough.

When he finished, polite applause rippled through the crowd, then the design jurors began their brief question-and-answer period. Duncan aced his response to the first inquiry about the challenges that building a sustainable winery might present for a client. He wrapped it up with a charmingly self-deprecating joke about how the only thing he'd recommend anyone turn a century-old bank barn into . . . was an updated bank barn.

After a few more jurors asked questions he handled with ease, one of them asked a gotcha question about how the manufacturing process of sustainable materials themselves could have negative environmental impacts. Duncan nodded thoughtfully and tucked his hands into the pockets of his chinos, momentarily stretching them taut over his thighs. He was comfortable and confident with the brief silence as he composed his reply.

"I think it's important to keep in mind that—"

Someone a few rows in front of her sneezed. Again, louder the second time, and it echoed in the sparsely occupied auditorium. Duncan paused mid-sentence to look away from the jurors and into the audience.

His eyes landed right on her.

Shit.

Temperance melted into a deep slouch. Through the crack between the seats in front of her, she watched Duncan smooth the front of his shirt and crack his knuckles on both hands.

"Continue, Mr. Brady," the gotcha juror said when Duncan hesitated.

"Ah—"

He hiccupped. Hard enough to make his shoulders jerk.

Oh, no.

No, no, no.

He tried again. "Ah—it's important to—" Another hiccup. A dark blush materialized at the upper edge of his beard.

One person in the audience chuckled uncomfortably, someone else cleared their throat. The jurors quietly shuffled papers.

Duncan's posture was stiff. He eventually managed to answer with authority, though without the finesse of his previous answers. The hiccups sounded painful and jarring, punctuating every other sentence. When the jurors no longer had questions for him, they thanked him and recommended he take a break and get some water.

Temperance slid out of her chair and bolted for the exit.

* * *

SHE'D almost made it to the external doors when she heard behind her, "*Stop.*"

Duncan was already striding toward her as she turned. Everything about his posture screamed irritation, but his eyes were pleading. "What the hell are you doing here?"

Hiccup.

Her heart felt like it was attempting an escape through her mouth. "I was *trying* to leave, and you stopped me."

"You shouldn't have been here at all, Temperance."

"I'm glad I was. I'm so proud—"

"I don't need you to be proud. I needed this to be completely separate from you." *Hiccup.* His jaw went taut. "Damn it."

When they were eighteen, they'd had such plans, full of youthful optimism and ambition and invincibility. Duncan had already enrolled in classes at LCC for that fall semester, so he'd applied late to the university's bachelor of architecture program. He'd be a semester behind Temperance, but they'd be together.

Then she'd gotten sick, and everything fell apart.

"I never imagined that just by being here I could be a distraction for you," she said.

Duncan dipped his head and squeezed his temples. "The fact that you exist at all has been distracting me for most of my life."

"I don't know how to respond to that. But the choices you made about your education are not my fault. They're also not my responsibility."

"I didn't want anyone to know about this until I was sure I could do it." He frowned down at her. "I applied late for the evening architecture program at Drexel. I still don't know if I got in. I didn't want anyone to know yet," he repeated, like he was trying to reason through his own irritation.

"Ah, Temperance. You're so used to being the smartest person in a room, but there's a lot you don't know shit about."

Temperance chose her words carefully. "No matter what happens with that, it doesn't diminish what you accomplished here."

His laugh was sour. "I know you think that's encouraging. But you're not getting it. It's *not* enough for me. I want more. I don't need people in my life making it easier for me to not achieve things."

"Duncan, you have the kind of family support that most people only dream of having."

"What the hell is that supposed to mean?"

"You were raised on affection. So you take the affection for granted. I was raised on expectation. It's not great—"

He cut her off. "You know what? I would *love* it if a single person in my life would set a high expectation of me. High expectations mean they believe you can fucking do it. Do you think anyone ever said to Harry, 'It's okay if you don't get into med school, bud—look at everything you already accomplished'? Or Patrick, for pharmacy school? Arden's thinking of applying to vet school. Nobody's tried to talk her out of that. And you—you've had your family's money, scholarships you didn't even need, you're so effortlessly smart and fearless and good—" He snapped his teeth shut and took a sharp breath through his nose. "You've always been playing tournament chess while I've been doing tic-tac-toe on the back of a fucking used napkin."

"I don't even know how to play chess."

Duncan's voice dropped into growl territory. "It's a metaphor, Temperance."

"Not everything has been easy for me," she said softly.

"Bullshit."

"Why are you so upset about this?"

Duncan tucked his hands into his pockets and let out a weary breath. He looked at the ceiling for a long time. "I wanted you to want to be with me as I am now. Not because I was doing—*becoming*—something more."

"How can you be more"—her voice broke, and her chin trembled—"when you're already everything?"

Finally, there was some tenderness in his eyes, but his voice had an edge. "Not yet. Not for myself." More applause came from the open auditorium door behind him. "I have to go."

He left her there. Alone.

CHAPTER TWENTY-NINE

Duncan

*D*uncan felt like a bag of hell.

The back of his neck was sunburnt in an inch-wide strip where he'd missed with the sunscreen, and his knees and ankles ached from hours of roof work two days ago. His eyes felt gritty from lack of sleep and from the sawdust that had drifted into them yesterday. His wrists were sore. Not because of anything specific—they were sore because sore was the default state for his wrists.

He stopped by the house that morning to grab coffee. Whatever he brewed down at the cabin always seemed to taste worse than anything he got anywhere else. Hell, he'd had better coffee at midnight in a Sheetz than what he was able to make for himself.

The kitchen was deserted, but there were signs of his family everywhere. One of Dad's novelty aprons was crumpled into a ball on the counter next to the stove, and a sweet trace of something baked and buttery lingered in the air. There was a blue-and-white porcelain vase of fresh wildflowers in the center of the island next to an overflowing wire basket of mail. A near-empty glass of iced tea sat in a fresh puddle of condensation next to a bottle of SPF 50 sunscreen with the cap popped open. At the barstool end of the island were a few empty wineglasses, all with a tiny eye of dried Syrah in the bottom. There was also a gin tumbler with two bone-dry lime slices inside, with a black satin hair scrunchie hugging the outside. Duncan slipped it off and lifted it to his nose, closing his eyes on the inhale.

Her.

He couldn't get it out of his head, the way she'd looked at his presentation. She'd been fresh-faced and wearing her big-framed glasses, in an old tank top and frayed denim cutoffs. Her hair was twisted up in a thick braid as it usually was, but she was windblown and a little frazzled, with strands of it coming loose all over. When he'd first seen her there in the audience, he thought he was hallucinating. Then she'd given him a tentative little smile and a raise of her eyebrows as she slid down her seat, and he'd almost lost what little composure he'd managed to scrounge up for himself.

When they'd argued in the little access hallway outside the auditorium, she'd looked like a pissed-off tumbleweed. He felt like a full-on bastard for how he'd treated her.

A small box addressed to him sat on the stack of mail on the island. He used the tip of his finger to snap the tape around the edge and pulled out five pairs of XL gloves made by different brands, each equally stretchy and made with lightweight cut-resistant fabric. Nitrile coated the contact surfaces across the fingers and palms.

Beneath the gloves was a crisp new bandana, still in the plastic. *White flag.*

There was a note on the packing slip.

TAKE CARE OF YOU.

* * *

BY ten A.M., he'd already responded to a handful of project inquiries and proposal requests in the Brady Brothers' email inbox, changed the oil on the Gator, and replaced a bent clamp on its CV boot. Now, he had a tractor torn apart to replace its driveshaft, engine grease up to his elbows.

He'd worn one of the new pairs of gloves. Not only did they protect his skin, they gave him a bit of extra grip. He could get used to this.

He was tightening the bolts to finish the job when he heard the shuffle of something large behind him in the open doorway of the equipment garage, then the characteristic sound of a breath being blown out through big donkey nostrils.

Out of an abundance of caution, Duncan had steered clear of Asparagus since his beard had come back in. Now, she came right for him with her head lowered and her tail swishing lazily behind her. Duncan stood and backed farther into the garage, and he braced for the pain of a headbutt or a bite on the shoulder.

Instead, she nuzzled the bottom hem of his shirt and pressed her forehead against his chest, making soft little chuffing sounds. Then she raised her head and nibbled his beard.

Duncan chuckled, pressed his forehead to the spot between her ears, and scratched her under the chin. She smelled warm and dusty, like sweet hay and sunshine. "I guess we really are friends now."

* * *

LATER that morning, Duncan found his parents in the tasting room. Their comfortable back-and-forth carried into the main space of the bank barn, peppered with laughter and Ma's intermittent and off-key singing during lulls in the conversation. Dad said something about the day already being "hotter than a goat's ass in a pepper patch," and by the time Duncan came into the room, they were laughing so hard they were crying.

The tasting room floor still bore the footprints of the animals that had come in seeking his abandoned pastrami sandwich at the end of spring. He'd smoothed out the edges of the prints himself with a carbide masonry file and filled each of them with a clear resin to bring them level with the rest of the concrete. Then he'd covered the floor with an agricultural-grade sealant. Now, the prints seemed to be an intentional design choice, and he was particularly proud of turning that embarrassment into an aesthetic win.

Dad rubbed oil into the reclaimed barnwood bar, and Ma did the same on the wine racks behind it.

"Hey," Duncan said, and they both looked up. He turned a chair around and sat on it with legs spread wide, propping his forearms on the backrest. "Got a minute? I need to tell you something." He waited until he had their attention before he continued. "I've been going to school again. In Linden, at the community college."

Ma tossed her cloth to a little tray on the sink behind the bar. Her face fell. "You kept a secret from us?"

"Ah—it's complicated. Mostly because if I failed out again, I didn't want anyone to know I'd even tried."

Ma said something under her breath in Spanish. "You didn't fail the first time. You gave up. There's a difference."

"Well, no, Ma." Duncan scratched his cheek. "I might not have been entirely forthcoming about the circumstances there. It doesn't matter, though. I wasn't ready then."

"What classes?" Dad asked.

"Gen ed, at first. Then their architecture diploma program. I'm starting at Drexel in the fall."

Dad finished a final swipe with his cloth and lobbed it into the tray with Ma's. He removed his gloves. "Say again?"

"I got accepted at Drexel, Dad. Just found out yesterday."

Dad pinched his thumb and forefinger over the bridge of his nose. "This is a two-weeks'-notice conversation, isn't it?"

Duncan's throat tightened. His heart raced. He'd wanted to have this conversation for most of his adult life, and now that it was happening, he felt like he'd stepped into a different reality. "I don't want to manage Brady Brothers, Dad. I don't want to be a general contractor. I should have told you a long time ago."

Dad looked up with lips pressed tight, but his eyes were soft. "When did you realize this?"

"Remember that summer we stopped at Fallingwater?" Duncan said.

"You were ten years old." Dad's voice was gentle.

Duncan cracked his knuckles. "Exactly."

"Oh, patito. That long?" Ma said.

"Why are we just learning about this now?" Dad asked.

Christ, where to even begin? It was simple, at first. Going back to LCC seemed a straightforward way to right one of his own wrongs.

As long as nobody else knew, the stakes were his alone. If he fucked up and failed out again, he wouldn't have to smile and nod at anyone's awkward expressions of encouragement.

He didn't fail, though. It was hard, but he was good at it, and that path he'd convinced himself he was too old and too overburdened to start down was suddenly right there in front of him.

"I don't want to have to look back and wonder where I'd be now if I'd just kept going," Millie had said to him once, in their first semester at LCC. That had stuck with him.

Later, the secrecy became more about how the hell to tell Dad he wanted out of Brady Brothers and less about school itself.

"You asked me to take over Brady Brothers five *weeks* before I started at LCC, Dad. I thought I could handle both. Hell, I *did* handle both," Duncan said. "I didn't want to let you down."

"You're my son, not a resource, damn it. You let yourself down by not doing this sooner."

"You're right. I did." Duncan's temper heated. "So I'm trying to fix it now, before I get any fucking older."

Ma made a noisy hum in the back of her throat as a warning for the language.

Dad spun a chair around and sat down to face him. Eye to eye. "Son, I gave you Brady Brothers because it seemed like you wanted it. You're damned good at everything you've ever done—"

"I'm good at other things, too."

"Well, *obviously*." Dad's brow furrowed. "But you didn't have to go to LCC to prove it. To anyone. And you don't have to do more now."

"That's exactly it, Dad. I didn't do it because I felt like I had to. I'm doing this for myself. I'm *earning* what I want."

"You already have everything you need here," said Dad. "'If you have built castles in the air, your work need not be lost; that is where they should be. Now put the foundations under them.'"

"Are you seriously sitting there, in a pit-stained Wawa T-shirt, quoting Thoreau?"

Dad lifted his chin. "I am a man of nuance and complexity."

Duncan sighed and closed his eyes to regroup. To Ma, he said, "Is he always this much of a pain in the ass?"

Ma simply pressed her lips together.

"You and Nathan are the Brady Brothers now," Dad said. "He's the one you need to be working this out with."

"I told you. I don't *want* to run Brady Brothers."

"How are you planning to pay for college? Loans? Why in the Sam Hill would you want to go into the same kind of debt your siblings have?" Dad said.

"You want to talk about money? Really? You two weren't exactly conservative with your decision to spend most of your retirement savings on this place."

"We're not talking about us."

"I have plenty of money." Duncan was intentionally vague. The money was yet another layer to this shit sandwich. How did he explain he could pay out of pocket for tuition without breaking a sweat? "Even if I didn't, the program is designed so students can keep a day job. I won't need loans."

"I don't think you're hearing what I'm saying, son. Brady Brothers can be whatever the hell you want it to be. You want to do green retrofits, sustainable architecture, whatever? Do it."

"I can't call myself an architect if I'm not a licensed architect, Dad."

"I was a contractor for forty years, son. I know the rules. You can get back to designing and drafting more, starting today. Get your plans reviewed and stamped by one of our architects, then move on to the next project."

"*I* want to be the one doing that, damn it." Duncan pressed his fist to the middle of his chest. "Jesus, did you ever try to talk Nate or Patrick out of their ambitions? Mal, or Harry? Or Arden?"

"You need to stop comparing yourself to the people around you," Dad said. "The only person you should compare yourself to is the person you were the day before."

"Look. I know you think all of this is helpful. I know you think you're creating opportunity for me by making things seem straightforward. But ask yourself—what is it about me, compared to every-one else in this family—that makes you feel like you need to make things easy for me?"

Dad was silent for a long time. He looked out the big window that overlooked Cloud Tide, nodding intermittently. Like he was agreeing with his own internal monologue. "Okay," he finally said. "You're right. And I'm behind you. All the way. But while we're on the topic of chasing dreams—" Dad glanced over to where Ma watched them by the bar. "Let's talk about Temperance."

Ah, hell.

Duncan cracked his knuckles and looked down at his boots. "What about her?"

"You can't sneak a sunrise past a rooster, son."

Duncan stood and dragged his hand over his face.

"How's she fit in to all this? You doing this for her?"

"*Jesus*, Dad. I just told you how I was doing this for *me*—"

"Look at this." Dad ran his hand along the edge of a joint in one of the open drawers behind the bar. "Dovetail joints like this are strong, but they take time and attention and skill. And if they break—what happens?"

"They don't usually break if they're done right—" Duncan said.

"Everything can break, Duncan. I know you've seen snapped dovetails before."

Duncan met Dad's gaze. "Each half leaves pieces of itself in the other side."

"Now, I'm not good at metaphors like your mother is—"

"I know what you're trying to do, Dad—"

"Is he always this much of a pain in the ass?" Dad echoed, look-ing to Ma.

Duncan sighed. "Temperance Madigan is too good for me. Al-ways has been."

"Nonsense," Ma said. "She'd be lucky to have you."

"You can't stick a flower in an asshole and pretend it's a vase, Ma."

"Now *that's* a good metaphor," Dad said.

Ma pinned him with a look. "Temperance is an egg. You squeeze her hard, and she remains strong. Gentle focus is what will crack her."

"I don't want to *crack* her, Ma."

"You know what I mean," she said.

Duncan hoisted his tool bag over his shoulder and gave her a one-handed hug and a kiss on the top of her head. "Your metaphors are weird."

Dad's laugh echoed in the big space of the barn behind them. "The asshole vase is weirder, son."

Ma cupped his cheeks with cool hands. "Love breaks us open to make a way for someone else to climb inside, patito. You should both be eggs."

CHAPTER THIRTY

Duncan

When Duncan bought his Huntsman suit in New York City on a trip to visit Mal a few years ago, he'd paid in full, and he'd paid in cash. But there was no amount of money, no degree of sartorial craftsmanship, and no measure of relative anonymity that would make him feel like he belonged at the Capewell-Talbot Foundation's annual fundraising gala that night. But there he was, overlooking a sea of glittering dresses, glittering smiles, and glittering flutes of expensive alcohol.

The event brought together the region's philanthropists, corporate leaders, and members of the healthcare community to raise money for the Capewell-Talbot Foundation. They chose a new venue each year, and tonight's gala was in Center City Philadelphia in an event space that had originally been an early-twentieth-century publishing house. Duncan had driven past it a dozen times over the years on his trips into the city, and the opportunity to finally get a look inside was one of the only things that made him able to stomach being there. It was classic Beaux Arts architecture, with liberal use of columns, arches, and elaborately carved moldings. Everything was magnified in size and ornamentation. An unflinching nosedive into grandeur. It wasn't Duncan's thing, but he appreciated the artistry of it.

It was the first fundraiser he'd ever been to, but instinct told him this one was impressive. He imagined wealthy folk were much more willing to part with their money when they got to wear fancy clothes and drink themed cocktails while doing it.

Inside the sunken atrium, a soaring dome of glass and steel dripped with crystal chandeliers reminiscent of dandelions gone to seed. Swags of sheer champagne-gold fabric hung between ivory marble pillars along both long walls, creating alcoves behind. Round tables were set with centerpieces of baseball-sized dahlia blooms in smoky pinks and creamy whites.

Duncan had one objective tonight: pay his dues to Corbin Madigan and Laine Talbot-Madigan.

The silent auction was set up along the open mezzanine overlooking the atrium. More tuxedoed butlers per capita roamed the auction area compared to the larger crowd below, passing bougie finger foods like prosciutto-wrapped dates and crab-stuffed shrimp. A bar sat at each end of the auction area—one serving themed cocktails, the other a Bloody Mary station with a truly impressive spread of fresh herbs, celery, citrus, and green olives the size of small plums. The bartender stood by to grate fresh horseradish or blend custom rim salts.

There was a canny intentionality to the way the items for bid were displayed, clearly meant to scratch specific itches in the human brain. Each item was placed far from the others to evoke a sense of exclusivity and scarcity—while still being close enough that everyone could see what everyone else browsed to amplify a sense of competition. Bidding was open for a fixed time frame of only two hours, generating urgency.

Duncan ignored it all, although he was thankful for the auction's condensed timeline. As soon as his money was locked in, he would get the fuck out of there. Then he could tell Temperance everything.

All things considered, he kept his composure admirably. The only times it slipped a bit were when he saw people who recognized him. Coleman Bello and his wife, Odessa, and Isaac Elias and his husband, Thierry, had come to him for a brief conversation as they browsed the silent auctions. Despite how pleasant and kind they were, he suspected they wondered what the hell he was doing there. When someone knew who you were underneath, it didn't matter how convincing the costume was.

Duncan hovered around the digital kiosk of the item he'd chosen to dump all his money into: two second-edition Jane Austen novels that were largely being ignored in favor of tropical vacations and ski chalet time-shares. A few people had stopped by to place bids, but they quickly moved on once they were outbid. Still, Duncan stayed close. He wasn't taking any chances.

There was movement behind him, closer than any other bodies had come to him all evening.

· Erik Uttridge appeared like a fart in an elevator—unexpected and entirely unwelcome.

"Declan," he said in greeting. "How's it going, my blue-collar brother?"

Uttridge didn't extend a hand for a shake, and Duncan didn't offer.

"Oh, you know, man." Duncan checked his watch and put on a tight-lipped smile, playing the role the other man wanted. "Hangin' out like a hair in a biscuit."

"Ever get that scrub sink on seven fixed?" Uttridge flashed his unnaturally white grin, waiting for Duncan to join in on the joke.

He didn't.

The atrium lights dimmed and brightened a few times, and the crowd below went quiet. From where he stood at the mezzanine, he could see the stage and the oversized digital clock to the rear of it that counted down the amount of time left in the auction.

Twenty-five more minutes.

A spotlight shone on the stage, where a woman in a sequined black dress and a crown of narrow salt-and-pepper braids approached the microphone and spread her arms wide. "Good evening, doctors, esteemed guests, and friends. Thank you all for being here tonight. I'm Dr. Moira Dawson, Domestic Relief and Aid's medical director, and this year's gala coordinator. I'm honored and humbled to see the largest crowd we've ever had for a Capewell-Talbot fundraising event. Your presence here is a testament to your unwavering commitment to people in need."

Uniform applause rippled through the atrium. It was a cultured sound, everyone clapping at roughly the same volume and tempo. Duncan wondered what it would sound like once the good doctors put away the thousands of dollars of top-shelf liquor he'd seen at the bars.

Dr. Dawson continued, "I have a few announcements to make before I welcome our fearless leaders to the stage. We've entered the final few minutes of the silent auction, so get those bids in now . . ."

"So are you a fan of Austen?" Uttridge said. "Women love that shit—"

Duncan cut him off. "What do you want?"

Uttridge scanned him with a shrewd once-over, and the jokey lilt in his voice disappeared. "You here with Madigan?"

"She's not here."

Twenty more minutes.

Uttridge gave him an odd look. "Yeah, she is." He went to the railing and pointed straight down. "She's right there."

Duncan took the bait, expecting that the man was fucking with him. He tucked his hands in his pockets and peered over the marble rail, and there she was. At the table in the front row closest to the edge of the atrium floor, partially obscured by the overhang of the mezzanine.

He felt like he'd been punched in the neck.

Her hair was up in a tousled braid that twisted around the top of her head. The dark blue dress she wore plunged low at the back, exposing bare skin well below the slope of her shoulder blades. When she moved, the beadwork on the fabric shimmered like a constellation.

In the seat beside her was a man Duncan could see clearly in profile. He'd met the guy once, when Temperance had brought him to the Brady Thanksgiving party years ago. Dr. Bodhi Rao's deep brown skin was flawless, his jaw angular to a trigonometric degree. During a lull for applause, Rao leaned in to whisper in Temperance's ear, and she nodded. After the applause, he draped his arm over the back of her chair. She stayed perched forward in her seat instead of leaning back into him, but Duncan would be a liar if he said they didn't look right together.

Hell. He'd never felt this separate from her. Might as well be a fish in love with the fucking moon.

Uttridge moved in beside him. He leaned forward with forearms on the marble. "Ahh, my condolences, man. I don't blame you for trying, though. She's the total package, even if she *is* frostier than her mom—"

"Walk away." Duncan straightened to his full height and met the other man's eyes, unblinking.

Uttridge did a double take. "Hey, man, I was just—"

"Immediately."

This time, the other man listened.

". . . please welcome Dr. Corbin Madigan and Dr. Laine Talbot-Madigan." On the stage below, Moira Dawson stepped backward from the microphone, clapping.

Duncan had been eighteen when he'd last seen the Madigans. But they both looked identical to how he remembered them. Laine Talbot-Madigan was a weapon personified—reed slim and sharp-shouldered in a silver sheath dress that matched a gleaming updo so blond it looked metallic in the spotlight. Corbin Madigan was the same height as his wife, with an air of old money that had nothing to do with his actual golden appearance, and everything to do with the tilt of his chin as he looked upon the hundreds of people below him. He'd looked at Duncan that same way on the day he'd cornered him in the hospital waiting room, staring down at him even though Duncan had at least eight or nine inches on him. He couldn't remember much from that day, but the words Corbin Madigan said to him were permanently etched on the inside of his skull.

"What if she gets sick like this again? How will you take care of her?

What she feels for you now—do you actually believe she'll feel the same after twelve years of school?

What can you offer her that she won't find better versions of outside this valley?"

There was conspicuous affection in the way the elder Madigans interacted with each other. They launched into a speech about how growing up in the area had shaped their lives and careers, playing off each other with a natural harmony and understated humor that almost seemed choreographed. Somehow that made Duncan dislike them even more.

". . . tonight, we're thrilled to announce the Helen Talbot Community Center," Laine said. On the screen behind her, a moving 3D rendering of a building appeared with a flourish of cinematic music. "With financial support from the Capewell-Talbot Foundation, and thanks to your generous donations tonight, this new center will fill many of the gaps in Vesper Valley's community services. There will be recreational and educational youth services, senior programs, nutrition programs, a food pantry, and more."

Below, Temperance had scooted even further forward to the edge of her seat. Her hands were in her lap, and she was motionless. Now, Bodhi Rao watched her instead of the stage.

Laine continued, "While we won't offer medical care, we plan to have an experienced staff of social workers and community organizers to connect residents to services and assistance they qualify for."

She went on about the three-year plan for the organization, but her voice faded to a monotone buzz until Duncan heard her say Temperance's name into the microphone.

"Many of you met Temperance when she was a teenager at this very gala. We are overjoyed to finally welcome her into the Capewell-Talbot Foundation family. Our Atlanta-headquartered program will be one of the first-ever child-focused initiatives of its kind, designed to address the very unique challenges that pediatric patients and their families face during natural disaster recoveries. With her public health and pediatrics experience, Temperance will bring a fresh perspective to our organization."

At that, louder applause. Behind Laine on the stage, Corbin pointed at Temperance, then put his hands together in a slow-motion clap that somehow felt patronizing.

"Dr. Madigan, stand up and let everyone see you," Laine said.

She didn't budge until the spotlight swung directly to her.

Applause erupted when Temperance slowly stood. She braced herself with fingertips against the white tablecloth, and when she wavered a little on her feet, Bodhi Rao subtly pressed a hand to the bare skin of her back. Duncan's pulse hammered inside his ears, and his teeth ached from the sustained clench of his jaw. He didn't need to see her face to know that she was very much not okay in that moment, and despite the sour flood of jealousy in his gut, he was grateful she had someone there to steady her. Even if it couldn't be him.

Ten more minutes.

Duncan ground his teeth. His relief that the auction would be finished soon was overshadowed by the need to get to Temperance. He'd figure out what the hell he was going to say once he found her.

CHAPTER THIRTY-ONE

Temperance

The atrium lights dimmed once her parents left the stage, and the small chamber orchestra began a string rendition of a five-year-old pop song. Temperance excused herself from the table, eyes still watering from the spotlight.

She needed to get the hell out of there, but a gauntlet of five hundred people stood between her and the exit. She'd made it five steps from her table when she was intercepted by a former fellow resident she'd gone out with a few times when they were both in their fourth year—she'd ended it after a good-night kiss somehow resulted in a sesame seed from his dinner stuck to her lip. Two more steps, and she was waylaid by a friend from her graduating class at Linden High who was one of the managing partners of the event-planning company running the gala. Then there was a neurosurgeon friend of her dad's, who, despite looking astoundingly like a sixty-something Chris Pine, she couldn't ever remember his name. "Why haven't we seen you in past years?" he'd asked, and Temperance pled being too busy with residency. Explaining that she'd been dis-invited from the complimentary ticket guest list after she'd rejected Capewell-Talbot money seemed like it might be gauche, considering the circumstances. Everyone was very nice, but Temperance's tank for dissembling was completely dry.

Her bullshit tolerance had maxed out as soon as the sole of her mother's left Louboutin had hit the stage.

Temperance excused herself by claiming she might've eaten a

bad shrimp. She hustled toward the back stairway to the mezzanine. She'd never jogged in heels before, but half a lifetime as a runner had the unexpected perk of making her sure-footed even wearing four-inch stilettos. Without slowing down, she grabbed a salt-rimmed paloma from one of the passing waitstaff's trays and lifted it straight to her mouth as she climbed the winding corner stairs. She'd go up, over, and out the staircase at the lobby end. Easy.

Layer upon layer of tension stacked in her chest, and it wasn't the good kind that made her bloodstream bolt with adrenaline. It was straight-up anxiety. Temperance paused on the stairs and pulled her phone from her wristlet to text Maren.

> You'll be relieved to know that mom and dad are as awful as ever

Tell them I said hi, lol

> They just announced to five hundred people that I was joining DORA

Aren't you?

> It's complicated

> Also, they seated me with Bodhi Rao

Tastykake?
Big night for you.

> I'm considering pulling the fire alarm

That's a felony, honey

> Think I can fake anaphylaxis in a room full of doctors?

Hang in there

Temperance was furious. Not only at her parents for the bait and switch, but at herself for falling for the bait in the first place. She'd taken on six figures of student loan debt to escape their influence, and none of it mattered. It was as if she'd spent years fortifying a bunker only to invite them inside and hand them a key.

She wanted Duncan.

There wasn't a doubt in her mind that if she called him, that minute, and asked him to come get her in Philly, he'd be there before the top of the hour.

She bobbled the phone when she tried to stuff it back into her wristlet, and it fell face-down on the marble stair below her. When she lifted it, the glass was spiderwebbed, and the screen was striped with blue and black lines, unresponsive to the swipe of her finger. "*Shit.*" Temperance stuffed it away, gathered her dress in her free hand, and hustled the rest of the way up the stairs.

The mezzanine level was brighter than the main floor, with recessed lighting that showcased the silent auction items. Enormous dome-shaped crystal chandeliers on the low ceiling threw millions of tiny needles of light. Champagne-colored carpet was so plush it was difficult to walk on in her heels. She slipped the damned things off and let them dangle from her free hand.

Duncan was there.

Near the mezzanine's marble railing.

Temperance couldn't move.

Dressed in unrelieved black, he was almost a shadow if not for the horizontal fold of a crisp white pocket square. His hair crested back from his face in a single tidy wave, and his beard was trimmed in a tight contour around his jaw. He nudged his chin up to straighten the already blade-straight collar of the dark button-down beneath his slim-fit suit jacket, then with a swift jerk of his arm, he pulled his sleeve back to check his watch. Everything about him seemed tactical—his stance, his clothes, even the way he moved.

"Duncan," she said, quietly.

He froze, hesitating for a moment before he raised his attention from his watch. By the time he looked up at her, she was halfway to him. This close, she could see the suit wasn't black. It was the dense, empyrean blue of midnight in August.

Blue suit. No tie. For a black-tie event. It was so very Duncan.

She'd never loved him more.

"Hi," he murmured.

He seemed far less surprised to see her than she was to see him.

"I have so many questions." She dropped her shoes and reached up to run the narrow lapel of his jacket between her finger and thumb. Beneath it, his heart pounded hard enough she could feel the beat against her knuckles.

"I can think of a few of my own." Duncan didn't move, but he tipped his head down to watch her touch him.

"What are you—" She skimmed her hand down his arm. The fabric was so fine it almost had a luster to it in the velvety light. "Tonight's tickets were a thousand dollars apiece. How—"

His low laugh was the darkest chocolate—deep and rich and a little bitter. He made a *tsk-tsk* sound with his tongue against his teeth. "Where are your manners?"

She leveled a cool glance at him.

The orchestra finished a piece, and a mellow sequence of chimes sounded from below to indicate the impending close of the auction. Duncan subtly glanced at his watch again. "Better not stand so close. Everyone will wonder who I am to you."

Temperance moved in so her breasts brushed his lapels. "Then I'm not standing close *enough*."

Duncan reached behind her waist and drew a finger slowly across the small of her back. Goosebumps rose in its wake. Her skin urged toward him on a cellular level.

Some of the tension eased out of him. His long exhale was hot against her hair. "I didn't think you'd be here tonight."

"I didn't either. I had some business to take care of with my parents."

"Same."

She flattened her palm against his chest. "I don't even know where to begin unpacking that."

"Best not try right now." He sounded distracted. Over her head, he watched tuxedoed event staff members collect the digital-bidding kiosks for each of the auction items.

Her belly turned over. "You heard their speech, didn't you."

"I did."

"I'm not going to Atlanta, Duncan."

A big, slow breath lifted his chest beneath her hand. "I believe you."

Thank god.

"Where are you sitting?"

"Nowhere. I did what I came to do."

She stepped back to look him in the eyes. "Please tell me."

There was an odd mix of deliberation and vulnerability in his expression. Paired with the halting breath he took—and held—Temperance knew his body language like she knew her own reflection. He wasn't going to answer her.

Hesitantly, he said, "I need you to trust me."

Temperance deflated a bit. Her hand slid away from his chest, but he intercepted it and lifted her palm to his mouth.

"Not here." His beard tickled her wrist when he kissed her. "We're very overdue for a conversation, though—" His eyes lifted to look past her head, but his mouth remained on her skin.

"There you are," Bodhi Rao said behind her. Duncan let go of her, and Temperance turned so fast her paloma sloshed over the rim of the glass.

Bodhi immediately turned his attention to Duncan. He extended an eager hand with a genuine smile. "Bodhi Rao. I'm an old friend of Temperance's."

Temperance turned sideways to accommodate Bodhi's outstretched arm. She gestured to Duncan.

"Bodhi, this is Duncan Brady. He's, ah—my—" Her brain stammered to a full stop. When Duncan moved beside her to receive Bodhi's handshake, his eyes met hers for just a blink, and the noise in her head abruptly quieted. With his gaze still latched tight to hers, she said, simply, "He's mine."

Duncan didn't look away from her, even when Bodhi snagged his hand and pumped it with unfiltered enthusiasm. His eyes were soft and dark as warm molasses.

"Great to meet you, man," Bodhi said.

Duncan finally turned his attention to Bodhi. "We met a few years ago, actually. Good to see you."

"You work with Temperance?" Bodhi's answering grin was sincere.

A tight-lipped smile from Duncan. "I do not."

Bodhi nodded encouragingly. "What field are you in, then?"

"I'm a contractor."

"Oh, per diem? Locum tenens? Nice." Bodhi crossed his arms over his chest and rocked back on his heels like he planned to stand there and chitchat all night. "Good money. Great flexibility." Bodhi nodded and nodded—had he *always* nodded that much? Temperance wanted to grab him by the chin and tell him to stay still. "Primary care? Hospitalist? Which agency you using?"

"No agency. I'm not in medicine." Duncan squared his feet with the width of his shoulders. "Construction contracting."

"Ahh." Bodhi's earnest energy short-circuited. When awkward silence stretched long, he said, "Well. I'll head back down. Nice seeing you, Duncan. Temperance, catch up later?"

She gave Bodhi a warm but noncommittal smile and wave. When she turned back to Duncan, she put her hand on his chest again. With him next to her, the ground seemed more substantial beneath her feet. "Can we leave?"

"Together?" A small smile hovered on his lips. "Think of the scandal, Dr. Madigan."

Abruptly, his expression fell. With hooded eyes, he looked past her shoulder again, unblinking. The fine hairs on the back of her neck rose, and she knew.

Temperance turned to watch her parents approach. She took a step backward to bring her body into subtle contact with Duncan's. He didn't budge, and his body heat radiated into her bare back.

"Don't leave before we've had a chance to thank you, Mr. Brady," Corbin said. He was using the voice he used on waitstaff at the Linden Country Club. It had always made her uncomfortable as a kid, though she could never pin down why. In retrospect, adult Temperance knew exactly why. It was the early inklings of her bullshit detector.

Laine leaned in and gave her a right-left-right cheek kiss, as if she'd been born and raised in Europe instead of suburban Philadelphia. With her face still pressed against Temperance's, she whispered, "At least you made it all the way through school. Better than your sister managed."

Temperance didn't lower her voice. "I'm thirty-four years old, Mom."

"Indeed. Which is why I thought you'd know better." Laine pressed closer and murmured, "Just, for the love of god, don't let him get you pregnant." Then she stood back and said, louder, "Temperance Jean. You look radiant. I'm so glad you didn't wear your glasses."

Duncan and Corbin were locked in a vise-grip handshake that made the tendons in their hands protrude. A squiggly vein popped out at her dad's temple, but Duncan remained placid. At the edge of Duncan's sleeve, some of his tattoos were visible—the lower part of a sneering skull doffing a top hat, and a scatter of stylized cherry blossoms. Her dad glanced at them and sniffed.

Like a curious cat, Laine clutched her wineglass to her chest and tilted her head sideways. To Temperance, she said, "So this is the reason you've been so hard to contact this summer."

Without missing a beat, Duncan lifted the paloma from Temperance's hand. He looked right at Laine and subtly slipped the edge of his tongue along the salt rim of the glass. Then he took a slow, deliberate sip. "I've kept her busy."

For the first time in her life, Temperance watched her mother *blush*.

"Well played, Mr. Brady," Corbin said. "All of tonight, really. I underestimated you for a long time."

"One thing we have in common," said Duncan.

"I'm very curious if Temperance knows of your passion for Austen."

Duncan raised his chin. "We're square now. We're done."

"Oh, for god's sake. Just say what you mean. Both of you," Temperance said.

"Would you like to tell her, or shall I?" Corbin said to Duncan.

Laine watched them over the rim of her glass.

A flush of prickly warmth began at Temperance's scalp and flowed down her neck and shoulders. "What's going on?"

Duncan's composure slipped, but for only a second. When he met her eyes, his lips tightened against his teeth, and he swallowed hard.

I need you to trust me.

"Your suit is quite nice, Mr. Brady," Laine said. "Isn't it curious to you, Temperance, how a man like Duncan might afford a five-thousand-dollar Huntsman suit?"

"One might also ask—what would possess a man like Duncan to spend fifteen thousand dollars on Jane Austen novels?" Corbin added.

Temperance's mouth went dry, and for a moment, the floor felt uneven under her feet. She snagged her paloma from Duncan and tossed back a piece of ice, pulverizing it between her teeth.

Softly, Duncan said, "They offered me money to stay away from you. And I took it."

She swallowed the ice while some of the shards were still big, and she nearly choked. "When?" Her voice was hoarse.

"I was eighteen, Temperance—"

"So, you came here tonight to—what?" She was going to be sick. "Pay off your debt?"

"The original check was for ten grand, though," Corbin said. "I assume you added the extra five for inflation, Mr. Brady? Truly—well played."

A void of emptiness ruptured wide inside her. Temperance swung back to face her parents. "Well, shit. Fifteen thousand is a real bargain, isn't it? Two million is my current valuation. Right, Mom? Fifteen thousand to two million in only fourteen years. That's some pretty remarkable appreciation on a capital asset, wouldn't you say,

Dad?" Temperance was shouting now, and she didn't care. "What is that—like, two hundred thousand percent?"

"Don't be crass, Temperance," Laine said.

Slowly, she turned to face her mother. "I'm not a pawn in your power game."

"I'm surprised by your indignation, darling. Money is why you're here tonight, too. Is it not?" Corbin said.

"Oh, fuck you, Dad."

"Behave yourself, Temperance Jean."

"Is this fun for you?" Temperance downed the rest of her paloma and set it down so hard on the nearby cocktail table that the ice rattled. "Is this the tense final-act moment where Duncan and I turn on each other? Argue in front of you two, so you can fan the flames? Control the narrative? Drive the young lovers apart?"

"Dear god." Laine sniffed. "I have no idea how you and your sister turned out to be so dramatic."

Temperance laughed. "Fuck off, Mom. You know what I think? You're doing this to distract from the fact that you bait-and-switched me about the clinic. Did you ever mean to help me, or were you lying the whole time?"

Corbin looked down his long nose. "This is what's best for you. It's a win-win. The community will get the services they need, and you won't have to be stuck here making sure they do."

"You don't get to decide what's best for me," Temperance snapped. Then she turned to Duncan. "And you. You've spent the last fourteen years upset with me for always doing what they wanted. But you did the same damned thing. You're a hypocrite."

Duncan stepped toward her. "Temperance—"

"No. You and I will talk about this later. *Away* from them. But right now, I'm going to remove myself from all three of you and go be pissed off for a while."

She picked up her shoes and left.

CHAPTER THIRTY-TWO

Duncan

*H*e'd been sitting on the porch at the Madigan house in Linden for an hour and a half when Temperance's little Corolla came down the lane. She parked next to his truck and closed the door quietly, and her shiny shoes made purposeful *click-click-click* sounds on the concrete path as she approached.

"I tried to call you," Duncan said.

"My phone is shattered. I went to the cabin. You weren't there."

He stood and looped his suit coat over his forearm. "Obviously."

She stepped past him and unlocked the door. "Are you here for some polite conversation?"

"Is that where you want to start? Or do we need to get the yelling out of the way first?"

Duncan followed her inside. Her boxes were still in the foyer, the same place they'd been earlier in the summer.

She tossed her keys on a marble-topped side table and kicked off her shoes. They clattered into the darkness of the cavernous house.

"You took the money, Duncan." Her eyes were sharp, glittering like shattered glass.

"Yes. I did. And if you'd have met me at the Boonies that night when I begged you to, you'd have known it. I tried to fix things. You never showed."

"You shouldn't have taken it in the first place. We were supposed to be a team. But you fell right in line with what they wanted."

"Corbin Madigan is a man who expects to be complied with, Temperance."

"Since when do you care about that?"

"When you were sick, I'd sit in the main lobby at the hospital every day after work, because that was the closest I could get to you. The third or fourth night, your dad glanced at me as he was leaving. The next day, he sat down next to me. 'You're the Brady boy,' he said, like he was *accusing* me of something, and I just blinked at him like a fucking idiot. Then he looked me right in the eyes and said, 'She was asking for you,' and I cracked a little. He told me he wasn't sure who I was until he saw the look on my face in that moment. He *comforted* me, Temperance. Patted me on the back. Told me he understood how much I cared. Then he gave me the check to disappear. I spent the next year thinking about how things would have gone if I'd responded differently. If I'd stood up to him then. Who we'd be now. I was trying to protect you."

"I didn't want a protector," she shouted. "I wanted a partner."

"How was I supposed to take care of you? We were still *kids*." His eyebrows were drawn over agonized eyes. "You had a mysterious illness that you were hospitalized for. I was barely out of high school, on my parents' health insurance, you were facing twelve fucking *years* of school." Duncan threw his hands up and let them fall to his sides. "How the hell am *I* the logical one here?"

"You're the one who paid for the clinic to use the community room at Linden CC, didn't you?"

"Why is it so much harder for you to accept things from me than from anyone else?"

"Answer me."

"Yes."

Temperance rubbed the center of her forehead. "The fifty-dollar tip at the bakery. The champagne at Rowan and Harry's wedding—"

Duncan cut her off. "If you reject what I try to give, you imply that I don't have anything of value to offer you."

"Damn it, Duncan. I don't want you to change your life because of me again. Set aside your dreams. You need that money—"

"What did you say to me once about being stripped of agency?" He got loud. He couldn't help it. "It's my *choice* to help you with the clinic. To spend it on people I love. It's *our* money, Temperance. The entire reason I kept it was for us."

"It feels like blood money. Or some fucked-up modern-day dowry."

"I know. That's why I paid back what they gave me. Plus inflation, by the way."

She didn't laugh, but her features softened. Progress.

"They used that money as a lever to get what they wanted. I did the same thing. The money stopped being theirs as soon as your dad handed me that check."

"What did you do with it?"

Duncan hesitated. "I invested it."

"How much is it now?"

"It's enough."

"See?" Anger flashed in her eyes. "Damn it, Duncan, I am asking to be brought all the way in on this conversation, and you're *still* being oblique with your answers—"

"Right now, it's about six hundred grand."

A breath whooshed out of her, and she stepped backward.

"It fluctuates, obviously," he clarified.

"Jesus. How? How is it that much?"

"Luck? I guess?"

"You could have told me." When he opened his mouth to reply, she held up her hand and cut him off. "And don't say you were trying to protect me again. *I* get to decide when I need to be protected."

"I was protecting *myself*. Nobody knew about the money, Temperance. Nobody knew about school. I needed to figure that out for myself first. Dad and Ma just found out three days ago."

Her shoulders sagged. She shuffled close to him and pressed her forehead against his sternum. They were quiet for a long time.

"I am so tired, Duncan. I just want to be loved for who I am. Not an ideal, not infallible. Not human capital. Just me. Let me mess up and be imperfect. I might have never been the girl you thought you fell in love with when we were teenagers. But I'm damn sure the woman who loves you now."

Temperance tucked her fingers into the waistband of his trousers and tugged him closer. She raised her head to meet his eyes.

"I want to kiss you," she whispered.

"You don't have to look so mad about it," he whispered back.

He settled his hands on her shoulders. His thumbs fit perfectly into the notches above her collarbones. He glided his hands up the sides of her neck, dipped his fingers into the sweet wisps of hair at her nape. He trailed the tip of his nose featherlight along her temple, then down the upper edge of her cheekbone. With his tongue, he caught the lobe of her ear, and drew it between his teeth. A full-body tremor went through him when she let out a groan of pleasure.

The vessels in his temples throbbed in unison with the ones in his groin.

"Duncan. Just kiss me," she breathed, angling her mouth toward his.

Finally, *finally*, he bent toward her. He felt the heat of her breath first, then the slow, sensual brush of her full bottom lip against his. "Open your eyes," he said against her mouth. "I love to watch what this does to you."

The moment seemed to hover suspended in time, a raindrop at the tip of a leaf. The staccato of her breath was hot against his lips. *"Please,"* was all she said. With every frayed thread of self-control he could summon, Duncan closed the distance between their mouths. He dropped fully into the kiss, inhaling a sharp breath through his nose, lifting her against him so hard it drew her up on the tips of her bare toes.

Her wavering moan was aching need and relief, and it echoed all the way to the darkest places inside him. At his waist, she slipped his belt free of its buckle. If not for the soft metallic clank, he wouldn't have noticed.

He kissed her open-mouthed and open-hearted. Between their bodies, she thumbed open the top button of his pants. The top of his erection breached the band of his underwear, and the whisper-light drag of her thumb across the slick tip was as erotic as if she'd used her tongue.

"No," Duncan said on an explosive breath. He stepped back.

Eyes glassy, lips swollen, Temperance said, "What?"

He pressed his forehead to hers. "Bed. Clothes off. Afterglow. Morning after. All of it."

"I don't need that."

"Damn it, Temperance." He huffed a bullish breath through his nose. "*I* do."

Duncan toed off his shoes and lifted her into his arms. Her room was in the back corner of the house, behind two curtained French doors. The sheets were rumpled on the big half-poster bed, and an overstuffed white comforter slumped off the bottom edge onto the smooth wood floor. A paperback romance book lay splayed open with pages down in the center of the mattress. He laid her down beside it, slid her bookmark into the pages, and sat it on the bedside table with care.

"Oh my god, that might be the hottest thing I've ever seen," Temperance breathed.

Duncan chuckled.

One by one, he drew silver pins from her hair until the coil slid down under its own weight, then he untwisted the braid. Standing over her at the bedside, he shucked his shirt off while she removed everything but her panties. A tiny triangle of bronze satin with black lace embellishments at the hips.

His mouth flooded like he was a goddamned animal. He swallowed so hard it ached all the way into his chest.

"Your panties will be on my death certificate," Duncan growled, dropping his pants.

She drew a finger up the center of the fabric. "You recognize these?"

"Yes." Duncan gestured with a sideways bend of his wrist. "Off."

"I haven't gotten to thank you for them yet."

"Thank me by taking them off. Now."

She propped up on her elbows and let her legs drop open at the knees. Just barely. "Come take them."

"No." He kept his eyes on hers. "I want your full participation in this."

A lock of her hair slid between her breasts when she dipped her head. "Is this a power struggle?"

"No." He grabbed her ankles and hauled her to the edge of the bed. "This is a course correction. And it's long overdue."

He bent over her body, skimming his teeth along her hip bones, the lower edge of her rib cage. Then he cupped a hand over the satin triangle between her legs. He twisted the slippery material into his fist. The fabric was soaked.

"Duncan." She arched off the mattress. "Take them *off.*"

Through the panties, he pinned her clit between the heel of his palm and her pubic bone. She rose off the bed, anchoring herself with two fists in the bedsheets. When he slid his thumb under the elastic of the crotch, her belly began to quake, and she took short, hissing breaths through clenched teeth. Duncan knew her orgasms as well as he knew his own. She'd come in those pretty panties in the next ten seconds if he kept it up.

He backed off.

Her frustrated whimper ended on a feral groan at the back of her throat. Duncan intercepted her hand on its way to finish what he'd started. He surged over her, restraining her arm above her head.

"Take off the fucking panties, Temperance," he said against her mouth.

The pale blue of her eyes was white hot, and in that moment, Duncan estimated his odds of getting headbutted in the nose were as good as anything else. She slipped her wrist free of his light grip and exploded into motion. He sat back on his heels as she hooked her thumbs in the waistband, nearly kneeing him in the face in her frenzy to get the panties off. She wadded them into a ball and hurled them across the bedroom, chest heaving.

He pushed her back to the mattress with a hand on her sternum.

Then he dropped to his knees beside the bed and dragged her to the edge again by her ankles.

"We good?" He ran his hands up the backs of her thighs.

"Yes." Temperance pressed her hands against her eyes. *"Please."*

With one hand shackled around her hip, he lowered his head between her thighs and fed on her like a man starved. Every stroke and tug of his mouth echoed the rhythm she set with her hands in his hair. Like he was her fucking marionette.

Her thighs clenched around his ears and her hips levitated off the bed. Duncan hooked both forearms under her legs and stacked his hands across her waist, locking his fingers together just below her navel. He flattened her against the mattress. "Stay *here*," he demanded.

She came like a storm, drenching and loud.

Duncan rose to his feet and thrust into a condom. In one fluid motion, he lifted her back from the edge of the bed and used his knees to spread her legs wide. He lay there for a moment, hip bones cradled by her still-shuddering inner thighs, his erection trapped tight between his pubic bone and hers.

"Wait." He exhaled hard and buried his face where her earlobe met her jaw, sucking the skin over her jugular with a wide-open mouth. Her pulse beat hard against his tongue. "Just breathe with me for a second."

"I'm already breathing." She drew her knees high against his rib cage to tilt the slippery center of her against his excruciating arousal. "I don't want to slow down."

The final thread in his frayed self-control shuddered like a pounded piano wire, but it held.

"I plan to take my time." He bit his teeth together so hard he saw stars. "We seem to be at an impasse."

"Stop talking." She pressed her heels into the mattress and canted her hips further upward, urging him to slide inside.

He pressed his hips down hard and rotated against her in a slow, broad circle.

Temperance sank her fingernails into his shoulders and hooked her ankles together at the base of his spine. She made another growly sound of frustration. "Why are you doing this?"

Duncan curled his toes and raised up to press his sweaty forehead to hers. "I hate how fast I blow my fuse with you."

"It's fine, we can always—"

"Listen to me, damn it. This isn't some idiotic toxic masculinity thing."

Temperance finally went still. Her eyebrows pulled together, and her chest rose and fell fast beneath his. Duncan raised on his elbows to fully take her in. Just once, her chin quivered. He had her attention.

"Every time you've come to me over the years—those were the only times I got to be that close to you. To touch you. To even *look* at you without worrying about whether anyone would notice. It never lasted long enough."

Tentatively, she cupped her hands around his face. She coasted the pads of her thumbs across his cheekbones. His bottom lip. His chin.

Every nerve in his body felt stripped raw. "I never knew when would be the last time, but I never doubted that someday—it would be."

On a shaky breath, she softly said, "You are such a pain in my ass, Duncan Brady. Stop talking and kiss me."

"No. We're doing this my way tonight." He wanted her like he wanted to breathe. "Do you understand?"

"Yes."

Duncan angled his hips back and up. He nudged inside her inch by searing inch, savoring each new depth he reached.

Lashes lowered, Temperance clamped her lips between her teeth and panted hard through her nose.

"Look at me," he grated out. Duncan withdrew completely, raising high over her. "The only way this is happening is if you watch me."

Her lashes lifted, and he sank his full weight into her with a solid, rolling thrust. Her burst of breath flared hot across his collar-bone. She arched her neck and squeezed her eyes shut.

"The whole time, Temperance." He was primed to the point of pain, but again, he pulled out. The brief pause was enough to bring him back from the edge. The throaty noise of frustration she made almost sent him right back over it.

He plunged inside her again. "Open." Another greedy thrust, all the way to the hilt. "Your." He rocked into her so hard her cheeks trembled. "Eyes."

When she finally looked at him again, her pupils were blown so wide her eyes looked black in the low light.

"You aren't playing fair," she rasped.

"I'm not playing at all." The bed slammed into the wall so hard the lamp flickered.

Her body flexed and bowed in counterpoint to his. "Please, *please* don't stop—"

"No more talking." He cut her off with a forceful churn of his hips. Again, and again. "Say my name or say stop. No other sound. No other words. Do you understand?"

Temperance clamped her teeth tight to her bottom lip, draining it of color. She nodded.

"Say it," he demanded.

"*Duncan.*" It was a plea, a curse. A prayer.

"Half my life, I've been trying to be okay without you." His lungs hitched on the words. "I don't *want* to be okay without you."

Temperance shoved her fingers into his hair. Her gaze locked to his.

"You were not just a phase." He hooked one hand behind her knee and gripped the headboard with the other. The sweat of their bellies was hot and slick between them.

"I am not better off without you." His voice broke.

Temperance was moaning now, fragmented little sounds of des-peration. Her thighs began to slip and shudder around his hips. She was the sun and he was a wingless Icarus, barreling recklessly into her heat. He released her leg and the headboard, holding her fast to his chest. He doubled down on his rhythm, pulse thundering in his neck and roaring in his ears.

"I will never"—he gulped air like a drowning man—"be over you."

She locked ankles behind his waist, opening more fully to his accelerated thrusts. *"Duncan."*

"You are not optional." Each word was punctuated by a labored breath. "You are necessary."

Temperance fisted her hand in the front of his hair. Her mouth fell open in a silent scream. A pink flush painted skin stippled with goosebumps. She jerked beneath him when she began to come, and every pulse of her molten heat stripped seconds away from his stamina.

Duncan's nervous system rocketed toward full overload. Again and again, she chanted his name, and a desperate refrain echoed in his mind with each of his powerful strokes. *I love you, I love you, I love you.*

"You're *mine*, Temperance. But it's not about possession." He was gasping now, struggling to speak. "It's about belonging."

Every fuse blew.

It felt tidal. Soaking and unrelenting and inevitable. Tears burned in his eyes and his vision blurred at the edges. He set his teeth against her shoulder, gently bearing down against the curve of bone beneath. Pleasure arced like electrical currents down his thighs, into his spine, his belly. His bloodstream. Everything inside him loosened. A frantic unraveling into the body of the woman beneath him.

* * *

DUNCAN rolled sideways onto his back. He brought her with him, and she curled against his side. For a while, they dozed in candlelight.

"No chance your parents are going to show up here, right?"

"God, no. I'm sure they're back in their swanky hotel room,

complaining about the linens and enumerating the myriad ways I've disappointed them."

Duncan grunted, and Temperance laughed.

"Wait, would you *want* them to?" She propped herself up on his chest with her chin on her fist.

"I mean—it certainly would drive home a point if they walked in on us naked."

Again, they laughed.

He twisted a lock of her hair around his finger. "Why didn't you ever want me to talk when we had sex?"

"It's petty."

"Tell me."

Temperance ran her fingernails gently down the center of his chest, then back up again. "Do you remember the first time we were together after we broke up?"

"I told you I still loved you."

"And you cried."

"I did."

"Then I cried," she said.

Duncan pressed his mouth and nose to her hair and breathed in, long and slow. "You did."

"Then the next time we were together, you said—"

"Ah, fucking hell." He put a hand over his eyes and groaned. "I said, 'At least neither of us cried this time.'"

Temperance sat up abruptly, looking down at his face. "I know the humor, the jokes—they're a defense mechanism. I just didn't—couldn't—"

"I should never have cheapened it like that." He rolled over to face her fully. "I'm sorry."

She cupped her hand around his cheek and leaned in to press a long, tender kiss to his mouth.

"Also," he murmured against her lips, "from now on, I need you to understand that I'll never shut up when we're naked together."

Temperance rolled her eyes and groaned. It escalated to a fizzy giggle when he rose over her and gently pushed her back to the mattress. She squirmed and nipped him on the shoulder, delving her fingers into his hair.

"Sexual filibustering." He pressed his mouth behind her ear.

They were both laughing when they began again.

CHAPTER THIRTY-THREE

Temperance

Temperance woke first, just after dawn. For nearly an hour, she lay with her head tucked against the slope of Duncan's chest, clothed only in strawberry-blond sunrise.

The sooty scent of blown-out candles from hours ago still hung in the air, and the clock in the bathroom seemed to tick slower than reality. With the tip of her finger, she traced the bands of muscle along the upper part of Duncan's ribs and made meandering swirls in the soft hairs on his belly and chest as he slept. She couldn't see his face, nestled below his chin as she was, but she felt when he began to awaken. How his chest rose and broadened in a big inhale beneath her cheek, and the way his thighs stiffened when he stretched his legs. The brief tightening of his palm on her naked hip as he tugged her more snugly against his side, and a quiet, contented rumble deep in his throat.

A quarter of an hour passed before either of them spoke.

"I've been afraid to talk, or even move, in case this isn't real." His words were hot against her scalp. "But I really gotta pee."

She chuckled and rolled to the side. "Me, too."

Duncan ran down to the hall washroom, and Temperance hurried to the bathroom adjacent to the bedroom, naked as a willow branch in winter. She was brushing her teeth at the sink when he came back to her, sliding his hands across her belly, curving his body around hers from behind. Their eyes met in the mirror over her shoulder.

"Can I use that?" he said.

"My toothbrush? Nasty."

"Temperance. We've been exchanging bodily fluids for half our lives. How is it nasty to share a toothbrush?"

"It just is." She rinsed her own brush and put it in the sink-top container, then nudged him backward with her butt to make room to pull out the middle drawer of the cabinet. There were brand-new toothbrushes and a hoard of travel-sized toothpastes in there, along with half a dozen other needful toiletries. "My parents have been traveling most of their lives. There're enough spare toiletries stashed in this house to stock a Walgreens."

Duncan plucked out a toothbrush and used her cinnamon toothpaste. After, he lifted her onto the bathroom counter and kissed her. Thoroughly.

"I need to run this morning." Her head fell back as Duncan worked his way down her neck with his mouth.

"No." He grumbled against her collarbone. "I'll be personally responsible for ensuring that you get an adequate workout today, Teacup." He bent low to press a kiss between her breasts. "Your heart health is one of my top priorities."

Her belly growled. Loud. They both froze.

"Was that— Did your stomach just growl?" He laughed.

Temperance dropped her forehead to his shoulder. "I'm so hungry."

"Food first. Then we're not leaving that bed until tomorrow morning."

All Temperance had brought for her brief stay at the house was nonperishable dry goods, fruit, tea bags, and wine. Her parents had strict rules about food when she or Maren came to the house: don't use the fridge (it was running, but in energy-saving mode, and they didn't want to risk anything being left there to spoil), make sure all trash is taken with them and disposed of (off-property), and don't eat anywhere in the house other than the kitchen (don't want to risk a crumb of something dropping and attracting vermin). So, Temperance and Duncan wrapped themselves in oversized bath towels and sat at the bar in the kitchen, chatting and sipping Empress Grey tea from Laine Talbot-Madigan's tulip-shaped Imperial Porcelain tea-cups. They ate bananas and date bars, fresh peaches from a Vesper Notch orchard, honey-roasted cashews as big as the end of Temperance's thumb, and macadamia shortbread biscotti from Fortuna's.

Then, they went back to bed.

* * *

"*PLEASE* tell me you have more condoms—" Duncan breathed.

"Black bag." Temperance pointed. "Over there. Outside pocket."

In seconds, he was off the bed. There was a distinct tan line at the back of his waist from all the hours at the lake. His butt was paler than the rest of him, and it bounced a bit as he vaulted toward her overnight bag. With his dark hair standing wild around his head, and the morning sun sliding over the convexities and concavities of him, he seemed almost mythical, like the magnitude of him was too much for this room. But there was a vulnerability to him, too. A sweetness. He unzipped the bag with youthful enthusiasm and let out a triumphant little growl as he withdrew the shiny foil square. A wave of tenderness crashed through her, sending her heart into her throat. Her bloodstream seemed to thrum toward him with purpose, like the moon urging high tide.

I love him. I am in endless, relentless love with this man.

From the bottom of the bed, Duncan crawled up the mattress on fists and knees, trailing kisses along the inner curve of her ankle, her calves, the softest part of her thighs. Teeth skidded gently over the upward thrust of her hip bone. "I love you, I love you, I love you," she breathed every time a kiss landed.

A wide-open mouth and a generous tongue closed against the lower curve of her small breast. Her back arched off the bed.

Duncan settled between her thighs, pressing inside her with a long, slow surge of his hips. Each cell in her body rang with recognition. Her nerve endings crackled like a lightning strike beneath her skin. Every feeling she'd ever felt for him coalesced to fill her up in that moment, and her body didn't feel big enough to contain it.

"I love you," she said again. Clear and calm and permanent.

"Temperance." Duncan rose over her, eyes bright, cheekbones flushed. His hair was exuberant chaos, waves spreading in all directions like a spent party popper. He grinned. "Stop talking, and show me."

* * *

LATER.

Duncan supported his weight above her, arms trembling.

"Let go." Temperance urged him to put his whole body on her.

He eased gently down, but the weight of him made an involuntary breath puff out of her open mouth. He was *heavy*.

She loved it.

"See?" The single syllable came out as an airy grunt. "You didn't hurt me."

"I still might," he whispered against her hair.

"I'm small, Duncan. But I'm not fragile."

"You're not small, you're bite-sized." He fit his teeth around the upper curve of her shoulder, then her chin. Her earlobe. She squirmed beneath him, even more breathless from laughter. "You're not fragile, either." Abruptly, he raised up to his elbows to cup her face in both hands. His eyes were soft, but his mouth was set in a serious line. "I had a dream last night."

Her hands went soft. Tender. "Oh, no."

"No, no—it was okay. Wasn't a nightmare. We were sitting around a campfire, and it was peaceful. Just you and me. Comforting."

"Were we naked?" she teased.

Duncan made a faux sound of annoyance. "You are *never* serious."

Temperance giggled.

"You always make it about sex."

More laughter.

"You remember that quote, *Love must be as much a light, as it is a flame*?" he said.

"Yeah."

Duncan pressed a kiss to the tip of her chin, then to her expectant mouth. "In the dream, you said to me, 'The flame *is* the light,' and then I woke up."

She searched his face for a long time. "Well. I *am* a poetic genius."

He groaned and dropped his face to the pillow. Temperance drew her knees up past his hips and locked her ankles at his back, skittering fingernails up his ribs, across his shoulders, into his hair. When he raised his head, they simply watched each other laugh.

She made a memory of the moment, like one of those little rectangles of glass with a scene etched inside.

* * *

DUNCAN snoozed, stretched out on the bed with a sheet over his lower half. Temperance sat beside him wearing only the plain white T-shirt he'd taken off the night before, indulging in her first-ever close examination of the tattoos on his arms. They ended at defined lines about an inch above his wrists, and again where his clavicle intersected with his upper arm. They all blended together in a colorful mosaic, though some were more vivid than others due to age.

He opened his eyes as if he'd sensed her scrutiny.

"So, what's the deal with all the tattoos?" Temperance said. "I have to know."

"I like tattoos."

"This is commitment, Duncan." She ran a finger along a remarkably realistic crow on his shoulder. It was mostly black ink, shaded with deep blues and purples.

"Well, you know about the first. My second was when I was eighteen and hotheaded. I wanted to hurt myself, but I got the ink instead. Then I couldn't stop."

"I'm sorry," she said, gently.

"Don't be. I love them. I'm just sad I've run out of space." He propped pillows against the headboard to sit up a bit.

Starting on the left, Temperance explored. She gently tugged his arm to lay it across her lap. His biceps was mostly covered by a wide cuff of the County Galway tartan, where his Brady ancestors were from. Below it was a light blue band to represent the Galician flag on Gia's side. A nautilus shell, a blue butterfly, and an especially whimsical fox intertwined with a rose on the inside of his left forearm. She laid her fingers to it. "What's this one?"

Duncan flexed his hand to make his muscles bunch beneath her touch. "*The Little Prince*, by Antoine de Saint-Exupéry. There's a fox, and a talking rose, and—" He cut off and looked at her with a tilted smile. "Christ. Never realized how weird it sounded out loud. There's a bunch of lines in it that resonated with me. 'The shame of it was that they loved each other. But they were both too young to know how to love,' and 'You become responsible, forever, for what you have tamed.'"

"Wow, you are a total marshmallow," Temperance teased.

Duncan pressed his free hand over his eyes and laughed. She bent forward to kiss the fox-and-rose tattoo.

"What about Dory here?" She ran her thumb along a blue tropical fish with stripes.

"That isn't Dory, you weirdo. Dory is a blue tang. This is an emperor angelfish."

"Oh, forgive me."

Again, that nervous laugh. "It's from the aquarium scene in *Romeo and Juliet*. That song was playing—'Kissing You'—right when we—ah—sealed the deal at the Boonies."

"You can say it." Temperance laughed and pinched him lightly in the biceps. "Oh my god, you *can't* say it. Right before we had sex the first time. How did you even remember that?"

He gave her a pained look.

She traced the faint stripes on the fish. "Duncan. I recognize this. *You* drew this, didn't you?" She sat up straighter and pulled his forearm closer to her face. "You designed *all* of these."

Duncan tucked his fingers in the front of his hair. "Yeah."

Temperance straddled his belly just above his hips. She pointed to each tattoo, and received a brief story for each. After, the only uncharted spot that remained was the soft interior of his right biceps. When she prompted him to lift his arm so she could see, he hesitated.

"I didn't design the one under there," Duncan said.

His reluctance only made her more curious. It had to be awful, like an amateurish scrawl of an eagle, or a kanji he thought read "strength" but was actually something like "dog water" or "arthritis."

Temperance leaned over him and slid both hands along his arm to lift it. "Come onnnn," she coaxed.

Duncan relented. He rested his hand behind his head and subtly flexed his biceps.

She planted her hands on his chest and pushed. "You *have* done that on purpose all these years."

He caught his bottom lip in his teeth, smiling. "Have I?"

Temperance scooted higher on his belly and bent to inspect the tattoos illuminated by the morning sun through the window. Duncan didn't take his attention from her face.

Her breath seized in her chest. Whatever it was, it was *beautiful*.

It was a rectangular image, a little smaller than the size of a playing card. Artfully done in shades of periwinkle, pink, and pale green, it was more faded than the others. One of his older pieces. Inside an intricate scrollwork frame stood a winged figure in the center, dressed in a flowing white robe and holding two golden chalices with a swirl of water flowing between. A single bare toe was dipped into water at the bottom.

It looked like an angel, but Duncan was far too secular to get a tattoo with religious connotations. The longer Temperance looked, the more he squirmed beneath her. With a self-conscious groan, he rubbed his eye with a knuckled fist. The gesture was disarmingly pure and a little bit anxious.

"It's a tarot card," he said. "It can mean a lot of things, apparently. For me, this one symbolizes persistence, patience, and peace."

Temperance laid her hand flat over the tattoo. His skin there was unbelievably soft. "It must have hurt."

Quietly, he said, "More than you can imagine."

Silence passed between them. The hairs on the back of her neck rose. "Duncan. What's the name of this card?"

His Adam's apple raised and dipped in a hard swallow. "It's the temperance card."

There weren't any words that could properly serve the emotions she felt in that moment. The feelings were bigger than language. She trailed her fingernails from his wrist to his biceps.

"This spot was where you got your bee with me that day. You covered it?"

"Look at the space inside the upper-right corner of the card," he said.

Temperance's hair dropped over her shoulder to glide across his chest. In the space he described was the tiny honeybee identical to the one on her ring finger. The ink was faded to a brown black, and it was small enough that it looked like it could be part of the design of the temperance card.

"Bee. For Brady." Duncan rubbed his thumb over her tattoo.

Temperance collapsed in a heap against his chest and cried.

Fourteen years they'd lost.

They'd grown and changed, but the ways they fit together had always remained the same. Time was the most precious currency there was, but it couldn't be created or generated like wealth. You simply needed to spend what you already had as carefully and intentionally as possible.

"What is it, baby?" Duncan said.

"I spent fourteen years missing you, even when you were sitting right beside me. I never stopped loving you, Duncan." Temperance held his face in her hands. "I think the way we loved each other was just too big for two eighteen-year-olds to know how to handle. We changed, and the world around us changed. But every version of me has loved every version of you, and deep down, I was always waiting."

"We both were. Right where we left us."

She was never letting him go again.

CHAPTER THIRTY-FOUR

Duncan

Temperance always refused to be the little spoon, claiming it made her too hot. The way she curled against him every night was a little bit ridiculous. A dainty espresso spoon curved around a massive soup ladle.

That morning, Duncan had awakened to her clinging to his side, a supple thigh hiked high across his midsection, her hand cupped gently around his neck. Her soft belly rose and fell against his hip bone, deep and slow. Strands of her hair clung to his beard, like he'd walked face-first into a spiderweb.

Gentle rain shimmered on the cabin roof. Milky-gray light and muted birdsong came through the open windows. It had been cool for August, so they'd left the panes cracked a few inches in the night. Duncan could *feel* the morning on his skin. Elemental and clean. The earth's first damp exhale of the day.

The rain was forecast to stop by midmorning; good news for the grand opening of the Cloud Tide Winery later that afternoon. Ma and Dad had posted flyers on dozens of community boards around the valley, and they'd even taken out an ad in the *Linden Local*. Duncan had nerves in his belly for the first time in as long as he could remember, but it wasn't about how years of his craftsmanship and project management would be on display today. Today's main event was more than a decade in the making. It would be the first time he and Temperance planned to publicly let on that they were together.

As carefully as he could manage, he twisted around to face her. Her arm slid down to lie across his chest, and he lifted her leg gently, so her knee didn't catch him in the crotch when she moved.

In only two weeks, they'd fallen into a comfortable routine. It was like their collective subconscious had taken a breath of relief and sighed: *finally*. They'd been in love with each other for more than half their lives, and at last being able to live inside that love felt like the world itself had changed.

"What do you want?" Temperance murmured in her throaty, sleep-fuzzed voice.

"Good morning," Duncan replied. "I want a lot of things. You'll have to be more specific."

"Your hand on my hip. You've been tapping your finger there for ten minutes now."

He balled his fist. "I'm sorry."

"You do that when you're waiting for something." Her sigh was a gentle rise of her chest against his ribs, and a warm breath up his neck. "Or when you're concentrating."

"I guess I was doing both. Waiting for you to wake up, and concentrating on your face. I want to draw you."

Temperance slid away and stretched, bendy as a braid of sweetgrass. "I need you to promise me something."

"Anything."

"I've seen how often stuff from your sketchbook makes it onto your skin." Her hair was fuzzy at her temple where she'd been pressed into his shoulder all night, and her eyes were solemn. "*Promise* me, Duncan. Promise me that you'll never tattoo my face on your body."

Duncan laughed and propped up on an elbow. "What? Why?"

"Have you *seen* how those turn out? They're cursed." She swung a pillow at him.

Duncan's reflexes were fast. He grabbed the pillow in his fist and yanked it—and her—toward him across the bed. Temperance let go at the last second, and he flailed backward. She bounced off the edge of the mattress and spun out of reach, bubbling with laughter. He chased her to the bathroom.

They showered together, as they did most days.

Temperance hip-checked him out of the hot water to rinse the shampoo from her hair. She lingered, playfully blocking him from the spray even after she was finished. He crowded her against the tile wall, and she shrieked at the cold. Their laughter was loud between the walls and the glass of the shower.

He was hard against her belly.

Temperance peered down and sighed melodramatically. "I think something's come between us."

Duncan smirked. "It's a *betweenis*."

He widened his stance for leverage to lift her against the wall and dipped his head to kiss her. But Temperance let her legs go slack and slid slowly down the tile. Her breasts dragged over his stomach, over his erection.

"What are you—"

She took him in her mouth, and Duncan nearly blacked out with the first slippery whirl of her tongue.

Her hands skated up the backs of his legs, pausing at his ass to dig in her fingertips. He was so swollen, so molten hot, so fast—it was almost painful. Thighs and calves tightening, his toes curled, squeaking against the bottom of the shower. If she kept up that same rhythmic pull and release, he had about sixty seconds—maybe thirty—

Duncan's knees went watery. He slapped his hands against the side walls of the shower to keep upright. He had to clench the cheeks of his ass to keep from thrusting unchecked.

"*Hnnnh—fuck—*" He palmed the back of her head.

Her soft laugh vibrated from tip to root. "Use your words, Mr. Brady," she murmured.

"We're supposed to be—oh my *god*"—he choked on the words when she gave him another deep, slow tug—"at the tasting room—"

"Actually, I changed my mind." She cut him off, reaching up to flatten her hand against his belly. "Stop talking, Mr. Brady." Another low laugh, another heavy drag of her tongue. "Right now, this *is* the tasting room."

* * *

THE tasting room grand opening at Cloud Tide Winery didn't include any actual Cloud Tide wine.

Ma and Dad decided they wanted to open Cloud Tide as a celebration of the valley community at-large, and to put the place officially on the map as an event and recreation destination. Proud to help kick-start the American offshoot of her family's winemaking legacy, Aunt Renata sent several cases of wine and spirits from Vega. There was a Spanish Tempranillo and a red blend, a Galician Godello, and an Albariño. The Mencía—another red—was so deeply pigmented it almost looked violet around the rim when poured into glasses. The Everetts also contributed several cases of Three Birds' signature red, an oak-aged Baco Noir, and a case of their bestselling white, a Traminette that had won several national and local awards.

Duncan and Temperance were an hour late.

The grounds had never been more beautiful, a prismatic explosion of color in every direction. Still damp from the morning rain, grapes glistened like dark jewels in the sunshine. The air was filled with the fizzy, far-off buzz of cicadas. The bee mural Duncan had painted earlier in the summer was attached to the side of the bank barn that faced the outdoor patio. Each individual piece of wood was slightly offset in depth and height from the piece beside it, giving it a different appearance depending on which angle you looked at it from.

He was proud of it.

The Bristow family's barbecue food truck was parked in the field to the west of the stone patio, filling the air with sweet, tangy smokiness. Millie had left for school in Michigan the week prior, but Birdie and Midge waved at them from the open front, rosy-cheeked in matching white aprons.

The sliding doors of the bank barn were open to the flat expanse of green lawn in front, as were the glass garage-style doors of the tasting room. Music played from outdoor speakers attached to the stone face of the barn, and sawed-off wine barrels overflowed with greenery and colorful flowers that Rowan had grown from seed earlier that spring. Pennant garlands in maroon and apricot were strung from the front corners of the barn to lantern poles that would light the path to the small gravel parking lot at night.

They managed to slip in relatively unnoticed, as large as the mingling crowd was. They each grabbed a glass of Vega Vineyards' Albariño from the tasting room bar. The wine was tart and intense, fresh as the North Atlantic Ocean air and Galician sunshine. To preview the tasting room menu, Dad had spent two days personally preparing hundreds of finger foods. Date-and-prosciutto sourdough flatbread was drizzled with honey from Florence Holley's beehives. Savory hand pies were filled with sweet tomatoes, caramelized onion, and herbs—all grown from seed right there at Cloud Tide. Peach bruschetta with basil and goat cheese from Bennett Goodwin's farm. Half a dozen others.

In the big barn space, they found a nook along the wall. Temperance stood by his side, close enough that the heat of her arm radiated into his. She felt entirely too far away after they'd spent the past fifteen hours in near-constant bodily contact.

"Feels weird," he whispered.

"Hmm?" She extended her pinkie to brush lengthwise against his.

"Being here. With you. Like this. I'm so conditioned to keep a reasonable distance from you. Making sure there were enough people between us, but not so many that it looked obvious that I was trying to avoid you."

"I have a confession." Temperance hid a soft laugh and a da Vinci smile behind her raised glass. "I always tried to stand where I could be seen by you."

Duncan chuckled. "Witch."

"Who will be the first to notice, you think?" She tucked her hand up the back of his shirt, flattening her warm palm against his skin.

"Definitely Frankie," they said at the same time.

Frankie was there to document the event in full photographer regalia—dressed in slim black jeans and a snug-fitting black T-shirt, equipped with a harness attached to two separate camera bodies over one shoulder. A battery pack for her flash hung from the opposite shoulder.

The music quieted, and Ma stepped up onto a makeshift pedestal created from a wooden wine crate.

"Hello, everyone." Ma paused and looked around the crowd. She smiled and made eye contact, like she was engaged in an intimate conversation instead of speaking to a crowd of nearly two hundred people. "First—thank you, *thank you* for being here. Maybe next time we have a party like this, we'll have some of our own wine!"

Everyone in the crowd raised cups and glasses, laughing.

"I think the most difficult part of doing a hard thing is making the choice to do it. This project of ours has been a labor of love for the last two years—heavy on the love and even more on the labor." Ma's eyes crinkled at the corners and lingered on Duncan. "It's been the hardest thing we've ever done. But once you begin, you're *in* it, you know? You get to stop fretting that you might have missed out on something extraordinary because you didn't try. And that's one of the things that makes it wonderful."

Duncan scanned the crowd as people nodded and murmured in agreement. Near the back wall, Malcolm watched Frankie shoot a photo of the Everett brothers. Sunshine beamed through the big windows along the northern face of the barn, making the wine in their glasses seem to glow from within. It made for an outstanding shot.

Shooting photos seemed to be an athletic process for Frankie, the way she bent and stretched and crouched. People were naturally eager to smile for her. She flitted around the crowd like a dark, beautiful dragonfly.

Mal swallowed hard and closed his eyes before looking down at the ground. The poor guy was in a hell of a lot of trouble.

Ma went on. "So. Family, friends. Strangers from around Vesper and surrounding counties who heard there was free wine here today"—she paused for laughter—"thank you for being here on this big day for the Bradys. Salud!"

Beside her, Dad raised his own glass and shouted, "Sláinte!"

The crowd quieted, and Ma stepped off the wine crate so Dad could take her place. The wood creaked and cracked as soon as he stepped up, and everyone gasped. Dad hopped off with theatrical flair, swinging a hand through the air. "Hell with it—don't need it anyway," he said, and the crowd roared. "Before I let you all get back to the party, I want to share the names of the first Cloud Tide wines we'll be perfecting over the next few years. The first will be Rosebud, a blend of reds named after our sweet Rowan, who helped set this family on a trajectory we couldn't have imagined or navigated without her. In more ways than one."

Rowan and Harry stood silhouetted in the open door of the barn. She had her face buried in the crook of his neck, and Harry grinned and waved on her behalf. He cupped a hand around his mouth and shouted, "That's my wife!"

"The second will be called Footprint, a Cab Franc." Dad hesitated. "Ah, when we do the tour of the tasting room, the inspiration behind that one will become clearer."

Somewhere in the crowd, Nate barked an obnoxious laugh. Duncan's cheeks got hot beneath his beard.

"Our Chardonnay will be called Afterglow—simply because Gia likes the name. My Gia gets what she wants." The crowd sent up a collective *"Awww,"* and Dad paused for an indulgent beat. "We have plans to plant a few more three-acre blocks with Spanish grapes. Hopefully they lead to some wonderful wine like the ones you're enjoying from Vega Vineyards right now."

Dad waited a moment, then turned to face where Temperance and Duncan stood. "And finally, I just want to say—it's about damned time." The crowd buzzed, and Dad waved his hand. "Sorry, that's not a wine name," he clarified with his arm pointed straight at them. "I'm talking about those two knuckleheads."

Heads swung around and bodies turned to see where he'd

pointed. Laughter and scattered applause followed. Frankie whooped and aimed her camera at them, and Colby Everett did the Colby Everett whistle that everyone in the valley recognized.

Temperance shone up at Duncan like the sun. She was gravity itself, and he'd been falling most of his life.

Finally, *finally*, it was time to land.

Duncan pulled her tight against his side, and the wine in both of their glasses tipped perilously close to the rims. "I'm going to kiss you now," he said.

With a thumb through one of his belt loops, Temperance crinkled her nose and tugged him closer. "About time."

Heart hammering his breastbone, Duncan dropped into the kiss. Her low laugh resonated into his mouth, and he laughed back. Nothing around them actually changed—the crowd still hummed with happy conversation, the sky remained the same celestial blue of Temperance's eyes, and the floor under his feet stayed intact. But for Duncan Brady, that simple connection of his lips to Temperance Jean Madigan's here in this public space was one of the most important moments of his life.

She was his, he was hers, and it didn't matter who saw them. They were together as a canonical part of the moment, no longer hidden in the background.

It felt simple and right and good, and simultaneously an extraordinary privilege, having this thing he'd been convinced over half of his life that he'd never deserve. The way he loved her was built into the architecture of his bones. It was as much his identity as the pattern on his fingertips and the chemistry of his blood.

And now everyone else knew it, too.

* * *

THE ribbon was cut, more wine was poured, and tours of the winery began.

Everyone was ushered back outside to mingle, and small groups were taken for tours. They began with the concrete crush pad outside the north face of the barn, where a combination of new and refurbished stainless-steel equipment sat ready for the first harvest in a few months. Rowan gave a narrative tour of how the grapes would pass through the crush process, then the group moved on to the inner parts of the winery inside the barn. Fully in her element, she was in effortless academic mode, without a trace of blush in her cheeks or a flare of red at the tips of her ears. She guided them to the production and lab areas—and she even made a joke about how awful her first attempt at fermentation was with the initial batch of fruit from last year.

In the barrel room, Duncan's personal touches were everywhere. The light fixtures were all LED, faucets were all low-flow, and the walls were insulated with a sustainable composite to minimize air infiltration. Bolted to the walls were racks made of kiln-dried chestnut beams from the demolished gambrel barn. Eventually, oak barrels would rest there to age reds, but since they were empty, the space looked more like a grown-up jungle gym. On the opposite side of the room sat several steel fermentation tanks. They diminished the rustic romanticism of the space, but they were necessary for the whites that wouldn't be aged in the barrels.

Throughout the day, they overheard Nate tell the story about Duncan's pastrami sandwich and the animal footprints in the tasting room's concrete four different times. Each recounting grew more absurdist and embellished than the last, finally landing on a fanciful rendition where Duncan had set the bait on purpose to recruit the animals to leave footprints as an intentional design choice. They also heard Dad tell Ace and Charlie about how *buttload* and *bunghole* were legitimate winemaking terms. It earned a giggle from Ace and an eye roll from Charlie. Ma had been close behind, and she'd snickered a little before she pinched her lips closed and poked him in the ribs with her knuckle.

Duncan walked behind Temperance as the crowd flowed. He ran a knuckle up her spine whenever the group squeezed together in a bottleneck. They indulged in lingering gazes, and they walked with arms slung low around each other's waists, hands tucked into back pockets.

They loved, visibly.

When they exited the barrel room into the open east pasture, Duncan saw something that made his heart stutter.

Corbin Madigan and Laine Talbot-Madigan were there.

Standing at the edge of a group of valley folks, they looked awkward and out of place, their posture tilted toward each other but their eyes unmistakably scanning the crowd. Both were dressed in casual clothing—khaki shorts and a pale green polo on Corbin, Laine in a flowy white-and-blue-striped sundress. They almost looked like normal people.

Corbin met his eyes across the crowd, and his chest expanded in a big, slow breath. With a subtle nod, he raised his wineglass the barest inch higher. At first, Duncan didn't react, but he didn't look away, either.

Beside him, Temperance leaned into him and tightened her arm around his waist while she chatted with the family of one of her former clinic patients. By how loose her posture was, she hadn't seen them yet.

Duncan nodded back to Corbin Madigan with a slight dip of his chin. Then he turned his attention back to Temperance as she wrapped up her conversation. Before he could speak, Maren came out of nowhere, putting her body between them and where the Madigans stood.

"Duncan," Maren warned. Her eyes flicked sideways before locking to his. She raised her brows. *Are you going to handle this, or do I need to?* her expression said.

Temperance smiled at Maren, but it faded fast. She tensed. "What's going on?"

Duncan glanced over Maren's shoulder. Corbin and Laine wound through the crowd, making their way straight to them.

His first instinct was to sweep her away. Run interference. Clearly, it was Maren's, too.

"I get to decide when I need to be protected."

Duncan slid his hand up Temperance's back. He pressed his palm between her shoulders and met her eyes. Softly, he said, "Your parents are here."

Maren's expression was thunderous.

Temperance frowned, glancing between her sister and him. "That's not possible. They're somewhere in California right now—"

Then she saw them.

Her jaw tightened, her back straightened, and Maren deflated with an annoyed sigh.

Duncan dipped close to her ear and murmured, "What do you want to do?"

Temperance took a bracing breath. After a beat of hesitation, she wiped her palms on her shorts and said, "I want to know why they're here."

"What can I do?" he whispered.

"Just be with me," she whispered back.

Maren turned sideways to accommodate their approach, but she didn't say a word. Duncan raised his chin and planted his feet a little wider. He kept his arm loose around Temperance's back, his hand tight against her hip.

"Phenomenal wine," Laine said by way of greeting, raising a crystalline glass of Vega Albariño. She swallowed hard, glancing at her daughters. "Hello, Temperance. Maren. You look well."

With Leo on his hip, Nate appeared behind Maren. She swung the baby into her arms and leaned back against him. Ace and Grey came a moment later, plowing into Maren from opposite sides.

A glance of understanding passed between Duncan and his brother.

"You can fight for someone, but you have to be sure they're ready to be fought for."

Grey blurted, "Who are they?"

Laine dampened her lips and looked down at the ground.

"This is your grandma," Maren said, "and this is your grandpa."

Ace only looked at them with mild curiosity, but Grey said, "Grandma and Grandpa are over there." He pointed to where Ma and Dad stood under a sprawling copper beech, laughing and chatting with people Duncan didn't recognize.

"Well." Maren hitched Leo higher on her hip and gave her parents a cool smile. "I guess that says everything, doesn't it?"

"Maren—" Laine's voice was strained.

Corbin interrupted. "We were in town on some business for the Helen Talbot Community Center and noticed the article in the *Linden Local* about the opening today." He spent a moment to take in the grounds and the winery behind them. "Impressive." He nodded, and his brows creased together. "Truly."

"Thank you," Duncan said, simply.

Laine said, "I hope it's okay that we're here—"

Temperance cut her off. "That depends on *why* you're here, Mom."

Leo said, *"Bluhdoo,"* and brought a fistful of Maren's wind-blown hair to his mouth.

The elder Madigans shared a look. "We wanted to close the loop on the grant," Laine said.

"It's official," Corbin said. "Capewell-Talbot has won the award, thanks to you."

"Congratulations." Temperance hesitated. "You could have told me that in an email, though. Or a phone call."

For the first time, the look Duncan saw in Laine Talbot-Madigan's eyes was something other than imperious coolness. It wasn't softness or vulnerability either, but it was close. She looked . . . human. Laine sipped her wine, then cleared her throat. "We'd like to invite you to be a part of the family organization—"

Maren cut in. "Temperance—"

"Please. Please hear me out," Laine said.

Nate put both hands on Maren's shoulders.

Cautiously, Laine began again. "We've worked with the board to facilitate your involvement—both of you—to whatever extent you'd like."

"It's time for the organization to move into the future," Corbin said.

Temperance looked up at Duncan, then to Maren, who lifted a single pale eyebrow.

Duncan held his breath.

In the distance, one of the Bristow sisters jangled the dinner bell that hung over the front window of their food truck.

Temperance turned toward the noise, and her eyes lit with determination. "I have an idea."

CHAPTER THIRTY-FIVE

Temperance

By the end of August, inspired by the Bristow sisters' barbecue truck, Temperance wrote a business plan for a mobile healthcare clinic that would serve the entirety of Vesper County. Not only would she be able to expand her reach, she'd also meet people where they were, fostering trust and connection along with providing healthcare for people who needed it most. The original plan was to start small with a focus on pediatrics, but after only a single phone conversation with Cole Bello, he was eager to explore the idea of expanding to include other primary care services. "We could have a whole fleet," he'd said. "Heals on Wheels!"

Maren and Temperance both would serve as members of the Capewell-Talbot board, in exchange for an annual endowment to Temperance's mobile clinic, plus college funds for Maren and Nate's kids if they chose to go someday—and regardless of their prospective field. Neither Temperance nor Maren was prepared to invite Laine and Corbin to Brady family functions—and they might never be—but it was progress.

Harry offered up space for her to park the mobile clinic in the lot at the Cora Woodward Maternity and Wellness Center. Construction was due to be completed on the center later this fall, and according to Rowan, there was a half acre on the property perfect for an extensive community garden to grow fresh, free produce. Temperance had so many ideas. To start, she planned to ask Harry about pet food drives, a donation-based bicycle program, and a Little Free Library on-site.

Duncan was on track to begin the evening architecture program in Philadelphia in mid-September. With Will's blessing, he'd work in a part-time capacity while in school, primarily managing the goings-on at Cloud Tide. Maren and Nate would manage Brady Brothers alongside a new general contractor they planned to promote from within. Once Duncan finished school in a few years, Brady Brothers would expand its licensed architect services under his guidance.

That night, Temperance got back to the cabin late after a dinner date in Vesper Notch with Rowan and Frankie. The sun was low in a lilac sky, shining like an amber ball through the wall of trees around the far side of the lake. Warm wind through the pines sounded like ocean waves, and the whirr of cicadas was so thick it sounded like a downpour on a metal roof.

In the grass between the cabin and the shore, a projector screen had been set up. Beside it, a small letter-board marquee read SECOND CHANCES ARE FOR WHEN YOU WEREN'T READY FOR THE FIRST. Duncan's truck was there, too, with gauzy mosquito netting suspended over the bed like a pyramidal tent. All around it on the ground, candles of different sizes were lit in tin pots.

Duncan jogged down the steps of the cabin to meet her. He wore a fitted charcoal V-neck and a pair of pale linen pants that did outstanding things for his strong thighs. Without a word, he slipped a hand around the back of her neck and bent to kiss her until she was dizzy. Temperance had to gasp for breath when he let her go.

"You know we don't have to have sex in the back of your truck anymore, right?" she breathed.

Duncan took her hand. "Come see."

Around the other side of the truck, a drive-in speaker pole was built into the ground. "How—" she began. It was the exact pole from the Boonies. Speaker 492, etched with their original engraving, TJ + D 4E. Attached to the top was a little white flag.

"I convinced Barney and Owen to retire pole 492 in exchange for a custom mural on the side of the concessions building."

"You *didn't*."

"Oh, I definitely did." He nudged the metal pole with his toe. "This thing's mounted in concrete."

"Does it work?" She ran her palm over the warm metal.

Duncan slipped his phone from his pocket and tapped the screen a few times. The opening notes of "Just Like Heaven" streamed from the speakers.

"Wow."

He chuckled. "Don't look too impressed. They're just little Bluetooth speakers sitting in there."

"I'm not talking about the mechanics of it, my love. I mean—all of it."

They left their shoes in the grass, and Duncan held the filmy drapes open at the tailgate of the truck bed to help her up. Inside, it was just tall enough for them to move around on their knees. He'd laid padding beneath an ivory shag rug on the floor, and an oversized dove-gray beanbag filled the entire back half of the truck bed. Plush blankets and fuzzy white pillows were strewn everywhere. LED candles and camping lanterns turned dim were strategically placed along the inner walls. There was a small wooden crate filled with blond and gold sunflowers, along with a bottle of wine on ice.

"I want to live here now." Temperance gathered the soft peach material of her cotton dress so she could climb into his lap.

"You like it?"

"I love it."

"What's on the big screen tonight?" she asked.

"Ah—still *Twister*." Duncan grimaced.

She settled on his thighs with her knees hugging his hips. She sighed with faux disappointment. "Second-chance romance stories are so *predictable*."

Duncan clamped his fingers around her ribs and dug in, tickling. Her body bent backward like a cattail reed, and she screeched with laughter. "Listen," he said, "it was either that, or *Shaun of the Dead*.

I have no idea why these are the only two movies Ma still has on DVD."

"I know, I know." Temperance giggled. "It's perfect."

"It's also very illegal since I didn't license it for a drive-in broadcast, so let's keep our fingers crossed we don't get caught."

"An authentic drive-in speaker pole doesn't make this a real drive-in." She laughed and crinkled her nose. "And anyway, we've got a close personal friend at the Vesper County Sheriff's Department now, remember?"

Duncan chuckled. He held her against him and kissed her, slow and sensual and soul-seeking. Temperance melted into him like sweet cream into coffee.

The sun was just a band of gold at the horizon by the time Duncan ended the kiss. When he spoke again, his words were soft against her mouth. "I want you, Temperance."

"I can tell," she teased, shifting in his lap.

"No, no. That guy's blatantly disregarding the emotional gravitas of the moment." There was an irreverent upward tilt to his gorgeous mouth, but it faded fast. His inky eyes grew solemn. "I mean—I *want* you, want you. I'm not letting this go again. I can't do never, and I won't do maybe. I want all of it. All in, and always."

She cupped his face in her hands. She never wanted to stop touching him—it felt like she had fourteen years of not touching him to make up for.

Duncan's brows were crowded close over determined eyes. "Do you remember, earlier in the summer, when you told me Capewell-Talbot was your backup plan?"

Temperance nodded and tucked back a dusky lock of hair from his forehead. She'd never seen him look more serious.

"Tell me why," he urged. "What did you mean?"

"I just—" She let her hands fall, resting them against his chest. The back of her nose tingled, and her eyes quickly filled with hot tears. "I didn't think I could exist where you were. It hurt."

"You're never going to need a backup plan again, baby."

She sniffed. "I thought *never* was for cowards?"

His beard couldn't hide the quick tremble of his chin. "In this case, *never* is only for the very most brave."

Duncan reached into the wooden box full of sunflowers and withdrew a little dark pouch. He deftly untied the strings at the top.

A ring.

Her ring.

Temperance reached out to touch the twinkling stone—a brief, questing nudge that lasted only a second. Her vision swam.

"It doesn't bite," Duncan teased.

The swell of her cheeks nudged tears free when she laughed. Joy made her feel loose-limbed, fizzy in her chest. "Hello there," she whispered to the ring. "I remember you."

"The moment we met each other, the clock started ticking on how much time we'd have together. We've already wasted too much of it. Be my wife, Temperance."

She pressed a fingertip to her chin and made a theatrically contemplative face. *"Hmm."*

Duncan groaned, and Temperance laughed up at the sky.

"Yes." She landed kisses on his forehead, his cheeks, his mouth. "Yes, yes, infinitely yes."

When he slid the ring on her finger, she said, "Are we finally going to be friends now, Duncan?"

"No, Mrs. B." His mouth arced into a smile against her lips. "We're family."

They didn't get to watch the movie.

CHAPTER THIRTY-SIX

Duncan

*L*et me take you to another place for this Queimada."

Flickering firelight reflected in the lenses of Ma's reading glasses, catching in the tiny crystals of the chain that looped down from each side. She lifted a wide, shallow ceramic pot from a wicker basket. Around the edge were twelve mugs with matching glaze, hooked by their handles.

The sun was setting earlier now. The Bradys—plus Frankie, who'd defaulted into in-law status now that Rowan and Temperance were part of the family—sat around the stone firepit in the grass between the house and the pond. By the hundreds, dandelion puffballs glowed in the rose-gold light of dusk. A gentle wind brought the sweet scent of dying leaves. An omen of fall.

"Everyone, close your eyes." Ma tipped her chin down to peer over the shiny frames of her glasses and waited for everyone to do as she said. She winked at Duncan and Temperance once the others closed their eyes.

Everyone had been so busy since August; this was the first night the Bradys had gathered for dinner in several weeks. It gave Duncan and Temperance a convenient excuse to bring everyone together for a bit of mischief. They'd looped Ma and Dad in on their plan, and Ma was especially delighted to play the role of accomplice by performing a Galician fire ceremony.

The Queimada.

"We're on a rocky cliff overlooking the sea." Ma dropped her voice low. "Dark wind brings you the sound of Galician bagpipes. The air is warm and damp, tasting of sand and salt. It feels inside your lungs as though you've taken some of the earth itself into you. Above, the roof of the world has been lifted, and you've never seen the sky so impossibly black and so impossibly vast."

Temperance leaned into his shoulder and whispered, "I don't know if I'm going to be able to get through this without cracking."

"They deserve at least a *little* bit of payback."

"What if they think we're serious, though?"

Duncan set his hand on her knee. "We'll keep them sweating for a minute or two, tops. That's nothing compared to their months of meddling."

Ma told everyone to open their eyes. On the picnic table at the other side of the campfire, she'd set out an array of goods. A bag of white sugar, a sack of coffee beans. A few oranges, and a thick-walled square bottle of spirits with the Vega Vineyards logo on the front.

"When I was a little girl," Ma began again, "Noche de San Juan was my favorite holiday. It is the way we welcome summer in Spain, a celebration of water and fire. My father used to tell a story about how the sun was in love with the earth. The summer solstice was the day it lingered with its beloved the longest. By lighting bonfires, we gave extra power to the sun so it could hold back the night and stay longer with its love.

"Since we had more important things to do on the summer sol-stice this year"—Ma paused to beam a smile at Rowan and Harry—"we'll celebrate belatedly with our Queimada. Hopefully I can remember the words."

She centered the clay pot on the table, then uncorked the square bottle of spirits and poured it slowly in. "This orujo represents the tears of the earth."

Even though Duncan sat several feet away, the bright and boozy fragrance of the orujo liquor made his nose tingle.

"Jesus," Harry muttered. He must have smelled it, too.

"Language," Ma said without looking up.

"Ah, pardon me for blaspheming during your pagan fire ceremony, Ma," Harry deadpanned.

"Hush."

Nate snorted a laugh. Ace and Charlie giggled.

"Like tears, we make it bitter." She used a knife to carve curling strips of orange peel into the pot, followed by a handful of coffee beans. Then she added a heaping scoop of sugar. "And sweet."

She stirred the concoction with the long-handled ladle. The grains of sugar grated against the ceramic.

Then Ma raised a ladle full of the queimada and used a small lighter to set the booze ablaze. When she lowered the flaming scoop back into the pot, the fire spread, licking slowly over the surface. She began the incantation in Gallego as she poured and stirred.

"Mouchos, curuxas, sapos e bruxas . . ."

Owls, barn owls, toads, and witches . . .

With a hypnotic rotation of her wrist, she stirred, scooped, and raised the ladle high, pouring a cascade of opalescent fire back into the pot.

". . . espíritos das neboadas veigas . . ."

. . . spirits of the misty vales . . .

The incantation continued, and the air was filled with the scent of caramelized sugar and the toasty brightness of the orange peels. When Ma finished, she placed a heavy lid over the pot, smothering the flames, and the world seemed darker.

Then she arranged the small ceramic mugs for pouring. She threw an orange peel and a few coffee beans into a thermos of hot apple cider for the kids, Mal, and Mercy, whose belly peeked out of a flowy pink maternity top.

"We will drink three times." Ma cut her eyes to Duncan and Temperance. "First, to banish evil spirits, and second, to purge the mind of bitterness. The final drink will infuse the soul with passion—"

That was their cue.

"Wait." Duncan stood.

Temperance followed suit. "We have something to tell you all."

Duncan looked down at her and let out a resigned sigh. "This isn't—" He hesitated.

"It's just—" Temperance paused for effect. She gestured between herself and Duncan. "This isn't working out for us."

A murmur went up through the group. Duncan and Temperance shared a sad glance. Her cheek dimpled inward where she clamped it in her teeth.

"What the *hell* is going on?" Arden blurted.

"We don't, ah—" Duncan sighed hard and slowly looked from person to person, lingering a little longer on Rowan and Harry. "We don't want to be engaged anymore."

More concerned rumblings. "What?" Maren whispered to Nate, and Mercy and Patrick clasped hands. Rowan gasped and started to stand, but Harry kept her seated with a gentle tug on her wrist. Malcolm crossed his arms, and Frankie sat forward with her elbows on her knees and her hands stacked over her mouth. Again, Arden said, "What the hell is happening?"

"So . . ." Duncan paused again for maximum effect.

"So," Temperance echoed. "We're just going to go ahead and get married."

For a beat, everyone looked confused.

Rowan leapt to her feet and ran to them, nearly knocking Temperance down with her hug. Duncan laughed and put his hands on their backs to steady them both. Frankie joined in on the hug, then everyone else piled in, like magnets snapping together. Dad pulled Duncan into the crowd. Little Grey was crying happy tears. Mal remained seated, but there was genuine warmth in his eyes as he watched.

Everyone backed away from the hug, grinning and talking over each other. Temperance had one hand pressed to her mouth, one hand pressed to her chest, giggling and trying to keep up with everyone's rapid-fire questions. "We got the license four days ago," she said. "We're doing a self-uniting ceremony—yes, we've already waited so long—you'll be our witnesses—yes, we have a date—no, no dress—"

Rowan's cheeks and ears were vivid red. She made a face and gently popped Duncan in the arm with a fist. "That was mean."

Harry laughed and shook Duncan's hand. He cut his eyes over at Rowan. "You have no idea the floodgates you've opened here. She's going to turn this into a contest."

"Oh, I think we can call it even now after three months of 'just be friends' shenanigans," Duncan said. "But if she wants to rumble—"

Mal approached. He didn't move in for a hug, but he allowed Temperance to hug *him*. "Congratulations," he said to Duncan over her golden head. "Maybe you won't be so goddamned insufferable now. The pining was excruciating. Truly."

"Well done, man, making this about you." Duncan laughed. He made a thoughtful face and cut his eyes over at Frankie as she closed in on them. "Hey, if you're looking for tips on strategy—"

"Absolutely not." Mal turned on his heel and strode away.

Frankie gave Temperance another hug and watched Mal go with her bottom lip pinned between her teeth.

"Red flags, Frances," Temperance said under her breath.

"Crème brûlée, Temperance," Frankie sang back with a wink.

"Huh?" Duncan said.

"You don't want to know," said Temperance.

A plume of smoke from the dying fire hazed the night sky. When it cleared, the stars seemed sharper against the endless black. Dad laid a few new logs on the fire. It sent up a whirl of tiny sparks, and the embers beneath rippled and flared. Temperance stared at them with a wistful smile on her face.

"Fire seeds." Duncan moved in behind her and wrapped his arms around her middle. He ducked his head and murmured behind her ear, "Stubborn."

She hummed an enigmatic little sound in the back of her throat. Goosebumps prickled the tiny hairs at her nape. "Hopeful."

"Stubborn, hopeful." He laughed softly. "Same thing."

The commotion died down, and everyone went back to their seats around the fire. Ma poured the queimada into the little ceramic mugs.

"You haven't told us," Maren said, still a little breathless. "When?"

Duncan and Temperance looked to Ma at the picnic table. She wore a small, secret smile. "Queimada isn't only for the solstice. Some do it to celebrate Hallow's Eve." She handed filled mugs to Dad, who passed them around the circle of Bradys. "Some do the Queimada at weddings."

Rowan's and Frankie's mouths dropped open.

"*When?*" Maren repeated, laughing.

"We were thinking . . ." Temperance trailed off and turned in Duncan's arms to face him. Her eyes were jewel bright in the firelight.

Duncan slid his fingers between hers to link their hands tight. It felt like he'd waited his whole life for this.

He looked up at everyone. Waited a beat. Then he smiled and said, "Right now."

ACKNOWLEDGMENTS

First and foremost: I'm grateful to the booksellers and librarians who loudly and unapologetically show up for romance. Purveyors of love, peddlers of feels—you have a superpower.

All the main characters of this book were created back in 2014 when I began writing what would become my debut, *Bend Toward the Sun*. I knew from the jump that Temperance and Duncan would have their own second-chance romance someday, but I'd actually had another couple in mind as the leads for my second novel. The short version is that we have my husband to thank for T.J. and Duncan's story existing right now. He was the first person to read an early manuscript of *Bend Toward the Sun* in mid-2020, and after finishing, he said: "Who's next?" When I told him, he (very firmly) objected. "It's gotta be Temperance and Duncan," he said. So— thank you, honey, for having such impeccable romance instincts. This was indeed the right time for them.

Since I'd originally thought I'd have a few years to figure out the details of T.J. and Duncan's backstory, I didn't really know them very well when I began drafting. I'd also never written a book on a deadline before. It was *really hard* to let people see my mess. I'm so lucky to have had a professional partner in this process who's one of the best in this industry: my editor, Alexandra Sehulster. Alex, thank you for repeatedly going all the way into the weeds with me to make this a story of the present rather than one of the past, and for helping me amp up the swoon factor to a whole new level. Your patience is endless and your talent is tremendous.

To my agent, Laura Bradford: thank you for persisting through my navel-gazing and my manuscript-length emails, and for helping me navigate the joys, frustrations, and realities of being a newbie author. Your wry humor and authoritative insight keep me grounded.

By far the best part of publishing a second book is that this time around I had a small but mighty group of readers and friends from the online romance community to share my excitement with. My endless love and appreciation go to Jocelyn (hashtag influencer) and Shelby for your outspoken social media ambassadorship of *Bend Toward the Sun* and for putting together a truly epic cover reveal squad for *Right Where We Left Us* literally hours before it went live because I forgot how calendars work. Thank you all—Allie, Ann, Ashley, Christina, both Courtneys, Danielle, Darrah, Emma, Izzy, Katherine, Lara, Mae, MC, Michelle, Nicole, Steph, Stephanie, Tonya, and Vanessa—for showing such love last September when *Right Where We Left Us* was officially announced. I'm so grateful.

Shout-out to NIGHT TRAVELER, whose songs I mainlined into my earholes on a near-daily basis while writing this book, and whose full discography would make a damned good soundtrack for a Cloud Tide streaming miniseries someday. (Showrunners, my agent's name is a few paragraphs up.)

To my family: Mom and Dad, thank you for never begrudging that I'm solidly middle-aged now and still figuring out what I want to be when I grow up, and for never having objected to the leaning towers of historical romance paperbacks I'd bring home from the library barely out of junior high. To my brother, Matt; my sister-in-law, Toni; and my nephew, Wyatt—thank you for showing up for me at local events and for being responsible for approximately half of my total book sales. Wyatt, please never actually read my books.

My three birds. It's probably going to be a while before you read this, but I want you to know: the way I love you is bigger than paper and ink can convey or contain. You and Daddy were my first cheerleaders, and I am so lucky and so proud you're all mine. Maybe someday I'll write books where I can take you up on your offers to illustrate them for me.

I already mentioned him here once, but he's important enough that he warrants a second mention. Keith: thank you for the miles and miles of walks around the neighborhood, helping me work out plot snags and the minutiae of character arcs. Thank you for allowing our life to be overtaken by fictional people. For giving up entire weekends with me so I could disappear into my writing dungeon. For all the perfectly grilled cheese sammies with pickles to fuel my body, and for your big love to fuel my heart and mind. You're still my favorite.

And finally—you, reader. Thanks for coming along with me to Cloud Tide. Let's be friends.

ABOUT THE AUTHOR

Jen Devon is a lifelong lover of love stories. She writes vivid, cinematic romances about imperfect people finding their perfect matches. A former ecology academic and adjunct biology professor, she now works in the internet tech industry and dreams of writing full-time. An avid gardener, photographer, gamer, and unapologetic nerd, she's also a mom of five (three kids, two rescue mutts) and lives in central Ohio with her engineer husband. You can find her online at jendevon.com.